# CIR
# MAXIMVS

# CIRCVS MAXIMVS

## A.D. O'NEILL

Black&White

**Black&White**

First published in the UK in 2024
This edition first published in 2024 by
Black & White Publishing Ltd
Nautical House, 104 Commercial Street, Edinburgh, EH6 6NF

A division of Bonnier Books UK
4th Floor, Victoria House, Bloomsbury Square, London, WC1B 4DA
Owned by Bonnier Books
Sveavägen 56, Stockholm, Sweden

This is a work of fiction. Names, places, events and
incidents are either the products of the author's
imagination or used fictitiously. Any resemblance to
actual persons, living or dead, or actual
events is purely coincidental.

A CIP catalogue record for this book is available from the British Library.

ISBN: 978 1 78530 638 9

1 3 5 7 9 10 8 6 4 2

Typeset by Data Connection
Printed and bound in Great Britain by Clays Ltd, Elcograf S.p.A.

MIX
Paper | Supporting
responsible forestry
FSC® C018072

www.blackandwhitepublishing.com

I am Martial of noble verse and wit,
Known throughout the world because of it,
Yet envy me not, for I remain of course,
Far less famous than Andraemon the horse.

**Martial,** *Epigrams 10,9*

He even killed some of the common people, merely because
they had spoken ill of the Blues.

**Suetonius,** *The Life of Vitellius*

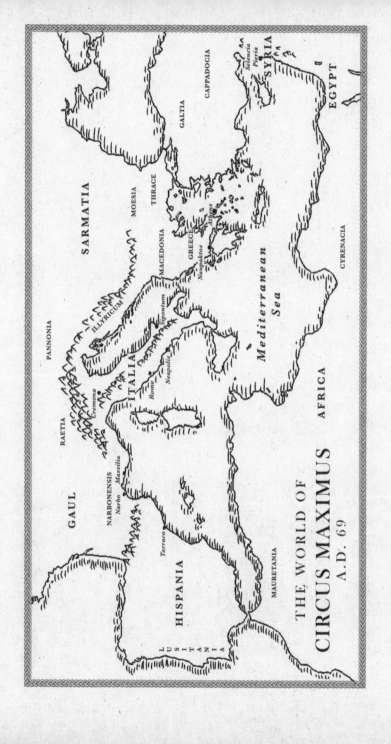

THE WORLD OF
CIRCUS MAXIMUS
A.D. 69

# INTRODUCTION

I N EARLY 1783 A SERIES OF EARTHQUAKES devastated the region of Calabria in southern Italy. As many as two hundred and fifty villages were either swallowed by the earth, inundated by mudslides, or swept away by tsunamis. There were over 35,000 fatalities.

One of the first visitors to the scene was Vivant Denon, *chargé d'affaires* at the French embassy in Naples. Denon's first task, as he saw it, was to determine the scale of destruction. His second task was to convince Louis XV, his king in Versailles, to send urgent relief. His third task was to help distribute the food, medicines and building materials that subsequently arrived by ship. But it was a fourth task, arising from an unexpected opportunity, that most concerns us here.

Denon – artist, writer, proto-archaeologist and later curator of the Louvre – had long been embroiled in a good-natured battle with rival ambassadors for possession of the priceless relics that were flooding the Neapolitan black market. Generally, such items came from the ruins of Pompeii and Herculaneum (then being excavated for the first time), but occasionally they emerged from other sources, too, such as old crypts, monasteries and private collections. And this is where the Calabrian earthquakes proved so providential. Huge new cracks had opened innumerable hidden chambers and subterranean vaults, some said to contain veritable treasure troves of antiquities. Hearing of some extraordinary discoveries, Denon, even in the middle of his charity work, wasted no time in personally inspecting as many of these sites as possible, as well as signalling his interest to the usual black-market dealers.

It was through the latter that he came to be offered a mysterious statue. Measuring a little over a metre in height, the marble horse, which had Arabian features, was depicted in the act of galloping – only two of its hooves touched the ground – and could not be displayed upright without additional support. It was adorned with a truncated harness and bore a cropped tail. One of its eyes was blank, possibly unfinished or neglected by the sculptor. A segment missing from the groin area appeared to have been plugged with gypsum. Most curiously, its left side – and only its left side – was heavily scarred, though it was difficult to determine if these marks had been purposely chiselled or came about as the result of damage or sabotage. Denon decided that the statue must have been part of a larger tableau, possibly featuring other horses, such as the life-size Horses of Saint Mark's that he had admired regularly during his years in Venice. When the dealer insisted however that the horse was an orphan, Denon claimed he was not interested unless the rest of the team could be located as well. The dealer lowered his asking price to fifty piastras. Denon bought it.

The piece, though Denon never found it worthy of display in the Musée Napoléon (the Louvre), thereafter became a key item in his private collection on Quai Voltaire in Paris. He never stopped puzzling over it and showing it off to visitors, possibly including Bonaparte himself. In letters to Isabella Teotochi,* an old lover in

---

* See *Lettres à Bettine, Vol. II* (Actes Sud, 2001).

Venice, he frequently confesses his frustration: "I am convinced the horse has secrets it wishes to share with me, yet the damaged groin means I am unable to establish even if it is a stallion or a mare!" Alas, when he died, in 1825, he had yet to solve the statue's mysteries, and it joined the rest of his curiosities sold at auction by his nephews.

The horse thereafter passed through the hands of various French collectors but did not appear in public until the *Vivant Denon, L'Oeil de Napoléon* exhibition in Chalon-sur-Saône in 2004. It was there that I viewed it while working on another project involving Denon. I remember being impressed by the creature's flowing mane and rippling musculature, while being puzzled, just as Denon had been, by the lopsided scarring. But I thought no more about it until 2013, when one of the exhibition's curators, art historian Hélène de Montgolfier, informed me of a remarkable discovery.

It seemed that X-ray scanning of the statue conducted by the Antiquities Department at the University of Burgundy had revealed a hollow core packed with what appeared to be bound parchment. After some bargaining with the owner, the investigating team had secured permission to remove the plug and extract the statue's contents. These turned out to be two exceptionally well-preserved codices from the first century A.D. Though the analysts, at that stage, had yet to open the fragile manuscripts – that was subject to further negotiations, not to mention supervision by the country's foremost antiquarians – the speculation, as you can well imagine, had reached something of a fever pitch.

Would the books contain some legendary lost text? Tiberius's autobiography? Claudius's history of Augustus's reign? The missing books of Livy's *History of Rome* or Tacitus's *Annals*? Or even (heaven forbid) something Gospel-related?

In fact, the books – the Cornelius Noctua Codices, as they came to be known – were about a subject that, to me at least, was infinitely more interesting. And yet inexplicably neglected.

* * *

Anyone who studies the history of chariot racing would find it difficult not to conclude that it was the greatest spectacle entertainment in human history. Only the failure of its principal venue, the Circus Maximus, to survive the centuries – the last recorded race was conducted there circa 550, after which the structure was pillaged into near non-existence – prevents it from assuming its rightful place in the popular imagination.

In fact, the surface area of the Circus Maximus was eleven times that of the nearby Colosseum. The entire arena was well over half a kilometre long and one hundred and fifty metres wide. At its zenith it could contain no less than 250,000 spectators (the capacity of the Colosseum was fifty thousand). Beast hunts, battle re-creations, athletic contests, religious festivities, military parades, novelty events and even gladiator bouts were all held there (the Colosseum was not completed until A.D. 80) but nothing was more popular than chariot racing. The four racing factions – the Greens, the Blues, the Reds and the Whites – were followed with fierce passion by patricians and plebeians alike. Numerous emperors were fanatical devotees. Even those who personally did not care for the sport acknowledged its importance to social cohesion and failed to attend the races at their peril. The charioteers, almost exclusively slaves and ex-slaves, were richer and more famous than most senators (Juvenal claimed that the earnings of a hundred lawyers could not match that of a single charioteer). The horses themselves were celebrities, their likenesses appearing in mosaics, frescoes, statues, cameos, drinking vessels, knife-handles, terracotta tablets and magic lamps. And monumental arenas, some patterned specifically on the Circus Maximus, multiplied throughout the empire for several centuries.

The fans, meanwhile, would not seem out of place in today's arenas. They wore faction colours, chanted team songs, gathered in specific sections of the stands, studied the form guides, gambled prodigiously, and naturally were held in disdain by contemporary intellectuals. "Let us turn to the idle and lazy common people," sniffed Ammianus Marcellinus. "Their home, their temple, their public assembly, their very reason for existence, is the Circus Maximus." Pliny the Younger was even more damning: "It astonishes me to see so many thousands of adults behaving like children. If they were attracted by the speed of the horses or the skill of the drivers, I could understand it. But it is the colours that they really care about, and were the colours to be exchanged mid-course they would instantly transfer their allegiance and desert the charioteers and horses they had previously cheered. Such is the popularity and importance of a worthless tunic."

This sort of contempt, which only ossified in the Christian era, no doubt accounts for the dearth of material about chariot racing in primary sources. The discovery of the Cornelius Noctua Codices – within a statue, it is now clear, of the mighty trace horse* Andraemon – therefore represents a thrilling advance in our understanding of the sport's history and culture (scholars of the period will, however, be pleased to note numerous incidents already mentioned by Tacitus, Suetonius, Josephus, Dio, Pliny the Elder, and so on). In recording his chronicles on parchment and hermetically sealing them for posterity we can be eternally grateful for Cornelius Noctua's unusual foresight, just as I am grateful to

---

* A four-horse chariot team consisted of two yoke horses (i.e., attached to the yoke) and two flanking trace horses. Of the four, the inside trace horse was considered the most influential.

Professor Hélène de Montgolfier for alerting me to the existence of the codices in the first place, and to M. Charles Clou and the University of Burgundy for allowing me to arrange a translation for this volume. In so doing, I have seen fit to edit freely for clarity, pace and occasionally suspense, as well as formatting the narrative into chapters. The singular structure – two parts of roughly equal length, the first spanning forty years, the second just nine weeks – is however the original author's.

# THE CHARIOTEERS' CREED

In the heat of the race the champion always finds extra.
Risk is the mother of greatness.
A life without challenge is a life without meaning.
The greater the odds, the sweeter the victory.
No pain is without pleasure.
No pleasure is without pain.
Every moment inside the Circus is immortal.
Every moment outside the Circus is training.
Master your horses or your horses will master you.
The existence of the hawk makes the eagle soar higher.
The ordeals of the journey enhance the lustre of the destination.
The race is never over until the finishing line is crossed.

# BOOK

## ONE

A.D. 30–69

# I

M Y FATHER, LUCIUS CORNELIUS PICUS, was impulsive but scheming, sensitive but scathing, generous but parsimonious, self-aggrandising yet modest – he was, in short, a mass of human contradictions. He also oversaw the Green Faction during its decades of greatest splendour and tumult, and was instrumental in the great saga of Corax of Campania and Alector of Arcadia. It is their story, as well as that of the Circus Maximus, that I intend to relate in these pages.

In the sixteenth year of the reign of Tiberius Caesar, my father was returning from an inspection tour of his shipyards in eastern Italy when he decided to make an unscheduled visit to the stud farm of the Sternini horse breeders. The farm, to which the Greens paid an annual stipend, was in a fertile corner of Picenum on the Adriatic coast, amid orchards of figs and grapes so succulent that seals were known to crawl miles inland to feast on them.

"So quiet you can hear a bee humming in the hills," my father muttered to Gryphus, his principal slave (it is to the recollections of both these men that I owe this account). "See if you can stir up some life."

As Gryphus – then lean, sprightly and clean-shaven – scrambled off to locate someone to speak to, my father surveyed the farm, which consisted of rolling paddocks, fenced-off yards and a modest training track. There were a few horses grazing in the pastures and, in one of the corrals, a raven-haired and curiously overdressed stable boy running two colts through their paces. My father was admiring the boy's command of the horses – he was leading them in increasingly rapid circles, whipping the long rein up and down – when Gryphus returned with a beaming fellow sporting a sizeable divot in his forehead.

"You must be Rutilius Oceanus of the Blues!" exclaimed the man, wiping his hands on his tunic. "But we didn't expect you until next week! Spare me a moment to round up the horses and fetch old man Sterninius. He's the one who still does the deals, you know."

"I would be most grateful," my father responded acidly.

It had always been one of his ploys to show up at his shipyards without warning, but this was the first time he had done so at a stud farm. And he was decidedly unimpressed. He continued admiring the stable boy, who had yoked the colts to a chariot and was getting them used to the snaffle and harness, when "Old Man" Sterninius (he was, in truth, no older than my father, though he liked to feign the prestige of age) emerged from the homestead.

"You're not Rutilius Oceanus," said he, shading his eyes against the sun.

"I am Lucius Cornelius Picus," replied my father. "The new *dominus factionis* of the Greens."

"The shipbuilder?"

"The same."

"Well, you're welcome at any time, of course, but I must admit you've caught us off-guard."

"As is plainly apparent."

Sterninius chuckled. "Come inside, then, and bring your slaves – I shall have some food and fine wine brought out for you."

"I am here to inspect your finest horses, not your finest wines. And my time is rather limited in any case. I must be back in Campania by the end of the week."

"You've come to purchase some horses?"

"I did not come to admire the scenery."

"But of course," said Sterninius. "I shall muster our finest stallions for your inspection."

There followed shouts and bangs as Sterninius shuffled around prodding his men to life. But in the end only two unimpressive fellows appeared – the divot-headed one who had welcomed my father earlier and an overweight groom who waddled into the stables, wiping his nose on a forearm.

"Beautiful day," muttered Sterninius.

"I did not come here to admire the weather, either."

There was an awkward silence – the only sounds came from the stable boy training the colts – until the groom came out with two bay stallions. Sterninius, visibly relieved, launched into a sales pitch.

"Prize racers each," he declared. "Each of Cappadocian pedigree, each four years old, each primed and ready for the track, each destined for greatness in the arena."

"Who was the sire?"

"Advocatus himself, outside trace horse in over one hundred victories in the Circus Maximus."

"Advocatus is here?"

"Alas, he died servicing one of the brood mares. What a way to go, eh?"

My father, offering not the slightest hint of amusement, circled the horses. "And these are really the finest stock you have for sale?"

"They are the finest horses available anywhere in Italy."

"What about those ones there?" My father gestured to the horses in the yard.

"They are not yet ready."

13

"To me they look more promising than the ones you *do* have for sale."

"They are untrained colts."

"They look comfortable enough on the long rein."

"That's just the boy – he makes them look comfortable."

"Are you sure they are not earmarked for the Blues?"

"For the Blues?" Sterninius had visibly tightened. "No, of course not. Those horses are not close to Circus-standard."

"Hmm. Then you will be able to yoke and harness the stallions here? So that I might determine their potential?"

"You want a . . . demonstration?"

"Is that not customary at this estate of yours?"

"My clients usually trust my judgement."

"Well," said my father, "I do not. Advocatus raced in only eighty-seven victories in the Circus Maximus."

Ashen-faced, Sterninius went to find his drivers – stud farms usually employ a retired charioteer or two to drive horses when necessary – but, as much as they searched, Sterninius and his divot-headed assistant could not find them. (Gryphus later claimed he overheard the men speculating that the charioteers had "gone to town", presumably Firmum.) So the overweight groom was appointed to the task.

This fellow, gulping and sweating, drove the horses up and down the track a few times, lashing them violently – my father noticed that the raven-haired stable boy had stopped to watch with disapproval – but the performance was so lacklustre that not even Sterninius could burnish it.

"Such a pity that my charioteers are indisposed."

"Try the boy," my father suggested.

"The boy is not a charioteer."

"Try him anyway. He could scarcely be any worse."

So the stable boy was called up from the yard. First, he went up to each of the horses, pressed his forehead between their eyes,

14

breathed into their nostrils and stroked them tenderly, seeming to communicate with them without saying a word. Then, after adjusting the yoke and harness, he stepped into the chariot and, at a signal from Sterninius, drove the stallions for a few laps around the track, with considerably greater horsemanship than the groom, though he had not once deployed the whip.

"There – you see?" exclaimed Sterninius. "They just needed warming up, that's all!"

The boy stepped off the chariot and, without so much as a murmur, returned to the yard to resume his work with the colts.

Sterninius turned to my father. "What do you think?"

My father stroked his beard.

"Would . . . would you like to see them run again?"

"No." My father ruminated awhile before nodding decisively. "I shall take them."

Sterninius grunted with apparent satisfaction. "An excellent choice, sir – you will not regret it."

"My slave Gryphus will help draw up the contracts."

"Indeed, indeed. And I shall pour some wine to celebrate. Sergius" – this to the overweight groom – "get the horses ready."

But as the groom started unhitching the two stallions my father frowned. "Wait a moment," he said. "Wait a moment. I believe there has been a misunderstanding."

"Oh?"

"I meant I would purchase the two horses in the yard."

Sterninius blinked. "The colts?"

"The same."

"But . . . but they are not ready, as I have said."

"Nevertheless, those are the horses I wish to purchase."

"I'm not sure I understand." Sterninius looked stricken. "You have not even seen them on the track."

"I have already observed them in action with the stable boy," explained my father. "Besides, my speciality for twenty years has

15

been the construction of *hippagines* for the transport of horses. Thus I am familiar with all the breeds. I know their temperaments. I know their shortcomings. And I can assess their potential as quickly as I can determine the quality of timber by examining the bark on a tree. So I want those colts there. I want them today. Kindly draw up the contracts."

"This . . . this is most unusual."

"That it may be, but that is in my nature. And one other thing."

"Yes?"

"The raven-haired stable boy – I wish to purchase him as well."

"Lentulus?" said Sterninius. "No, no – you don't want Lentulus."

"You seem very disposed to telling me what I don't want, Sterninius."

"But you don't understand. The boy is not right – in the head, I mean. Trust me when I tell you this, if you trust me on nothing else."

"He seems perfectly normal to me," my father observed, "if a little quiet."

"He is not just quiet, he is mute. You have no idea what his former master did to him. He is less a boy than a beast, I tell you. No, no . . . you want nothing to do with Lentulus."

All this had been spoken within earshot of the boy, who nonetheless continued his work with the colts – banging copper sheets to simulate the din of the arena – as if completely oblivious. Unnerved – for Sterninius seemed sincere for a change – my father decided not to press the matter. He went into the homestead, finalised the contracts, and within an hour was rattling off in his carriage, along with Gryphus, his driver, his attendants, and the two freshly purchased colts. The stable boy, he noticed on his way out of the estate, had meanwhile headed into the pasture to round up two new horses.

The procession had barely travelled a mile, however, when a flock of ravens erupted from a millet field and wheeled overhead, their shadows dappling my father's face. And my father, who could be acutely superstitious when it suited him – he had a particular weakness for omens involving birds – decided that this represented nothing less than a sign from the gods. He would curse himself for ever if he did not trust his intuition. So he ordered the driver to turn back to the stud farm, where he formalised the purchase of the raven-haired slave boy over the renewed protestations of Sterninius.

"You will regret this, I tell you," the breeder growled. "That boy has misery branded on his hide – on his very soul."

In fact, "Old Man" Sterninius survived long enough to witness the entirety of his stable boy's racing career, and like innumerable others would claim to have been integral to his discovery. As for the boy himself, when he arrived at the Greens' estate in Campania, he was taken aside by the chief steward to be to be stripped and washed, at which point my father was called in to see something remarkable. And when he beheld the hundreds of scars, welts, ridges and burns that thatched the young lad's body from neck to toe – the boy himself was staring into middle-distance with his tormented black eyes – my father, who could be terribly emotional at times, admitted that he could "scarcely contain a tear".

That, in any event, was how Corax of Campania, as he came to be known, was acquired by the Greens.

# II

Very different were the circumstances by which my father purchased Alector of Arcadia.

Since the Green Faction's inception in the dying decades of the Republic, its principal training track had always been on the eastern side of the Field of Mars. But since this unbarricaded space, crowded in by the temples and playing fields of Rome, provided little privacy for the testing of horses and tactics, the faction had also maintained a track in Campania not far from Vesuvius (when based on the mountain, the slave army of Spartacus had raided the estate for its horses). Nevertheless, my father, upon assuming the role of *dominus factionis*, considered this property too distant from the Circus Maximus for convenience, and he despaired of the region's notoriously languid atmosphere, which he feared was having a corrupting influence on the faction's training staff and charioteers.

As it happened, it took some years before he fielded a satisfactory offer for the estate, but among the early landowners he sounded out, in a bid to offload it, was the Augustan senator Gnaeus Marcius, an old family acquaintance. This meeting took place either shortly before or shortly after the acquisition of Corax – the two events being so tightly bound that my father would not later be able to disentangle them.

Marcius at the time was residing at his luxurious seaside villa at Baiae. Here, amid his fishponds, cascades and terraces cluttered with statues, he received my father cordially, listened politely to his offer, and graciously declined. "I'm afraid, dear Picus, that I'm far too old now to be purchasing new estates. I already own so many mansions, villas, vineyards and tenanted lands that it's beyond my power to keep track of them. But I'll tell you what I shall do. There's an old friend of mine, Publius Vinicius – I assume you've heard of him?"

"The consul?"

"And governor of Asia for some years. I happen to know he's staying for a while at his villa on the other side of Neapolis – I dined with him last week – and I'm certain he mentioned his interest in purchasing land in this area. I shall notify him of your property's availability at once."

"That's very kind of you, Marcius, but when do you think you might receive a reply?"

"My courier Philantos will deliver a letter and return directly with his response."

"My dear Marcius, I must depart here well before nightfall – much too soon for your courier to get to the other side of Neapolis and back."

Marcius smirked. "You've not met Philantos," he said.

With that, the old senator scribbled some details on a scroll and called for his courier.

This turned out to be a sparkling-eyed, flaxen-haired young boy bearing an aspect of unnatural self-confidence.

"Philantos," said Marcius, "do you see this gentleman here?"

"I see him," replied the presumptuous lad, surveying my father with indifference.

"I want you to deliver this message to Publius Vinicius on his behalf. Do you remember the villa of Publius Vinicius? You have carried messages there in the past."

"I remember."

"Then make haste and use our swiftest horse. I require Vinicius's answer before my guest departs."

"Oh?" the boy sniffed. "What's in it for me?"

"The standard treat, and no more."

"It's a tall order, what you're asking. How do I know this fellow won't be leaving within the hour?"

"My guest, for all his pressing engagements, will leave only after you return. It is therefore only good manners to make him wait not a minute longer than necessary – would you not agree?"

"I say again, what's in it for me?"

"You will get a slice of fig pie as normal."

"And a cup of wine?"

"Very well, and a cup of wine."

The boy – no older than twelve – snorted, accepted the scroll, and hastened off.

"My word, Marcius," scoffed my father when the lad had disappeared. "I've never seen anything like it!"

"Quite the cockerel, isn't he?"

"But to speak to you with such impudence – a mere slave boy!"

"A slave boy, perhaps, but it's difficult not to indulge Philantos. He has been, you see, the finest messenger boy I have ever owned. Fast, reliable, indefatigable, and master of all the shortcuts between here and Beneventum."

"But there are limits to how much you should tolerate, surely? It sets a bad example for the rest of your slaves."

"If all my slaves were as efficient in their duties as Philantos, I might happily suffer their insolence as well. Would you care to purchase him, by the way?"

My father frowned. "And why would you be offering him for sale, if he is really as invaluable as you suggest?"

"For a start, there's a small matter of prudence. Did you not notice that I had to seal and stamp that scroll?"

"I did."

"Well, that's because Philantos has demonstrated a fondness for reading my correspondence in the course of delivering it, then gossiping about the contents later."

"Unforgivable!"

"And that's not the worst of it. Because you will by now have noticed my new wife, Valeria."

"Of course."

"And you will agree that hers is a singular beauty, to whose allure a poet would struggle to do justice?"

"My dear fellow," my father said, "you're not suggesting—?"

"No, the boy has not made any advances on her – not yet." Marcius chuckled. "But, as sure as Mars consorted with Venus, he will attempt to do so one day – I can see it in his eyes. And I tell you honestly, as old as I am, and as young as Valeria is, I am not at all confident she will be able to resist his charms. It would thus be an enormous relief for me if you took the boy off my hands and kept him far out of my sight – not to mention the vicinity of my wife."

My father shook his head. "And as delighted as I would be to help, dear Marcius, I am not sure I need a courier right now, as exceptional as he might be."

"I thought perhaps you might have another use for him."

"Oh?" My father, who was very prudish at heart – he would cover my eyes if a stallion so much as sniffed a mare in our presence – raised his eyebrows. "What makes you think that I might have suddenly developed such inclinations?"

"No, no," Marcius clarified quickly, "I mean as a charioteer."

"A charioteer – why? Has he had any experience on the track?"

21

"None, I grant you, but I am convinced he would learn the skills very quickly. He regards no activity as beyond his capabilities, and is entirely impervious to fear. Are those not the very qualities that are essential in a charioteer? How is that faction of yours coming along, by the way?"

There followed a lengthy digression during which my father detailed, with much purgative pleasure, the many unforeseen problems he had encountered as *dominus factionis* of the Greens, including his ongoing frustration with the lack of support afforded by "that death adder Tiberius", who by then was devoting most of his time to degenerate activities on Capri. (On a clear day the emperor's island residence could be spotted from Marcius's front balcony: "I swear," laughed Marcius, "I've seen falcons drop from the sky as they swoop over the place, so toxic are the fumes that emanate from it.")

By this time the sunlight was gilding the western wing of the villa and my father said he would need to return to the estate, "as much as it grieves me to miss the reply of Publius Vinicius. But perhaps," he added tactfully, "you could have your courier deliver the reply to me personally at the estate tomorrow? In that way I might test for myself his aptitude on the track."

"I am sure Philantos would be delighted to visit your estate at any time," Marcius replied mischievously. "But what makes you think that you will not be receiving the message, when he has already returned with it?"

"Returned with it, has he?"

"He is in fact standing behind you right now."

My father swivelled in his seat, finding to his astonishment the boy, with barely a sheen of perspiration on his forehead, staring down at him triumphantly.

My father gasped. "Are you really trying to tell me," he asked the lad, "that you rode all the way to the other side of Neapolis and back again while I have been sitting here?"

"With enough time for some reading on the way," replied the boy, thrusting out an unsealed scroll. "Publicius says he would be happy to inspect the property you have for sale, but while he is not without interest, he must warn you that he is already committed to purchasing a separate estate north of Cumae."

My father was speechless, accepting the scroll without even reading it. But the boy, he discovered, had not yet finished.

"And I can be a charioteer," he declared, "if that's what you're talking about. I can be the greatest charioteer of all time. You just wait and see. I can be anything."

And at just that moment, my father claimed later, he heard a cock crowing in the distance – another sign from the heavens, he decided, that it would be foolish to ignore.

That, in any case, was how Alector of Arcadia, the Greek Rooster, began his famously flamboyant career with the Greens.

# III

M Y FATHER AT THE TIME HAD A PENCHANT for naming his new recruits after the birds of land and sea, as well as assigning them alliterative towns, provinces and regions the boys themselves had not even visited in their dreams: hence Pelicanus of Pannonia, Cygnus of Cyrenaica, Pavo of Peloponnesus, Aquilinus of Aquitania, Columbus of Calabria, Graculus of Gades, Mergus of Magnesia and Halcyon of Heliopolis (mercifully he tired of this predilection before naming the boys after the vulture, the screech owl and the dunghill cock).

These were some of the apprentices whom Corax of Campania (the Raven), and Alector of Arcadia (the Rooster), joined for stable-hand duties in their first years at the Campania estate. It was, need-less to say, a task at which Corax immediately excelled. Not only did he sleep with the horses in the stables, even on the most frigid of nights, but he was the first to inspect them in the morning, the last to settle them in the evening, and often the only one around to comfort them during storms and volcanic eruptions. He was meant to learn the finer points of equestrian welfare from the faction's senior *veterinarii*, but he had his own methods of leg binding, wound-dressing and hoof-trimming, not to mention his personal variations on traditional equine diagnostics, which in most cases proved demonstrably superior to those in practice. It was said that he could determine a horse's age without looking at its teeth, test it for fever simply by touching it under the jaw, and detect if it had worms merely by pressing his ear to its belly.

"Small wonder," my father observed later, "that 'Old Man' Sterninius did not want to see him sold."

The tragic fate of Silvanus, at the time the Green Faction's finest outside trace horse, eloquently illustrates the boy's abilities. After exhibiting lameness in the right foreleg, Silvanus was sent to Campania to recuperate under Corax's supervision. After four weeks the horse seemed sufficiently improved for the veterinarians to declare that he was ready to race again in the Circus. But Corax – in a display of vocal protest all the more striking for its rarity – insisted that Silvanus was not nearly fit enough for the arena.

"I tell you solemnly," he said, planting himself in front of the veterinarians as they attempted to remove the stallion from the stables, "that if Silvanus runs without another month's rest his foreleg will crack."

The veterinarians hesitated – Corax even in his youth could be daunting when he spoke – but in the end they scoffed. "The beast's bindings will be enough to keep his leg in one piece. That is, if your wrappings are of a sufficient standard in the first place."

Six days later, Silvanus was swinging around the eastern turning posts at the Circus Maximus when there was a snap so loud that a collective flinch rippled through the crowd. Silvanus buckled and the other horses in the team came sprawling down on top of him. Eutychus of Dalmatia, the faction's most promising young charioteer, was very nearly killed in the chaos. Silvanus himself was dragged by ground attendants into the spoilarium and mercifully dispatched.

When informed of the tragedy, Corax said nothing, but he retreated to the stables, stony faced, and did not appear again for hours. I do not believe he cried, because Corax never cried – except on one occasion, which I shall mention in time – but I have no doubt he lamented his failure to advertise his objections more vehemently.

"Had I known of his protests I would have prevented Silvanus from racing, of course," my father told me later. "Even as a boy, Corax was worth a thousand of those pompous quacks."

Corax would go on to have innumerable more opportunities to prove his worth, and my father – who saw in the lad's grasp of horses something akin to his own extrasensory feel for the density and pliability of wood – would congratulate himself repeatedly for observing the auguries and turning back to the Sternini stud farm.

My mother, on the other hand, was much less enamoured of Corax. A matronly and forthright woman – the one person on earth, apart from unhinged emperors, capable of intimidating my father – she could never tolerate anyone with a gloomy disposition, convinced that dourness was a self-inflicted and deeply selfish malady. She liked to appear at the training estate occasionally to admire the horses and the hard-bodied physiques of the charioteers – she was quite shameless about such things – but Corax only made her nose curl. "That boy wears the mask of tragedy," she sniffed. "Mark my words, some drama will one day befall him – something will make us wish he had never been born."

She was, in contrast, much taken with Alector, whose cocksure manner appealed to her love of the theatre. "That boy wears the mask of comedy," she declared. "He will bring joy wherever he goes."

For that matter, my father was also fond of the Rooster, seeing in his swagger a theatricality that would generate much popularity in the Circus. But to the boy's companions on the estate – the slightly older apprentices in particular – Alector often seemed less charming and amusing than arrogant and impudent. He had, for instance, a penchant for outrageous pranks, such as when he slapped mustard on the fundaments of four horses about to race (the team, driven by a charioteer who had recently insulted Alector, bucked and bolted and ploughed through a barrier at the end of the track); or when, having been ordered to clean out the stables, he dug a hole outside the door of the sleeping quarters, filled it with horse dung, bellowed "Fire! Fire!" at the top of his lungs, and watched with great amusement as the boys piled one after another into the pit.

He was also disinclined to squander his time on the welfare of the horses, insisting that it was charioteers that won races, not their steeds. Nor was he disposed to perform the customary body- and discipline-building exercises, arguing that he already possessed every quality necessary to be a champion charioteer and no amount of rope jumping or weightlifting was going to make him any stronger or faster. He was eager to take up the reins of a chariot team and frequently did so anyway when no one was watching.

Meanwhile, my father continued to use him as a courier and once even dispatched him with a personal greeting to Valeria, the fetching young wife of the boy's former master Gnaeus Marcius (while Marcius was absent, as an additional tease). My father reckoned that Alector was such an exceptional rider that, should he somehow fail to make the grade as a charioteer, he would certainly become the best jubilator* in the empire.

Indeed, Alector once prevailed upon my father to prove his superior horsemanship to the other boys. So my father had a faction flag buried at a nominated point outside Neapolis and then sent out the apprentices to retrieve it. As it happened, the other riders found Alector galloping out of sight before they had ridden more than half a mile from the estate, and they were still negotiating a difficult bend under the Aqua Augustus, north of the city, when they spotted the Rooster again, already waving the green pennant, flashing over their heads on the aqueduct itself – this elevated network being one

---

* A rider who wove between chariots to issue instructions during a race.

of the means by which he had spirited around the region with such preternatural swiftness.

The boy's triumphalism after this victory, and indeed everything about his bearing, should have made him insufferable to the ascetic Corax, and vice versa. But curiously the two boys, so different in philosophy and temperament, were on remarkably good terms in those early years. Corax, for instance, would invariably single out Alector's horses for special attention before and after races, just as Alector would spare his sombre friend the mockery he so enthusiastically meted to their fellow stable boys – and in fact would shield him from ridicule at every turn.

Perhaps it was a matter of chance, since both had arrived at the estate at roughly the same time and found themselves branded immediately, and mistakenly, as brothers. Perhaps it was Corax's secret admiration for Alector, a fellow slave boy who refused to be cowed by anyone, regardless of status. Or maybe it had something to do with Alector's genuine awe at the physical sufferings that young Corax had so evidently endured.

Whatever the case, it would become a source of great wonder, to those who knew them only later, that the two epic rivals had once been the firmest of friends.

# IV

THE CHARIOTEERS' CREED, called the Code of Romulus after the notional founder of the Circus Maximus, remains something of a cultish dogma in which pride, lust, resentment and greed are swirled together in an intoxicating brew that inebriates as many as it invigorates. Charioteers are encouraged to fixate on the one motivation that most empowers them – self-indulgence, honour, freedom, revenge – and bow at the altar of the corresponding god: Bacchus, Honos, Libertas, Nemesis. They repeat articles of the creed as mantras: *In the heat of the race the champion always finds extra; The greater the odds, the sweeter the victory; No pain is without pleasure; The race is never over until the finishing line is crossed.*

Naturally my father arranged for his champion charioteers, young and old, to visit the training estate now and then to stir this bubbling pot. Among the former variety was the aforementioned Eutychus of Dalmatia, at the time predicted to become one of the greatest charioteers of all time (he retired rich and famous but not especially great, as will be seen); among the latter was the retired freedman Durius of Sicily, not quite the oldest charioteer ever to have raced in the Circus – that was Curtius of Bononia, whose grandsons cheered him through his final race – but arguably the most sated and content.

"Look at me," Durius would exclaim to the apprentices. "Thirty years ago, I was a slave boy like you. I was a chattel. I was a piece of furniture. I was a donkey. A pig. A hound. A flea. But then I was discovered by the Green Faction. I trained, like you, as a charioteer. I trained hard. I never stopped training. I trained so hard and so relentlessly, in fact, that I had no time to question whether I was happy or sad. And if I was frustrated at times, it was only because I could not wait to drive horses in the Circus Maximus. Because I could see like an oracle into the future and knew that I had within me the ability to be a first-rank charioteer if only I made the right sacrifices. So I allowed myself no distractions. I permitted myself no self-pity. I committed myself, mind and body, to the cause. And what happened? I became a biga* driver in the Circus. I was soon the *best* biga driver in the Circus. I became a triga driver. I was soon the *best* triga driver. I became a quadriga driver. I was soon the *best* quadriga driver. I was a champion. I consorted with consuls. I cavorted with singing girls. I made love to the wives of senators. I was no stranger to imperial palaces. I was celebrated by the Divine Augustus himself. I received the golden laurel from his godly hands. I won millions of sesterces for my masters. I won many more millions for myself. I became a freedman. I remain a freedman. I shall die a freedman. And look at me now."

Durius usually contrived to appear before such assemblies reclined on a couch balancing a cup of wine in one hand and a bunch of grapes in the other, fanned by half-naked slave girls – the very picture of Bacchanalian glory.

"I live in the most luxurious house in Stabiae. I have villas all around the mainland and on Ischia. I am bathed in scented oils and

---

* Two-horse chariot.

priceless perfumes. I eat peacock brains off golden plates. I drink wine out of silver chalices. When I appear on the streets people clear a path for me. They offer me tributes. They offer me food. They offer me their daughters. I want for nothing. I have not a care in the world. I concern myself not about the machinations of the senate, the status of the army, or the trading price of wheat. I wake when it pleases me, eat when it pleases me, fornicate when it pleases me, and attend the Circus when it pleases me. No one, not a soul, tells me what to do. And to those who might say that I live a life of decadence I say this." At this point he would lean forward and cast a sweeping look across the eager young faces arrayed before him. "Of course I do. Because I came from nothing, from less than nothing, to be an emperor of the Circus Maximus. Because I risked my life for my own freedom. Because again and again I escaped the greedy fingers of Charon. Because in amassing my victories I became one of only six *milliarii** in Circus history. Because the sun has clearly shone on me, as it is shining right now, and it is not for me to argue with the sun. And any one of you boys here today – even you, my granite-faced friend – can one day be like me."

Legend has it that on this occasion he was referring to Corax of Campania, though I suspect that, even if this were true, the Raven would have been unmoved by such singular attention. But rumour also has it – and this I find less difficult to believe – that Alector was particularly receptive to Durius's exhortations that day, furiously nodding his head and muttering, "That will be me. That will be me!" As for the rest of the Durius's claims, I can verify that they are true, barring the expedient omission that he had also raced for the Reds and Whites at various stages in his career. I chanced across him one day at the baths of Rhegium, when he was in his seventies, and his zest for life remained undimmed, allowing for a

---

* Winner of a thousand races.

certain chagrin that his celebrity had been eclipsed by the likes of Corax and Alector.

Less favoured by the gods, it must be said, were the multitude of charioteers who had been physically ruined on the track. Among the most common injuries were shattered pelvises, dislocated shoulders, torn ligaments, amputated limbs and fractured skulls. Charioteers forced by such disabilities into early retirement were a pitiful lot, hobbling about lamenting what might have been; and since it was not considered desirable for them to haunt the arenas and certainly not the training tracks, for "the good of the Circus" they were obliged to fade as swiftly (and as far away) as possible. It is therefore one of my father's many great legacies that he refused to ignore these broken men entirely, being instrumental in securing a subsistence fund for those most in need, as well as complimentary seats in the Circus Maximus on race days, and even a well-tended Cemetery of Charioteers, just outside the Capena Gate, for those who had already crossed the final finishing line.

Neither did he seek to have their ugly fates hidden from the apprentices. He made a point, in fact, of turning misfortune into motivation. The head trainer at Campania in those days, Phoebus of Thrace, himself something of a cripple, was the chief conduit of such bracing truths. "A quarter of you will retire maimed!" he would roar. "A quarter of you will die. A quarter of you will become moderately successful. And a quarter of you will be rich beyond the dreams of Croesus. Which is it to be? Do you baulk at the possibility of injury or death? Or do you see a priceless opportunity to break your shackles and soar among the gods?"

Here he would return to the Creed. "Risk is the mother of greatness! It was challenges that made Hercules a god! The ordeals of the journey enhance the lustre of the destination! Navigate your way through the reefs of destruction" – nautical metaphors have always been popular with charioteers – "and you will see the lighthouse on the bluff! And you will anchor, when you retire, in the harbour of contentment! And if by chance you do sink early beneath the waves, remember that there is no greater honour than to expire in the Circus. History will remember you long after the emperors' names have faded on their plinths. And as for consuls, scribes, generals, gladiators – they would need to live for a thousand years to be as half as famous as a *milliarius*. Think of Durius of Sicily! In these parts he is more famous than Tiberius, and a good sight more popular to boot. Think of his prizes! Think of his laurels! Think of his memories! Did you not see the look on his face when he was here? I tell you honestly, I can imagine no greater reward than for a man to live out his days basking in the light of his own glories. Oh, that I could live like that! Oh, that I had been good enough to *deserve* that. Oh, that I had trained hard enough to warrant that reward. And now, alas" – stroking his misshapen leg with gnarled fingers – "my only hope is to achieve greatness through the miserable likes of you."

Phoebus of Thrace might not have been a top-rank charioteer, being the victor in only thirty-three races in the Circus Maximus. He was not even the best of trainers (though he, too, would later claim to have been integral to the discovery of Corax and Alector). But it would be churlish not to acknowledge the evergreen poignancy of the retired sportsman resigned to envying comrades who have somehow accomplished everything that he, for various reasons, has sadly failed to achieve.

# V

UPON HIS BIRTH MY FATHER HAD BEEN AWARDED the cognomen Picus, after the woodpeckers that were at that moment drumming in the trees outside the family home, and it is to be supposed that this distinction – for previous members of the Cornelii family had been named after sea creatures – served to cement his allegiance to the avian world. As to whether this name influenced his destiny, or merely signalled it, is a subject for philosophers; suffice to say that his woodpecker-like eye for the quality of timber would in time take him around the empire – to the forests of the Pyrenees, Bithynia, Macedonia, Crete, Parnassus, and even Cimmeria – and claim for him the title of Rome's premier mast-hunter. It seemed inevitable, therefore, that whereas my grandfather had always been prone to assess men using seafaring metaphors – "He sails close to the wind"; "He's full of bilge"; "He tacks this way and that" – my father in turn would become partial to analogies involving wood – "He's a fine grain of man"; "He's as tough as cedar"; "He bends like a palm tree".

He expanded the family business everywhere from Spain to Syria – shipyards in half a dozen ports, timber plantations in as many provinces – and proved more than capable of assuming the captaincy itself when his father succumbed to gout and apoplexia. Already in his mid-thirties at the time, he was convinced he would pilot the Cornelii business to its days of greatest glory.

But something inexplicable was afoot. The chief shipbuilding rivals of the Cornelii were the Rutilii, originally of ancient Etruscan stock, and a more prestigious family insofar as their far reaches harboured at least one former consul. Their new "captain" was Quintus Rutilius Oceanus, the same age as my father but otherwise as dissimilar as it was possible to be: short, grim-looking, unde-monstrative and "as cheap as a boxwood chest". And yet Oceanus was somehow securing shipbuilding commissions that my father assumed would be his own, in some cases even claiming contracts that had been in the Cornelii family for decades.

My father could not fathom it. Rutilian vessels were jerry-built, they were riddled with woodworm, and in storms they broke apart "like wicker baskets". He began to wonder if Oceanus was bribing or blackmailing; if, against all evidence, the little fellow was some sort of criminal mastermind. It was only when he discovered that, concurrent to taking over the family business, his rival had also become *dominus factionis* of the Blues – more or less an honorary appointment at the time – that he saw the wood for the trees. Oceanus was leveraging his position as president of that chariot racing faction – the one most favoured by senators, ambitious equites and opportunistic civil servants – to generate business opportunities for himself.

My father knew at once what needed to be done. The Cornelii, after all, had long been passive followers of the Greens, the one faction that was even more popular than the Blues. And my father, through the construction of horse transports, was already on good terms with its many breeders, scouts and quartermasters. So now was the time, with the position conveniently vacant, to capitalise. He would become *dominus factionis* of the Greens. And, just like Oceanus, he would make the most of this association to win contracts where his own faction was most popular – among the military, the plebeian aediles, the merchant class, the artisans, and the common people themselves.

For a man with such tenuous connections to take over a faction so swiftly and comprehensively would not be possible today, when racing structures are so much stricter and more impenetrable. In the days of Tiberius, however, the sport was going through a painful period of transition. The sallow and depraved emperor's personal antipathy for public spectacles had a direct bearing on the number willing to fund them. There was a general feeling in the chariot racing fraternity that these were years that had to be endured, with some stoicism, before a new light appeared on the horizon. And this hesitancy proved enough for my father to storm in and take over without resistance – becoming, overall, the thirteenth *dominus factionis* in the Green Faction's recorded history.

The passion, the inexhaustible energy, the skills of command, and not least the innovations he brought to chariot racing, would prove legendary. They would change the sport for ever. For which some credit must go to Quintus Rutilius Oceanus for spurring him to action in the first place, and thereafter providing the sort of rivalry – alternately bitter and good-natured – that my father had always believed was crucial to success.

It is sweetly ironic, therefore, that both Oceanus and my father would become best known for what they did *not* do, rather than for what they did: Oceanus as the shipbuilder who travelled only once by sea (a traumatic maiden voyage had left him unwilling ever again to risk the waves), and my father as the *dominus factionis* who witnessed just one race in the Circus Maximus – a race, arguably the most famous in history, which naturally I shall cover in due course.

# VI

WHEN HE FOUND TIME TO VISIT THE ESTATE in Campania during a particularly hectic season of shipbuilding, my father was presented with a most memorable scene. By this stage Corax and Alector had commenced full training, and my father, convinced that both would soon be champions, arrived expecting to field encouraging news about their progress. Instead, Phoebus of Thrace hauled the two boys forward, his hands clamped around their necks, and hurled Corax to the ground.

"Take a look at him, my lord," he spat. "A wilful, disobedient boy who will never amount to anything on the track. I'd send him to the silver mines if I had my way!"

My father was dumbfounded. "Whatever has he done?"

"It's what he *hasn't* done that's the problem."

"And what exactly is that?"

"He won't lash the horses. Refuses outright to do so! I ask you, what good is a charioteer who cares more about the horses than he does about winning?"

My father surveyed Corax, who had pushed himself to his feet. "Is it true, boy? Look at me for a moment."

Corax raised his melancholy eyes.

"You do not whip the horses? Even in the final lap?"

Corax continued to look pained.

"Ha!" sneered Phoebus. "What did I tell you, my lord? There's something wrong with the lad! I've promised to flog *him* if he doesn't follow orders!"

My father, shuddering at the thought, turned his attention to Alector. "And what has this one done wrong?"

"What has he *not* done wrong?" exclaimed Phoebus, now shaking the Rooster. "Hijinks, insolence, truancy – you name it! From a boy who's been here three years now, too, can you believe it?"

My father had been expecting nothing else. "But on the track?"

"On the track he is performing below expectations."

"How so?"

"Because he's been infected with the stupidity of his cheerless chum here! Because he too refuses to lash the horses!"

My father frowned. "You too choose not to use the whip?" he asked Alector.

"I use it, of course I use it."

"Aye!" said Phoebus, shaking him again. "But so lightly that it might as well be a gnat's sting!"

"That's all the horses need from me," countered Alector. "It's the charioteer that wins races, not the whip."

"What did I tell you?" chortled Phoebus. "The sprite's fallen under the influence of raven-boy here! Do I have permission to flog them both, my lord?"

Alector began to protest. "The horses can be trained—"

"Close your beak, you noxious cockerel!"

"I tell you, the horses can be—"

"I said shut your maw!" Phoebus's hands were around his neck.

My father intervened. "There's no need for that – let the boy speak for a moment."

Alector took the opportunity to shake the trainer off. "I said the horses can be trained to respond to the trumpet's blare. Corax here

38

has already done so many times. The blare, he's proved, is more motivating than any whip."

"The blare?" asked my father.

"Have you ever heard anything like it, my lord?" Phoebus sniggered. "These two have been training the horses to respond to the sound of the trumpet."

"The trumpet?"

"We blow a trumpet here at the start of the sixth lap, to signal the final two laps to the drivers – to warn them to get the whips cracking."

"A signal, you say?"

"It was my idea, because we have no lap counters."

"And these boys" – my father indicated Corax and Alector – "they believe the horses can be trained to gallop faster upon hearing this blare?"

"Have you ever heard of such a thing?"

"But is there any truth to what they say?"

"What does it matter?" said Phoebus. "No trumpets are used to signal the final laps in the Circus Maximus."

"Not yet," said Alector.

"Quiet, rooster-boy!"

My father, ruminating a moment, looked at Alector and Corax – the latter was still staring into the middle distance – and arrived at a decision. "Let me see this," he said. "Let me see it in action."

"My lord?"

"A race, I mean."

"But my lord—"

"Do as I say. These two boys against our finest apprentices."

"You mean to say you—"

"Just do it!"

"If . . . if you insist, my lord."

With conspicuous reluctance, Phoebus summoned three senior apprentices as well as one young charioteer who had already raced in the Circus Maximus. This made for six chariot teams in all, and it took an hour for all the horses to be marshalled and harnessed at the makeshift starting line. But when it came time for the race, Alector was already exhibiting his customary cockiness, grinning and gesticulating and inviting all to admire him. Corax was expressionless as usual.

The rope barrier was dropped and the race began.

The experienced charioteer immediately bolted out to the lead, followed by the senior apprentices with Alector well behind and Corax bringing up the rear. And for my father this was a dispiriting sight, not least because the boys' refusal to use the whip seemed to be costing them dearly. But by the third lap, when the other teams no longer responded so readily to the lash, Alector had made up enough ground to be midway through the pack with Corax close behind, tactically blocking the stragglers. And so it proceeded for the next two laps also, with Alector inching his team ever closer to the lead and Corax continuing to obstruct his rivals.

A groundsman hoisted a trumpet and blared out a note.

And now – just as the other charioteers began whipping their horses violently – Alector's horses abruptly seemed possessed. With nary a lash they surged past the other teams, assuming the lead and extending it all the way to the finishing line, completing the race five chariot-lengths ahead of the nearest competitor.

Corax, having played his supporting role to great effect, came a creditable third.

As Alector performed an impromptu victory lap, celebrating as though he had achieved a famous victory in the Circus Maximus, my father turned to Phoebus. "You were seeking to flog the boy," he snapped, "when perhaps it is I who should be flogging *you*."

"But, my lord," whimpered Phoebus, "the trumpet ... the trumpet is not used that way in the Circus – as I have already noted."

To which my father, climbing back into his carriage, repeated with great satisfaction the words of Alector.

"*Not yet.*"

# VII

THE QUESTION OF WHO IS RESPONSIBLE for the trumpet blast that now signals the sixth lap in the Circus Maximus remains a matter of historical dispute. Was it my father, who made the suggestion to the stewards and magistrates? Was it Alector, who first brought the idea to my father's attention? Corax, who trained the horses to respond to the sound? Or even Phoebus, who introduced the practice to the training track? As is often the case for the beleaguered historian, attribution remains difficult to pin down. What is indisputable is that my father, not for the first time in chariot racing history, had deviously altered the rules to furnish the Greens with a subtle if short-lived advantage.

He was no less active in uniting the other factions in order to pursue the interests of chariot racing in general. In this capacity he met frequently with his arch nemesis Rutilius Oceanus as well as the *domini factionum* of the Reds and Whites (in those early years, Gratitidius Iuvenlis and Pedius Facilis respectively). Here, in tones of expedient civility, the men discussed such matters as the financial disposition of the sport as a whole, the merits of expanding into the provinces, and the lamentable condition of the Circus Maximus itself.

Of particular concern was the increasingly lawless behaviour of race-day crowds. Spectators were flashing mirrors at the horses, they were throwing spiked balls and pottery shards, they were rolling around drunk and rioting in the stands. In fact, the *domini factionum* have always been highly ambivalent about faction partisans, thriving on their numbers and enthusiasm, but sharing a vigorous disdain for the individuals themselves. Nevertheless, they were able to fashion the prevailing unruliness into yet another reason for imperial indulgence. In Augustus's reign there had been seventeen race days per annum; now there were just twelve. Clearly the plebeians were getting restive because they had too few opportunities to expel their tensions.

Unfortunately, Tiberius had by this stage appointed a humourless magistrate of public events, Titus Caesonius, whose only purpose seemed to be to nip in the bud any proposal for imperial funding. My father therefore appealed for a meeting with Tiberius himself.

"The emperor is not interested in your silly games," Caesonius sneered. "Nevertheless, I shall pass on your request, just for the satisfaction of having it officially declined."

It was a surprise to everyone, then, when Tiberius agreed to meet both my father and Rutilius Oceanus at the earliest opportunity. He added that some apprentices should be brought along so that he might "keep a finger on the state of our youth". My father duly selected Corax and Alector, his most promising young charioteers, while Oceanus chose two lads from his own faction, including the future champion Crudelis of Utica. All these met up in Misenum, where they were to be conveyed, along with a cargo of exotic delicacies, across the waters to Capri in an imperial trireme fresh from Oceanus's shipyards. But at the last moment Oceanus, panting with anxiety, could not bring himself to endure even such a modest voyage, and was forced to relinquish his boys to the command of my father.

"It's fortunate that the seas are so smooth today," teased my father, "or I, too, would be thinking twice about risking my life in one of your godforsaken tubs."

On the island they were bustled by Titus Caesonius up many flights of rock-hewn stairs – a carriageway had been cut nearby, though Caesonius's clear intention was to make them sweat – and down some winding paths, through some heavily guarded gates, and into the palatial Villa Jovis, where my father was alarmed to see scantily clothed youths cavorting in the shadows. In lush gardens overlooking the sea, Tiberius – pale and bony, with diamond flakes of skin hanging from his face ("He looked like a birch with peeling bark," my father observed later) – was reclining on a fallen oak under thick-foliaged mastic trees.

"I find my skin can no longer tolerate the sunlight," the emperor wheezed, "so I hide in the shade like a salamander. Line the boys up at once, whatever-your-name-is, so I might inspect them."

"Of course, Caesar."

My father went about arranging the boys in a line, fussing in particular over Corax and Alector while expounding on their talents and predicting great things to come. "I promise you," he assured the emperor, "that you will find no better chariot racing apprentices anywhere."

Tiberius, however, ordered the boys to turn one way and the other and raise their arms and legs. "Why is the one on the left swathed like a corpse?" he asked.

"Corax dresses that way to cover his scars, Caesar."

"Scars?"

"He was beaten mercilessly by a former master."

"His flesh is marred, is it?"

"Very much so, Caesar."

The emperor grunted and transferred his attention to Alector. "And the other one? Why is he looking so impertinent?"

"What's that mean?" demanded Alector.

"You see?" snorted Tiberius, turning as if for an apology.

"It's true Alector is unusually self-assured," my father conceded, "but not without reason, Caesar, considering his outstanding horsemanship."

"I care not about horsemanship," scowled Tiberius. "What about the other ones there?"

My father was forced to admit that he knew nothing about Oceanus's apprentices apart from the fact that they were training for the Blues. "Though they can hardly for blamed for that."

Tiberius appraised the two lads from several angles and motioned to a functionary. "Have them taken into the villa and oiled," he said, before turning back to my father. "You can keep the other two for yourself." Then he settled back, looking impatient. "And now get down to your other business, whatever-your-name-is, for I have much better things to occupy my attention."

As Oceanus's boys were whisked away and Corax and Alector wandered off to explore the gardens, my father, increasingly perturbed, lowered himself onto a cypress log and tactfully proposed the extra race days – something, he said, that was "in the clear interests of Rome".

But the emperor, who seemed more interested in scratching loose skin from his face, looked him up and down. "Rome's interests?" he growled. "What about the emperor's interests?"

"Caesar?"

"You know what I mean. Reward the people extra days in the Circus and you only give them more opportunities to gather in groups and hatch plots against me."

"I am aware of no plots, Caesar."

"Oh really? What do they say about me in the Circus now? What do they call me?"

"Since, Caesar, you are seldom there, they have no reason to say anything."

"Cease humouring me – what do they say?"

44

My father settled on a deflection. "I can tell you honestly, Caesar, that I have heard not a word of criticism about you in the stands. But that is only because I also avoid the Circus on race day."

"You too?" The emperor had raised one of his unruly eyebrows.

"I'm afraid so, Caesar. You see, the possibility of injury or worse to my horses and charioteers is something I simply cannot tolerate. Thus I never attend the races, for fear of witnessing something unbearable."

"It has nothing to do with the rabble?"

"The rabble, Caesar?"

"The mobs, the plebs – are you really telling me you enjoy their company any more than I do?"

"I cannot say whether I enjoy it or not, Caesar, since I am never there." Then my father, sensing that Tiberius was wearying of him, decided to risk candour. "But as to what they say about you elsewhere, Caesar, well, if it's anything like what I hear in the streets . . ."

"In the streets?" Now the emperor leaned forward. "And what pray tell do they say in the streets?"

My father girded himself. "They call you an absentee landlord, Caesar, more interested in perversions than the fate of Rome."

"They say that, do they?"

"I'm afraid so, Caesar."

Tiberius thought about it and chortled. "Yes, I imagine they would. The ingrates have no idea how much I've done for them – no understanding at all of the intricacies of good administration. They just go on stoking their little resentments, as they always have. It's like a fire, you know. A thousand fires are one thing, but put them together and you have a conflagration. Do you know what Augustus told me?"

"What did he tell you, Caesar?"

"That chariot racing is the most dangerous cult in Rome, and its acolytes the most fearsome. The raging fires kindled in the Circus scared even him. Such destructive powers, he said, can be contained by only the most tireless of leaders, and harnessed by only the most manipulative."

"Leaders like you, Caesar."

"No," scoffed Tiberius, "I have no interest in stoking fires. Nor do I have any desire to hitch my fate to a chariot. That is not my way. So forget about your dreams of more race days, whatever-your-name-is. What else did you come here to petition for?"

My father, adjusting as rapidly as possible, blurted out the Guild's other proposals – including more Vigiles in the arena and the relocation of the beast hunts to the Circus Flaminius – and for the very first time he raised the issue that would become a lifelong obsession: the reconstruction of the stands of the Circus Maximus. "Which, as I'm sure you already know, Caesar, with your commendable interest in fire risks, are made of highly flammable wood, made even more volatile by the number of cookshops that infest the outside of the arena."

"Now that would truly make for a conflagration, would it not?"

"It would be a terrible and avoidable tragedy, Caesar."

"I suppose you are suggesting that the stands be made of marble?"

"They need not be marble. There are certain species of fireproof wood, as I'm sure you'll remember, from your days as a general in Germania."

"Raetian larch, I assume you mean?"

"Precisely, Caesar."

"You wish to see Raetian larch used in the Circus Maximus?"

"I am convinced that such a timber would retard the progress of any fire, just as I am convinced that such a fire is inevitable."

"You have consulted seers?"

"I have consulted my expertise in wood."

"Well, I *have* consulted seers. And they tell me that the Circus Maximus will indeed one day burn. There will be a conflagration, you may count on it – and do you know what I say to that?"

"What do you say, Caesar?"

Tiberius narrowed his eyes, his tongue flicking lizard-like across his lips. "I say, well and good. Let the whole thing go up in flames, for all I care. A charred hole would be preferable to that dung pit. Its absence might even draw me back to Rome."

My father found both prospects appalling. "I see," he said evenly. "I see. Then that is your final word on the matter, Caesar?"

Tiberius made a dismissive gesture. "I'm too old to change my mind now. And too proud of my financial discipline to waste money on racetracks. So no, you won't be getting your Raetian larch. Or any of your other silly requests. Caesonius was right. You are like overfed children always squealing for cake. Give me this, give me that, damn the expense, the fate of Rome depends on it. I called you in only to satisfy myself that nothing had changed. And clearly nothing *has* changed. Be off with you, you whining brat, and expect no favours from me."

"Of . . . of course, Caesar."

My father bowed and retreated, swiftly marshalling Alector and Corax – the latter was staring wistfully at the sea – before making a raid on the Villa Jovis and rounding up Oceanus's freshly oiled apprentices as well. Whispering, "Come with me and don't say a word!", he raced the boys down to the harbour and bundled them into a fishing boat, instructing the captain, "Row like the Tritons are chasing you!"

Whether or not my father was fortunate to get away with this – there were so many catamites on Capri by that stage that the emperor might not even have noticed that his new acquisitions had disappeared – it was only a few months later that the Aventine side of the Circus Maximus was partially destroyed by fire, seeming to fulfil my father's predictions and those of the emperor's seers. Nevertheless, Tiberius, as if personally to punish him, mandated financial relief only for those home-owners whose properties had been damaged. The factions were forced to summon their own emergency finances, drawn chiefly from aspiring consuls and praetors, to restore the arena's stands. Thus, the whole unsettling audience on the island had served no purpose but to remind my father that no favours would be bestowed upon the Circus until Rome was blessed with an emperor prepared to "hitch his fate to a chariot".

And though he did not know it then, he had already glimpsed two future emperors, luxuriating in the sordid chambers of the Villa Jovis, who would one day do just that with a vengeance.

# VIII

IT WAS NOT LONG AFTERWARDS, as it happened, that my father was back at the estate watching Corax and Alector go through their paces – Alector in particular was swerving and accelerating with remarkable audacity – when he noticed two young men perched on a mound overlooking the track, one lean and chinless, the other plump and jowly. And when he ordered Gryphus to expel them, fearing they might be spies for rival factions, he was informed that the slightly older and slimmer youth was in fact Gaius, the son of Germanicus.

"Germanicus?" said my father, fondly remembering the charismatic and ill-fated general. "Why yes, now that I think of it, I am sure I saw him carrying a young boy on his shoulders once."

"The lad has been staying with Tiberius on Capri."

"Oh?"

"He has been adopted by the emperor, in fact."

My father, wincing, remembered the debauched figures in the Villa Jovis. "Yes, I recall seeing him there as well. But what has brought him here now?"

"Eutychus of Dalmatia invited him, master."

"For any particular reason?"

"He is a passionate fan of the Greens."

My father nodded. "Like his father before him," he noted, and was about to look away when another question occurred to him. "And the other fellow? The one devouring the chicken leg?"

"I believe that is his companion, Aulus Vitellius."

"Aulus the son of Lucius Vitellius? The consul?"

"Just so."

"But I thought the Vitelli were diehard followers of the Blues?"

"I'm not sure, master."

"No matter, I suppose," decided my father, looking back at the track. "It will do us no harm to have supporters in high places for a change."

He nonetheless claimed later that a shiver of premonition ran through him at that moment, for reasons he could not quite articulate, and when he turned back to the mound, after the race, the two young men had vanished "like autumn leaves on a late November breeze".

# IX

IT WAS AROUND THIS TIME THAT I, Manius Cornelius Noctua, was born. They say one can remember nothing earlier than one's third year and yet I am haunted by memories, real or imagined, of our sprawling home in Campania, its many rich and fragrant woods, my frenetic and domineering mother, and our children's nurse about whom I will have more to say later. What I do *not* remember is the presence of my father, so consumed was he in the business of ship-building and the management of the Greens. Nor do I recall anything of the Campania training estate – I am not sure if I was ever taken there – though I remember well enough its lavish replacement off the Via Latina seven miles southeast of Rome. Here the track was precisely the same dimensions as the Circus Maximus; the stables were warmed in winter and well-ventilated in summer; there were barracks for the apprentices and training staff; there were comfort-able lodgings for my father and his guests; there were elegant statues of Venus, Consus and Neptunus Equestris flanking the drive; there was even, at the entrance, a triumphal arch, bedecked with Green pennants, like something commemorating a great military conquest.

I also remember the move from Neapolis to Rome with a baggage-train of goods and a gaggle of household slaves. Corax and

Alector made the trip at the same time, albeit without the baggage and slaves, so I can well imagine their mounting excitement as the marshlands, pinewoods and barren fields yielded to sweeping farm-yards, vineyards and market gardens, and finally to the impressive villas, towers and mighty aqueducts sweeping towards the temples and tottering tenements of Rome.

For me, the arrival meant settling into our commodious new home halfway up the fashionable environs of the Caelian Hill. For Alector and Corax it meant taking up residence in their freshly timbered quarters at the Via Latina estate. Here, with their training stepped up in quantity and intensity, in prepara-tion for their Circus Maximus debut, there were precious few opportunities to roam around sightseeing. Nevertheless, my father, amid all his other engagements, took time out to escort them on a personally guided tour of Rome – "Alector wide-eyed and excited," he said, "and Corax looking as though he were on his way to a beating."

Never would two slave boys from rustic Italy have experienced anything like it: the surging currents of jostling limbs, stabbing elbows and skins of every shade; the chanting priests, hassling hucksters, shrieking shopkeepers and snarling soldiers; the carts and carriages, hounds and horses, load-bearers and lashing lictors; the deeply rutted streets slippery with mud and lime dust, fruit peels and flower petals; the constant cacophony of howling and hissing, cursing, cackling, whistling and wailing; the reek of burning incense, smouldering sulphur, fermenting dyes and week-old blood in slaughterhouse sluices.

"I took them to the Trigarium," my father told me. "I showed them the training grounds of the Greens and Blues. We visited the Theatre of Pompey. The Baths of Agrippa, where some of our chari-oteers were bathing. I guided them through the Forum Augustum and the Forum Magnum. I led them up the Capitoline and pointed out the legendary bronze chariot team above the Temple of Jupiter

Optimus Maximus. I made sure we visited the Circus Flaminius. And of course I escorted them through the Circus Maximus itself."

The Circus at this stage was not looking at its best. The stands were of swollen and splintering wood, livestock from the nearby Forum Boarium* was corralled on the track between festivals, and the unregulated vaults under the arches were crowded with brothels, gambling shops, trinket stands and filthy food stalls. To new arrivals, however, it must have presented an overwhelming sight: the monumental gateway that glowed and sparkled in the sun, the Wall of the Milliarii glinting with inlaid gold, the pillared porticos climbing higher than three storeys, and the faction flags rippling on poles mounted equidistantly around the rim.

The boys were greeted by the curator of the arena and ushered though chambers and tunnels into the arena itself, where everything seemed to invite further awe: its seventy tiers of seats; its arched ramparts and battlemented towers; its starting gates of intricate latticework; and its magnificent profusion of altars, shrines, statues and temples.

"The Circus is the cosmos and the cosmos is the Circus," my father proclaimed (I would later hear this little speech many times). "See the gods that stand grandly on its periphery; see the temples of Ceres, Flora, Luna, Magna Mater and Venus Obsequens; see the twelve gates in honour of the twelve zodiacal signs; and on game day see the chariots flash around the track like meteors in races dedicated to the planetary gods."

Reaching the central spina, where mighty columns stood amid shrines and pavilions, he guided the boys up the steps, saying, "And here we stand on the Earth, with the gods of the harvest, the dolphins honouring Neptune, and the fountains representing the lakes and rivers of the Empire." He gestured to the hill. "And there

---

* The Cattle Market.

53

on the Palatine the palace of the emperor alongside the Temple of Apollo, the Temple of Magna Mater, and the house of Romulus himself."

He introduced to the boys Myron's great statue of Hercules, confiscated from Greece; the statue of Eros by Praxiteles; the gilded statues of winged Victoria and Cybele riding a lion; the colonnaded statues of the immortal charioteers Pompeius of Syracuse and Caramallus of Bruttium; the mighty pink granite obelisk imported by Augustus from Heliopolis; the sacred palm tree from Thebes; and the various recesses where the *spartores* hurled water across the smoking hubs of passing chariot wheels.

Alector, meanwhile, was beaming, like "a general contemplating a battlefield, a god overlooking Elysium", while Corax wore "a beetled brow and squinted eyes, like a captain surveying a ship for leaks".

But when they descended to the track, the latter became unusually vocal. "What is that?" he asked, pointing to a water channel that ringed the arena.

"Why, that is the *euripus*," my father informed him. "Installed by Julius Caesar himself, to prevent wild beasts from leaping into the crowd."

"Wild beasts?"

"From the hunts that amuse the crowd between races."

"But the channel narrows the track and increases the probability of collisions."

"I have said so myself!" my father agreed, laughing. "I have argued repeatedly for the beast hunts to be relegated to the Circus Flaminius, but the accursed Tiberius refuses to allow it."

My father imagined Corax would be pleased with this answer, but the boy was now prodding the sand with his foot. "The surface is unyielding," he declared. "The track at Campania was easier on the horses' hooves."

"I have said that too!" my father noted. "But the races are not until next week, remember, and the groundsmen wait until the last moment before adding the cushioning layers. Otherwise, all their hard work might blow away in the wind or be washed away in the next storm."

My father thought that this, too, might placate Corax, but now the boy was staring at the sheets of polished steel that had been affixed to the corners of the arena. "And what are those?"

My father swelled with pride. "They are mirrors, recently installed at my own suggestion, so that the crowds might follow what is happening on the other side of the spina. There is too much cluttering the centre of the arena already, as you yourself have observed."

Corax was already shaking his head. "The reflections will spook the horses. They will crash at the turns."

My father chuckled. "You underestimate the chariot horses of the Circus Maximus, which have become inured to all sorts of distractions."

"I tell you, the horses will baulk and crash."

"You had better listen to him," Alector urged, "for Corax knows of what he speaks."

Now my father had no reason to doubt Corax's prescience on equine matters, but neither did he fancy going back to the Guild and arguing that the steel sheets, for which he had spent so much time lobbying, should be removed upon the objections of an apprentice charioteer.

"Well," he said evasively, "we shall see how things turn out next week."

And, swiftly changing the subject, he continued the tour of the arena.

I have been reliably informed that at least six other apprentices were with my father that day, including the future champions Mergus of Magnesia and Cyrus of Cyrenaica. But it says much about their subsequent histories that my father, when recounting this episode, would mention only two.

# X

A WEEK LATER OUR ARMENIAN SLAVE Gryphus took the boys back to the Circus for their first experience of the races. Gryphus, who upon his later manumission awarded himself with the royal name Tigranes, was at that stage yet to develop the many affectations of grooming that would soon come to define him. But even in those days he was a prissy taskmaster, like a conceited schoolteacher, not averse to boxing the boys' ears or striking them with a birch cane if they transgressed. (He was also gifted with a prodigious memory upon which I have relied heavily for the first half of this chronicle.)

The races were part of that year's Apollinarian Games and images of Apollo festooned the streets. First on Gryphus's agenda was claiming a vantage point on the Via Tuscus to view the *pompa circensis* preceding the races. Leading the procession that day were acrobats, dancers and standard bearers in animal skins; then came the consuls in chariots studded with gems; then the magistrate of the games in a tunic embroidered with palms; then the sons of nobility under a blizzard of flower petals; and finally a long chain of trumpeters heralding the principal chariot teams themselves.

Tarracius of Spain, with over seven hundred victories the most successful of the faction's charioteers at that point, and Eutychus of Dalmatia, the most promising of the younger brigade, were the official representatives of the Greens. Corax and Alector, well acquainted with both men from the training estate, were "visibly perplexed" by the extreme response their appearance now generated. The Greens partisans "went wild with adulation". "Marry me, Eutychus!" cried the women, straining against the barricades and baring their breasts. And "All power to Tarracius!" bellowed the men, baring their teeth. Nor were their horses overlooked: "Hail Ferrox!" the people exclaimed, and "Excelsior, Diresor!" and "May the gods empower you, Corynus!"

The appearance of the Blues charioteers, by contrast, elicited nothing but disdain. "Down with Hierax!" sneered the Greens fanatics, throwing nutshells and vegetable scrapings. And: "May he yoke black horses!" And: "May the fires of Tantalus swallow you, Vibius!"

But the greatest commotion – and it was an unusual one, for Reds charioteers traditionally inspired no great hostility – came with the appearance of Taurus of Crete. Only the second *essedarius** to establish a prolonged career in the Circus Maximus – the first was Atlas of Mauretania – Taurus was a notorious brute for whom no tactic was too outrageous. Deviously taking advantage of the new rules that permitted charioteers to carry curved blades – ostensibly to cut themselves free from the reins in an emergency – Taurus employed his own dagger to sinister effect, slashing wildly at other charioteers, stabbing at horses and slicing through their harnesses. No single charioteer in history had ever been responsible for such mayhem. Though fans of the Reds insisted that he was a gentle giant, with five young children to support, he had simultaneously

---

* A gladiator who drove chariots.

become the Circus's most sinister villain and its most lucrative drawcard.

Selected for the first race, to ensure the crowds arrived early, Taurus's mere presence in the starting stalls was enough to get the masses roiling. Tiberius himself was not present, of course, but Gaius the son of Germanicus and his close friend Aulus Vitellius were installed in the pulvinar beside that year's consuls Valerius Asiaticus and Gabinius Secundus. Corax and Alector were perched with Gryphus high in the stands at the Caelian end – a position much favoured by faction tacticians owing to its commanding view of the track.

There was an ear-shattering roar when the starting gates burst open and the eight quadriga teams erupted into the arena. Taurus of Crete, driving a widened chariot with bronze bulls' heads mounted on the hubs, was already thrashing the charioteers to his left and right with a multi-thonged whip studded with snake fangs. This gained him half a length before he had even crossed the breakline. Then, expertly shifting his pelvis and twisting the reins, he steered for the inside track, falling into second place behind Amarantus of Apulia as the horses rounded the first turn.

Corax, anticipating carnage when the horses were frightened by their reflections, now leaned forward expectantly. But as it happened the stallions, though they veered slightly off course, survived the first corner without incident. Thousands of eyes shifted to the polished mirrors to watch the chariots on the far side of the spina, before returning to the track when the teams curled round the western *metae* and swung into view again. And so it played out for the next few laps, the horses baulking but not deviating significantly when they glimpsed their reflections, prompting Gryphus – who had also accompanied the boys on their earlier tour of the Circus – to echo my father.

"You see," he said to Corax, "the horses are better disciplined than you thought."

Taurus of Crete, unable to take the lead, meanwhile continued stabbing and whipping to no great effect. He crossed the line third overall, alighted from his chariot, kicked up dust and made obscene gestures to the crowd. The winner was the Greens' new star, Eutychus of Dalmatia.

Afterwards, as much of the crowd drifted off to lay more bets, the *bestiarii* herded into the arena the first of the day's four-legged sacrifices. Lions were chained to leopards, jackals to hyenas, bulls to bears, and, once these had torn each other to pieces, and the skulls of the survivors smashed, the carcasses were carted off through the Porta Pompae to be fed to pigs and the destitute.

Corax stared.

Then, in the second race, after the sun had risen high enough to flood the arena, his worst fears came true. Three teams came down at the turns when the stallions were spooked by the mirrors. Four of the horses were wheeled off to the spoilarium with broken legs. Two of the charioteers were stretchered off, dazed and bleeding.

Then there was another beast hunt in which rhinoceroses, hippopotami and long-necked camels* were shot down by imperial archers, to wild cheering from the crowd.

Then came another chariot race involving Eutychus and a furious Taurus of Crete, in which two horses died and one charioteer was carried off with injuries to his hips and spine.

Then came a comedic interlude involving foxes with flaming torches attached to their tails, bear cubs fighting with young hyenas, and warthogs negotiating a narrow plank over sharpened spikes.

The fourth race was for debuting charioteers in bigas. Four of the teams crashed at the turns and one unfortunate apprentice,

---

* Giraffes.

trampled under a hail of hooves, died on the spot – his career snuffed out before it had chance to begin.

By this time it was noon and into the arena came the *damnati* for the midday executions. The condemned men were lashed with whips and struck with clubs, the parricides were sewn in sacks with vipers and crocodiles, the thieves were crushed between iron spheres, and those accused of treason were dropped through a hatch into a cage of ravenous wolves. Some of the crowd took the opportunity to stock up on bread and brew and make lightning visits to the brothels under the exterior arches.

Then Taurus of Crete was back, so incensed about his previous losses that he was not only stabbing at his opponents but reaching out and dragging them from their chariots. Two drivers crashed at the turns and three horses snapped legs.

Then came a fight between thirty armoured *bestiarii* and sixteen bulls. The sand of the arena by this stage was so blood-soaked that fresh sawdust had to be distributed over the wettest patches and blowflies as big as bumblebees clouded the air.

In the sixth race, so many teams piled into each other that the intervening entertainment, meant to involve a leopard-and-cheetah race, had to be delayed as the arena was cleared of dead and broken bodies.

"This is not a circus," Corax hissed through clenched teeth. "This is a slaughterhouse."

According to Gryphus, "The boy ended the day in the spoil-arium, making sure that the fatally injured horses, which included a number he had trained personally, were dispatched as quickly and painlessly as possible."

The sheets of polished steel were removed from the Circus two days later.

# XI

BEFORE I TURN TO THE RACING CAREERS of Corax and Alector, which of course cover three distinct phases, I must try to account for the unprecedented level of anticipation that accompanied their debut in the Circus Maximus.

To familiarise them with the noise and rituals of the arena, the boys, as was the custom, had spent three years as *moratores*, attending to the horses and charioteers before and after races. This was the sort of task at which Corax excelled: no team under his supervision left the starting stalls with inadequate wrappings, frayed harnesses or poorly greased axles. He was so adept at soothing agitated horses, too, that he seemed able to inspire even the lowliest nags to perform well above expectation. Accordingly, he became something of good luck charm, even to those charioteers generally irritated by his sullen nature, and the Greens partisans rewarded him with much unsolicited celebrity. "I hope the boy Corax is in charge of the horses today," was a common refrain. And: "Look at how content the horses are – it must be young Corax who settled them."

Needless to say, Alector was much less suited to such a role and even managed to delegate many of his more mundane responsibilities to Corax. But he, too, was a welcome sight in the stalls, joshing and jesting and taunting the charioteers of rival factions. "Hey, Calchas," he might say, "why are you sweating so much? You're dripping like a stew pot." And: "You know, Lacerta, the red looks good on you – it will match the colour of your arse when you get spanked after this race." And, most boldly of all, considering his age: "Hey, Protogenes, don't you think you're a little young for this? I've eaten cheeses that are older than you." Even those charioteers disparaged by his jibes were said to enjoy his ribbing.

But most famously there was the moment during the Victory Games when young Alector, called upon by Pelorus of Spain to adjust his chariot's yoke-piece – Corax was otherwise occupied – either by accident or design managed to be busy with the task when the starting gates sprang open, so that when the team burst onto the track, he was still astride one of the middle horses. And that was the way he remained – grinning, whooping, feasting on the amusement of the fans – even after Pelorus, seeing his team falling hopelessly behind, tried to whip him loose. But Alector only jumped monkey-like from one horse to the other, all the way to the finishing line, at which point he dismounted and spent so long bowing and waving to the crowd that the ground attendants had to drag him forcibly from the track. Pelorus afterwards insisted that the lad should be caned. "And if you can't do it," he told my father, "then I shall gladly do so myself!" But my father, who was terribly amused by the whole affair, ended up trading Pelorus to the Whites instead, leaving Alector to spend the next twelve months bragging to envious comrades that he was already "broken in" as a charioteer, having completed seven laps in the Circus Maximus while "you can only dream about it".

These reasons, in any event, along with rumours of the Rooster's astonishing feats on the training track, help to explain the exceptional number of people that piled into the Circus to witness the two apprentices in their debut, at a time when biga races were invariably low on the card and aroused little interest. Such was the size of the crowd, indeed, that three spectators clinging to the scaffolding on the Aventine side fell off and later died of their injuries.

The Greeks were especially vocal that day, for my father, as he did with all his recruits, had invented for Alector a highly fanciful background – that he was the grandson of Alector of Epirus, the legendary hero of the panhellic games – and Alector, delighted to have any sort of pedigree, came dressed for the part in a long chiffon robe with a ribbon tied around his head.

Corax – supposedly discovered as a new-born babe in a stable, possibly birthed by a mare – was meanwhile sporting a padded tunic and leggings which, as usual, covered his frame from neck to toe.

In the race itself the Rooster proved even more impressive than expected. Thanks in no small part to the expert blocking tactics of his friend the Raven, he shot exuberantly out of the starting stalls, hugged the leading teams for five laps, and upon the trumpet's blast really cut loose, overtaking all the others and crossing the finish line a full four lengths ahead of his closest rival. His celebratory antics during his victory lap, which included crowing like a rooster, were so extravagant that they verged on self-parody and, in the way of such things, earned him even more admirers.

In his six subsequent biga races, over four successive games, he was victorious in all but one, dropping to second only when Corax unexpectedly abandoned his blocking duties to leap off and attend to some fallen horses. But at the time Greens charioteers were dominating race days in general, widely attributed to their sleek chariots and superb new horses, so no one could be certain how much the Rooster himself was responsible for his own success. Incensed, Alector thereafter insisted on racing mid-ranked horses in older style war-chariots, and he still managed to win comfortably.

By now he was itching to race in quadrigas against senior charioteers, but my father in his wisdom decided it was best to hold him back, partly out of fear of what might happen to Alector's confidence if he were soundly beaten, and partly to squeeze every drop of anticipation out of his budding champion's long-awaited four-horse debut. And, meanwhile, Alector for the first time was invited to the home of Gaius, the son of Germanicus, where he caroused with Eutychus and many charioteers considerably older than he, amusing them with his willingness to participate in all manner of revelry. Corax, uninterested in such decadence, invariably retired to the stables to groom the horses and perform his body-strengthening exercises alone.

Then, completely out of the blue, Taurus of Crete advertised his wish to race against "the chicken" Alector, an announcement that was unprecedented for two reasons. First because experienced charioteers were averse to showing much interest in lowly novices, and second because the Red Faction was a notional ally of the Greens, assisting us in blocking manoeuvres on race days, and the charioteers were nominally cousins on and off the track. For a Red therefore to deride a Green in such an ostentatious manner, and a mere biga driver at that, seemed amply indicative of Alector's rising status.

Nevertheless, the taunts grew bolder. Taurus claimed that he had "always had a taste for poultry". He said that in the Circus "he would roast Alector alive". The boy was "a pullet, not a rooster" and represented no serious threat to a "fighting bull" like himself. In fact, Taurus went on, if he were beaten in the Circus by "the gosling Greek" he would be too ashamed to show his face in the arena ever again.

Naturally this made Alector even more determined to take him on. "A chicken, am I? Ha! I bet I could turn that cow on a spit!" Together with Corax, who had seen far too many horses brutally flayed by Taurus, he beseeched my father to make it happen. And, when expectation could scarcely be wound any tighter, my father caved in.

I well remember the race because I, at five years old, was among the spectators that day, along with Gryphus, my mother, and some of our household slaves. It was my first visit to the Circus Maximus and I was tremendously excited. My father – who by that stage was spending race days pacing restlessly around the courtyard of the Via Latina estate – claimed on the other hand that he was "unusually calm and confident, awaiting the courier with the results". I recall distinctly the poor visibility, for a thick fog had descended on the arena and the chariot teams were difficult to discern through veils of mist (in my innocence I assumed that the Circus always looked that way). Views of the track were so diminished, indeed, that there was even some debate between stewards and ground attendants about whether the races should proceed at all. But ultimately so many spectators had crowded into the arena, chiefly in the lower tiers, that it was judged unwise to postpone.

As for the race itself, it was even more thrilling than expected. When they erupted from the starting stalls – Taurus was wearing a gladiator helmet and gold cuirass; Alector had affixed red plumes to his head like a rooster's comb – Taurus immediately turned his attention not to Alector but to Corax, having clearly identified him as the real reason behind the Rooster's success. As they crossed the breakline he was raking Corax with his whip and slashing at him with a sword-sized blade. Corax, who was as strong and nimble as any gladiator, was well equipped to dodge and deflect such attentions, and by the time the teams had completed the first lap Alector was six lengths ahead.

Abandoning his initial strategy, Taurus began lashing his horses and chasing after his real quarry, the chariots by now careering around the track at such velocity that they were stirring up great whorls of disturbed mist. By the third lap Taurus had edged so close to Salutarius of Verona, who was in second place, that he was able to seize the charioteer, wrench him off his feet and fling him across the back of his horses like a bundle of rags. Then, with his path clear, he started closing in on Alector.

It was neck and neck for the next two laps. At times it looked certain that Taurus would outpace his young opponent; now and then it looked as though he was close enough to decapitate Alector with his blade; and all the time he was whipping his team so violently that mists of blood mingled with the fog. But when the trumpets blared for the sixth lap, the Rooster and his horses, still largely unlashed, took a decisive lead, ably defended by Corax, who had made up enough ground to box Taurus against the spina, the furious gladiator hurling his blade, his whip and a chunk of railing at the Raven in a frantic effort to break free. In the end, Alector crossed the line in first place with Corax second and Taurus a humiliating third.

That wasn't the end of it, though, for Taurus, launching off his chariot, attempted to hide behind the turning posts and dislodge Alector as he swung around the corner on his victory lap. But, in anticipation of this, Corax wheeled in and smacked the gladiator to the ground. Cruising past in his own chariot, Alector then taunted Taurus with moos and bellows as the crowd laughed uproariously. Enraged, the gladiator sprang to his feet and attempted to chase the upstarts around the track only to be restrained by ground officials. When he disposed of these, too, a cadre of Vigiles charged in and, not without sustaining a few black eyes and bruises, managed to barricade him against the barrier as Alector and Corax departed via the Triumphal Gate. Flinging off his helmet and cuirass, Taurus later skulked through the Porta Pompae and, true to his word, was never seen in the Circus again.

Apart from all that, I remember the striking moment at the end of the day, as the mist flattened on the track, when the crier called for silence and announced that the great Tiberius Caesar Augustus had just passed away at Misenum. This solemn news generated no great misery in the crowd – beyond a certain sense of dislocation that accompanies the demise of any significant leader – but when the crier declared that the Senate had already chosen a new emperor, Gaius the son of Germanicus, there were ripples of enthusiasm that built to a crescendo as the spotty-faced princeps materialised on the pulvinar, resplendent in a gold-and-purple-fringed toga and looking for all the world like a deity perched on a sea of clouds.

The crowd in unison acclaimed him.

"CALIGULA . . . CALIGULA . . . CALIGULA!"

A bold new era in the Circus Maximus had begun.

# XII

NOTWITHSTANDING CREDIBLE RUMOURS that the new emperor had personally arranged to have Tiberius smothered in his sick bed, Caligula's reign could scarcely have started more auspiciously. He hosted public banquets, distributed money and grain, put an end to crippling taxes, and embarked upon huge new building projects. He was energetic, effusive, merciful and generous – the reincarnation, it seemed, of his much-loved father. Most importantly, as far as chariot racing was concerned, he mandated more race days – for the Lupercalian Games, the Cerealian Games, the Palatine Games, the Concordian Games, the Consualian Games and the Saturnalia – and met frequently and enthusiastically with the Guild of Factions. And, while he refused to relocate the beast hunts to the Circus Flaminius – "I like to see a sprinkle of blood on the dust" – and seemed curiously dismissive of any proposal to reconstruct the Circus Maximus in fire-resistant wood – "I have grander plans that that" – he did promise more imperial involvement in the sport. "Just you wait and see," he told the *domini factionum* with his impish grin. "Just you wait and see." He was particularly candid with my father. "The Greens will rule the Circus as I rule Rome," he confided, before echoing Augustus:

"The crowds of the Circus Maximus are like a chariot team, dear Picus, and I intend to drive that team to victory."

For the *domini factionum*, this flurry of new races meant that scores of horses and charioteers had to be recruited and trained at all haste. It was at this point that my father decided to release Corax from his blocking duties and turn him, as rapidly as possible, into a first-rank charioteer. He had visions of the Raven and the Rooster, his very first discoveries, becoming "the yoke horses that lead the Greens to victory for the next ten years". Nevertheless, Corax's first forays in his new role evinced little improvement as the sombre young charioteer returned again and again to his blocking duties – almost as if he considered it immodest, or plain rude, to assume the lead.

In the end my father had to take him aside. "You want to earn your manumission, Corax? You want to retire from the 'silly slaughterhouse', as you call it? Then you will get to your destination so much quicker if you win, lad. Win and win again. And for heaven's sake use the whip, boy, even if it is only lightly. The horses can take it. They *enjoy* it. Not every lash has to wound, you know."

After this exhortation Corax, who respected my father more than any other man, made a concerted effort to improve. He even deployed the whip occasionally. But overall, despite recording his first two Circus victories, his performances continued to be disappointing. So my father settled on a strategy he would later regret.

He had always favoured the philosophy, borrowed from General Gaius Marius, that battalions become more motivated when divided into cohorts and set against each other in the spirit of competition. In the case of managing the Greens, this meant separating the faction's army of trainers, quartermasters, scouts, groundsmen, grooms, surgeons, sweepers and stablehands into divisions, offering bonuses to those who were most industrious, and occasionally introducing outside experts as a means of enhancing rivalry. To give just one example, he relocated some of his most trusted craftsmen from the shipyards into the carpentry workshops, secretly instructing them to "show these spoke-whittlers how a proper chariot should be made". And while the shipbuilders took some time to master the new craft, their very presence seemed to inspire the existing wainwrights and wheelwrights to greater experimentation, so that, using developments derived from both parties, the Greens' workshops were soon churning out the sleekest and sturdiest of chariots – mulberry and wickerwork models so light that they could be lifted with one hand, yet so strong that they could survive hundreds of runs – while simultaneously the wheelwrights' techniques of pegging and steam-bending brought countless improvements to the construction of my father's ships.

But it is one thing to manufacture rivalries in shipyards and faction workshops, and quite another to contrive them among the charioteers themselves. My father knew such manipulations were fraught with danger. He knew the whole ploy could unravel. But, enjoying his own craftiness, he decided he would take the risk anyway, counting on his ability to contain any consequences before they caused too much damage.

Thus it was that he instructed the trainers to inform Corax that Alector had been saying unflattering things about him behind his back. That Corax would never amount to anything. That he wasn't even particularly good at blocking. That he, Alector, would have won many more races had he not been relying on "the wax-hearted Raven". That he would never forgive Corax for prioritising fallen horses over victory.

Corax, my father was disappointed to learn, received all these calumnies in his typically imperturbable fashion. He did not seem particularly offended. After all, there was hardly a charioteer at the estate who had not been the victim of Alector's colourful jibes. More to the point, Corax's performance in the Circus did not noticeably improve. So my father, increasingly cavalier, decided that Alector should take the blocking role in a race in which Corax was principal charioteer. Alector, as he expected, bridled at the very thought.

"What's the meaning of this?" he demanded, confronting my father as soon as he arrived at the estate. "You know I am no blocker."

My father was still easing himself out of the carriage. "It will do you good to try it for a change. It will make you a better charioteer."

"I could not be a better charioteer than I am already. I pluck the reins like the strings of a harp. Why waste me as a blocker? Do you not want the Greens to win?"

"I want you to perform the same role that Corax has consistently performed for you. You owe him that much, as I'm sure you'll agree."

"Has Corax put you up to this?" asked Alector, narrowing his eyes. "Is that what you're saying?"

"That is none of your business."

"Well, I don't believe it. That's not the way Corax thinks."

"You might be surprised at the way Corax thinks."

"But it's a waste of my talent, I tell you. And a waste of Corax's talent. He knows his limitations. He is not worthy of the Incitatus Team."

"The Incitatus Team might have a different opinion."

"This is madness, I tell you. You've not seen Corax as a leading charioteer. He looks as though has no idea what to do – like a eunuch at an orgy."

This insult, such as it was, was of course relayed later to Corax.

As for the race itself, it remains a matter of contention whether Alector contrived the circumstances that unfolded or merely took advantage of them (I am inclined to think the latter). In any case, Corax, driving the Incitatus Team, was in the third lap, about to bear down on the Whites charioteer Fortunatus of Moesia, when he felt his chariot being buffeted from the inside track. Symmachus of Gaul, a Reds charioteer, was grinding against him. He was steering

71

his horses into Corax's team. And Corax was dumbfounded. Symmachus was a first-rank charioteer, not a blocker, and first-rank charioteers never demeaned themselves with such lowly tactics. So Corax urged his horses on, still trying to overtake Fortunatus. But Symmachus was curiously persistent. He seemed keener on diverting Corax than he was in taking the lead. Corax flicked his whip. Symmachus was lashing his own. He was driving Corax away from the spina. The two chariot teams were ploughing into each other. The harnesses were tangling. The wheels were grinding together. Corax made one last desperate attempt to wrench free but it was too late. His axle snapped, his chariot broke apart like a head of lettuce, and wheel pins went spinning through the air. With reins looped around his waist, Corax was ripped off his feet, dragged across the track and very nearly trampled by Symmachus's stampeding horses.

By the time he had cut himself loose – he had been dragged thirty lengths and only his padded tunic prevented serious injury – he was well past the western turning posts. Launching to his feet to settle his team, he saw Alector flashing past, shouting, "Castor and Pollux!"

This might require some explanation. "Castor" and "Pollux" as they were popularly known – their real names were Coryphaeus and Polyclus – were identical twin brothers in the days of the triumvirate. During a famous race in the Circus Maximus, Castor was torn out of his chariot into the path of Pollux's horses. Unable to stop, Pollux trundled over his brother, killing him instantly, then went on to complete the last four laps and win the race. The story was told repeatedly as an example of the ruthless principle to which all charioteers were expected to adhere: that sentiment has no place in the Circus Maximus, that winning is always paramount. Pollux was revered as a hero.

This notion might have assuaged Corax but for one detail. Symmachus of Gaul, who had suffered no injury of his own, was a well-known companion of Caligula's who had feasted and gambled many times with Alector. So it was conceivable, if not likely, that the two had conspired to obstruct Corax during the race in order that Alector might have an excuse to claim the lead and maintain his near-perfect record.

As he performed his victory lap, Alector cruised past a bleeding Corax, who was guiding his horses towards the Porta Pompae.

"Castor and Pollux!" he shouted again – desperate, it seemed, for some sort of acknowledgment. "Castor and Pollux, remember?"

But Corax, mute and stony-faced as ever, led his team from the arena without once shifting his gaze from the horses.

# XIII

THOUGH CALIGULA HAD NOT BEEN PRESENT on the day of the crash, he was there at the Circus to witness a grimly determined Corax finally make good on his potential – winning race after race by significant margins – and could not help noticing that the fame of the Raven, after several months, was fast approaching that of the Rooster. Not that Corax – who typically eschewed victory laps, accepted laurels only under sufferance, and quitted the track as soon as he was no longer required – had done anything to court popularity. He was not even comfortable with adoring faction partisans, unlike Alector, who loved mingling with his fans, especially those who were young, female and open to suggestion.

"That charioteer of yours with the long black locks," the emperor said to my father one day. "What is his name again?"

"I believe you are talking about Corax of Campania," replied my father, knowing full well that Caligula remembered the charioteer's name.

"That's right, the Raven – talks very little, doesn't he?"

"He is very discriminating with his words, it's true."

"It's funny," Caligula chuckled, "but I believe there are actual ravens that talk more than he. Certainly other birds." At that very moment Caligula was reclined on a sofa with a flightless parrot perched on one hand and an apple in the other. He was taking nibbles out of the fruit and proffering fragments to the bird with his tongue.

"I have said as much myself," admitted my father. "Do you recall, Caesar, the raven that inhabited the Forum some years ago?"

"The one that was given a lavish funeral when it died?"

"Indeed. Well, the canny bird told Corax that he would one day become the most famous raven in the empire. Which, coming from that particular bird, was no small honour."

It was one of my father's many half-baked stories and even Caligula, who had a weakness for fanciful anecdotes, did not look convinced. "Nevertheless," he sniffed. "I'm not sure I like him. The way he never smiles. The way he always seems on the verge of tears."

"Corax never cries, Caesar."

"The way he wears his hair down to his shoulders."

"He is only concealing scars on the nape of his neck."

"The way he never comes to my feasts, for that matter. I've hosted every other charioteer from the Greens and Reds, so why not him?"

"Corax is extremely private, Caesar."

"His is the sort of privacy that makes me suspicious."

"There are things that happened in his childhood – the very thought of them would make a statue weep."

"*Ouch!*" The parrot had nipped the emperor's tongue. "You naughty little brute! I'm not made of brass, you know!" He glanced at Aulus Vitellius, who was lounging on a sofa nearby. "Not all of me, at any rate. Nevertheless, where were we? Yes, yes, the Raven. To me he seems more like a Blues charioteer than a Green. What do you think, Aulus?"

Vitellius said through a mouthful of grapes, "We'd take him, should you ever decide to get rid of him."

"Yes, I'm sure you would, you beast." Caligula looked back at my father. "But really, Picus, what is so impressive about him?

I understand he crashed the Incitatus Team at the Concordian Games recently – is that true?"

"That was a most controversial incident, Caesar."

"You are not implying there was something untoward, I hope? Because I heard a vile rumour that Symmachus played some role in the crash."

My father, mindful of Symmachus's intimacy with the emperor, took refuge in diplomacy. "I am duty-bound to defend Corax, Caesar, just as I am obliged to defend all my charioteers."

"Still," Caligula persisted, "I have questions about him, you know. If he is worthy of the Incitatus Team. If the grimness of his manner might infect them somehow."

"He personally trained the horses, Caesar, so he must have had some positive influence."

"Still, I wonder if the team might be even better if driven by someone else. Someone with a more conducive temperament. Eutychus, perhaps. Or Alector. Or even me."

"You, Caesar?"

Caligula, sharing a wink with Vitellius, grew cagey. "Enough of that," he said, launching to his feet. "Let us go for a walk, while you tell me more about our horses. Your plans for the Megalesian Games. And faction politics – you know I can never get enough of partisan gossip."

As they wandered through the palace's richly ornamented corridors – Caligula was still balancing the parrot on his fist – my father made sure he painted a rosy picture. Enthusiasm for chariot racing had never been greater. Even with all the new race days, the plebs just couldn't get enough. They were lining up outside the arena in the middle of the night. They were buying all sorts of racing knick-knacks. They were dressing in faction colours (Caligula had waived the rule mandating togas in the Circus). They were conspicuously more content and better behaved, and immensely grateful to their emperor for providing them with such spectacular diversions.

76

Caligula chuckled. "Aulus thinks I go too far in my support of the Greens."

"Not at all, Caesar – better devotion to one faction than feigning indifference to all."

"The people love it when I appear in the pulvinar, don't they?"

"Their cheers are sincere, Caesar, I can promise you that."

Caligula made a wistful sound. "You know, I dearly wish I could appear more often, but there is so much work to do. Work, work, work. The responsibilities of an emperor are more than any mortal man can bear."

"And you are much more than any mortal man," returned my father, who could recognise a cue for flattery. "I only wish my horses were as inexhaustible."

He went on to detail, with considerable tact, the measures he had implemented to take the strain of the additional race days off the teams. Shorter races – five laps, four laps, even three. The last race of each Games would be a *diversium*, in which only the two best performing teams would compete. And there would be a new race, a *pedibus ad quadrigam*, in which charioteers would sprint one lap on foot before leaping into their chariots to complete the remaining six.

"Very ingenious," Caligula said, depositing the parrot on a ledge. "I don't know how you conceive of such things."

"It was Corax of Campania who suggested many of these innovations, Caesar."

"Hmph," said Caligula, now yoking the parrot to a toy chariot. "Always thinking of the horses, isn't he?"

"It's his weakness, Caesar."

"Pity he doesn't think more of the crowds – they like a man with charm, you know."

"Corax's charm is an acquired taste, I'll grant you that."

They were on a Palatine balcony overlooking the Mercian valley. The bird was hauling its little chariot back and forth along the ledge.

In the sunlit Circus Maximus below, groundsmen were sprinkling decorative chrysocolla\* in preparation for the Megalesian Games. Ex-sailors, skilled in rigging, were unfurling canvas awnings across the upper tiers. Augustus's great Egyptian obelisk was casting a sundial-like shadow across the track.

"What do you make of that needle?" asked Caligula, noticing my father's gaze.

"The obelisk? I have a special fondness for it," my father admitted, "since it was the Cornelii who constructed the freighter that brought it to Rome."

"A magnificent vessel."

"Indeed. I used to play in the ship when I was a child. It was where I first learned to recognise the qualities of timber."

"Such a pity it was destroyed in that storm."

"I admit I shed a tear."

Caligula smiled cagily. "Then how, dear Picus, would you feel about a new commission? For another great freighter?"

"Caesar?"

"To import another needle from Egypt – even bigger than the one brought here by Augustus."

"Bigger?"

"It's already waiting for us in Alexandria, but as yet we have no vessel with sufficient capacity to transport it."

My father blinked. "Are you saying, Caesar, that you require a ship as large as the one built for Augustus?"

"Larger, I should think."

My father's imagination was reeling. "Well, it would require the sturdiest woods, of course. And it would take a considerable time to construct. A suitable mainmast alone might take months to—"

---

\* A green copper silicate.

"I want it ready to sail by next spring," Caligula said. "Do you think it can be done?"

"Yes, yes . . . of course, Caesar. Anything can be done, with an appropriate amount of dedication."

"With the appropriate amount of money, I think you mean."

"It would not be cheap, admittedly."

"Well, I want you to spare no expense – none whatever."

"Of course, Caesar, of course." My father, thrilled, found himself gazing down upon the Circus again. "A new obelisk, bigger than the existing obelisk. That will certainly—"

"Oh, don't misunderstand me," added Caligula, frowning. "This new needle is not intended for the Circus Maximus."

"Caesar?"

"I want it installed in an entirely new arena. That's what I've been meaning to tell you, dear Picus. And it's why I have resisted too many improvements to the Circus Maximus."

"A new arena?"

"I've already had the site surveyed and cleared. It will be a sparkling new circus, constructed entirely of marble, and filled with statues of the great charioteers."

My father was awed. "Caesar, I don't know what to say." For a moment he reflected on the two factors that had motivated him to take over the Greens in the first place – the good of the sport and the good of his business – and this new project seemed like the culmination of both dreams simultaneously. "If this arena is built as you suggest, the factions will be forever indebted to you. The *plebeians* will be forever indebted to you. I've said for years that the Circus Maximus is a fire trap, but now that—"

"The plebeians can mind their own business," Caligula snapped.

"Of . . . of course, Caesar."

"I already support their favourite faction – is that not enough for them?"

"Yes, yes . . . I mean . . ."

"The new circus, you see, is not designed to take the place of the old one. Rather, it will be custom-made and highly specialised. Reserved for private engagements, with hand-picked crowds."

"A private arena, Caesar?"

"A bespoke, emperor-worthy arena."

"Yet the same size as the Circus Maximus?"

"The track will be, of course," confirmed Caligula, affecting a wicked smile. "Oh, just think of it, Picus! A new chariot racing arena in Rome, magisterial in size, exquisite in construction, and reserved for only the most discerning and well-behaved audiences! A track where Eutychus can race the finest horses. Where Alector can race the finest horses. Where *I* can race the finest horses! Did you ever believe such a thing would be possible? Is your mouth not watering at the very prospect?"

My father nodded, desperately fixing an approving expression on his face. But this, he later claimed, was the moment he first truly wondered if the emperor "had started to lose his marbles".

There was a rattle of tiny wheels as the parrot zigzagged across the ledge, the toy chariot trundling behind it.

# XIV

THE SITE CALIGULA HAD SELECTED for this new circus was marshy land under the Vatican Hill in the northwest of Rome. While the area was cleared of shanties and undesirables, drained and shored up, then laid with foundations for its elegant arena, my father was occupied supervising the construction of the immense freighter necessary to transport the majestic obelisk, along with its equally weighty plinth, across the Mediterranean from Alexandria. He had "rarely been busier or happier", despite his misgivings about the private circus and his inability to devote much time to the Greens.

Gryphus, who in my father's absence was keeping track of all developments in the Circus, was able to report that Corax continued to grow in stature but remained aloof and unsociable. Alector, on the other hand, while still the crowd favourite, was for the first time showing signs of fatigue (which Gryphus attributed to his late-night mischief-making with Caligula). To confront the latter problem my father, as soon as he found the time to visit the estate, appealed to the Rooster's formidable pride.

"You do know that Corax is close to eclipsing you on the track?"

"He might well eclipse me for a few moments," Alector returned indifferently, "but he will quickly move on, like the moon, and my sun will blaze brighter than ever."

As for Corax's unremitting dourness, my father in his wisdom was inclined to agree with Columella – that a stallion denied the company of mares will eventually go mad – and decided that the Raven needed to be "loosened up", as it were, with female companionship. Now the family at the time had a Cytherian slave girl called Xenia, slender as a stylus, tawny of skin, lithe of limbs, spearlike of gaze, and exuding an effect on men seldom seen since the days of the fabled Helen. In Campania she had been a kitchen maid who performed as "kingfisher" during our feasts – she netted fish from our interior pond to be promptly fried and served – but so numerous were the guests who, eyeing her beguiling movements, became instantly besotted and offered huge sums of money for her purchase – and even, in the case of one senator, tried to have her abducted – that my father was forced to relegate her to the back rooms. And though he here made use of her for a while as a personal masseuse and a bath attendant, I am satisfied he had no carnal interest in her – he was, as I have noted, rather prudish about such matters – and in any case my mother, who had grown rather protective of the girl, soon recruited her as a personal handmaiden and children's nurse, in which capacity I first came to know her.

In order to set her up with Corax, therefore, my father had to wait until my mother was absent from Rome, visiting family in Messana, before moving swiftly.

"I hear your old wounds have opened up again," he said to the Raven at the Via Latina estate (Corax's boyhood scars by this stage had healed into a remarkable patchwork of ridges and cicatrices, some so deep that they were still prone to bleeding under pressure). "Gryphus tells me that after a minor accident last week your tunic was soaked in blood."

"The wounds will heal."

"And they could get a lot worse before they get better, too. Well, I happen to know a Greek who is an expert on the dressing of wounds. I shall arrange for you to receive some attention at once."

"I always use my own dressings."

"Your dressings are meant for horses."

"Then they are good enough for me."

My father sighed. "Enough of this stubbornness, Corax. You cannot properly apply ointments to your own back, and horse ointments at that. No more arguments. I shall be leaving as soon as I finish my inspection, and you will be in the carriage with me."

At our home on the Caelian my father showed off our ebony chairs, citruswood chests and pantherwood table – I sometimes think he was prouder of his furniture than he was of his children – and then became remarkably ill at ease, muttering non sequiturs and swinging his arms and instructing Corax to take a seat so that "everything can happen as the Fates dictate".

I know all this because I, as a bashful six-year-old, was present that day, half hiding behind the couch. Corax, who was sitting alone on a chair at the other side of the room, noticed me after a while and stared with a puzzled expression, as though he had never before beheld a well-fed child. It was not the first time I had been in the presence of a great charioteer – Tarracius of Spain, for one, had dined with the family on numerous occasions – but I could not unfasten my gaze from the man, so curiously magnetic was he.

Then Xenia breezed in and, upon seeing Corax, came to a halt, her expression flattening.

"Oh," she said. "Are you the chariot driver?"

Corax took a long time to respond. "I am Corax of Campania, my lady."

"You have some wounds that need attention?"

"I have been ordered to wait here for a Greek physician."

"*I* am the Greek physician," announced Xenia.

Corax stared at her for a few moments before shaking his head. "I did not expect this, my lady."

"Then what *did* you expect, a bonesetter of gladiators?"

"I gave it no thought, my lady."

"And why do you call me 'my lady' when I am a slave like you?"

Corax was unable to respond.

"My name is Xenia," she said.

"I have no wish to offend you, Xenia."

There was a tremendously awkward pause. Finally, Corax started rising.

"I am sorry to waste your time, Xenia. I shall be on my way at once."

"What are you talking about?" said Xenia, who had been serving my mother long enough to acquire some of her feisty ways. "I have a task to perform."

"It is not a task for you."

"Why? Do you think I have not treated men before?"

"You have not treated me."

"And what is so different about you?"

Corax gave her a pained look, as though imploring her not to ask any more questions. "We should not argue in front of the boy," he said instead.

It was the very first time anyone had said such a thing – considered my feelings in the heat of a domestic dispute – and it endeared Corax to me permanently.

Xenia glanced my way and almost surrendered – I am convinced of it – before resorting again to inflexibility. "Enough of this foolishness, Corax of Campania. Go through to the changing room and remove your tunic at once."

"I cannot do that."

"Then what am I to tell my master? The one who gave me specific orders? Do you wish to see me flogged?"

In reality, my father – who I later learned was eavesdropping in the next room – would never have marred her flawless flesh, as Xenia surely knew. But her willingness to indulge in such distortions is itself revealing. As for Corax, the possibility of such a punishment worked on him in ways she could never have imagined. His slab-like face creased with the thought, he swallowed, he nodded solemnly, and with palpable reluctance he allowed himself to be led off to the changing room, where Xenia drew the curtains.

I do not know exactly what transpired in the room, of course, but they were in there so long that my father emerged from hiding and seemed on the verge of taking a peek before noticing me and drawing back, red-faced.

I do know, however, that Xenia spent the evening sobbing inconsolably, and I could not work out why my father, enjoying his supper, looked so wicked and pleased.

# XV

I T IS FASCINATING TO SPECULATE how matters might have developed had the relationship between Corax and Xenia been allowed to develop without interference. Corax, looking supremely sheepish, began visiting our home regularly in order to spend time with her amid the box hedges of my father's roof garden. Occasionally he brought along gifts – tasteless baubles – which she accepted with a rebuke, insisting that he should not waste money on her (while simultaneously fighting an appreciative blush). Corax spoke little but always tenderly; Xenia continued to resort to good-natured directness. They agreed that chariot racing was a cruel pursuit, good only as a means of attaining freedom, and Xenia urged him to think of his life beyond the arena. At the same time she started visiting the Circus Maximus regularly, in the company of myself and our household slaves, and could not stifle audible gasps of delight whenever Corax won, and resounding sighs of disappointment when he lost.

Meanwhile, to my father's great satisfaction, Corax mellowed enough to mingle with Greens fans and converse with the select few – children, cripples, injured soldiers – who were permitted to mingle with the charioteers outside the Triumphal Gate once the races had ended. In one notable instance, he met with a stuttering Gaulish boy by the name of Becco who had come with his family all the way from Tolosa. "Your bravery suggests a man of great consequence," Corax assured the lad tenderly, little realising that young Becco would reappear, decades later, at a crucial juncture in his destiny.

But if my father was content with these developments, my mother was very much less so. Still convinced that Corax was selfish and ill-fated, she claimed to be concerned chiefly for the fate of Xenia who, after my older sister died in infancy, had become to her something of a surrogate daughter.

"He will bring her nothing but tragedy," she told my father one day, as he was sorting through his bills of trade. "One does not need to be an augur to see that. Why in the name of all the gods have you allowed such a union to develop?"

My father shrugged. "The two of them are very different, to be sure, but they balance each other perfectly – and that is what makes them so good for one another."

"What is wrong with Xenia, that she needs to be balanced?"

"She needs a man to love and protect her, and Corax is the most devoted man I have ever known."

"Devoted to self-pity, perhaps. He is *damaged*, I tell you. What happens if she bears him offspring? I swear, the babe itself will be covered in burns and welts, so deep are the scars on its father."

"Well," my father said, "they have grown fond of each other very quickly, that much is certain, and there is nothing we can do about that."

"On the contrary, there is a great deal we can do about that. I remind you that Xenia is my slave."

"You cannot order her not to love him."

"I might not have to."

"Hmph." My father, never eager to pry into my mother's schemes, got back to his bills. "All will follow as the gods dictate."

By this stage, in record-breaking time, Caligula's prize obelisk, together with its massive pedestal, had been imported from Egypt in my father's freighter and installed on the spina of the Circus Vaticanus.* But my father had still to be reimbursed for the huge expenses – craft, crew, insurance policy – because the emperor, in a delirious spending spree, had all but bankrupted the treasury paying for all his palaces, theatres, amphitheatres and private gardens, not to mention the Circus Vaticanus itself. And just when my father mustered the courage to seek compensation in person, Caligula ordered the construction of two new pleasure craft, complete with temples, gardens, fish tanks and even stables, and my father, dazzled by the prospect, opted to save his appeals for another day.

The industry necessary to complete the huge new yachts nonetheless provided sufficient diversion for my mother to put her plans into action. She started by heading out to the Via Latina estate and confronting Corax in person.

"What is the matter with you?" she barked. "Why do you insist on insinuating yourself into poor Xenia's life? Have you never thought what would happen to her if you died in the arena? Or are disabled in some foolish accident? Like so many others in your trade?"

My mother spoke at a sensitive time in the history of chariot racing, for there had been a succession of freakish accidents leaving five charioteers either dead or permanently maimed. In one bizarre incident, Liber of Pannonia was racing in second place when the leading chariot collapsed and sent a whizzing wheel into the middle of his forehead. He was killed instantly. But since he was still bound up in his reins he remained propped up in his chariot as his horses raced all the way to the finishing line, earning him the unenviable distinction of being the first corpse to win a race in the Circus Maximus.

---

\* The obelisk is currently the centrepiece of St Peter's Square. The Augustan obelisk from the Circus Maximus adorns the Piazza del Popolo.

Corax, glancing apologetically in my direction for some reason (I was in the family carriage nearby), seemed unsure how to proceed.

"Lost your tongue, have you?" my mother snarled. "Well, just think about other people for a change. If you truly love Xenia you will detach yourself from her at once. She has many men with their eyes on her already, including slaves many times more charming than you, but they are not selfish enough to court her while they remain slaves. And I have told her exactly that – that you cannot be much of a man if you cannot do her the courtesy of waiting for your manumission!"

Corax, still with eyes averted, asked in a low voice, "And how did Xenia respond to this?"

"What does it matter what she said? She is an innocent slave who seeks to harm no one! And now you, a reckless charioteer, destined to die on the track if I am not mistaken, risk ruining her entire life to satisfy your transient lusts! No, I shall not allow you to swamp her life in misery!"

And, without waiting for further response, my mother bustled back into the carriage and ordered the driver to whip the horses repeatedly, itself a stinging rebuke of Corax (I saw his tortured eyes watching us as we rattled off).

At the very next meeting in the Circus Maximus, as it happened, the great Greens charioteer Tarracius of Spain, driving as a freedman for only the thirtieth time, was jolted out of his chariot during the sixth race and impaled upon his own dagger. He died at his home two days later. Similar to Corax, in that he did not care for celebratory excess, Tarracius was a sort of father figure to the younger charioteers. At his funeral, which was attended by a hundred thousand mourners, his grieving widow, whom he had only married upon his manumission, threw herself on the funeral pyre. With her pockets filled with pitch, she ignited like a torch.

If she had the powers of a goddess my mother could hardly have engineered a more sobering scene.

Corax, in any event, ceased coming to our home on the Caelian. Xenia was puzzled at first, then angry, then distraught. My mother, who had long urged her to forget all about him – "Very serious allegations have been made about his character" – now claimed, with feigned reluctance, that she had heard on good authority that Corax had already pledged himself to three other women, two of them common prostitutes from under the arches of the Circus Maximus.

It is a matter of personal shame that I never revealed the truth. But I, as much as anyone, lived in mortal dread of my mother's wrath.

Nevertheless, Xenia managed to steal away one afternoon to the Via Latina estate – at great risk, for Caligula was then taking advantage of any beauty who took his fancy – and confronted Corax in the stables. I was not privy to their exchange, and Xenia herself has never deigned to discuss it, but I like to imagine that she asked him if it was true that he had proposed to other women. And I picture Corax, pained by his inability to explain, stolidly refusing to say too much while keeping his eyes lowered – perhaps, when pressed, raising them just long enough to beg her not to ask any more questions.

He had, of course, no way of knowing that it was my mother who had been cultivating the sordid rumours. Nor did he know at the time – no one did – that she had already settled on his replacement. And he would have been mortified to learn just who that replacement was, and just how successful this new suitor would turn out to be.

When Xenia returned to our home, in any case, she was weeping convulsively. And this time it was my mother, not my father, who at supper looked both wicked and pleased.

# XVI

I T IS NOT FOR ME TO OPINE on matters of the heart, least of all those relating to the feminine sex, since my only love from earliest memory has been that of wax tablets, rolled scrolls and bottles of fragrant inks; I am a historian and sometime poet (of no great renown), but never much of a lover. Those waters, tested very tentatively in my youth, proved alternately too frigid and too warm for my liking, and I retreated with haste to the safety of my books.

Nevertheless, I feel confident in stating that Xenia accepted her new suitor so swiftly into her life more as a means of provocation than anything, trusting, no doubt, that word of their union would soon reach the ears of Corax and jolt him to his senses. Unless my recollections have been distorted by age or wishful thinking – which, as a historian, I admit is always possible – she was unnaturally stilted during those early meetings, laughing too frequently, making too many admiring comments, and altogether behaving much less candidly than was her nature. I am equally confident, however, that such artifice turned to affection with unusual rapidity, and that affection turned just as quickly into genuine love. It was the sort of progress that would have been remarkable, even shocking, had her suitor been any man other than Alector of Arcadia. But in this much, at least, my mother was not wrong – the Rooster, with his sunny personality, sparkling eyes and cheeky nature, was manifestly more attractive than the Raven.

Regarding his own motives, I am perhaps no more qualified to speak, since my experiences have always been hesitant and confounding, while Alector by then was already a seasoned lover. And yet I believe I can state without hesitation that Xenia was no regular beauty to him – something to be discarded after feasting, like a plum-stone – and that she did, indeed, represent the first time he had genuinely surrendered his heart.

It was my mother who, during one of my father's absences, had invited Alector to a feast – with a couple of other less winsome charioteers, just to furnish him with a flattering contrast – and my mother who dressed and perfumed Xenia for the occasion, and my mother who made sure that she served the table, and my mother who reeled out one of her overbearing introductions: "Have a look at her, Alector, is she not beautiful? Her name is Xenia, you know – a Greek, just like you."

Whether or not this was truly the first time Alector had beheld her – he claimed later that, with his keen eye for beauty, he had already noticed her in the stands of the Circus Maximus – the look I saw in his eyes at that moment was the same mixture of awe and mortality that I had previously observed on Corax. And it seemed clear to me that, for all the ladies that had melted under his gaze, Alector had never himself been liquefied by a woman as he was that day in Xenia's presence. I believe he was robbed of words, sapped of confidence, struggling for a proper reaction – a cockerel who had suddenly turned into a tit. It is notable, too, that when Xenia, becoming conversational in her affected way, asked him from where in Greece he hailed, he replied that in truth he had never been to that land – a notable response, I think, because to any other woman I am sure he would have lied.

He returned to the house many times after that, bringing gifts that unlike Corax's were exquisite, and staring deeply into Xenia's eyes, and telling her stories, and making her laugh and sing, and eventually making her swoon. A brief chronicle here would help put everything in context. Xenia had enjoyed Corax's company for six months, and truly loved him; when he rejected her, she grieved for perhaps another three months before being introduced to Alector; after four months with Alector she adored him as surely as she had loved Corax; and their union continued, as will be seen, for some months after that.

All of which brings me to the question of how Alector found out about Xenia's previous relationship. And if I can state without doubt that he did not learn about it from Xenia herself, or my mother, or my father, or any of our slaves, it is only because I know for certain that the informer was me.

You would be right to ask why I would do such thing. To which I can only say, well, perhaps some of Alector's mischievousness had rubbed off on me. Or perhaps I was ashamed of my mother's brazen manipulations. Or maybe I was still so fond of Corax that I felt compelled to deflate his successor with the truth.

"She was Corax's sweetheart, you know."

Alector, who was in the tablinum waiting for Xenia to appear, flashed at me one of his dazzling smiles. "What's that, young man?"

"Xenia," I told him. "She loved Corax, and Corax loved her, before you came along."

He looked perplexed for a moment. "Why do you say such things? Did Eutychus put you up to this?"

"Not at all. I just thought you should know." And like a cockroach I scuttled off.

Now I do not know if Alector confronted Xenia about this revelation, or questioned my mother, or mentioned it to other charioteers, but it was around this same time that news of the new pairing finally found its way to Corax. And the Raven, by all accounts, was quietly devastated. In truth, I believe he had merely postponed his union with Xenia until he had earned his manumission, secured his future, and retired from chariot racing. He was naïve enough to think that Xenia, having been so inexplicably spurned, would wait patiently for him to return. But now he felt betrayed and even mocked – by Xenia, by Alector, and possibly even Caligula (the possibility that the emperor had orchestrated the new relationship became a popular rumour). In any event, the tension between the two charioteers thereafter seemed to overwhelm the Via Latina estate – one only had to pass through the entrance arch to feel it in the air – and reverberated through the crowds of the Circus Maximus, who feasted on such scandals, and flooded into the arena precisely to find out how the drama might play out.

Under the circumstances my father, back from launching the emperor's floating palaces onto Lake Nemi, might have been delighted. Corax was performing better than ever. But Alector, too, had reclaimed his previous form in the arena, either to ward off the challenge from Corax or simply because he had suspended his nocturnal escapades with the emperor. And yet, despite all this – or perhaps because of it – a whole new crisis now emerged.

There was a wealthy landowner at the time called Gnaeus Lorius Tranquillus. And this fellow, notwithstanding his name, was so overbearing that some of his slaves conspired to kill him in his sleep. When the plan failed, the ringleaders were promptly executed, but Caligula, who had passed through a period of physical illness and emerged into a state of perpetual madness, decided that the remainder of the man's slaves – two hundred of them, across several estates – should be punished as well, as a warning to other malcontents in their ranks.

He announced that a special race would be held in the Circus Maximus, in the middle of the annual Agrippinian Games, in which the slaves would be laid flat out on the track, in twenty scattered clusters, as eight chariot teams raced around them at top speed. Caligula himself had selected the eight participating charioteers, including Corax of Campania and Alector of Arcadia.

When Corax got wind of this, he vowed that he would never participate in such an atrocity and demanded that all his fellow charioteers follow suit. But in the end only Magnus of Noricum, a dwarf charioteer whom the emperor had included for novelty value, agreed to withdraw. Corax's continuing exhortations, meanwhile, culminated in a dramatic confrontation between himself and Alector that was witnessed by several at the estate – the unprecedented volume of words, as much as their meaning, testifying to the intensity of the emotions at play.

"Stop your braying, you choleric mule," Alector growled. "Why make life harder than it already is?"

Corax glared at him. "Are you saying that you feel no shame about driving in this race?"

"Did I say I was happy about it? But the race will go ahead with or without us – that much is certain."

"And you are prepared to trample over your brother and sister slaves, is that it?"

"It's exactly because I am best placed *not* to trample over them that I am willing to participate."

Corax scoffed. "You cannot bear to disobey your great friend the emperor, I suppose?"

"My decision has nothing to do with Caligula, you whinnying fool."

"Do you deny that you have caroused with him? Visited gambling dens and houses of ill repute? Dallied with women of low character? And continue to do so?"

Alector bristled. "Are you calling Xenia a harlot, you crow?"

The Raven and the Rooster, restrained only by onlookers, surged towards each other like rutting stags, snarling at each other with flared nostrils and bared teeth – both men swollen with long-brewed tension, both of them trying to work out who should be most offended, and both of them enervated, in the end, by their mutual affection for Xenia.

In the event, the punitive race was run in front of a crowd so uncharacteristically muted that Caligula's mad cackles rattled around the arena. True to his word, Alector managed to avoid striking even a finger as he weaved dexterously around the track and won the race by thirty lengths. But as many as forty slaves were struck by pounding hooves or chariot wheels, and of these ten died later in the spoilarium.

For refusing to take part Magnus the dwarf had his ears lopped off and was exiled from the city of Rome. He later became Corax's most reliable friend and confidant. Corax himself escaped punishment only because my father somehow convinced the emperor that the Raven had been forced to pull out, against his fervent wishes, owing to the ligament problems that had famously plagued him. The increasingly unhinged Caligula was clearly suspicious, however, and it was with a sense of great dread that my father arrived at the Palatine a few days later, in response to a personal summons.

The emperor, on a dais in the throne room, was wearing Grecian robes and chained for some reason to the curule chair. The magisterial chamber, the windows of which Tiberius had sealed with crimson curtains, was dissected by a solitary shaft of slow-creeping sunlight. Other revellers, costumed as mythological figures, were reclined in the wine-red darkness.

"Did you know what that useless stargazer Thrasyllus once said of me?" Caligula asked my father, without lowering his eyes. "He said I had as much chance of becoming emperor as I had of riding across the Bay of Baiae. Well, now that I am emperor, I have decided to do just that. I shall ride across the Bay of Baiae. Not across the waves, but across a bridge. A new bridge. A bridge of boats. I'm assuming your woodcutters and plankers can throw something together? I want it done at all possible haste, you know – no wasting time in debauchery, you hear?"

My father, who had prostrated across the floor in the Parthian style – for that was the way that visitors were now compelled to greet the emperor – got to his feet, relieved. "Of course, Caesar – it will be my honour to get the construction underway immediately."

"And I want to drive a chariot, you know. A quadriga hauled by a full complement of horses."

"I shall make sure you have the finest chariot available."

"I don't want a fast one; I want a handsome one."

"I shall have it fixed with the most precious gems and gold fittings, Caesar."

"And I want to drive the Incitatus Team – I assume you can arrange that as well?"

My father fought a grimace. "Of course, Caesar, if that is your wish."

"It is my wish, of course it is."

"Then it will be my pleasure to prepare the horses as well, Caesar."

Caligula sniffed, suddenly transfixed by a mosquito hovering in the shaft of light.

My father hesitated. "Will that be all, Caesar?"

Caligula, his nose curling, was still tracking the lugubrious insect.

"Caesar – is there nothing else I can do for you?"

Caligula jolted out his trance and stared intently at my father for a few moments, as if just remembering where he was.

"Oh, there's a contract you must sign," he said, gesturing to the darkness. "Aulus Vitellius over there has it with him. Did you bring your signet ring?"

"Contract, Caesar?"

"Why yes," said the emperor. "For the transfer of Corax of Campania to the Blue Faction. I arranged it this morning. It will be good for the Greens to be rid of him. He is trouble, you know – trust me, I see iniquity in him. I sense that he is cursed."

Then, the matter settled – for my father was altogether speechless – he looked up again.

"Now where is that mosquito? You've made me lose him, Picus! I'm not happy about this. He is an eagle in disguise, you know! Where are you, little eaglet? You shall not get my liver! My liver is not for you!"

And on and on he went, giggling and squirming and tugging on his chain.

# XVII

I T HAS ALWAYS BEEN COMMON FOR CHARIOTEERS to drive for different factions, and my father himself had been responsible for numerous high-profile transfers. This, however, was the first time such an arrangement had been thrust upon him, and he was particularly distressed, to the point of tears, because he loved Corax as much as he loved his son (indeed, I am inclined to say with the detachment of age, considerably more so). So it was with genuine heartbreak that he informed Corax of the news, and with much sincerity that he wished him the best of fortune even while racing for the Blues.

"As far as I am concerned," he told Corax, embracing him, "your every victory will be a win for me."

"And you will always be my master," returned Corax, who was never surprised by the cruel workings of men.

My father even forewent the customary ritual whereby various calumnies are disseminated regarding a transferring charioteer – that he is a drunkard, a reprobate, that he was unpopular with his teammates – in order to placate the faction acolytes. But, as it happened, the circumstances were in this case so well-known that not even fickle fans were moved to generate scurrilous rumours.

And consequently, Corax was one of those rare charioteers who could simultaneously be loved by followers of both the Blues and the Greens, as well as widely admired by fans of the Reds and the Whites.

Within the Blues camp itself, Corax's presence had an instantaneous effect, bringing as he did an exemplary discipline that had been sorely lacking from the well-financed but ill-managed faction (I have this on the authority of Blues charioteer Crudelis of Utica himself). He inspired the others to forgo their rich foods and wine, he ended their practice of attaching silly ornaments to their harnesses and finials, he introduced more expertise and better sanitation to the stables, and he altogether improved things in a thousand different ways. He was meanwhile respectful of, if not overly friendly with, the Blues' *dominus factionis* Rutilius Oceanus, while reserving a particular loathing for Vitellius, whom he knew to have been integral to his transfer.

As a result, the Blues as a whole improved appreciably on the track. Corax himself had never been better, winning race after race by commanding margins, his unchanging expression – for he never smiled, no matter how great the victory – becoming the stuff of legend. But even Alector was now less demonstrative in victory, seeming to have found a purpose greater than mere glory – this said to be the love of the mysterious enchantress who had previously cast her spell on Corax – and, naturally, this had the fans clamouring for a race between the two mortal enemies and erstwhile friends.

But my father, perhaps with the tacit cooperation of Rutilius Oceanus, stubbornly resisted the temptation. It might have been some sensitivity to the feelings of Xenia; it might have been some deference to his own emotions; and it might, again, have boiled down to sheer showmanship – wringing every single drop of anticipation out of what was tipped to be the greatest showdown since Auchenius of Rhodes raced against Eros of Moesia (who was sleeping with Auchenius's mother at the time).

Unfortunately, my father did not get the chance to choose, because Caligula by then had transitioned into a state of constant delirium. The less money there was to waste, the more he found to spend. The heavier the weight of personal responsibility, the more reckless he became. He was condemning citizens to death at the slightest provocation. He was having people tortured in front of him at feasts. In the Forum he erected a huge golden statue of himself which was dressed every morning to match whatever he was wearing that particular day. His sexual depravities, meanwhile, were too numerous to be recounted here.

And simultaneously there were so many chariot races, gladiator bouts and beast hunts that the city's arenas had to be illuminated deep into the night by blazing braziers. Nor was the emperor a mere spectator. At the Floralian Games he declared that Eutychus of Dalmatia was the greatest charioteer of all time, worthy of a statue in the Temple of Jupiter Optimus Maximus, and awarded him with twenty thousand gold pieces on the spot. Then, having made this infallible judgement, he announced that he would race against Eutychus in the Circus Vaticanus – a god against a demi-god – to demonstrate the truth of this declaration. And so it was that, barely a week later, before an embarrassed crowd of senators, equites and courtiers, he crossed the finishing line a full twenty lengths ahead of Eutychus, who promptly announced that it was the Emperor Gaius Caesar Optimus Maximus who was, in truth, the greatest charioteer of all time.

But when an account of this race filtered into the streets it was greeted with more derision than admiration. It was noted that Caligula had been driving the Greens' fastest stallions, the Incitatus Team, while Eutychus had been lumped with "four sway-backed cart horses no one has ever heard of". It was observed the race had been conducted under controlled supervision far away from the Circus Maximus. It was a matter of speculation that Eutychus had been paid handsomely to tighten his reins. Moreover, while it was generally accepted that Eutychus was an outstanding charioteer – the closest thing to a *milliarius* that there was at the time – he was clearly no longer a match for either Corax or Alector.

If the emperor were truly great, the fans asked, then why then did he not race against the Raven and the Rooster? And in front of the public at that?

It is not known how these sentiments made their way to Caligula. Perhaps he overheard something on one of his nocturnal expeditions. Perhaps some suicidal courtier informed him personally. Or perhaps he arrived at the realisation spontaneously, in a rare moment of self-awareness.

In any event, at the next meeting of the Senate – to which he came adorned flamboyantly in Greens regalia – the emperor pouted and tittered and sang himself to sleep during the debates, which concerned such dreary affairs as tax rates in the provinces and the disposition of the imperial legions, until someone dared to ask about the appointment of new senators. And suddenly, histrionically, Caligula awoke.

"New senators?" he said, giggling wickedly. "I tell you honestly, I would rather have Incitatus in here than any of you lot. He would be a damn sight more entertaining. Make a lot more sense than most of you, too. And be a lot better looking, for that matter. What say you, gentlemen? Incitatus for senator? For consul, perhaps? For emperor even, when I join Jupiter?"

He surveyed the distinguished faces around him, finding a mixture of aversion and hesitant smiles, as if the senators were desperately trying to convince themselves that the proposal was some sort of jest.

"Oh, what boring sacks of chaff you lot are. I can bear it no longer!" The emperor sprang to his feet. "But if you really want to see the next consul in action," he said, flouncing across the floor, "you might come to the Circus Maximus at the Cerealian Games. The two of us shall be racing together, you know. Me and Incitatus, that is, against Corax of Campania and Alector of Arcadia. Now *that* is a contest that should settle once and for all, without an iota of a doubt, who is the greatest charioteer of all time!"

He halted at the door and surveyed the senators with another exasperated sigh.

"Oh, look at you now – just look at you! You'd sooner be dressing up like Egyptians, I suppose! Or pursuing your little peccadilloes, I fancy! You've simply no idea – I can tell! – what an impotent, inglorious and insalubrious lot you are!"

# XVIII

THIS ANNOUNCEMENT, WHICH OF COURSE came without any consultation with my father or Rutilius Oceanus, caused great consternation within the camps of the Greens and the Blues. Both Alector and Corax were considered excessively headstrong, albeit in dramatically different ways, and there was ample reason to suspect that, in the heat of a race against the emperor, neither would allow himself to lose. It scarcely helped that, following his voluntary humiliation in the Circus Vaticanus, Eutychus of Dalmatia had become a figure of withering ridicule, showered with abuse in the street – "Hey Eutychus, if I pay you enough will you lose to my grandmother?" – and the very amount that Caligula had gifted to him quickly becoming the notional price of a man's honour: "I wouldn't agree to that if you offered me Eutychus's twenty thousand gold pieces."

Of the two, it is perhaps paradoxical that the Rooster was thought to be the more reasonable. Then again, he was still directly under the influence of my father, the man he most respected, and Xenia, the woman he most loved. And both were adamant that Alector would find no gain in beating a living deity. Any fleeting gratification would only end with his being flung from the Tarpeian Rock. Or tossed into a cage of starving bears. It did not really matter how he would be killed; what was certain is that his execution would happen. No sensible man – no man with prospects, no man who truly enjoyed *living* – would do such a thing. For these reasons alone my father and Xenia were confident that the Rooster would swallow his pride.

And yet they could not be certain. Because losing to Caligula, when everyone could see the whole thing was a charade, was one thing. But losing to the Raven – who, like Alector, was exactly one win away from become the youngest double-*centenarius* in chariot racing history – was quite another. Even if Corax were executed immediately after victory, Alector would be haunted and humiliated for the rest of his life.

And the Blues were having great difficulty with Corax. He had not specifically told them he intended to win, but neither would he confirm that he was willing to lose. Pressure was applied to him in such a ham-fisted way – "If you fail to do your duty, we will crucify you before the emperor does" – and by such a ham-fisted envoy – young Aulus Vitellius himself – that it only proved counterproductive. Corax refused to speak to anyone. And went about training his horses as usual.

Hastening back to Rome from Misenum, where he had been inspecting some new battleships, the Blues *dominus* Rutilius Oceanus tried frantically to pierce the charioteer's armour. But Corax did not even appear to be listening. So a despairing Oceanus appealed to my father.

"You must make the lad see sense, for both our sakes. He will listen to you, Picus, even if he will not listen to me."

"You overestimate my powers, Oceanus."

"Then who might we turn to, if not you?"

My father stroked his beard for a while and then said, "There is someone, perhaps, but it's a last resort. Because it will possibly make him more stubborn than ever. Can you convince him to meet me at the Temple of Venus Erycina?"

"The one on the Capitoline or the one on the Quirinal?"

"There's one on the Quirinal? I didn't know that."

"Very well, the one on the Capitoline. But why, Picus – what are you planning to do?"

"No," my father decided, "it is best that you do not know, so nothing can be inferred from your bearing."

Thus it was that Corax was ordered to visit the Capitoline at a specified time, and thus it was that the Raven, looking very grave, entered the gloom of the temple and found himself alone except for a hooded worshipper standing near the sacred flame. And he was heading towards this person, assuming it to be my father, when he abruptly drew up in his tracks. Because now the identity of the figure, even heavily disguised, had become unmistakable.

"You must forgive me for this deception, Corax," said Xenia, throwing back her hood. "But I would not be here if I did not love you."

Corax, I have been reliably told (my father was watching from the darkness), lowered his gaze at once.

"Is it true what I hear?" Xenia went on. "That you cannot bring yourself to lose this silly race against the emperor? That you would have yourself killed on some foolish point of honour?"

Corax, like a chastened hound, had not raised his eyes.

"What has become of you? The man I knew would never have given himself over to such childish nonsense. Do you wish to die, is that it?"

Corax was mute.

"Do you think you are making some point to the slaves? That you must win the race for them?"

Still no answer.

"Well, I tell you this, as a handmaiden myself – no wants to see you executed for no reason, least of all the slaves."

"If I win or if I die," Corax now said, almost in a whisper, "it will—"

"Speak up, Corax, I cannot hear you."

"If I win or if I die," Corax repeated, louder, "it will not be for the slaves."

"Oh?" Xenia said, frowning. "Then who will it be for?"

Corax looked up and spoke in a heartfelt whisper. "It will be for you."

Struck dumb for a moment, Xenia very nearly lost her composure. But she rallied.

"Win for me?" she said, choking out the words. "Is that what you said? What are you talking about? If you really wish to do anything for me, you will *lose*! Do you hear me – you will lose!"

Corax, looking supremely pained, again averted his eyes.

"What is the matter with you, Corax? Have you not listened to a word I've said?"

"I'm afraid I must—"

"*What?*"

"I'm afraid I must be true to my feelings."

He turned to go, impervious to Xenia's further appeals, and had almost reached the stairs when my father erupted from the shadows.

"Corax!" he exclaimed. "My dear Corax. You must excuse us – both of us."

The charioteer halted, humbled.

"You must know that we love you. And you must know that we would not be saying these things if we were not concerned for your welfare. You must tighten your reins – you *must*."

Corax said nothing but his brow creased.

"Alector intends to do so, so why can you not do so also? There is no shame in this."

Corax looked up. "Alector intends to lose?"

"He does, of course he does."

"You know this for a fact?"

"Of course I do," my father said – but his eyes flickered.

Corax thought about it for a moment and then nodded. "I do not blame you for trying," he said, and made to leave.

My father blocked him again. "Corax, please. Think of the rest of us. If you do not lose this farcical race, others might suffer from association . . ."

Corax shook his head. "I no longer race for the Greens."

"But Alector does."

"Then that is Alector's decision, not mine."

"But Corax – if you try to win then Alector will try to win also. You know this is true."

Corax hesitated.

"He will try to beat you. And then he will be punished as surely as you will be punished. And I will be punished as well. And who knows what will happen to Xenia?"

Corax looked my father in the eye, then over his shoulder at Xenia, and for a moment he appeared to waver. But then he rediscovered his resolve. "I say again – that is entirely a matter for Alector."

"Corax—!" my father cried, turning to Xenia with alarm.

But the Raven, raising his own hood, was already marching down the stairs and dissolving into the crowds of the Capitoline.

# XIX

**A**LECTOR WAS NOT INFORMED OF CORAX'S STUBBORNNESS; quite the opposite, he was given every impression that the Raven had also agreed to "play Eutychus". Nevertheless, my father sensed some uncertainty in him, even suspicion – Alector, after all, knew Corax better than anyone – and so, after another extraordinary meeting with Rutilius Oceanus, it was agreed that there was only one course of action which legally and ethically would absolve both factions of all responsibility.

Alector of Arcadia was granted his freedom in a hastily arranged manumission ceremony the evening before the race.

Corax of Campania was similarly granted his freedom by his new owner Rutilius Oceanus.

Both men, my father noted with bleak satisfaction, chose to honour him with their freedman's titles: Lucius Cornelius Alector and Lucius Cornelius Corax. The latter's decision reportedly bothered Vitellius much more than it irritated Oceanus.

In fact, the younger Vitellius, whose devotion to the emperor was as expedient as it was total – he had already attributed his pronounced limp, the result of Caligula's crashing into him in a chariot, to "toppling down some stairs" – now seemed hellbent on clipping the Raven's wings. He first tried to poison Corax's horses, and when this failed for lack of opportunity – Corax never left the vicinity of his team – he settled on poisoning the charioteer himself, on the morning of the race. But even this proved not entirely successful when Corax, tasting something acrid in his gruel, flung the bowl across the room.

The Raven had nonetheless ingested enough of the concoction to be shivering and bilious when he arrived at the Circus Maximus. Though it was a gloomy spring day, with flecks of rain swirling around the arena, the stands were so laden with people that the timbers were groaning and creaking noisily. There was an unusually high representation of slaves. I myself was there with a retinue from the family household. Xenia, infuriated, did not attend. My father was pacing around the Via Latina estate as usual.

The race was to be a *pedibus ad quadrigam* – one lap on foot followed by six in chariots. The foot-race element had been enough for Caligula to perceive an advantage, for he was lean enough to be sprightly, whereas Alector and Corax had never been much adept at the sprint.

Corax and Alector took their places at the breakline, the three chariot teams held in place behind them, and waited wordlessly in the chilly April air, not even glancing at each other, until there was a blast of trumpets – the horses jolted and whinnied – and Caligula, flamboyantly costumed as Apollo, minced into the arena, strumming a harp and wallowing in the adulation of the crowd (which, in fact, was pointedly subdued). Alector bowed to the ground in acknowledgement of the emperor, as was now mandatory, but when Corax attempted to do so he keeled over and vomited on the track. The crowd, not having yet heard of his poisoning, assumed this to be an indication of great anxiety or disgust, and a ripple of laughter, followed by a smattering of applause, coursed around the arena.

Caligula, interpreting the reaction to Corax as scorn, laughed also, bade the Raven to rise, and handed his harp to a ground attendant. Alector, keeping a wary eye on both of them, later told my father that he "never felt more ill at ease in the Circus or less enthusiastic about a race". Corax pushed himself upright, wiping vomitus from his lips.

Caligula abruptly took off.

There had been no trumpet blare, no dropped *mappa*, no signal from the presiding magistrates, nothing. And for several crucial moments both Corax and Alector stood in place, fully expecting the emperor to return to the line. But then, as a rising murmur in the crowd became a howl, they realised that a living deity enjoys the prerogative of making his own rules. The race had begun.

Belatedly the two charioteers took off as well. The spindly shanked emperor, far ahead, had a risible running style, all excessively pumping limbs and wildly bobbing head, but there was no denying he had achieved a substantial lead by the time he reached the first turning posts. Alector quickly made up some ground but Corax, hobbled by both his size and his illness, looked as though he were ploughing through snow.

The Incitatus Team, having been marshalled into place at the breakline, were ready to take off as soon as the emperor arrived, well ahead of Alector. He sprang into his gold-banded chariot, dismissed the ground attendants and blurted down the track for the second lap, whipping the stallions furiously. When he reached the first turning posts Alector had just launched his own horses in pursuit, and Corax was still trudging down the track on the Palatine side. For a moment it looked as though Caligula would lap the Raven before he had even reached the breakline, but Corax managed to leap into his chariot and take off just as the emperor caught up with him.

The two teams were racing side by side for a few moments, one lap apart. But the further they travelled the more Corax's skills became manifest. He gained ground on Caligula's team. He churned dust in the emperor's face. He took the turn and hurtled down the Palatine side, determined it seemed to catch up.

But it was Alector who was of course best placed to make a serious challenge. When the third dolphin was flipped the Rooster had closed the gap to a mere two lengths. He could already have taken the lead. Caligula was clearly a fraud, barely apprentice standard. With no sense of timing and little feel for the reins, he was *hindering* the Incitatus Team. But Alector, fighting the urge to overtake, was reminded constantly of his vow to my father. Of his promises to Xenia. Of being a loving husband. Of the prospect of retiring as a freedman. Of the glories that awaited him after he relinquished victory in this one ridiculous race.

Then a series of exclamations alerted him to some new sensation. Sparing a glance behind, Alector saw Corax's team thundering up on the outside track – as if this were the final lap! The madman was going at full gallop! He was going to make a dash for the lead!

Now Alector battled with conflicting emotions. One moment he was loosening his reins – he could not permit Corax to overtake him – and the next he was tightening them again – he could not allow himself to get ahead of the emperor. Then he was watching, passive and queasy, as Corax drove his stallions alongside his own team. Then the Raven was rattling past him. And then overtaking Caligula. The crowd was on its feet. The emperor himself looked stricken. The three teams were now taking the turn for the fifth lap and he was starting to fall behind.

But Corax, with vomitus still dribbling from his mouth, stubbornly persisted. He was *extending* his lead. He clearly had no intention of restraining his horses. He had committed himself wholly to victory.

Alector noticed the humiliation on Caligula's face. And, more than that, the sense of helplessness and desperation. The living god was thrashing his horses and shrieking commands but, even with the Incitatus Team going full tilt, even with his jubilator shouting encouragement in his ear, he could not make up ground. But neither could he lose gracefully. So, with Corax charging further and further ahead, he rolled his eyes and wavered as though over-come with a sudden ailment. He released the reins. He pulled out of the race.

Alector waited no longer. There were two laps to go and it was down to him and Corax. He whipped his horses. He cut loose. He tore past the emperor. He was convinced he could catch up because Corax's chariot team could not sustain such a frenetic pace all the way to the finishing line.

By the start of the seventh lap, they were neck and neck. Some track officials tried to stop them – the Incitatus Team was at the side of the track and Caligula was being attended to by physicians – but, to great bellows of approval from the crowd, Corax and Alector tore past. They raced at a ferocious speed around the turning posts to the Palatine side and charged down the straight – verily as though this were the last race in the last games on the last day of the world.

A half-hour later, when a courier on frothing steed arrived at the Via Latina estate and delivered the result, my father mulled over the news and nodded resignedly.

"I suspected it would be that way," he sighed. "It was written in the stars. In the wheelings of the birds. Yes, I knew it would end up this way."

# XX

T HE RESULT WAS OF NO CONSEQUENCE TO CALIGULA, who had already declared the whole race null and void. While still in his chariot it had become clear to him that he had been "poisoned by forces unknown" (it was of course Corax who had been poisoned), that his stallions had been struck by darts fired from the spina (it was in fact Corax and Alector's horses that were later found to have barbs in their hides), and that Incitatus in particular had been the victim of some sinister sabotage.

In this last matter he was not, as it happens, entirely mistaken. When Corax was still racing with the Greens he had complained bitterly about the pampering of Incitatus, who in the imperial stables was eating gold-flaked oats and sleeping on feather pillows. The stallion, Corax assured my father, would be ruined by such indulgences. And my father, who was fond of saying that you can kill a tree just as easily by overwatering as underwatering, was inclined to agree. Now it so happened that visiting Rome at the time was Quintus Creticus Tenax, a wily horse breeder who owned a stud farm north of Massilia. And this Tenax was an expert in "masking" horses – that is, replacing champion racers with inferior lookalikes, usually for gambling purposes but also to prevent the horses from being overworked or otherwise coming to harm. So my father commissioned him to trim and rebrand a middling white stallion to resemble Incitatus and, with the connivance of sympathetic imperial grooms, managed to switch this lesser horse with the real Incitatus in the middle of the night. Caligula never even noticed.

Ironically, it was the very fact that the emperor would not be driving the genuine Incitatus in the *pedibus ad quadrigam* that later became problematic. After all, everyone wanted Caligula to lead so decisively, or at least put up such a creditable display, that neither Alector nor Corax would be too ashamed to lose. And so a last-minute plan was devised to switch the horses again – an ambitious effort that was easily thwarted by the emperor's officious new body-guards. No evidence could be found to link either Corax or Alector to this subversion, but Vitellius, eager to support the emperor, was happy to make public his "grave suspicion" that the Divine Caligula had been victim to some sinister operation in which the competing charioteers had played no insignificant part.

In the end, both the Raven and the Rooster were lucky not to have been executed; Vitellius for one was calling for the ultimate punishment. It is not known exactly why Caligula chose to be merciful. Perhaps he was intimidated by Corax's newfound status as "Prince of the Slaves". Perhaps he retained some affection for Alector from their days of mutual revelry. And perhaps both charioteers were saved by the startling fact that neither had actually won the race. For when they flashed across the finishing line their teams were so inseparable that no one – the magistrates, the stewards or the crowd – could determine who had come first. It was a dead heat. It was the most famously inconclusive race in Circus Maximus history.

Corax was exiled from Rome for a distance of seven hundred miles. Alector, less culpable, was banished to his "homeland" of Greece. Both sentences were immediate and indefinite. Corax headed west in the middle of the night, farewelling no one but my father, who was weeping so much he could barely speak. Alector by contrast decided to make a great show of his own departure, parading with a vociferous army of supporters to Sipontum, where he embarked on a merchant ship while promising to return "as soon as Little Boots is sent to the cobblers".

As it transpired, Caligula's downfall was accelerated by the disastrous *pedibus ad quadrigam*. Infinitely worse than being despised in the Senate is becoming a joke in the Circus. Sensing a change in the public mood, he drifted into even greater excess. He called for more gladiatorial bouts, more beast hunts, more public executions and more chariot races. He very flagrantly, as opposed to surreptitiously, began poisoning Blues horses and charioteers. When he was openly jeered in the Circus Maximus, he had Blues supporters hauled out of the crowd and thrown to the tigers. When the booing persisted, he ordered the awnings stripped from the upper levels, on a blisteringly hot day, because "the Circus is dedicated to the sun".

Those praying for his demise soon included my father, who had become increasingly exhausted trying to distance the Green Faction from its most prominent patron. There were several ill-conceived assassination attempts orchestrated by generals and courtiers, some in the Circus Maximus itself, but when Caligula survived all of these, he only deemed himself more invincible than ever. He claimed to be Hercules. He claimed to be Jupiter. He said that any attempt on his life was illogical because he could not be killed. But then, during a break in the Palatine Games less than a year after the *pedibus ad quadrigam*, while passing through a narrow passage connecting the Circus to his palace, the living deity was swooped upon, clubbed, kicked, stabbed and beheaded – brought to a most illogical end at the age of twenty-eight.

For a week or two, Eutychus was mocked as a possible new emperor, though "twenty thousand gold pieces should be enough for him to see him abdicate".

As for my father, all that remained was to deal with the status of Xenia. Distraught over the result of the remarkable race, in which both her former partners had chosen personal pride over devotion, the sublime slave girl at first retreated into melancholy, then bitterness, then despair, and finally a resolve to forgive and forget, for she belatedly accepted that what she most wanted was to be with her pig-headed lover, to exert her sensible influence over him and to stand with him in exile where he needed her more than ever.

Accordingly, my father manumitted her in a moving ceremony in which many tears were shed, for truly no one wanted to see her leave. But leave she did, with all our goodwill, all her meagre possessions, and all the gifts that we had showered upon her.

And I tell you honestly that no one knew until the very last moment which direction – east or west – Xenia intended to travel, or with which of the two birds, the Raven or the Rooster, she was intending to nest.

# XXI

I T WAS AROUND THIS POINT – the first year of Claudius's reign – that Albus of the Esquiline first appeared in Rome. Albus was neither a trainer nor a breeder, neither a charioteer nor a *dominus factionis*, but he would become one of the most influential figures in the history of chariot racing. No one was sure where he came from – his accent combined traces of several disparate provinces – but the most convincing story held that he was a former legionary who had been sentenced for some indiscretion to hard labour in the salt mines of Vicus before escaping and re-emerging with a whole new identity (if nothing else this neatly accounted for his bleached appearance and habit of coughing up clouds of white dust). Nor did anyone know his precise age – he was so hairless he did not even sport eyebrows – except to say that with each year he seemed to acquire another layer of fat – "like a tree which annually takes on a new ring" – and in time he became so prodigious that folds of skin oozed around his chair and made him seem as one with the furniture, immense and immovable.

Albus owned a tavern on the Esquiline, the Cornigera, which was immensely popular in its day not for its appearance – a ramshackle building with a yawning entrance covered with horsehair blankets – or for its interior – rows of splintered benches in a crypt-dark chamber – and certainly not for its food – rock-hard bread, greasy stews and wine so rank that dogs cocked their legs wherever it was spilled. Instead, it had earned its great renown simply by being the most brazen and successful gambling den in Rome. As such, it was constantly crowded with tradesmen, shopkeepers, builders, soldiers, sailors, merchants, freedmen, guardsmen, travellers and Vigiles – anyone, in fact, who was interested in laying a bet.*

Over this temple of iniquity Albus presided like a high priest, usually from a smoky little room at the tavern's rear, but also from the roof itself, where he would sit sunning himself like a seal on a rock, quaffing wine, waving away flies, and presiding with imperial majesty over all that he surveyed (the tavern was high on the Cispian spur). And it says much about his status in Rome that he became a fondly sought-out landmark of the Esquiline, without ever being abused, mocked or targeted by blunt objects, despite the innumerable gamblers who were ruinously in his debt.

Albus's power, which was mysterious as his origins, derived from his peerless knowledge of everything that was happening in Rome. He seemed better informed than the emperor and more prescient than a seer. He had spies in the imperial palaces, in the Praetorian Barracks, in the head offices of the *cursus publicus*,† and most especially in the stables of all four racing factions, where his men were not above determining the condition of the horses by sampling their urine and sifting through their dung.

He also maintained an elaborate system of messenger pigeons to alert him to all significant happenings around the empire. My father at around the same time established a similar system, involving dyed

---

* Officially gambling was banned except during Saturnalia; unofficially it thrived throughout the year.
† The imperial postal service.

pigeons to inform him of race results, and would later claim to have been the pioneer of this practice in Rome (to the apparent chagrin of Albus, who otherwise cared nothing for what people thought of him). But it must be noted that, beyond such minor disagreements, the relationship between Albus and my father – between Albus and all the *domini factionum* – was mutually beneficial and respectful, with the gambling king routinely informing the *domini* of charioteers who were betting against their own factions, and the *domini* in turn furnishing him with priceless morsels of inside information with which to determine his odds.

In any case, it was Albus who, owing to his unimpeachable contacts or innate wisdom or supernatural powers of divination, was the first to declare that Xenia would head west. The odds he offered on this outcome were so short that many speculated that he must have had access to an informer in our household, while just as many decided it was a wild guess borne of ignorance of a woman's proclivities (Albus had never been known to enjoy the company of any lover, female or otherwise).

But it mattered little in the end, because – as in most cases – Albus was completely right. He made another fortune on the outcome and further enhanced his reputation as the most knowledgeable man in Rome.

Xenia had gone to join Corax.

# XXII

DENIED ASSISTANCE BY IMPERIAL DECREE, Corax had slogged across Italy and Narbonensis, avoiding the towns and cities, stealing through the Alps, hunting for hares and fish, lighting fires with flints, sleeping in caves and cattlefolds, and sipping melted snow. At one stage, when he was at his weakest, he was given shelter by a kindly hermit who restored him to health with berries and herbal drinks before sending him on his way. But, in general, the people he encountered, Gaulish tribespeople and bandits mainly, were as inhospitable as the city dwellers, and if they did not slit his throat, it was probably because they sensed in him a man who was already dead.

He ended up in Tarraco on the east coast of Spain, where a monumental arena, popularly known as the Circus Augustus, had been erected at prodigious expense. In fact, despite the Senate's objections to the expansion of chariot racing beyond Italy, Spain already boasted a number of circuses – at Gades, Merida and Toletum – which regularly throbbed with rowdy crowds. And here, with his competition comprised chiefly of talent not quite skilled enough for Rome, Corax quickly became the province's most successful and celebrated charioteer. His winnings did not match those that he had accrued from the Circus Maximus, even accounting for the substantial cut that had once been claimed by the Greens and Blues, but he was a free man making his own decisions and beholden to no one – except, of course, Xenia.

I have found no witnesses to their reunion and I am reluctant to speculate how Corax reacted to her reappearance in his life, beyond assuming he was very moved. The two must have been quickly reconciled, in any event, for Xenia had been gone barely six months when we received a letter from Spain informing us that they had been married. And though Corax continued to drive chariots for a living, against her better judgement, she must surely have been satisfied with his ambivalence about the trade, for he continued to exhibit no great delight in his victories and little inclination to mingle with faction administrators or even his fellow charioteers. That he was popular at all was due only to his exemplary talent and his unassailable integrity.

My father, on one of his regular visits to his timber plantations in the Pyrenees, made a digression to Tarraco to visit the couple at their home just inside the city walls, where he found them so content – "Xenia bickering lovingly, Corax wearing her rebukes with silent affection" – that he could not help shedding a tear. He made sure they were comfortably off – passing over a few bags of gold from the sale of one of Caligula's unused yachts – and vowed to do everything possible to have Corax's exile rescinded (though at this possibility Xenia was conspicuously silent).

My father, who also went frequently to Greece to confer with shipping and timber agents there, made a similar visit to Alector, who at that stage was lodging in Elis in preparation for the Olympic Games. Here he found a man who, like Corax, was adjusting as rapidly as possible to a different standard of sport. The Greeks of course are the fathers of chariot racing but have no great circuses, no great crowds, no great stud farms, and few consistently great horses or charioteers. They also have a curious habit of viewing sporting endeavours more through the eye of the philosopher than the fanatic (which I am happy to concede might be an indication of their refinement).

Yet still they honour their greatest sportsmen in verse, in exquisite statuary, and with considerable charity. A charioteer who has "raced for Hellas" in the Roman games, and certainly in the Circus Maximus, will never again have to pay for a meal or a room at an inn. And this is where Alector found that my father's contrived history of his Greek origins paid unexpected dividends, for he was cheered to the echo upon his arrival at Patrae, acclaimed by unprecedented crowds whenever he raced, and fêted everywhere with feasts and music. Even Alector of Epirus, the heroic charioteer whom my father had claimed was the Rooster's grandfather, crawled out of his deathbed to point out their obvious physical resemblances ("a head, a torso, four limbs and not much else," my father laughed).

Swiftly establishing himself as the provincial champion, not unlike Corax, Alector was also living with a beautiful, bickering woman, not unlike Xenia. But this, it turned out, was just one of a succession of new lovers, for the Rooster had resumed with a vengeance his life of promiscuity and short-lived affections. In truth, he was stunned and deeply hurt – he admitted this openly to my father – by Xenia's preference for the Raven. Coming as it did after he had dispatched dozens of letters from Greece assuring the slave girl of his abiding devotion, her decision seemed to him inexplicable. He could only speculate that some jilted lover from his past had gotten into her ear, and he cursed himself for not impressing upon her the magnitude and sincerity of his love while he had a chance. All the women in the world could not eclipse her memory, he declared, none could equal her beauty or purity of soul, and no one could claim anywhere near the same compelling effect on his heart. He saw it as his mission now to win her back, even if that meant destroying Corax in the process. And he had consulted innumerable oracles and marketplace astrologers who had assured him that such a day would indeed come to pass.

"Nothing is surer than this," he told my father. "I shall meet Xenia again one day. I shall see her face, and I shall race before her in the Circus Maximus, before I die."

My father was deeply troubled by this statement of intent, chiding himself for pitting the two men against each other in the first place, cursing my mother for her scheming ways, and damning Caligula for further complicating matters with his madness. As for Albus of the Esquiline, I am not sure if he ever became aware of Alector's audacious prediction, or opened a book on the possibility, but I have no doubt the odds would have lengthened appreciably as year after year evaporated like steam.

# XXIII

A T HIS VERY FIRST MEETING with the new emperor Claudius, my father, true to his word, lobbied for the return of Corax and Alector, pointing out, in as diplomatic language as possible, that their exile had been not simply unjust but counterproductive, for in their mandated disgrace both had proved more popular than ever. This sentiment was backed up by appeals from the Guild of Factions and the newly founded Guild of Charioteers, as well as sundry petitions delivered by the plebeians to the pulvinar of the Circus Maximus.

It all seemed so indisputable that my father could not work out why the stammering emperor continued to prove evasive. "N-N-Now is not the t-t-t-time," Claudius invariably replied. It became tempting to suspect the malignant presence of Aulus Vitellius and his equally devious father Lucius, both of whom, having buried Caligula, had seamlessly wormed their way into the new emperor's inner circle. Neither man would welcome the prospect of Corax or Alector returning to Rome, just as both continued to do everything possible to sabotage the Green Faction in general. They had already conspired to have some of my father's shipping contracts transferred to the Rutilii, strengthening the finances of the Blues, and had even, in a particularly egregious show of spite, convinced Claudius to sink my father's beloved super-freighter – the one that had transported Caligula's obelisk from Alexandria – to form a breakwater at the new harbour of Portus. My father felt especially aggrieved by this, as he considered the vessel his masterpiece and had adored escorting visitors throughout its hold, pointing out the quality of the timbers and anticipating many monumental voyages in its future.

The Vitelli had also tried talking Claudius into pledging allegiance to the Blues, if only for the sake of balance, but here the emperor proved admirably resistant, publicly declaring a preference for no faction and dressing the pulvinar in no particular colour. He had always been a fixture in the Circus – appearing as the imperial figure-head whenever his nephew Caligula was absent – and continued to do so as emperor, without visible enthusiasm, for his real passion was for the game of dice. Nor did he exhibit much interest in regulating chariot racing, or approving the many ideas that my father proposed for fireproofing the Circus, or expanding the arena's capacity, or doing anything apart from reconstructing the starting gates in marble (an incongruous flourish that only came about when he discovered an excess of the stone left over from one of Caligula's aborted building projects). He also left the Circus Vaticanus to be taken over by the army as a marching ground and had the imperial stables – the ones in which Incitatus had been lodged – transformed into a barracks. Those in the chariot racing fraternity who had been hoping that he would be equally as passionate about the sport as his predecessor, without perhaps the partisan extravagance, were duly disappointed.

Nevertheless, my father never ceased making his appeals on behalf of Corax and Alector, until one day Claudius, in his convoluted and metaphorical manner, provided an explanation of sorts for his prevarications.

"Have you ever been to Gaul?" he asked.

"Many times," my father replied, "in order to inspect its timber plantations."

"Oh? And where m-m-m-might you say are the best trees in that province?"

"Most certainly at Jura, Caesar."

"What about Mount Vogesus? Have you ever visited there?"

"Just twice, Caesar, though the Cornelii once purchased a great deal of timber from those slopes."

The emperor nodded. "Then did you know that there were once so many trees on Mount Vogesus that they were f-f-f-forced to c-c-c-compete with each other for sunlight and grew to a height of a hundred c-c-cubits or more?"

"I have heard as much," admitted my father. "Though I never of course saw those forests in such profusion."

"Of course not. And do you know why that is?"

"Why, Caesar?"

"Because so many great trees had been removed from the slopes, in order to build your ships, that the soil had l-l-loosened and been washed down the m-m-m-mountain, burying whole villages at the foot of the hills – did you know that?"

My father smiled. "What is always required – and what was clearly lacking in the case of Mount Vogesus – is the skilful management that balances the needs of the mountain with the requirements of the shipyards."

"Skilful management is indeed the mark of a great l-l-l-leader," the twitching emperor agreed, "and a l-l-l-leader's greatest virtue is the resolve to rule for p-p-posterity."

"I cannot disagree with that, Caesar."

Claudius, who had been slumped in a wickerwork chair, now leaned forward and spoke with unusual fluency. "Then I ask you to picture in your mind one solitary tree that is left standing on the mountain when all the other trees have been felled," he said. "This tree, with no competition for the sunlight, stands brightly on the slope – noble, majestic and visible to all for many miles around. But at the same time it is stripped of all protection, it is weathered harshly by storms, it bends to breaking point in winds, it is weighed upon by squirrels and hawks, and it becomes the sole meal for parasites. And so it is that this great tree, for all its majesty, can be toppled with a few well-aimed strikes. And so it is also that the tree might be better off, for its own welfare as well as that of the mountain, if it were hidden within groves of other t-t-trees."

My father did not miss the implications of this remarkable little lecture. Claudius had witnessed the parsimony and abhorrent behaviour of Tiberius, he had seen at close hand the excesses and depravity of Caligula, and he had watched from the sidelines as both men were schemed against and ultimately killed. His whole life, then, had become a precarious balancing act designed to avoid the sort of hostility that might lead to a similar fate.

In short, Corax and Alector would not see their exile repealed because it was another Caesar's responsibility; the popularity such a pardon would bring would be short-lived, and the political cost would be potentially life-threatening. In other words, Claudius had resolved to keep an even hand on the tiller at all times, even if this meant that innocent men were stranded in waters far behind.

Sensing this, my father very reluctantly suspended all his attempts to get the Raven and the Rooster exonerated of their crimes, and for a long time we genuinely believed we would never again see the two men in Rome.

# XXIV

THIS IS NOT TO SUGGEST that chariot racing did not continue to prosper. In fact, when I look back upon those days, I must confess that I remember little of my studies, my home life, or even of my family and friends, and yet everything – with startling precision – about the unusual happenings to which I bore witness in the arena. I would go so far to say that I identify whole years not by the names of the consuls, or even by the stage in the emperor's reign, but by the sights and sounds that enthralled me in the Circus Maximus.

I remember, for instance, the immense swarm of bees that, having escaped the imperial apiaries, one year descended on the arena during the Floralian Games. First to notice the awesome cloud in the sky were the spectators in the upper tiers, their tremulous mutterings alerting the rest of us to some incoming phenomenon. And when the bees settled on the Triumphal Gate – attracted, no doubt, by all the flowers that had been garlanded there – everyone cheered and whistled, inferring a blessing from Flora herself. The visitors remained in place for an hour or so, humming away contentedly, until the fourth race, whereupon an ear-shattering roar from the crowd – Cyrus of Cyrenaica had collided with Diogenes of Thebes – seemed to startle them, for abruptly they launched into the air and fell not merely upon the spectators – everyone ducked and fled – but upon the track itself, where the horses panicked, the charioteers lost their bearings, and there were so many collisions that the races had to be suspended until the bees in their caprice decided it was time to move on.

I recall also the year that the Tiber, in one of its periodic inundations, flooded the arena to the depth of a cubit, but the stewards decided to proceed with the races anyway, so that the nautical terminology that had long been applied to chariot racing achieved newfound pertinence as the horses flounced like porpoises through the water, the charioteers steered their vessels like helmsmen, and the chariots themselves floated like genuine *naufragia** whenever they crashed and broke apart.

I was there the day when the hapless Felix of Dacia – arguably the unluckiest charioteer in Circus history – smashed into one of those same *naufragia* at the Caelian end, the twin actions of his horses hurdling the shattered chariot and his own vehicle jolting over the wreckage somehow combining to catapult him into the air, still wrapped in reins, so that he landed in another chariot – no one could believe it – standing beside the rival charioteer but facing sideways, attached to his horses but looking directly at their flanks (one can only imagine what the horses made of it), still struggling to control them, still hoping to win the race, until the next turn when he was wrenched from his footing, his own horses ran over him, he broke two limbs and everyone fell about laughing.

I witnessed, too, the subsequent races when Felix's luck only seemed to worsen. On one occasion he was leading by four lengths, on track for his first-ever Circus victory, when some imbecile – possibly with a financial interest in the result – flung mice onto the

---

* Shipwrecks.

track causing Felix's team to shy and crash. And later, in perhaps the greatest humiliation of all, his stallions were secretly administered emetics before a race – my father cannot be ruled out as the culprit, since by this stage Felix was driving for the Blues – and discharged their bowels during the fifth lap, so that Felix crossed the finishing line dripping with horse dung, the crowd once again laughing him off the track.

I was there on the memorable day when Androcles returned to the Circus with his ancient lion, the one that, recognising him as the saviour who had years earlier extracted a thorn from its paw, refused to attack him and instead became his pet. (After a suspicious number of subsequent appearances over many years, it must be said, it became obvious that this "eternally grateful lion" had been replaced on at least one and possibly two occasions.)

I was there, too, on the day that Amplus the Elephant charmed the crowd by blowing a golden trumpet, the merry creature responding so favourably to acclamation that, even after the beast was led out of the arena, each new hurrah would bring a musical response from far beyond the walls, the crowd thereafter cheering and pausing – a hundred thousand people holding their breath – until an increasingly distant trumpet blare was heard, causing them to laugh so heartily that they forgot about the races entirely.

I remember, too, the novelty race between Philisticles the Magician and the Reds charioteer Fuscus of Caesariensis. As they swung around the turning posts for the last time, Philisticles, who was sporting a conical hat and robes intricately patterned with gold thread, had fallen a good two laps behind Fuscus, who had slowed his own team purposely to mock his flamboyant opponent. But suddenly Philisticles flung incendiary powder at the track ahead, and when the clouds of smoke dissipated it was now Philisticles who was in Fuscus's chariot and Fuscus, astonished, who found himself in the chariot of Philisticles. Not only that, but Philisticles appeared to be wearing a Reds tunic and Fuscus was robed in jewels and gold thread. No one in the arena could work out how it was done. Seconds later, Philisticles drove the winning horses across the finishing line and the crowd, so close to jeering, erupted into spontaneous cheers. (Nor was that the end of it, for when Philisticles accepted a special laurel from that year's consul – no less than Lucius Vitellius himself – he tossed more of his magical powder on the pulvinar floor and disappeared in another cloud of coloured smoke, only to reappear, moments later, on the middle of the spina, wearing a dove on his head and a smile that was brighter than the sun.)

And, though I was not there personally – for by that stage I had lost all interest in chariot racing (a temporary disaffection upon which I shall expand upon shortly) – I am compelled to follow up on the story of Felix of Dacia, for reasons that will later become evident.

After the string of unfortunate accidents I have already recounted, Felix seemed finally to have achieved some success – he had claimed second place on three occasions and seemed set to claim his very first Circus victory – when by chance he tripped over a horrifically diseased beggar in the Forum Boarium – that at least is the legend – and from this very brief contact contracted *Elephantias Graecorum*. Sporting swollen features, ulcerated ears and suppurating skin, he was manumitted through the mercy of his *dominus* (he was by that stage racing with the Reds) and retired to a lepers' hamlet in Liguria. But he could never quite relinquish his dream of a victory lap in the Circus Maximus and, his health rapidly deteriorating, he applied to that year's consuls, Antistius Vetus and Suillius Nerullinus, to be allowed one final race in the arena. That this was eventually authorised, even under the tightest of limitations, was considered something of an aberration at the time, and many suspected that the poor fellow was being set up for more ridicule.

In the event, the grotesquely afflicted Felix, covered with black protuberances and leaking sores, raced his chariot around the track seven times – his opponents, a few volunteers from across the factions, made a show of not even coming close – and crossed the finishing line weeping so violently that the crowd, which had first been inclined to revulsion if not mockery, began chanting his name.

"FELIX . . . FELIX . . . FELIX . . . FELIX!"

It was, by all accounts, an intensely moving scene. And those of us who had secretly been hoping for some reprehensible behaviour to sigh about in the libraries were duly disappointed. Even Claudius, who was in the pulvinar that day, ordered a golden laurel to be deposited on Felix's head – he could not bring himself to do so personally – and the unfortunate charioteer, having enjoyed his single moment in the sun, returned to Liguria where he was struck by lightning not six weeks later.

But his death did not mean he was entirely forgotten. News of his fate travelled swiftly through the provinces, reaching the ears of Alector – who proposed a toast, as was his custom, to a fallen comrade – and to Corax, who was later to prove grateful that he had been so sympathetic to Felix when they were racing together in the Greens.

# XXV

C LAUDIUS'S ANNOUNCEMENT THAT HE WAS ANOINTING his plump and pustular Nero as his successor was, I am convinced, a cunning ploy designed to forestall a Vitellian assassination attempt, for the unlikely heir was even more fanatical about the Greens than Caligula had ever been.

But, if this was Claudius's intention, it proved a fatal mistake. His new wife Agrippina the Younger, Nero's mother, is rumoured to have suspected that her husband's stated preference was a ruse, and so moved to finish him off before he could officially change his mind. The expert poisoner Locusta – already notorious in chariot racing circles for having prepared the powder that Corax ingested prior to the famous *pedibus ad quadrigam* – brewed up a concoction that was smeared over one of the emperor's mushroom pies – or so the story goes – and he expired in the fourteenth year of his reign, at the age of sixty-three.

My father, who had spent most of the man's reign fearing that his faction was about to be usurped as the imperial favourite, might therefore have had reason to feel relieved. But Nero's natural father was the detestable Gnaeus Domitus Ahenobarbus – who as praetor had once tried to swindle charioteers out of their prize money – and his mother Agrippina was "the most venomous viper ever to slither out of a pit". The boy Nero was uninspiring in looks, effete in manner and greedy of disposition – "Caligula without the breeding," my father said.

Nevertheless, the first years of his reign proved, to the chariot racing fraternity at least, similarly promising. He added two removable light towers to the spina of the Circus Maximus for night events, he embossed the zodiacal signs on the twelve starting gates, he improved the drainage and built up the flood defences, and he doubled the number of night patrols around the arena. He forbade beast hunts (my father was elated), widened the track over the *euripus* (the barrier no longer being required), installed perfume sprinklers on the top tiers (crowds were now showered with distillations of narcissus and sandalwood), and on extra special occasions had the track coated with crystals of selenite, so that the chariots churned up plumes of sparkling dust. He also cleared the soldiers out of the Circus Vaticanus, convened frequently with the various chariot racing guilds, promised to stamp out cheating and unruly behaviour, and pardoned Corax and Alector sixteen years to the day since they were sent into exile.

But this last gesture was largely academic. Corax had already retired from racing, reportedly at the insistence of Xenia, who feared for his life in the increasingly chaotic Spanish circuses. The very model of Stoicism – I believe he had officially embraced the philosophy by this time – he tried his hand at other careers – ostler, wainwright, harness maker – before inevitably accepting, with his wife's grudging consent, that any trade other than breeder and trainer of horses was a waste of his singular talents. And so, using the money he had scraped together from his many victories (as well as that gifted to him by my father), he purchased a parcel of land in the hills of Tarraco – close enough to the Circus Augustus that cheering could be heard when the wind was blowing in the right direction – and set about establishing what would become, in time, the most famous and successful stud farm in Spain. Visiting again for both business and personal reasons, my father found a man more talkative than he remembered but otherwise largely unchanged – still hospitable, still ambivalent about chariot racing, and still most at ease with his horses.

"He informed me for some reason that he had buried all the accoutrements of his racing career. Victory crowns, celebratory figurines and decrees, inscribed goblets and platters, team tunics, ceremonial helmets – everything. He'd just thrown the lot into a deep pit and covered it with earth, never to be exhumed, never to be thought about again. But by stating all this in an unusually loud and emphatic voice, he seemed more intent on making a statement to Xenia than confessing anything to me.

"And in any case, I felt the warmth of the fires still raging within him. And I saw the bleeding wounds that had dripped upon his soul. He had learned to accept the supremacy of the cruel and the corrupt, yes, but it was clear that he was shielding dreams of something better inside. Truly, he was like that olive tree in the Forum of Megara upon which victorious soldiers used to hang their belts and greaves, and which in time absorbed these pieces of armour into its bark, sometimes concealing them completely – that was Corax with his grievances."

In short, my father claimed it was obvious even then that Corax, not unlike Alector, dreamed of reappearing one day in the Circus Maximus. But without any reason to do so – since he was nominally retired – he had settled on siring sons to one day take his place. Alas, the first two of these boys were stillborn, and the fate of the third I shall cover shortly.

As for Alector, he continued to drink so greedily from the cup of life that inevitably he went too far. In the northern Peloponnese he bedded the young wife of a well-known shipping merchant, the son of a Cilician pirate who had settled there under Augustus, and this hot-tempered fellow – Theodoros was his name; my father knew him personally – proved not the least inclined to magnanimous cuckoldry. Claiming that vengeance was his "divine right", he and his henchmen pursued a half-naked Alector all the way to Patrae, where the Rooster slipped out of the harbour on the first boat to Corinth. There, warned that his life was still in danger, he secured passage to Ephesus where he remained in hiding for six months. Then, prematurely deciding it was safe, he ventured back to Greece, was chased again across the Peloponnese, fled again for Corinth, and ultimately resolved, for eminently sensible reasons, to resume his racing career in the eastern provinces. But it proved an endless struggle to earn enough money in the region's dilapidated hippodromes and dusty open-air tracks. My father found him one day in Antioch "racing against drunkards and acrobats" and decided at once to "plant him in firm ground" by appointing him head trainer at the new Greens training estate in western Syria. From there Alector was to roam around the region promoting chariot racing, scouting for potential charioteers and preparing the most promising for Rome.

"He was as cocky as ever," my father reported, "insisting that Rome had not seen the last of him and determined still to claim Xenia from Corax. 'She should have married me,' he said, downing his wine. 'No son of mine would ever perish in the womb.' And yet for all his bluster I sensed that he was putting on a show, like a tree blazing with colour before the winter sets in – defiance being his own way of concealing his wounds."

Nor did Alector enjoy success in generating sons, despite his intemperate remarks about Corax. There were even rumours that he was "more capon than rooster". And then, when one of his many conquests did bear a child, the unfortunate mother died within months, leaving Alector to take the infant into his care and raise her as best as he could. This girl, the famous Selene of Syria, would grow up to become his staunchest defender, fondest critic and best friend.

# XXVI

I N THE SEVENTH YEAR OF THE REIGN OF NERO, when the emperor was twenty-three, I was a young historian studying the rituals of Etruscan cults and the collected works of Lucius Lucceius. Despite my father's fervent desire for me to write a history of the Green Faction – and notwithstanding the work I had put into that very endeavour – I was passing through a transitional stage where my early enthusiasm for chariot racing had given way to an equally passionate disdain. I had begun to view the sport's participants, chiefly the charioteers, as gullible and grievously exploited. I had begun to see its followers – the heaving, frothing, chanting crowds – as illiterate and puerile. Worst of all, I had started to view my father as the king of hypocrites. For while he would work himself into a lather over the supposed spying tactics of competing factions, he would the next moment blithely dispatch his own operatives to infiltrate rival estates; while he would gnash his teeth over the "unscrupulous" and "criminal" sabotage antics of the Blues and Whites, he would simultaneously bribe other factions' moratores to insert wax pins into their chariot axles (a trick as old as Hippodema); and while he would fume and stamp over the "brazen cheating" of competing officials on race day, he would in the next breath order a platter of fine food and wine to be sent to a steward or games magistrate "in anticipation of mutual celebration".

In short, my cosy belief that the sport of chariot racing, especially as practised by my father, represented what the noble Hesiod called "good strife" – invigorating rivalries that stimulate progress – had given way to the conviction that the only strife it generates is almost exclusively bad – soul-sapping fanaticism, self-righteous resentment and an ever-increasing appetite for conflict and conquest.

Nevertheless, I was still residing at the family home – my father no doubt foresaw that I would one day realise that politics, my new passion, was a sport as venal and bloody as anything in the arena – when one night, as I was half-asleep in bed, I could not help over-hearing some commotion in the atrium. A visitor had arrived and my father was speaking to him in the sort of high-pitched whispering that attracts attention even while aiming to avoid it. I flung on a robe and went to investigate.

Standing in the shadows, flanked by pillars, I beheld – in the light of a single oil lamp, which was reflecting on the pool – my father next to a man I struggled to identify. Wearing a long-sleeved tunic cinched over woollen trousers, the visitor was rugged of physique, granite of face, soulful of eyes and close-pruned of hair. I reckoned his age at around forty-three or so. Fragments of the conversation drifted to my ears.

"I cannot do that," I heard the man say.

"But you must!" my father was arguing. "There is no danger, I promise you!"

"It is not a matter of danger, but preference."

"But the arena is your home – your theatre."

"I've already been away too long."

"Come now, are you really saying that you would ride all this way and not visit the Circus Maximus?"

"My mission is now complete."

139

"Then stay at least the night – one night, two nights, five. The place is yours. I need to speak to you."

"No . . ."

"But you are loved here. You are a son to me. You—"

It was at this stage that the mysterious stranger, following my father's gaze, turned and noticed me watching from the shadows. And I heard him say something that rent me like a sword.

"We should not argue in front of your son."

I was speechless. But if this was truly Corax of Campania – an older, stockier Corax – then how was it that he had he recognised me – pudgy and bearded, swathed in darkness – while I had not recognised him? And what in the name of the gods was he doing here in Rome?

Fearing, perhaps, the answers to these questions – and embarrassed that I had been caught eavesdropping – I retreated like a six-year-old to the safety of my bedchamber and listened intently until I heard the front door being opened and closed. And only later did I learn the reason for his visit.

For some years, it seemed, Corax had been dispatching to my father his finest horses, which in turn became some of the Greens' most successful racers: Paezon, Blandus, Mariscus and Panchates among them. He had even provided mares – including the great Galata and Ballista – in an era where faction stables were stocked almost exclusively with stallions. Simultaneously he had managed to extend equine careers in both directions, sending to Rome horses that were just three years old and others that were well over fifteen. But a new colt in training, he informed my father, was the most promising horse he had ever trained.

Andraemon, a shimmering white stallion, combined prime Numidian stock with the finest elements of the Spanish and Cappadocian breeds. He was a superlative mixture of speed, endurance, intelligence and temperament. Sired by the champion racer Stellus, whom Corax himself had driven in the Circus Maximus, he was already an exemplary leader, dominating teams, guiding them, and setting the pace – on the track, in the stables, even while grazing.

Delighted to hear it, my father urged Corax to send the horse from Spain at once. But a month went by and there was no sign of anything arriving at the ports. My father fired off a letter, seeking clarification – had the horse been injured? had someone fallen ill? – but received no answer. A month after that, with the inaugural Neroian Games looming ever closer, my father was frustrated but refused to give up. He was counting on Corax to be true to his word. And he was right.

What had happened was this. Xenia maintained a small number of milch goats whose buck, Cupido, was much loved by all on the farm including the horses. Andraemon was so fond of the beast that he would not travel anywhere without him. In arranging transport to Rome, therefore, Corax had no alternative but to seek passage for Cupido as well. But at the Tarraco docks he found no captain willing to put to sea with a goat, which on ships are considered the very worst of luck, and this left Corax with only one solution.

He promptly put together a pack of victuals, tools and horse medicines and, retracing the route he had negotiated twenty-one years earlier, escorted Andraemon and Cupido a thousand miles across Spain, Narbonensis and Italy, all the way to Rome. It took exactly two months, travelling at a strictly regulated pace, to reach the Via Latina estate, where he relinquished the horse to the capable hands of the grooms before making a brief digression to my father and heading home. The dangers of the expedition had not concerned him in the slightest. But the full story proved more remarkable still.

Andraemon and the billy goat, it turned out, were special to Corax for very personal reasons. It seemed his beloved son Falco, whom he was grooming as an expert horseman, had adopted Cupido and kept him almost permanently at his side. But one day, while the boy was performing training exercises alone and unsupervised, his pony, possibly spooked by Cupido, bucked him onto a fence. The boy's head struck a beam and he died on the spot. He was five years old.

When Corax found the child's body he was devastated. It is said he wept for the first and only time in his life. He watered the earth with so many tears, legend has it, that a great chestnut tree later sprang up on the site. Andraemon, meanwhile, having witnessed the tragedy from the other side of the paddock, came forward to nudge and console Corax, and thereafter became excessively protective of the goat, as if the beast had absorbed the boy's spirit – as if, by guarding Cupido, he might somehow keep Falco alive.

I cannot say how much of that is true but I do know that I thereafter started to take a keen interest in the development of the stallion, and was delighted when it fulfilled all the potential of which Corax had boasted. And when my father came to contriving a story to help explain the horse's fondness for Cupido, I was moved to say that it would be better to stick to the original anecdote, which was infinitely more impressive than anything that might be summoned from the imagination.

"No," my father protested, "the truth is too personal to Corax. He would not want it to become public knowledge."

"Very well," I said, "then allow me to think of something new. Corax at least deserves something tasteful."

It was only when I started to invent a worthy tale, back in my quarters, that I realised what was happening. My resolve was weakening. My resistance to chariot racing was breaking down. So, embarrassed, I made no attempt to spin a fanciful new story – in the event, the truth got out anyway – and it took a few more years, and another extraordinary event, to return me fully to the Circus.

# XXVII

**A**N INSIDE TRACE HORSE LIKE ANDRAEMON, however exceptional, still needs three other horses to make up a quadriga team, and my father had just the stallions in mind. Pertinax and Postumus (the latter had been born after his sire's death) were half-brothers imported from the wilds of Commagene. Immensely, deceptively powerful – so powerful, legend has it, that as colts they had dragged twelve pillars up a steep hillside to the palace of the King of Scythia – they were my father's first choice for the new team's yoke horses. ("Like trees, the most durable horses come from the harshest of environments," he always said.) As for the outside trace horse, it could only be Olympius, a grey stallion born in the shadow of Mount Olympus. Sired by Pegasus, the "winged" horse Alector had driven many times to victory in Greece, he was as swift as a gazelle, as proud as a lion, and as hardy as a rhinoceros. By the time my father purchased him, on the recommendation of an Athenian timber merchant, he was already a champion of the Isthmian and Nemean Games, and the Greeks – who have always regarded the outside trace horse as the most important racer in any team – were both thrilled and mortified at the thought of losing him to the Circus Maximus.

There was some expectation that Olympius would bridle under the command of the equally strong-willed Andraemon, and vice versa, but the two trace horses proved instantly compatible. In fact, the whole team came together more quickly and harmoniously than could ever have been expected. They seemed to be veritably champing at the bit to flaunt their combined talents in the Circus Maximus.

In the event, their first driver was Lotus of Loadicea, a charioteer so imperturbable and unassuming that my father had encouraged him to take up Corax's mantle in the Circus. But Lotus exhibited no great affinity for horses, no preternatural skill at the reins, and a painful air of affectation whenever he attempted to manufacture a steely Corax-like visage. Nevertheless, he benefited enormously from one of my father's silly stories – that the Raven had anointed him as his successor and passed to him the secrets of equine communication – and gained considerable popularity as Corax's torchbearer, while inadvertently keeping the memory of the exiled charioteer alive.

In his first race with the Andraemon Team, Lotus drove the horses to a creditable second. In their second race he lost by a single length. In their third he won by two lengths. Over the course of fifteen subsequent races the team's improvement, though unremarkable, was promising enough for him to claim the presumptive title of their permanent charioteer.

But then his career was stunted by an unmentionable scandal. For some months the charioteer, after every victory, had been observed steering his team to the benches beside the pulvinar and there tossing a rose to the Vestal Virgins. The gesture had always seemed innocent enough, but the crowds, paying more attention now that he was driving the Andraemon Team, noticed that that his flower seemed directed to one Vestal in particular. Still, no one really wanted to believe anything untoward, until someone – rumour has it that it was Vitellius himself – contrived to have the two of them caught *in flagrante delicto* at Lotus's villa. The Vestal was, of course, buried alive in the vault near the Colline Gate; Lotus was banished by Nero, with some reluctance, to Mauretania, where he wilted into obscurity.

The team's second charioteer was the freedman Cometus of Cyprus. Cometus, originally called Cedrus, had acquired his new moniker after a celebrated incident in which his chariot scraped so long against the spina that it caught fire and trailed flames all the way to the finishing line. Something of a crowd favourite, he guided the horses to solid if unremarkable victories and seemed destined to become their permanent charioteer. But along the way Cometus had become devoted to the new cult of Chrestus, even to the point of requesting that all his winnings, beyond mere subsistence payments, should be redirected to its priests.* Now my father, whose own beliefs were erratic – he was fond of saying that the only true god was Fortuna, and Albus was her prophet in Rome – was, like most of the *domini factionum*, prepared to tolerate any religious conviction so long as it did not have any adverse effect on a charioteer's performance. But Cometus's faith seemed to be steering him off course. When one of the cult's underground temples collapsed, killing a score of worshippers, the sombre charioteer spent more time soliciting donations than he did in training. And when my father confronted him about this, Cometus insisted that there were more important things in this world than chariot racing – an unspeakable blasphemy for a charioteer. Nevertheless, he somehow convinced my father to join him at one of the cult's many rituals.

My father returned shaking his head. "In form it was little different from a Mithraic ceremony," he told me. "A lot of prayers

---

* According to Christian lore, St Peter was crucified, upside down, in the Circus Vaticanus.

and chants and earnest expressions of brotherhood. But some of the sentiments expressed in their homilies were – how can I put this? – *incompatible* with chariot racing."

As he described them, I was reminded of the austere philosophies of Diogenes the Cynic. "You should be careful in rebuking Cometus," I warned, "for faiths thrive in persecution."

"Do you really think a *dominus factionis* might not know that?" my father returned, laughing.

In the end, Cometus became so devoted to his creed that he would not participate in any feast, spurned all victory marches and parades, and refused to complete any race in which a fellow charioteer was injured. He was like Corax without the scars. As a last resort my father tried to turn his faith into a motivation – "Think of all the prize money you can gift to your prophets!" – but Cometus all of a sudden seemed to think of *himself* as a prophet. He was leading his fans down to the Tiber and dunking their heads in the water, for heaven's sake.

It was time, clearly, for something to be done. For my father to do what he had secretly been itching to do for months. It was time to hand the reins of the Andraemon Team to "the Rooster's Rooster" – Alector reborn.

# XXVIII

ALECTOR'S ACADEMY IN SYRIA had already furnished the Greens with some of the finest charioteers of the era, including Primulus of Prusa, Calliopus of Cappadocia and Cedrus of Cyprus. Alector, for all his youthful indiscretions, was a masterful recruiter and trainer. He began by travelling with his daughter Selene to any eastern hippodrome that was hosting a race, be it Antioch, Pergamum, Damascus, Tyre or Caesarea, sweeping into the arena in a copper-spangled chariot, performing a few charges and dexterous moves, and then bellowing out his mission to the assembled crowds.

"I am Alector of Arcadia, famous champion of Rome! The legendary quadriga driver whose illustrious career was cut short by the depraved Emperor Gaius! Know you any lads who are ready to risk death in the arena? Know you any slaves skilled with horses? Then send them to me in the Amuq Valley for assessment and training! Great fame and even greater prize monies await your slaves – not to mention you, you greedy bastards – in the Circus Maximus, the temple of dreams!"

The boys who survived his ruthless culling process were then put through a training course that was part Phoebus of Thrace, part

Durius of Sicily, and part Platonic philosophy (which Alector had somehow acquired during his years in Greece). He would regale them with his singular take on Plato's chariot allegory: "Driving yourself through training – driving yourself through life! – is like driving a biga drawn by two horses, one interested only in earthly pleasures, the other fixated on eternal glory! The champion charioteer is the one who finds the precise balance between the two – between *hedonism* and *thumos* – while the straggler goes around in endless circles!" (That he himself was in no position to scold others about the dangers of hedonism seemed never to trouble him.)

He further assured his young apprentices that learning how to race a chariot was all the wisdom a man would ever require: "You keep on your feet, you stay alert to your enemies, you seize your opportunities, you steer through adversity, you draw back when necessary, and you head constantly for the finishing line!" He even became mystical: "The charioteer in his purest form is not an agent of destiny, but a commander of destiny! He does not respond to the elements, he controls them!

"Look at me!" he roared. "I came from nothing and I supped with emperors. I was the idol of men and the heartthrob of women. I was loved throughout the empire. I could have been anything! I *should* have been anything! Yet pity me not for I remain happy. I challenge you, in fact, to name any man who is happier than I! And all because, when I was your age, I listened with great respect to my seniors and trainers" – he truly said this, according to Selene – "and I learned how to master a chariot team!"

But he had never schooled anyone whose talent reduced him to envy until he recruited the young Thracian charioteer Delphinius of Doriscus. Dusky and statuesque, with sparkling white teeth and a well-trimmed beard – not to mention a certain ingenuous charisma; Selene was secretly in love with him – Delphinius was as impressive on the track as the youthful Alector had been. In his first official race, in the hippodrome at Damascus, he trounced vastly more experienced charioteers by the length of the straight. He was equally adept in the biga, triga and quadriga. His main flaw – which Alector attributed to his background as the pampered stablehand of a perfume merchant's widow – was his poorly developed taste for blood. Delphinius won not to defeat his opponents but simply because he did not know how to lose. And he was alarmingly sentimental at times, almost Corax-like, such as when he pulled up in the middle of races to assist fallen comrades. Alector – for whom "wax-hearted" was the gravest of insults – lectured him about the fabled charioteers Castor and Pollux, to which Delphinius, who was very well-educated for a charioteer, frowned and said, "Have you not heard? That legend has been revised."

"Revised, has it?"

"It's true," insisted Delphinius. "Records have been unearthed that prove that Pollux did not run over his brother on that fabled day, but actually stopped to assist him, and was subsequently sent to the quarries for his impertinence. Then his brother stopped racing in sympathy, and he too was sent to the stone pits. And since neither of them ever repented – to their last day they were proud of what they did – 'Castor and Pollux' has become an expression of charioteering brotherhood, not a commitment to victory at all costs."

(I can confirm this personally, as I myself was the one who discovered the true story – in the writings of Lucius Lucceius, no less – and passed it on to the Guild of Charioteers.)

But Alector, as usual, was unmoved. "Aye," he said, "do you think me a dullard? I too have heard that story, and trust me, such piffle would never have held water in my day."

"You are saying you do not accept the revision?"

"Why should I?"

"And you seriously object to the spirit of charioteer brotherhood?"

"To the spirit of charioteer idiocy – yes, I do." Alector thrust a finger into Delphinius's chest. "Listen to me, Perfume Boy – if I ever live to see you stopping again to assist a fallen charioteer I shall personally leap onto the track and give you a horse-whipping."

By the time my father decided that Delphinius was ready for the Circus Maximus – Alector himself claimed there was still much work to do – the boy was already a champion of the eastern hippodromes and a hero of the Syriach Games. The lad was convinced, as Alector had been, that he would be the greatest charioteer of all time. And when he arrived in Rome where, despite all Alector's misgivings, he proved an instant sensation – driving with such verve and skill that he made middling horses look like champions – there seemed every possibility he would be just that. My father, seeing history repeat itself, disseminated the rumour that the boy was actually the son of Alector, the "Rooster's Rooster" – a notion that proved immensely popular among the fans – and there were urgent calls for him to be united immediately with the Andraemon Team. But my father, at first, was resistant. "A great chariot team requires only four stallions, not five," he would joke.

Speculation arose that my father disfavoured Delphinius because he did not personally own him (roughly half of charioteers at any one time remained the property of their original masters), but in truth his hesitation was just another ploy to stir up anticipation. It was also a concession to the feelings of the senior charioteers, who were always rankled when the best horses were assigned to newcomers. So my father was not particularly flustered when both Lotus of Laodicea and Cometus of Cyprus discounted themselves for wildly different reasons, nor especially alarmed when the other first-rank charioteers decided that the Andraemon Team was possibly cursed (my father himself might have strategically promulgated the notion).

"It's time to step up, lad," he told Delphinius, as if issuing a call to arms. "It's time to drive the Andraemon Team."

The effect was instantaneous. With Delphinius helming them, the horses, already brilliant, became practically unbeatable. In one six-month period they won so many successive victories – fifty-five, a Circus record – that Albus of the Esquiline ceased offering odds on them. They could race four times in one day and still have as much energy in their last race as they had in their first. They were to other chariot horses what dolphins are to seals. They were more popular than gods. Their likenesses appeared on walls, on floors, on lamps, in figurines. They were so peerless that during a *pompa circensis* a crazed fan of the Blues threw hot coals over them, blinding Andraemon in the right eye. But since the stallion seemed otherwise unaffected – the Greeks, for one, have always believed that trace horses are better half-blind – he became only more popular, with "one-eyed" fans covering their right eye-sockets as an expression of affinity.

Thus it was that, as Nero entered the tenth year of his reign, my father seemed to have reached the pinnacle of his reign as *dominus factionis*. It was true that he was getting old – almost seventy – and hobbling about on a hickory cane. It was true, also, that he was facing financial difficulties relating to the shipbuilding business (which I shall glance upon shortly). Nor could it be denied that the Green Faction was struggling to deal with its mounting expenses, owing partly to persistent overreach in trying to establish a presence in the provinces. Nevertheless, we had the most electrifying chariot team, the most flamboyant and popular new charioteer, and the passionate support of the emperor. It seemed, indeed, that my father, as he flirted for the first time with the prospect of retirement, had nothing left to prove – that nothing could possibly go wrong.

And then came the catastrophe.

# XXIX

**M**OST RESIDENTS OF ROME THAT NIGHT\* were alerted by the smoke, the clamour, the howls of distress, or even the tremendous heat and glow. My father on the other hand claimed he sensed the disaster "in my bones, as a mother senses some tragedy to her offspring". For some days, he said, he had been aware of sinister omens in nature – the fleeing of birds and insects, the tensing of trees – and was "fully anticipating some sort of calamity". True or not, I can confirm that he was the first in our neighbourhood to raise the alarm, hammering on my door – by this stage I was living in a separate residence down the slope of the Caelian – and ordering me to the scene of the emergency. The Circus Maximus was on fire.

The blaze had started under the arches on the Palatine side, in one of the accursed cookshops that my father had always argued were an invitation to disaster. When we arrived, the flames were racing up the rear of the stands and the emergency cisterns were empty. "The river!" my father exclaimed. "Let us bring water from the Tiber!"

---

\* 18 July A.D. 64.

He frantically organised a chain of people to transmit buckets through the warren of streets to the Circus, and it says much of the people's affection for the arena that there was no shortage of volunteers willing to risk their own lives in the effort. But – as my father admitted later – it "was like trying to fell a tree by snipping off a twig". The water, no matter how high anyone could hurl it, sloshed around at ground level as the flames sped ever upwards, propelled by fierce gusts – it was a windy summer's night – and the intense flammability of the ancient wood. Soon the Circus was a giant torch, squealing, hissing, howling and raining fiery timbers around us. Then the Palatine itself – and all the surrounding hills – were alight. It was not just the Circus Maximus that was burning – it was the whole of Rome.

Yet my father, dumbstruck, would not leave the vicinity of the arena. Even when the others had fled, he stood frozen in the heat, his beard frazzling and tears evaporating on his cheeks. It took all my strength to drag him away from the toppling stands. We found refuge in the vaults under the Circus, but even here the temperature was furnace-like and the smoke eye-stinging. Nor did it seem entirely safe, for we could hear the great structure crackling and collapsing above us. But we could not escape through the sewers because the connecting channels had been purposely blocked after an attempted theft of charioteer prize money. It is not even certain we would have survived the night had we not found a winding corridor to the Mithraic Temple, which in turn led us to a stairway rising to the Aventine side of the outer arena.

When we flopped out – I believe it was morning, but the smoke was so dense it was impossible to say – the fire was still raging. Nevertheless, the most voracious flames had already consumed the Circus and moved on. My first concern was naturally for our own properties – my mother and her retinue, mercifully, were in Massena – but when I managed to reach the Caelian, dodging collapsing walls and weaving between torrents of people, I found my own place miraculously untouched. The family home, constructed largely of Raetian larch, was similarly unscathed. The training grounds of the Field of Mars were blanketed with ash but otherwise unchanged. So too the estate off the Via Latina. The horses were safe. The Andraemon Team was unharmed. All the Greens charioteers – barring Cometus of Cyprus, who had died trying to rescue some fellow cultists – were alive and well.

The majority of Rome, needless to say, was much less fortunate. Those who survived the disaster scarcely need reminding, but by the time the conflagration had fizzled out only three of the city's fourteen districts remained intact. Lost for ever were scores of temples, palatial villas, priceless treasures, cherished libraries, exquisite gardens, sprawling markets, huge swathes of residential buildings, and untold thousands of citizens.

Yet my father did not seem to care. He was not even roused by the wails of women, or the appalling stench of roasted flesh, or by fleeing animals, or the progress of the still ravenous flames. Rooted in place at the base of the Aventine, with ash and embers swirling around him, he could not shift his welling eyes from the husk of the Circus Maximus, barely visible though it was through a fog of smoke.

"I said that this would happen," he kept saying. "I told everyone for years."

Inevitably Nero ventured down from Antium to inspect the ruins. With all four *domini factionum*, the arena's curators, and the imperial architects Severus and Celer, he marched into the smoking Circus to find a tangle of carbonised beams across the track and the spina mantled with snowlike ash. Even the Triumphal Gate and the marble starting stalls were scorched. The emperor, though, clamping a *mappa* over his nose, seemed curiously buoyant.

"Oh well," he said to my father, "you always said the place was a fire trap."

"I did," my father whispered blankly.

"Still, it might be a good thing, you know."

"A . . . a good thing, Caesar?"

"Why yes," said Nero, blowing his nose. "Because now there will be no objections, no hint of resentment, when I build a new Circus in its place."

"A new Circus . . .?"

"Made entirely of marble this time. With a giant statue of Jupiter on the spina. Beside a colossal statue of me. I tell you, Picus, you will want to keep yourself alive just to see the sparkling new arena I shall erect in my name!"

It was at that moment, my father claimed, that he saw in Nero the same madness that had devoured Caligula.

The reconstruction, for that matter, was much easier said than done. Even the emperor, since the Palatine had not escaped injury, seemed consumed in the building of an immense new palace, the Domus Aurea, with its three hundred rooms, ornamental gardens, artificial lake and revolving banquet hall. The colossal statue of himself, sculpted by Zenodorus, never quite made it onto the spina. And, meanwhile, chariot races were conducted in the Circus Vaticanus – entirely inadequate in seating capacity – the Circus Flaminius – entirely inadequate in shape – and even in the shell of the Circus Maximus itself – entirely inadequate since parts of its stands were still collapsing.

Nor did the reconstruction proceed with any vigour. Building materials were scarce, the imperial coffers were empty, and the homeless were getting restive about the emperor's priorities. Rumours that he had purposely destroyed the city exactly so that he might rebuild it meant that whenever he appeared at the races he was jeered and heckled. The Green Faction did not escape suspicion, for many were of the belief that Lotus of Laodicea's relationship with the Vestal Virgin was the proximate cause of the conflagration in the first place. There were even scurrilous suggestions that my

155

father had ignited the fire by his own hand, just to see the Circus refashioned to his favoured specifications.

Thus the arena, when it finally began to rise from the ashes, was built not of marble, not of Gabine blocks or even Raetian larch, but of more ridiculously flammable wood. And the crowds were a fraction of what they had been. The people were too exhausted to care – unable to sleep owing to all the builders' drays that were lumbering through the streets in the night, and incapable of rest during the day because of all the hammering and pounding from the construction sites. Even Albus of the Esquiline found it difficult to make a profit, despite his legendary role in the fire (the last flame had reputedly been extinguished by one of his toxic brews). The great expenses necessary to mount imperial games were looking prohibitive. The atmosphere in Rome was febrile. Rats had been spotted eating mice. Seagulls were scrapping with pigeons. There were the first mutterings of civil war.

Perhaps the only positive note, if it can be called that, was my complete surrender to the embrace of the Circus, ten years after I had forsaken it. The absence of chariot racing, not to mention the marginalisation of its principal temple, had forced me to appreciate like never before its crucial role in the culture and welfare of Rome. I decided that life was a whole lot less colourful, and certainly not better, without it. This grudging acknowledgment served to reconcile me with my father – to the extent that we were ever estranged – and saw me resume my role as chariot racing's first official historian.

The extraordinary events that the Great Fire precipitated, I can therefore verify from eyewitness accounts and first-hand experience. And this is what you will read hereon.

# XXX

To APPRECIATE FULLY THE AUDACITY of my father's next decision, as well as its irresistible logic, there are certain factors you first need to consider.

The first was that, even to those of us generally scornful of such things, the omens of some new tragedy for the Green Faction could scarcely be ignored. In our courtyard a dead hawk had been discovered with an asp writhing in its gullet. In Campania a white foal had been born blind in the right eye like Andraemon. At the Via Latina estate cracks of such magnitude had appeared in the statue of Neptunus Equestris that the four horses had split and broken apart.

The second is that by now, to revive Claudius's analogy, my father was like a tall tree standing alone on a hillside. He had been the Greens' *dominus factionis* for as long as anyone could remember, and while no one could gainsay his achievements or the extraordinary influence he had exerted on chariot racing, there were no shortage of rivals yearning to see him cut down. Foremost among these were the faction's most generous patrons who, with no small amount of hubris, fancied that they could do a better job. Nor is there any point denying that my father in his old age had become

157

less summer oak than winter poplar – pale, mottled, losing his leaves, rooted in watery ground. His eyes were glaucous, his face was like an old parchment, and he had become sufficiently forgetful of people's names that Gryphus, no sapling himself, felt compelled to accompany him everywhere just to kindle his memory and smooth over the inevitable misunderstandings.

You also need to consider the surprisingly poor state of his shipbuilding business, a considerable percentage of whose profits had long been long redirected to the Greens. The Great Fire was damaging enough – nobody was ordering new vessels, and timber supplies had been forcibly requisitioned by the navy – but the most debilitating problems predated the catastrophe, for management of the shipyards had for some time been in the hands of my older brother Larus, who – there is no way of saying this kindly – had demonstrated none of my father's administrative flair. Such was the mess he made of it, in fact, that my father – who could not bring himself to admit anything openly – was spending most of his time sorting out the accounts and issuing countermanding instructions from afar. Which of course only further distracted him from chariot racing when he could least afford it. Nor did there seem any chance that Larus was competent enough to take over as the Greens' *dominus factionis* when the time came, or even assist my father in some quotidian capacity – that role had been assumed by Gryphus, whom my father was seriously considering anointing at his successor (an unprecedented promotion for a freedman).

My father was also fielding much of the blame for the downfalls of the champion charioteers Cometus of Cyprus and Lotus of Laodicea. Just a few years previously, the sentiment went, he would never have allowed Cometus to become a zealot or Lotus to lose his prudence. The old man is slipping, was the whisper on the wind. It's only the success of the Andraemon Team that's keeping him in place.

And what about those illustrious horses? They had become so successful that they seemed to be singlehandedly holding the faction together. They had racked up over two hundred and fifty Circus victories – leading in over one hundred and forty of those races from start to finish – and had amassed over fifty million sesterces in prize money. Naturally, therefore, they were also loved by the emperor. And, naturally, it took no great powers of divination to see where this was leading. Nero, like Caligula, would sooner or later request to drive them in competition. He had already done so in public parades.

Those who knew of Incitatus's decline were appalled to think that a similar fate might now befall the Andraemon Team. And inevitably there were calls for preventative measures. Find four lookalike chariot horses, my father's rivals suggested, and disguise them just as you did to Incitatus. To which my father almost agreed. He almost summoned Quintus Creticus Tenax from Massilia to exercise again his masking skills. But he was not convinced it would work this time. The Incitatus deception was too widely known, and there was every possibility that Nero, coming from such disreputable stock, would be inclined to suspect something.

So – considering his wavering foundations and the uncertain status of the faction – what he did next might seem remarkably foolish or incredibly brave. But in truth he was frustrated by the endless rebuilding of the Circus Maximus, he was weary of racing his best horses in unsuitable arenas, and he was as committed as always to expanding the sport throughout the provinces.

In any case, without consulting the faction patrons or anyone else, he had the Andraemon Team split up and sent to distant shores – Pertinax, Postumus and Olympius to Syria, there to be managed by Alector and his daughter Selene, and Andraemon to Spain, where he would be reunited with Corax at his stud farm outside Tarraco.

Delphinius of Doriscus would remain in Rome, but the horses would only return when "the auspices are more favourable". By which we took my father to mean "when the emperor's reign is at an end".

It was a dangerous thing to hope for at the best of times, as subsequent events proved.

# XXXI

WHETHER HIS FACULTIES HAD DIMMED OR NOT, there is no doubt my father was capable of a shrewd answer when necessary, as I witnessed myself when, joining him on his maiden visit to the Domus Aurea, we were confronted in the shimmering corridors by a deceptively good-humoured Nero.

"I must let you know how dismayed I am with you, Picus," chuckled the emperor, wagging a finger. "To send the Andraemon Team away without notifying me – it was your decision, I've been told?"

"Entirely my decision, Caesar."

"Then you will no doubt enlighten me as to your purpose. The people's passion for the Circus binds them together in a time of suffering. Why then remove Rome's most beloved horses at the height of their glory?"

"You will need to indulge me, Caesar, when I say that I am a man of some wisdom – yes, I think the prerogative of age allows me to claim that. And it was my judgement that the sentiments inspired by the Andraemon Team were becoming less noble than dangerous. I mean to say, the great passions aroused – even when they were ostensibly harmless – were clearly *displacing* affections that would be better directed elsewhere. If you know what I mean, Caesar."

"Are you saying" – Nero frowned – "what *are* you saying?"

"I am saying," my father replied portentously, "that the plebeians were worshipping horses as they should have been worshipping their emperor. And that such an unnatural diversion is fraught with ungovernable perils, as you would no doubt agree."

It was the sort of cunning persuasion at which my father excelled – part flattery, part sinister implication – and it proved enough to bamboozle the emperor for a few precious moments.

"I was . . . I was intending to drive them in the arena, you know," he managed.

"It is the first I've heard of it, Caesar."

"Then you did not send them to distant shores for that reason? Precisely so I would have no chance to do so?"

"That was the furthest thing from my mind," my father insisted. "Though, were the team still in Rome, I would advise you against driving them in any event."

"Oh? Not drive the fastest horses the Circus has ever seen? What pray tell would I gain from that?"

"You would have everything to gain, Caesar. Because a victory with the Andraemon Team would only invite your enemies to claim that the horses had won the race, not the charioteer. But a victory *without* the Andraemon Team – now that would be indisputably glorious, because no one, anywhere in the empire, would then have any reason to question your skill."

We were at that moment standing upon an immense multi-coloured mosaic showing the empire from the wilds of northern Britannia to the frontiers of Parthia. Nero considered my father's argument and chortled heartily. "Your vision is sharp, dear Picus, though your eyes are clouded."

"I see with more than my eyes, Caesar."

"And I am not convinced you are not wilier than you ought to be." The emperor turned to me with a snigger. "He is well named after the woodpecker, this father of yours – so adept at finding weak points and hammering away until he draws nectar."

It was not much of an analogy but I laughed politely.

"All the same," continued Nero, fluffing his toga. "I am prepared to respect your reasoning in this instance, dear Picus, and to trust that the Andraemon Team will do much to glorify Rome in the provinces."

"They are your ambassadors in equine form, Caesar," replied my father, by now almost collapsing from all the energy it had taken to flatter and deceive.

Indeed, to maintain their form on the track, the three horses in Syria were raced in the hippodromes there to great acclaim – Alector himself, despite his age, had driven them on a number of occasions – just as Andraemon had resumed his role as trace horse in the circuses of Spain. Both the Raven and the Rooster had strict instructions to guard the horses closely, to hide them at a moment's notice if necessary, and to report on all aspects of their form and condition. My father still planned to have them brought back to Rome "at the earliest opportunity".

As it happened, that moment arose much earlier than expected. After winning a few highly contrived races in the Circus Vaticanus and the partly rebuilt Circus Maximus, Nero decided to take the provinces by storm. My father, dreading the news that the emperor would be heading for Spain or Syria, prepared to dispatch frantic warnings to Corax and Alector. But it turned out that Nero, with his celebrated fondness for Hellenic culture, had an entirely different destination in mind.

Prudently buttering up the local populations with unprecedented tax cuts – the Greeks were relieved of customs duties in perpetuity – he ordered all four of the panhellic games to be held within one year and, to no one's surprise, won over a thousand chariot races in succession (including a number in which he had not even participated). The calls from my father's rivals for the return of the Andraemon Team became even more pronounced as the emperor's Grecian sojourn grew prolonged. But my father deferred repeatedly to his "old man's wisdom" and urged patience because "this is not over yet".

In fact, long and bitter experience had taught him to always hold something in reserve. Permit me to give you an example. One of the faction's wheelwrights had discovered a means of stabilising our chariots by adding iron rims to the outside of the wheels. But in secret testing it was discovered that these rims, while preventing the wheels from breaking apart, also slowed the chariots down significantly. So the wheelwright made a crucial refinement: he retained a rim on only the right wheel, the one that bore the added pressure in the turns. And while this still impeded the charioteer marginally in the straights, it furnished him with much greater confidence in rounding the corners, meaning that he was appreciably faster over the course of seven laps. But rather than introducing this race-winning modification immediately, my father in his wisdom decided to keep it a closely guarded secret until the Greens desperately needed an advantage. Because he knew the rim would be copied by the other factions within a month or so of its introduction.

Notwithstanding some complications with this philosophy – the wheelwright responsible threatened to sell his design to the Blues if he did not receive exorbitant extra payment (my father was forced to have "a little chat" with him in the company of an old gladiator friend) – he was determined to hold the Andraemon Team in reserve as well. He would recall the horses only when they were absolutely, indisputably needed. And – more importantly – absolutely, indisputably safe.

Then Nero, plumper than ever, returned from Greece with a boatload of victory trophies and pilfered statues. In an awesome twelve-horse battle chariot he squeezed through the specially widened Triumphal Gate of the Circus Maximus, which under cranes and scaffolding was resuming its familiar shape, and deposited his trophies at the base of Augustus's obelisk before hosting a celebratory banquet in the Domus Aurea. And since he there, over suckling pig and marinated goose, gave every indication of having achieved everything he set out to prove – he even announced that he had retired from chariot racing "weighed down with accomplishment" – my father's rivals were adamant that it must now be safe enough, surely, to bring the Andraemon Team home.

The pressure was almost overwhelming. I admit I expected my father to buckle. But I was simply not aware at the time how accurately he had sensed the future, and how prescient his caution would turn out to be. I could only watch, with a historian's disinterested wonder, as over the next eighteen months catastrophic events piled up on one another like out-of-control chariots in the Circus Maximus.

# XXXII

**W**HAT I DID NOT KNOW, and should perhaps have guessed, was that my father's far-reaching vision was derived almost exclusively from Albus of the Esquiline. Indeed, the gambling king's betting odds were so accurate that for years people had exploited them to assess all sorts of possible outcomes. What are the odds that the corn bill will pass in the Senate? What are the odds that Bruccius will be acquitted at his murder trial? What are the odds that Spiculus the gladiator will remain faithful to his new lover Ursula? Eventually Albus, who was anything but a dope, became purposely misleading unless substantial money was pledged in advance. But with the *domini factionum* he was usually willing to share his wisdom on credit alone.

In any event, when Nero's downfall seemed all but inevitable – the treasury was empty, the provincial governors had deserted him, the army was in open rebellion, and the emperor himself was cowering in his golden palace – my father made a clandestine visit to the back room of the Cornigera, where Albus's blubber had so completely folded over his chair that he seemed to be floating in mid-air.

"How long will the emperor last?"

"Three months," Albus told him flatly. "Sooner if he does not flee. Nothing can change that now."

"And his replacement?"

"Galba seems most likely."

"Galba is not a Caesar."

"The people have had their fill of Caesars."

"I see," said my father.

In chariot racing circles Galba was best remembered for the extravagant games he had financed when praetor. Elephants had walked on tightropes and chariots had been driven by dog-faced monkeys.* Since then, my father had met him only once, in Spain, where as proconsul he had expressed open admiration for Andraemon. But, apart from this idle remark in the governor's box of the Circus Augustus, Galba had exhibited no great enthusiasm for chariot racing.

"Be sparing in your relief."

"I beg your pardon?" My father was jolted out his reverie.

"I can see it on your face," Albus observed. "You think Emperor Galba will be harmless. You think it will be a return to the days of Claudius."

My father was never surprised at Albus's capacity to read minds. "You suggest that Galba is unstable?"

"I suggest that Galba is no leader."

"Who then will replace him?"

"Come back in six months and ask me again."

When Nero was compelled into suicide and the Senate declared Galba emperor, much as Albus had predicted, my father's rivals were quick to call for the return of the Andraemon Team. But my father, haunted by the gambling king's warnings, insisted it was too early.

---

* Baboons.

Emperor Galba initially encouraged public spectacles, despite a lamentable lack of funds, and even hastened the rebuilding of the Circus Maximus. But in November the Greens very nearly lost their most symbiotic festival, the Plebeian Games, the unthinkable averted by just one victory. Exasperated, my father's rivals insisted again it was time to bring the horses home. My father, pale and sleepless, argued that it was still too early. His rivals went away to whisper among themselves. My father returned to the smoky room in the Cornigera.

"You said that Galba would not last long," he told Albus.

"He won't."

"He seems stable enough."

"Would you like to bet on it?"

"No . . ." My father sighed, considering the possibilities. "How much longer, then?"

"Four months at most."

"Who then are the frontrunners to replace him?"

"Your best bet is Flavius Vespasianus."

"Vespasian?" My father knew Vespasian as a ruthless general in Syria. "I have not heard his name mentioned."

"You have heard it now."

"Hmmm." Vespasian favoured no faction and if anything seemed fixated on gladiator bouts. But then my father frowned. "Best bet?" he asked. "You say he's my 'best bet'?"

"What of it?"

"Are you suggesting that he is a good bet – or a good outcome?"

"I am saying there is another horse in the race – a name will you not care to hear."

"Say it anyway."

Albus sniffed. "Vitellius."

"*Vitellius?*" my father asked. "*Aulus* Vitellius?"

"None other."

"You are not serious?"

"I like the idea no more than you do."

"*Vitellius*," my father muttered again.

Following his years of sycophantic fraternising with Caligula and Claudius, Vitellius had made every effort to entrench himself in a similar position under Nero. But Nero, thanks in no small part to my father's vigorous scheming, had grown weary of the man's ceaseless lobbying for the Blues. And Vitellius – dismissed unceremoniously from the palace, and with his father no longer around to rescue him – had experienced a rapid decline in prestige. He was living in a garret, surviving on slops and cabbage leaves, when Galba had appointed him, despite a conspicuous lack of qualifications, as commander of the legions of Lower Germania.

"I thought he was torturing barbarians," my father said. "I thought we had seen the last of him."

"He is popular with his troops."

"Popular? How?"

"Vitellius knows how to bribe and blackmail."

"You think by these means alone he might become emperor?"

"Would you like to bet against it?"

"No," my father said, paling at the thought. "No . . ."

Shortly afterwards, when Galba was decapitated in the Forum, my father had every reason to fear the worst. But the new emperor, it turned out, was neither Vitellius nor Vespasian but Otho, Nero's boon companion of yore. And since Otho was if anything inclined to favour the Greens, in honour of his dearly departed friend, my father's rivals argued it was time, surely, to bring the Andraemon Team home. My father went to the Cornigera again.

"You never mentioned Otho," he said.

"I had no reason to."

"Otho is now emperor."

"Otho is a teaser pony."

"You are saying that Otho, like Galba, is just warming the throne for another?"

"Would you care to bet against it?"

"No," said my father. "No . . ."

A few weeks later Otho threw a lavish Lupercalian Games at which he appeared in the Circus Maximus looking as relaxed and cheerful as Nero had in the early years of his principate. My father's rivals said it was time, now more than ever, to return the horses to Rome. My father told them he had been reliably informed that Otho's position was not as secure as it seemed. His rivals asked him to name his sources. My father refused to answer. His rivals wondered if he had been consulting augurs and oracles again. My father was evasive.

Two months later, when his forces were wiped out at the First Battle of Cremona, Otho stabbed himself to death and Vitellius, still in Germania, claimed the title of emperor.

My father's rivals, making no apologies for their hypocrisy, were suddenly distraught. "What are we to do now? With that monster heading for Rome? Are the Andraemon Team really safe where they are?"

My father, despite his sagging features, was looking like an oak again. "I shall order Corax and Alector to withdraw the horses completely from public view."

"But shall we ever see them again?"

"Let us see how events unfurl."

Vitellius took months marching from Germania to Rome, halting at every town on the way and feasting so frequently that his food taster died of obesity and his own girth doubled in size. My father barely recognised him when he was summoned to the Domus Aurea.

"Well, well, if it isn't Picus of the Greens. Is your faction ready?"

"Ready for what, Imperator?"

"For a war?"

"The Greens are always ready, Imperator."

Vitellius – beet-faced, sweaty, wiping pastry crumbs from his lips – lanced my father with a glare. "I was there, you know, standing alongside Caligula and Nero as they rained favour after favour on the Faction of the Frog. I saw how you personally bathed in their beneficence and cared not a whit for scruple or mercy. And I know, too, how you used your influence again and again to conspire against me. I have a long, long memory. It is only out of formality, then, that I warn you to expect some changes. Some corrections, as it were, in the spirit of the game."

My father nodded wearily. "I expected little else, Imperator."

"Perhaps some consolidation is required, would you not agree?"

"Imperator?"

"A merger of the Greens and Reds, perhaps? Both factions are riddled with corruption. Your supporters are collectively a rabble. So why not smash them together and see if something fresh can be squeezed out?"

"And what might you call this unwieldy merger? The Browns?"

Vitellius chuckled. "What does it matter? The Purples, perhaps, in honour of the emperor?"

"Calling them the Purples would make it difficult for you not to support them, would it not?"

"Interesting point. Then the Golds? How about that? You cannot say that some gold in the arena would not brighten things up?"

"There would still be only three factions, and the Circus needs four."

"Three factions are sufficient, it seems to me. Already the best horses are spread a little thin. Where pray tell is the Andraemon Team, by the way?"

"The horses, Imperator? Or the artworks?" This was a pointed reference to Nero's mosaics and statues of the team, which had been ripped down and ejected from the palace.

"You know what I mean."

"The horses themselves are resting."

"Yes, 'resting'. Cluvius Rufus in Spain tells me Andraemon has not been seen in the arena for months. I believe the same can be said for the others in Syria. It makes no difference to me. 'All Rome is a circus' – did not one of my predecessors say that? Well, one thing is certain, Picus – the emperor wears a different tunic now. And he will drive his faction to victory – you can be assured of that."

My father was silent.

"Oh, be off with you, you scruffy old tree cutter," growled Vitellius, belching explosively and reaching for another tart. "Your decrepitude, like your faction, disgusts me."

In the following months Vitellius – who in the lower quarters had been renamed "Vesuvius" owing to his immense size and propensity for emitting noxious gases – went about reclaiming the Circus for his favoured faction. He helped Rutilius Oceanus poach the best horses from rival stables. He turned the Circus Vaticanus into a Blues training track. He built new stables exclusively for the Blues. With the help of Locusta, he poisoned some of the Greens' best horses – Zosimus, Crinitus, Cursor, Mirandus, Linon and Paratus – and killed or maimed some of its finest charioteers – Cinnamus of Cyzicus, Venustrus of Venetia and Suren of Armenia (missing Delphinius of Doriscus only because Delphinius was already guarded day and night). He crucified supporters of the Greens merely for wearing team colours in public. He issued a wildly inflated tax bill to the Greens management team and demanded immediate payment. He threatened the faction's benefactors. He seemed hellbent on seeing the Greens eliminated entirely.

The Greens scraped home to win the Victory Games in the deciding race. They *lost* the Portunalian Games in the final race. They lost the Roman Games by two races. They lost the Cerealian Games by three races. They had never in history lost three games in succession. And next in line were the Plebeian Games. Vitellius had declared they would be the biggest, most flamboyant in history – two weeks of unprecedented spectacle and celebration. He was even bringing back the beast hunts, albeit separately from the race day, while the races themselves, at the end of the games, would be "a decisive moment in the history of Rome".

My father visited the Cornigera, where he had to be cranked onto the roof because Albus was lounging beside his pigeon loft.

"What are the odds," he asked hoarsely, "of Vitellius falling like the others?"

"Shift to the left, will you – you're blocking the sun."

"Yes, yes, of course." My father waddled across the roof. "What are the odds of Vitellius collapsing?"

"I offer no odds on that."

"Why?"

"Because the future of Rome has never been more uncertain."

My father stifled a grimace – Albus in full sunlight was a sobering sight – and forced himself on. "What about Vespasian, then? Are his troops not massing in the east? Has he not been declared a rival emperor?"

"That much is indisputable."

"Then do you give him no chance of marching on Rome and deposing Vitellius?"

"That his legions will march on Rome is inevitable. As to whether they succeed depends on how Vesuvius holds his ground. Even I cannot predict that."

"Military matters are beyond your purview?"

"Military matters are only part of this war," said Albus. "Vesuvius, you see, will be fighting on a multitude of fronts. In the Senate. In the hearts of the people. In the back alleys of Rome. In the Circus Maximus itself. A victory there will be worth a thousand on the battlefield."

"Are you saying," my father asked, leaning on his cane, "that merely by winning the Plebeian Games for the Blues, Vitellius might retain power over all of Rome?"

"By destroying the Greens, Vesuvius will symbolically crush his greatest enemy and take a stranglehold on the principate."

"But the Greens . . ." My father could scarcely bring himself to say it. "The Greens are already half-crushed."

"Then I suggest you do everything in your power – for your own sake as well as Rome's – to address the problem before it is too late." Albus waved away a fly. "You will need your greatest horses. Your best charioteers. And no small amount of luck. But it's not impossible. Two thousand to one. But not impossible."

My father hobbled away from the tavern feeling like an instrument of the gods. As if the decision had already been made for him. He spent two hours with Gryphus composing letters before summoning couriers and dispatching them to Spain and Syria. The Andraemon Team, finally, were to race again in the Circus Maximus. Corax and Alector had five weeks to get the horses back to Rome. Their lives would be in constant danger. The fate of the faction – the fate of the whole empire – depended on them.

It is the story of this remarkable two-thousand-to-one odyssey that comprises the second book of my chronicle.

# BOOK
## TWO
21 OCTOBER–22 DECEMBER A.D. 69

# I

SINCE MY FATHER'S TWO COURIERS LEFT ROME at roughly the same time, Corax should have received his message a week before Alector. But there was a storm in the western Mediterranean and the irresolute captain of the Spain-bound vessel put in at Sardinia and then hugged the coast all the way the way to Tarraco. Hence the two letters arrived just two days apart.

The one to Corax – written in Gryphus's meticulous script, as my father's own handwriting by that stage was all but illegible – read:

> To C. in H.T. [Spain], *many good wishes from Rome,*
>
> *V. has now authorised the L.P.* [Plebeian Games] *culminating in one day of twelve races. As never before, it will be F.V.* [the Blue Faction] *pitted against F.P.* [the Green Faction]. *I have decided that AN.* [Andraemon] *needs to be returned to R. to partake in these races. This is imperative. Send him by boat as before and a deputation will greet him when he arrives at Portus. AL.* [Alector] *will escort the other horses and all will be reunited in R.*
>
> *All best wishes, L.C.P.*

I should not have to tell you that "send him by boat" was a ruse lest the message were intercepted. My father knew very well that Andraemon would not be able travel on water unless his obsession with Cupido's welfare had diminished or the captains of the sea had miraculously overcome their nautical superstitions. The horse and goat would need to travel overland again, and clearly would need as much notice as possible. As such, my father would have been mortified to learn that his dispatch did not reach Corax until the twenty-first day of October. Corax's previous overland journey, during the reign of Nero, had taken two months. Now, less than half that time was available.

According to Magnus of Noricum – the earless dwarf who had become his closest friend and most trusted assistant – Corax read the message expressionlessly before passing it over. "The day has come," he said solemnly.

Magnus read the scroll swiftly and looked up. "There is not much time."

"No time to tarry."

"I shall not let you down, Corax – whatever the cost, I shall not let you down."

"No," said Corax.

"No?"

"I shall have to do this myself."

Magnus frowned. "But it is my mission, Corax – we agreed on that."

"I cannot expect you to make such a journey in less than four weeks."

"I never expected it to be easy."

"It is too much to ask of one man."

"Then it is too to ask of you."

"And there are your duties here on the farm. Xenia will need assistance."

"Xenia will need *your* assistance, Corax – have you forgotten your pledge? The very reason you delegated the task to me in the first place?"

Corax looked away.

Magnus handed back the message. "I can do it, Corax. Live or die, I can do it. Leave the journey to me, as we planned, so that you may fulfil your promise to your wife."

Corax stared into the distance for a while before tearing himself loose and heading down the slope. Briefly Magnus thought he was heading for the stables – as though, his mind made up, he was intending to prepare Andraemon at once – but instead he made for the sacred chestnut tree, the one that had sprung up on the site of his son's death.

This was a deeply significant move. Corax only went there when he felt the need to commune with the spirit of his dead son Falco – to seek the highest form of clarity or absolution. And to Magnus, now, there seemed little question as to what the Raven would be asking. When Corax had taken Andraemon to Rome the first time, after all, Xenia had been furious. She made him promise that his first responsibility was to her, not to the Greens. And Corax had agreed. He reminded her that he cared for racing no more than she did. That he spurned the charioteers' creed as a poison. That he did not follow the fate of his horses and had no interest in the careers of other charioteers. That he avoided, for that matter, all news from Rome. But he had given his word to my father and that was that.

"You will not do it again?" Xenia had demanded.

"I will have no reason to do it again."

"That is not a proper answer."

"Then I promise to make no more pledges that you do not know about."

"I have your word on that?"

"You have my word."

Presently Magnus watched as Corax stared at the great tree. Trying to divine the right course of action, seeking a clear path – something that would allow him to take command. And in truth, though he had refrained from saying it, Magnus was not sure that he alone was experienced enough to regulate a horse's pace and diet on such a long and urgent journey. He feared, moreover, the complications that would arise from the political turmoil. And the worsening weather. And whatever measures had been taken to stop them from reaching Rome. The task, if he were honest, was really a two-man job. With much planning and many precautions, in time that was simply not available.

He watched as Corax read my father's message repeatedly – as if the text itself might conceal an answer, some hidden command, some crucial piece of information. Then something seemed to puzzle the great charioteer; he glanced across at Magnus, and marched back up the slope, looking very stern.

"Who is 'V'?" he asked.

Magnus tightened. "I believe Picus means the emperor, Corax."

"And who is the emperor?"

"Are you sure you wish to know?"

"I would not be asking if I did not."

"And are you certain it will have no bearing on your decision?"

"Just answer the question."

Magnus replied, "The new emperor is Vitellius, Corax."

Corax stared down at him, as if he had misheard. "Aulus Vitellius?"

"Aulus Vitellius."

"Aulus, the son of Lucius?"

"I'm afraid it is true."

"The man who poisoned me?"

"The same."

"How long have you known this?"

"I heard something at the Circus Augustus."

"When?"

180

"A few months ago . . ."

"Yet you never mentioned it to me?"

"Would there have been any benefit in doing so?"

Corax reflected for a while, his nostrils dilating. Then he rolled the letter and turned for the stables.

"Corax!" cried Magnus, rushing to catch up. "Corax, have you made your decision?"

"Yes," breathed the Raven, not breaking his stride. "Yes, I have."

# II

OBVIOUSLY, I CANNOT SAY PRECISELY what was going through Corax's mind at that moment. Magnus's verdict on the matter, which accorded with that of my father, is not without merit. "Corax saw that there are only two types of justice in this world: that which is seized and that which is meted out by chance. And sometimes, as rare a comet, there is a combination of the two – an opportunity that cries out to be taken."

Nonetheless, though I cannot claim to have known Corax as intimately as either Magnus or my father, I prefer to think that the Raven, as a Stoic, would not have allowed himself to be driven by such base emotions. I prefer to think that personal grievances would have hindered rather than driven him. I suspect that the involvement of the emperor merely convinced him that the mission would be inordinately difficult and that, given such exceptional circumstances, he decided he had no real choice.

At the same time, I have little doubt that my father wanted and expected him to be involved. I am certain that he was relying on Corax's unquestioning loyalty – his willingness to do anything, no matter how arduous or time-consuming, for his spiritual father. I am also inclined to think that – being manipulative as always, and not fully understanding the nuances of Stoicism – my father had included references to both Vitellius and Alector precisely to stir up in Corax a dormant sense of rivalry. To sharpen his senses and quicken his pace. To ignite in him the desire to beat his slave brother to Rome. To turn the journey into a uniquely long and challenging race

It was of course for precisely the same reasons that he included a reference to Corax in his letter to Alector.

*To A. in S., [Syria] greetings from Rome,*

*V. has now authorised the L.P. As never before, it will be the F.V. pitted against the F.P. I have decided that O., P. and P. [Olympius, Pertinax and Postumus] need urgently to be reunited in Rome with AN. C. will escort that horse. You must take the others by sea. Spare no expense. Ensure that the ship puts in at as few ports as possible. I have alerted my agents and associates along the way.*

*All best wishes, L.C.P.*

(I have a draft of the original letter in front of me now. And I note with amusement my father's confidence that Corax would escort Andraemon to Rome – though I do not know, in truth, if he was ever aware of Corax's "arrangement" with Xenia.)

Alector's noble daughter Selene – years later, the first female charioteer to race in the Circus Maximus – remembers the afternoon the letter arrived. A fierce storm was howling through the Amuq Valley – the surrounding mountains were curtained by sheets of rain – and she was busy in the stables, trimming the hooves of Pertinax, when her father burst in brandishing the scroll and looking "as happy as a Phrygian fig pecker".

"Get the horses ready. Are they all here? Get them ready. They'll need to be inspected. Get all your tools together, too. The medicines, everything. And keep your voice down. We need to move fast."

He was speaking in such a maniacal rush that she could barely understand what he was saying.

"Whatever is the matter, Father?"

"We have four weeks. No, twenty-six days. No – less."

"Twenty-six days for what?"

"Keep your voice down."

"Twenty-six days for what?" she whispered.

"To get to Rome, of course – for the Plebeian Games."

"We are going to Rome?"

"At all speed."

"With the horses?"

"Naturally."

"To see the Circus Maximus?"

"What else?" replied Alector, chuckling at her look of awe.

Selene's whole life had been spent listening to her father's boastful stories about Rome. He spoke of the city so often, and so lovingly, that she could not comprehend why he had not already returned there.

"That bastard Vitellius cannot be allowed to get away with this," he went on.

"The emperor himself is involved, Father?"

"He wants to destroy the Greens. He's wanted to destroy old man Picus – all of us – for years."

"The horses will save the Greens?"

"The horses and their charioteer."

"Delphinius?" asked Selene, unable to suppress a surge of excitement. "Are we to see Delphinius in Rome?"

Her father glanced at her crossly. "Delphinius? Forget about Delphinius – I know him much better than you do. Forget about him, I say. He is not nearly as good as I was."

"He will drive the horses though?"

"We shall see about that. And keep your voice down."

"No one can hear us here, Father."

"Keep your voice down, I tell you."

In fact, the legions of Syria were firmly in the camp of the rival emperor Vespasian, and the notion that it was unsafe to speak aloud was largely illusory.

"Shall we inform Icelus?" asked Selene, referring to the estate manager.

"Icelus and Gorgias – they will find out soon enough anyway. But no one else."

"When do we leave?"

"We can reach Seleucia by morning."

"Are you saying we should leave tonight?"

"Why not, if we hasten?"

Selene found herself both alarmed and thrilled by the sudden turn of events. But she still found time to be cautious. "Can we really get to Rome in time for the races, Father?"

"We have to. The Greens cannot win without us."

"But you are certain the horses will be fit to race, after so many days at sea?"

"They raced at Antioch – and won – two days after arriving here, did they not?"

"What about Andraemon?"

"Our horses are more important than Andraemon."

"But he is being returned to Rome as well?"

"So the letter indicates." Alector passed it to her.

Selene's eyes raced across the text. "It says 'C.' will be escorting him."

"Corax," hissed her father.

"Corax of Campania?"

"More pity the horse."

"But you always said he was good with horses."

"Good with horses but not much else. We shall beat him to Rome, even with his substantial head start, even though we travel twice as far – we shall beat him, I tell you. We shall consign him to

185

second place, where he has always belonged, and the goddess Xenia will return to her senses at last."

Selene, who had heard her father eulogise Xenia so often that she fantasised about being her daughter, scanned the letter again. "But the message mentions nothing about Xenia going to Rome, Father."

Alector, staring into the storm, snorted. "Oh, she will be in Rome, all right – you may count on it. The goddess will be in Rome. She chose Corax because he was safe, secure and *damaged*, but in truth she has always adored me. There is no doubt about that. I have always been her greatest love. She will make sure she is there in Rome, by hook or by crook, you can wager on it. To greet me. To apologise to me. To admit the truth."

As her father stood there under the eaves, his tousled hair dripping water, Selene realised that he was at that very moment staring towards Rome. In fact, now that she considered the matter, she had often seen him staring wistfully in that direction. She had always assumed he was admiring the breadth of the estate, or surveying the horses, or planning some alteration to the pastures, but clearly his focus had always been on the distant metropolis. Pining for Xenia. Recalling his rivalry with Corax. Hoping desperately for an order, a magical permit – an official excuse to return.

Abruptly he emerged from his musings, shook himself, and glanced at his daughter with sparkling eyes.

"Get those horses ready. Pack some hardtack and wine. And keep your voice down."

The thunder boomed.

# III

I AM NOT SURE WHY, other than bald hubris, Alector assumed that Xenia would be accompanying her husband to Rome. In fact, Corax had resolved not to inform his wife about the extent of the journey, at least not until it was too late to hinder him. In a rare display of mendacity, he advised her that he and Magnus would be absent for a week or two, escorting Andraemon to the races in the Narbo hippodrome.

"Oh?" she said, carrying radishes in from the garden. "And why do both of you need to go?"

"We have just received a letter from Picus," explained her husband, "urging us to be especially protective of the horse's welfare at this time."

"Why?"

"There is great unrest across the empire."

"Then why are you going to Narbo at all?"

"That commitment was made months ago."

"It is the first I've heard of it."

"Did I not mention it before?"

"Hmm." Xenia had Medusa-like eyes that she trained upon her husband ruthlessly. But Corax, to his great advantage at times like

187

these, had always been made of stone. "Well," she said, "I expect you back in early November at the latest. There are mares to be foaled and you know old Atticus can no longer do it."

"I have taken that into consideration," Corax told her, which was true enough – he had already made arrangements with a local veterinarian.

"Very well, then," said Xenia, clumping the radishes in a pot. "Then you had better get back to work. I expect the south fence to be repaired before you go."

"You are a good wife," Corax told her, extending a hand to touch her before abruptly changing his mind. He turned instead for the stables.

There was so much still to do. Implicit in my father's message – "a deputation will meet him when he arrives at Portus" – was an order to send a decoy Andraemon by ship, in order to dupe imperial spies in Spain and Italy. So Corax made a show of leading a meticulously masked stallion down to the port and securing passage, along with a stable boy, on a cargo lighter bound for Rome (he had already sent the courier – the one who delivered my father's message – back to the city to warn the Greens in advance). Then, without even saying a proper farewell to Xenia – he had entrusted the true details of his expedition to the serving woman Melussa – he departed with Magnus and Andraemon under the cloak of darkness and disguise.

Riding a cavalry horse, Corax was wearing the Capricorn-embossed cuirass and helmet of the First Adiutrix legion (whose legate, based in Tarraco, was a devoted follower of the Greens). Beside him, Magnus, wearing a cloth around his head to conceal his missing ears, was at the reins of a covered wagon hauled by two horses – Tuscus, a conspicuously patterned yoke horse, and Andraemon, trudging along on the right with his scarred left side hidden from view. The great trace horse had been dyed chestnut with boiled walnut shells, had his mane trimmed, his bony excrescences concealed under leg bindings, and a prodigious fake tail attached where previously there had been only a stump.* Cupido was dyed with lampblack and concealed at the rear of the wagon.

Counting on their officious bearing to ward off curiosity, the two men, still recognisable figures in many parts of Spain, travelled at a swift but inconspicuous pace up the Via Augusta, taking refuge amid trees whenever they sensed trouble, and resting behind barns and granaries during the brighter hours of the day. They negotiated a wide detour around Barcino, the first major settlement in their path, then plied the mule tracks to the west of Emporiae, the famous port city of the Greeks, and it was only when the frontier of Narbonensis came in sight that they committed themselves fully to the coastal road.

"See it?" Corax asked.

Magnus, snapping to attention, had to squint, and squint hard, because he had "circus eyes" – scraped and stained by years of upraised dust. "A frontier post?"

"Just so," said Corax.

As they rode closer Magnus made out a crumbling, palm-flanked fort with some cavalry riders milling around on their steeds.

"Leave the talking to me," said Corax, assuming the lead as two spear-wielding guards stepped out to intercept them.

"Hail Vitellius!" exclaimed Corax, giving a pectoral salute.

"Hail Vitellius," responded the swarthier of the two guards – unshaven and hairy-legged.

"Or Augustus, or Imperator, or whatever the tub of lard is calling himself now," added his fair-haired companion, surprising Magnus with his disrespect.

"Where are you heading?" asked Hairy Legs, circling the wagon.

---

* To prevent them getting tangled in the reins, the tails of chariot horses were routinely cropped.

"To Rome," replied Corax. "Carrying personal goods for Cluvius Rufus, proconsul of Hispania Tarraconensis."

"We know Rufus well enough," noted Hairy Legs. "He passed here – when was it, Brixius, four months ago?"

"The Ides of June," replied Brixius.

"In an awful hurry, he was, to get to his chum Vitellius."

"I have a permit," announced Corax, producing a rolled document.

"From Cluvius Rufus?" asked Hairy Legs.

"From the legionary legate in Tarraco."

"Permits from First Adiutrix carry little weight around here."

"In the absence of the proconsul, it will have to do."

"Have a look, Brixius."

Brixius took the scroll and started reading, his lips moving. Hairy Legs took to poking around in the rear of the wagon.

"A goat?" he asked Magnus. "Why do you carry a goat?"

Magnus, remembering Corax's order, remained silent.

Hairy Legs frowned. "What's the matter with you, Stumpy – have you no ears?"

Magnus, fielding a discreet nod from Corax, cleared his throat. "You might be surprised," he muttered, then raised his voice. "But the goat you speak of is a mascot – nothing more."

"You're taking a legionary mascot to Rome?"

"Capricorn is a talisman, sir – a charm like no other."

"He looks like any ordinary goat to me."

"To First Adiutrix he is more than that – he is a battle standard."

"Then why would First Adiutrix part with its battle standard? In times like these especially?"

"They have other mascots."

"You, perhaps? You look like a mascot yourself."

"Not me," said Magnus, with another glance at Corax. "I am too useful in the stables."

"Doing what?"

"I dust the stallions' balls."

It was the sort of barracks humour much favoured by soldiers, and Hairy Legs, smirking, was about to respond when Brixius, followed by the mounted Corax, appeared at his side.

"Like he says," he confirmed, holding up the scroll. "The permit mentions household goods."

"Maybe so," said Hairy Legs, gesturing. "But a lampstand? A vase? Who needs such items urgently?"

"Our lot is not to ask questions," insisted Corax.

"Then maybe you can guess why Cluvius Rufus did not ship his furniture to Rome?"

"Cluvius Rufus does not trust boats – the reason he himself does not travel by sea."

"I thought you did not ask questions."

"The preferences of Cluvius Rufus are well known in Tarraco."

"Hmm, let's have a look." Hairy Legs took the scroll and scanned it. "This says you have the right to accommodation at the waystations of the *cursus publicus*."

"That is correct."

"Have you done so already?"

"We have."

"Did you meet Fulvius the Frog-faced?"

"I know of no one with this name."

"What about Lucanus Plancus?"

"Neither do I know of him."

"Yet they are in command of the waystations between here and Emporiae."

"If they were present, we did not meet them."

"What about Sabina the She-Wolf, who entertains visitors along this route?"

"We have no time for such women."

"What type of man does not?"

"The type who is in a hurry."

"To get furniture to Rome?"

"To make the delivery and return. We have no wish to dwell in that cesspit a moment longer than necessary."

Hairy Legs made an approving sound. "'Cesspit' is right. It's for insubordination in Rome that Brixius and I were posted to this backwater, you know." He rolled up the permit and returned it to Corax. "All right, never let it be said we held up a lampstand belonging to a friend of Vitellius."

"Or Vesuvius," added Brixius, "or Vomitus, or whatever he calls himself now."

Corax nodded, relieved. "Then we are grateful for your understanding and hope to see you again on our return."

"Now that would mean you are extremely lucky indeed," said Hairy Legs, and he spat into the dust before assuming an air of confidentiality. "May I offer you some advice, my legionary friend?"

"You may."

"Whatever the true reason you and your testicle-tickling chum are avoiding the waystations – and think me no fool – you would be wise to lodge at them from now on. There is much mayhem in Gaul, even more than usual, and many shifting allegiances. Some legions remain loyal to Vitellius, others have declared for Vespasian, still others are of mixed intent. Take it from me, you will need to make use of every refuge you can find."

"We shall keep it in mind," said Corax, genuinely grateful for the information – and for not being held up any longer than necessary – and without further ado he and Magnus rode off past the frontier post and headed for the crossroads at Narbo, at which point the highway became the Via Domitia.

It was 26 October and there were twenty-two days remaining to the first race in the Circus Maximus.

# IV

I T IS ONE OF THE MANY CHARMING FOIBLES of charioteers that, having spent their years of training requiring little experience with matters of money, they inevitably have no idea what to do with it when they start amassing fortunes. Recognising this, my father did his best to protect his best drivers from financial predators while simultaneously urging them not to squander their earnings on gold-digging courtesans and fleeting indulgences. In the case of Corax and Alector, though, the former was naturally Spartan, while the latter was already fixed in his profligate ways well before his exile from Rome. In Syria, even with the responsibility of fatherhood, the Rooster continued to fritter away his winnings on feasts, singing girls and knick-knacks for his daughter, counting on funds to materialise whenever he really needed them.

So it was that, arriving at the docks of Seleucia Pieria with Selene and the three horses – who were not masked in any way – Alector was genuinely puzzled when all the ship captains he approached refused to accept the ill-judged offers he made for passage to Rome.

"There are too many unlucky days in late October to launch a boat now," protested one.

"The open sea at the start of the storm season?" scoffed another. "How much money have you got?"

"Seventeen days to Rome?" sneered a third. "Not bloody likely."

Alector could not fathom it. "It's as though we're being prevented from travelling by higher forces," he told Selene.

"The captains might change their minds if you offered a larger sum," she suggested.

"I've offered everything I can afford."

"Then call upon the goodwill of the Greens."

"Goodwill is a poor substitute for gold."

"I mean, pledge some amount on behalf of Picus – he is well known around here as a shipbuilder, is he not? His reputation might go a long way."

"You are very shrewd for your age, you know that?"

"It is an honour to hear such things from you, Father."

And so, after promising twenty thousand sesterces if he, his daughter and the three horses were delivered within seventeen days to Rome, Alector managed to secure passage on an Egyptian cargo lighter called *Horus*. But they had not even boarded the vessel when news arrived that the harbour had silted up, owing to the week's torrential rains, and no ship would be able to cast off for at least a week. Alector was distraught.

"In the name of all the gods, how shall we ever make it to Rome now?"

Selene, however, scrambled around the shipping offices and discovered that the *Concordia*, a freighter from Portus, had been piloted out of the harbour in anticipation of the blockage and was anchored offshore where it was taking on its cargo. This, as it happened, was a vivarium of exotic beasts heading to Rome to be slaughtered in one of Vitellius's beast-hunts. The animals had been transhipped in open water but in doing so a few had slipped into the sea, leaving enough room aboard for three horses.

The beast-master, a Parthian named Izates with claw marks all over his face, nevertheless refused to let Alector claim the vacant space, insisting that his own animals needed all the room they could get. But in this he was overruled by the captain of the ship, a Greek called Sippas who had once seen Alector race at the Thessalonica hippodrome. Thus, the blindfolded stallions, with some difficulty, were rowed out on a skiff and, soothed attentively by Selene, winched aboard the *Concordia*, which already reeked like a bear pit.

Stuffed nose-to-tail in the hold were striped hyenas, desert jackals, Arabian ostriches, Jordanian leopards and Mesopotamian lions, as well as many other strange beasts with wicked horns and ugly humps. It took Alector and Selene three hours, working with the ship's carpenter, to erect screens to separate the jittery stallions from this agitated menagerie. Then, with his daughter by his side, the Rooster scaled the ramp to slake his thirst, roam around the deck and flirt with a female beast-handler ("Rather attractive," admitted Selene, "despite a missing arm"). But he could not avoid the attention of a raven of exceptional size and shimmering blackness, which appeared on the mainmast, in the rigging, on the taffrail, and everywhere he went, stalking him incessantly, watching him unblinkingly, and giving no indication of its purpose.

"From which country came the raven?" Alector asked Izates.

"What raven?" snarled the crotchety beast-master.

"The raven right there on the crossbeam."

"I assure you, horse-lover, there is no raven in my vivarium, for why would the residents of Rome care for something that drops shit on them every day?"

Alector approached the captain. "How long has that bird been on your ship?"

"Never have I seen it before," replied Sippas, shielding his eye. "Though ravens are good to have on a boat, for they rid the decks of vermin."

"There are plenty of other creatures aboard that would readily rid your decks of vermin."

Sippas chuckled. "Then the raven will go hungry, and with no great suffering, I'd say, for it is already a plump-looking bird."

For a while Alector tried to shoo it off ("Clearly disturbed," Selene told me later, "though of course he would never admit it, by the notion that Corax was surveying his every move"), before retreating with his daughter into the stinking hold.

# V

I N FACT, THE RAVEN AT JUST THAT MOMENT had more on his mind than speculating about the progress of the Rooster. Having avoided the city of Narbo, where he had raced a few times as a charioteer, he and Magnus crossed into a region of foetid marshland and dense forest, encountering so many indications of military activity that they decided to take respite at one of the relief stations, just as the frontier guard had recommended.

There were stables, a tavern, a pigsty, a few hay ricks and a nondescript inn. The station manager, a twitchy ex-cavalry officer called Pennus, exhibited no particular suspicions about their permit – his eyes swept so rapidly across the text that Corax was not convinced he could read – and seemed inordinately happy just to have visitors. Even in the stables there were only a few bony steeds – an alarming sight for Corax, who had been planning to camouflage Andraemon amid other horses.

"I thought this place would be busier," he noted.

"We have seen just two couriers pass through this week," admitted Pennus.

"Why is that?"

"Trouble down the road. The army has commandeered all the best mounts."

"They cannot be allowed to take our own horses."

"I shall make sure they do not," Pennus assured him. "In the meantime, help yourself to the broth my wife is preparing."

Corax and Magnus repaired across the road to a tavern called The Hind, where, in order to keep a close eye on the stables, they secured the table nearest the window. The place stank of fried onions and vinegary wine.

"What did you think he meant by trouble down the road?" Magnus asked.

"We shall find out soon enough."

Barely had Corax uttered these words than a legionary tribune, identifiable by his studded leather breastplate, drew up outside on a large grey gelding. Doffing his helmet, he went to Pennus and chatted amicably for a few minutes before becoming distracted by the new horses.

"He might recognise Andraemon," whispered Magnus.

"*Quiet*," Corax snapped – Pennus's wife was approaching with their drinks.

They sipped the acrid wine and watched, as idly as possible, as the tribune examined Tuscus and Andraemon. He looked at their hindquarters, their torsos, their heads, paying particular attention to Andraemon's patchy left side and sightless right eye. He asked something of Pennus, who gestured to the tavern, then he nodded, mounted his steed, and went on his way.

"He might be riding off to inform someone," Magnus suggested.

"Or he might be just riding off."

"Lucky we kept Cupido in the wagon."

They ate the lumpy broth, chewed on the rock-hard bread, and Corax – taking advantage of a multi-coloured map on the wall – described from experience the roads ahead, the major towns, the topographical features, the character of the locals and the locations where they should reunite if separated. Magnus, meanwhile, spared a moment to speculate about the rest of the Andraemon Team.

"They will need to be travelling on a swift vessel," he observed, "if they are to make it in time."

"A boat as swift as the horses themselves," Corax agreed. "And that is not even—"

But he was rudely interrupted.

"Your own horses look unusually swift."

The two men turned to find the legionary tribune – the same one they thought had ridden off – installed at a nearby table with a severe look in his eyes. They had not noticed him enter.

"Excuse me, my friend?" Corax asked.

"I said those are swift-looking horses you have out there. Very swift."

Corax was unblinking. "Know something about horses, do you?"

"Enough to know that they were not bred to draw wagons."

"Is that so?"

"It is so. They are chariot horses. You know and I know it."

Silence from the whole tavern – silence even from Pennus's wife, who had stopped to listen in – until Corax spoke again. "Many cart horses come from circuses in these parts, my friend. But we know little about their background, I regret to say, because they were supplied to us at the last minute in Tarraco."

"For what purpose are they supplied, exactly?"

"We are transporting furniture to the proconsul of Hispania Tarraconensis, who currently resides in Rome."

"And for that he needs chariot horses, does he?"

"He certainly needs his goods quickly." Corax turned away, as if to indicate that the conversation was over, but the tribune persisted.

"And it does not bother you that one of those stallions has been masked?"

"Masked?" asked Corax, eyebrows raised.

199

"You know what I mean. I examined the horse closely. I saw the scars, the welts, the brands. Such markings remain, no matter what efforts are taken to conceal them."

"You seem to have taken a great interest in one of our horses for some reason."

"I take a great interest in the horse it resembles."

"And what horse does it resemble?"

The tribune sneered. "You know the one I mean."

The subsequent silence, as tight as a hawser, was broken by Magnus, laughing boisterously.

"Of course," he said. "Of course! Why do you think we call him Andraemon? Champion of the Circus Maximus? Truly, all that's missing is a goat." And he chuckled heartily, as if the idea were plainly preposterous.

The tribune looked at Magnus with narrowed eyes, as if debating whether to cut him down. But eventually he scowled.

"The horse *did* look like Andraemon," he said. "And some black-guard has tried to disguise him as that famous stallion. Whether it was you or some previous owner, that I do not know. Nor do I want to know. And for that you can count yourself lucky. I am not familiar with the laws of Tarraco, or whatever shithole you come from, but blinding an old hack, scarring its side and trying to pass it off as a champion chariot horse should be a crime. It should be a capital offence. It diminishes the circus. It diminishes us all."

Then, as Corax and Magnus watched expressionlessly, he drained what was left of his wine, slammed the goblet on the table, and stormed out to remount his gelding and gallop away.

It was 28 October and there were twenty days until the races in the Circus Maximus.

# VI

IN ROME THERE WAS A PROFUSION OF BLUE BANNERS, blue pennants and blue-painted store fronts; all the flags rippling above the Circus Maximus were blue; even the bronze quadriga team surmounting the Temple of Jupiter Optimus Maximus was adorned in blue. To my father it meant more than a mere declaration of war: Vitellius was clearly trying to redeem himself, in the eyes of his fellow Blues at least, for betraying the faction's finest charioteer twenty-nine years earlier.

Albus of the Esquiline held much the same view. "Vesuvius," he told me, "has bet his entire personal fortune on the outcome of the Plebeian Games, did you know that? Not to mention half the riches of the imperial treasury. So it's not just the fate of the empire that he is wagering on these races – more importantly, at least in his own mind, he is staking the reputation of himself."

I never ceased to be amazed by the eloquence of the grotesque man in the rancid gloom at the rear of the Cornigera. I had already consulted him regularly on the history of chariot racing – his meticulous records are now stored in the imperial archives – but was visiting him presently in my capacity as a Greens liaison officer, my father being too preoccupied to appear in person.

"Be that as it may," I managed, eager to get down to business, "what are the odds of the Andraemon Team being intercepted en route to Rome?"

"Have you ever laid a bet on in your life, lad?"

"Never," I admitted, not without pride.

"Then let us dispense with the gambling terminology."

"That would be much appreciated," I said. "How likely is it that the horses will be prevented from reaching Rome, then?"

"Difficult to determine. Did you know that Vesuvius has engaged the services of his most ruthless poisoners and cutthroats?"

"The same ones who've been killing our horses and charioteers?"

"Not them," replied Albus. "This is a special, extra-judicial hit squad he used in Germania – disgraced legionaries and pardoned murderers, mainly. He has sent them out to kill your horses, or permanently hobble them, before they can get close to the Circus Maximus."

I was chilled. "Then he already knows that the Andraemon Team is on its way?"

"Who would not suspect it?"

"Where then will the killers strike – do you know that?"

"At the ports if you give them a chance. He has sent assassins to Portus and Ostia, of course, but also to Puteoli, Neapolis and Tarentum in the south. And Brundisium, Traentinum and Sipontum on the Adriatic coast. Alector will be at great risk when he makes land."

"Vitellius knows – you know – that Alector is coming by ship?"

"Who would not suspect it?"

"What about Corax?"

"Vesuvius does not yet know that he is taking the land route."

"Then how do you know?"

"I know if a bee dies in Baetica," said Albus, and the pigeons cooed on the roof.

For some reason I shivered. "So these assassins you speak of – Vitellius has sent none of them north?"

"None. And the progress of Vespasian's legions makes that region difficult to negotiate anyway."

"Where now are Vespasian's legions?"

"Third Gallica has crossed the Julian Alps."

"You know this as a fact?"

"I know if a mouse dies in Macedonia."

"Then they could soon be in Rome . . ."

"If Vesuvius does not marshal enough support, of course. And if he does not win the Plebeian Games, even more so."

I thought about it. "Are the assassins corruptible? Can they be paid off?"

"All assassins are corruptible. But you would need to pay grandly."

"How so?"

"Vesuvius has offered twenty thousand sesterces to anyone who injures one of the horses. For killing one, with tangible proof, forty thousand sesterces. Twice that amount if the horse is Andraemon. And for capturing Andraemon, and bringing him to the Blues' stables alive, one hundred thousand sesterces."

"Vitellius hopes to race Andraemon in the Blue Faction?"

"If the Greens are destroyed, what difference does it make?"

"I suppose so." I started getting to my feet, deciding my father would need to know the news as soon as possible. "Very well, then I thank you again for—"

"Wait a minute." Albus was squinting at me. "Wait a minute. You can't really believe you can get away like that?"

"I beg your pardon?" I had almost banged my head on the hanging lamp.

"It's a trade, lad – now more than ever."

"You want some intelligence from me?"

"Your father must have warned you to expect that."

"Yes, of course," I said, reseating myself. "Forgive my haste. What is it that you wish to know?"

"Delphinius of Doriscus – where is he?"

"Resting in his villa, which is heavily guarded."

"He is definitely there – not a decoy?"

"I have spoken to him personally."

"They still might get to him."

"I don't see how."

"You don't have to. They can find a way."

"Delphinius is aware of all the dangers," I pointed out, "and he is determined to race in the Plebeian Games."

"But will that be for the Greens?"

"Why do you say that?"

A vaporous smile. "I merely urge you to be ready for anything, lad. What about your chariots?"

"Our chariots?"

"I'm sure you know of which I speak."

When I worked out what he meant, I glanced at his bodyguard. "Do you mind if we keep this private?"

"Garrulus never discusses what he hears in this place."

"His name suggests otherwise."

"He is mute. Hence the nickname Garrulus."

"I'd be happier if he were deaf."

Albus shrugged. "Garrulus," he said, "kindly leave us for a few moments."

With no apparent resentment, the guard pushed through the horsehair coverings and disappeared.

I dropped my voice to a whisper. "If you refer to the iron hoops on the wheels—"

"Of course I do, lad."

"Well, my father intends to have them installed two days prior to the Games."

"Two days?"

"The charioteers need time to practise."

"Two days gives the Blues ample time to adapt their own chariots."

"We intend to train in secret."

"With all your charioteers? That makes for a very loose secret."

"We are confident we can prevent this one from getting out."

"*I* heard about it," said Albus.

"And how *did* you hear about it, by the way?"

"I know if a hare dies in Heraclea," said Albus. "And don't ask me again about my sources, lad, as I've run out of witty boasts."

"Then how many others have learned about it – do you know that?"

"If you mean Vesuvius, you can rest easy. Because I, unlike others, know how to keep a secret."

"And you will continue to keep it that way?"

"Until your father gives me a reason to change my mind."

I figured it was as much as I could expect. "Very well," I said, rising. "Then I shall no doubt be seeing you again soon."

"Short odds that means tomorrow," said Albus, returning to his boards. "And send Garrulus back in on your way out, will you?"

As it happened, I did not return to the tavern the next day, but only because we were dealing with a whole new crisis. The cargo lighter carrying the decoy Andraemon had somehow arrived at Portus in advance of the courier that Corax had sent to warn us about it (we later learned that the courier's ship had hugged the coast, despite promises to the contrary). And this meant that Corax's stable boy, frantic, decided to leave the horse aboard and race fifteen miles to inform my father in person. But by the time everyone from the estate had bustled out to Portus – even my father, wheezing asthmatically, joined the expedition – the horse had disappeared. "Snatched," according to the trembling captain, "by a cur bearing a blade as long as a bowsprit."

The decoy Andraemon had been taken. So how long could it be before his captors worked out that the horse, not blind in the right eye, was not really Andraemon?

# VII

MAGNUS WAS BY NO MEANS A SENTIMENTAL MAN. Years of mockery and exploitation, not to mention his exile on a point of principle, meant that his heart had calcified into a cartilage-like lump. Nevertheless, he felt very much beholden to Corax, who, twenty-four years earlier, upon hearing that he was drinking himself to death in the taverns of Lusitania, had ridden six hundred miles to rescue him.

"Corax of Campania," Magnus had exclaimed, plonking down his goblet. "What in blazes brings you to this dung heap?"

"I've come to see a hero."

"Then you should try looking at your own reflection."

"On the contrary, I see one right now. May I take a seat?"

"You may take whatever you like. How did you recognise me, by the way?"

Corax, never adept at recognising jokes, squeezed onto a bench. "How could I ever forget you? After what you did that day in the Circus – refusing to race over those slaves."

"You refused as well."

"But I went unpunished. You did not."

"You were punished later."

"On a point of foolish pride, yes. You, on the other hand, were punished for your courage."

"Courage, eh?" Magnus shifted uneasily.

"Courage, definitely. Make no mistake – on that day you made yourself the biggest man in Rome."

Magnus laughed. "A welcome conceit, Corax, but I hope you've not ridden all this way just to flatter me?"

"No indeed. I've come to offer you work."

"What sort of work?"

"In the Circus Augustus."

"Not in exhibition events, I hope? I've had my fill of novelty races."

"Certainly not in novelty races."

"Or ordinary races, for that matter. Did you not hear? My pelvis was sledgehammered by Caligula's henchmen. I still have no feeling in my hips, and am all but useless with the reins."

"Nonetheless, you would still retain enough touch to be a jubilator, would you not?"

"I've never ridden as a jubilator in my life."

"The best of them are lightweight like you, and few can match your feel for horses. I shall have a word to faction management in Tarraco."

"And why would they listen to you, when they must have jubilators of their own?"

"They trust me on such matters. And I can further make it a condition of my loyalty."

"Oh?" said Magnus. "And why would you do something like that?"

"Because you are my brother, whether you like it or not."

"Your brother, am I?"

"My brother in exile. In grievance. In virtue."

"Certainly not in talent."

"All the same, it is my responsibility to look out for you," insisted Corax, reaching over to seal the dwarf's goblet with his hand. "To make sure that you don't drown in a vat of wine."

207

And that, in short, was how Magnus of Noricum went from self-pitying drunkard in Lusitania to jubilator for the Spanish Greens and trusted stablehand on Corax's stud farm.

Presently he was alone on a leaf-carpeted donkey path, steering the wagon now yoked to Tuscus and the cavalry horse. Corax was a quarter-mile behind, riding Andraemon with Cupido running alongside. The tense encounter at the waystation, together with the increasing volume of soldiers on the Via Domitia, had prompted the two men to separate temporarily in case they were ambushed.

It was mid-afternoon and a chilly grey fog had settled in. The path, snaking through steep hills, was flanked with towering, creeper-covered trees which might have been concealing anything – from wild beasts to brigands – but Magnus, partly so that Corax could keep track of him, was declaring his defiance in song:

"Life is short, no doubt,
And time takes its toll,
So remember always this simple truth,
And sing with all your soul."

There was a flicker of movement in the forest – Andraemon and Tuscus nickered – but this only encouraged Magnus to bellow even louder:

"While you live, shine,
Cast your light like the sun,
For light defeats the darkness,
And this life we have but one."

A huge conifer groaned and cracked and came cleaving through the fog and crashing across the path ahead, thumping dead leaves into the air.

The horses reared up. Magnus flailed at the reins. Two sword-wielding bandits sprang from the trees.

"Halt there!"

One of the bandits – bearded, shabbily dressed, stinking of sweat – was already mounting the wagon. "Try nothing, little man, or I'll slaughter you like a lamb."

"No need," said Magnus with his most disarming smile. "The horses have stopped as you see."

"Arms?"

"Say again?"

"Where are your arms?"

"I have no arms."

The bearded bandit was already frisking him, however, extracting a dagger from his tunic and a short sword from under his feet.

"What do you call these?"

"You would struggle to skewer a rodent with those."

The bandit dug his blade into Magnus's throat. "Then perhaps I should skewer you?"

Magnus tried to laugh. "You had better hurry, whatever you do, for I have an escort behind me – an escort of soldiers."

"Of course you do – that's why you travel on this mule track."

"I'm telling you, I have an escort."

"Why? What are you carrying?" The bandit called out to his companion, who was inspecting the rear of the wagon. "What is he carrying, Judoc?"

"Furniture!" came the response. "Nothing but furniture!"

The bandit jabbed Magnus again. "Have an escort for furniture, do you?"

"Very important furniture, intended for the emperor in Rome."

"Of course it is."

"I have a permit," Magnus said, reaching under the blanket beside him.

"*Careful*," the bandit hissed, pressing his blade.

"A . . . a permit," Magnus repeated, holding up the scroll. "From the legionary legate at—"

The bandit plucked the scroll from his hands and flung it over his shoulder. "We care nothing for your fancy words here." He leaned in to pierce Magnus's skin. "Pass over your money, dwarf."

Magnus winced. "I have no money."

"Like you have no arms? You'll be lucky if I don't slit your throat now, just for—"

But then there was some commotion behind them and the bandit drew back. "What is it?"

Judoc squinted down the path, frowning. "A goat."

"A what?" The bearded bandit landed on the ground to have a better look. Magnus, also turning, saw Cupido prancing out of the mist.

"The dwarf's escort," the bandit sneered. "Rope it."

"You had better not touch that goat, either," Magnus warned.

"Why? Does it belong to the emperor, too?"

"I tell you, you should not touch that goat."

The bandit scowled. "Rope it, anyway," he told Judoc. "Before it gets away."

Judoc was about to do so when there was an explosive whinny and a riderless stallion came bursting out of the fog and thundering down the path. The brigands drew back as the horse kicked out, trying – it seemed – to protect the goat.

"Calm the beast," ordered the bearded bandit, clearly shaken.

"It wears a military bridle," Judoc noted.

The bandit glanced warily at Magnus and back. "Then we'll take the wagon and join the others."

"And the dwarf?"

"I'll take care of the dwarf."

Magnus, caught off-guard, tried to squirm away but the bandit was already back on the cart, towering over him. The horses were shifting, Cupido was bleating, Andraemon was rearing, and in the middle of it all a blade was heading for his throat.

Then Magnus heard a whistle and felt a swirl of mist. He heard a sickening *crunch*. He felt a spray of droplets on his skin. And, coming to his senses, he saw that the bandit had something buried in his face.

A hatchet.

The bandit had not seen it coming. He had not even had time to blink. He wavered on the wagon for a few seconds, his arms loosening, then thumped back onto the path.

The man called Judoc wheeled around, saw his partner twitching on the ground, and fled for his life into the forest. It had all taken barely a dozen heartbeats.

Magnus, breathless, turned to find a barrel-chested soldier limping out of the trees. He had to blink many times, just to be sure, but it was definitely Corax. Bearing an unsheathed sword. With mist swirling around him like smoke.

Making swiftly for the fallen body, the Raven verified that the bandit was dead, pressed a foot into his chest and wrenched the hatchet from his face.

"Corax . . ." Magnus breathed, astonished. "I didn't know you could do that!"

Corax grunted ambivalently. "Neither did I, until I tried it."

Magnus thought about it for a moment and then brayed with laughter. "Of course! Of course! *In the heat of the race the champion always finds extra!*"

But Corax – either appalled that he had killed a man or affronted by the notion that he was still under the tyranny of the charioteers' creed – was in no mood for celebration.

"We need to find a way up this track," he growled. "There are surely more bandits in the woods. Night is falling. There could well be rain. So wipe that grin off your face, get off your arse, and help me move this tree."

It was 30 October and there were eighteen days until the races in the Circus Maximus.

# VIII

O N THE MORNING OF 1 NOVEMBER, two days after my meeting with Albus of the Esquiline, Delphinius of Doriscus was crossing the atrium at his luxurious villa, which was a mere arrowshot from Vitellius's ancestral home in the Servilian Hills, when he noticed an imposing young woman waiting beside the fountain.

He blinked. "Who are you? And what are you doing here?"

"I am here to massage you," replied the woman.

"Why? I have my own masseurs."

"Picus decided they could not be trusted."

"He did, did he? And what makes him think I can trust you?"

"I have been Picus's personal masseuse for three years."

"Oh really?" Delphinius tried to be sceptical – he had never seen the girl before, though she must have been credentialled enough to get past the guards – before deciding to be amused. "Well, then," he said, "I suppose I could do with some loosening up before my meal. Yes indeed, I've not had a decent massage in weeks. What is your name, girl?"

"Narcissa."

"A grand name for a slave." He looked her up and down – she was unusually well-muscled, even for a masseuse – and nodded approvingly. "All right, then, come this way, Narcissa – we will see how good you are with your hands."

Delphinius, by his own admission, was not particularly skilled with women. Part of his attraction to them, in fact, was his beguiling awkwardness. Nevertheless, as a champion charioteer, he had never been shy about making the most of his celebrity, and over the years he had accumulated as many conquests in the bedchamber as he had on the track. He was particularly active in the week leading up to a major race day, when charioteers, in the name of relieving tension, were encouraged to disport themselves with as many partners – man, woman, child or beast – as they pleased. So perhaps, he wondered presently, Picus had sent this vixen – she really had the most wicked air about her – purposely to calm his nerves? To reward him for his obedience?

"Have you ever massaged a charioteer before?" he asked, as they arrived at the caldarium.

"I know how it is done."

"It's an art all of its own, you know."

"If you say so."

"Much different than pumping and stretching the flesh of old men."

"The principles are the same."

"The principles, perhaps, but not the men." Delphinius swiftly disrobed. "If you know what I mean."

The girl, however, merely pointed to the slab. "Lay flat on the table."

"You really intend to massage me?"

"I have my instructions. And not much time."

Strangely impressed by her indifference, Delphinius climbed onto the marble, lay flat on his stomach, and tried to relax as she got to work – roughly kneading the muscles of his shoulders and back.

"Your hands are sweaty," he told her.

"That is your sweat, not mine."

"I think you might be nervous."

"I have no reason to be nervous."

"Do you not know who I am?"

"You are Delphinius of Doriscus."

He waited for more – "the most famous charioteer in the empire", "winner of eight hundred and eight races in the Circus Maximus" or some such thing – but she was alarmingly quiet. Just prodding at his back with her slippery hands. Delphinius felt curiously hollow.

"You are driving in the Plebeian Games?" she asked finally.

"I beg your pardon?"

"I asked if you are driving in the Plebeian Games."

"Well, of course I am driving in the Plebeian Games. That is exactly why Picus sent you here, is it not?"

"That's right." She squeezed his shoulders for a while. "And you expect to drive the Andraemon Team?"

"Naturally I expect to drive the Andraemon Team. No charioteer can draw as much out of them as I can. Why? Do you know of anyone more appropriate?"

"That is not what I mean."

"Then what did you mean?"

"Nothing important," she said.

Finches were cheeping in the garden. There was the tinkle of water from the fountains. The *clang clang clang* of distant hammering. Delphinius hoped he hadn't intimidated her. He was enjoying the conversation, as curious as it was.

She pressed her hands between his shoulder blades. "What I mean to say," she went on, "is that there are other factors, are there not?"

"Such as?"

"The horses, for one."

"What about them?"

"Do you even know where they are?"

Delphinius was surprised. "I have no knowledge of their whereabouts."

"You have no idea what port they are aiming for, or if they are in fact now in Italy?"

"Such information has not been shared with me."

"Nothing slipped through inadvertently?"

"Nothing." Delphinius wondered if the girl was probing him for information. It was not unknown for household slaves to be bribed by gambling syndicates. "Nothing at all."

She got back to squeezing his neck, almost throttling him. He was on the verge of complaining.

"There are rumours," she said at length, "that a decoy Andraemon was sent from Spain, and that the emperor himself recognised that it was not the real horse."

"Where did you learn that?"

"I heard someone talking about it."

"In the Picus household?"

"That's correct."

"Hmm," said Delphinius, "it's news to me. A decoy? Really?"

"So they say."

"I shall need to inform Picus about this, you know. Such information, true or not, is not meant to be gossiped about."

Silence for another minute or so – the girl, who had drawn back, seemed to be unwrapping something – and then the mysterious interrogation continued.

"Then you've not heard," she asked, "how the genuine Andraemon is being brought to Rome?"

"Of course not. I've been stranded here for weeks."

"And you would not tell me in any case?"

"I *could* not tell you in any case. They let me know nothing here. I am surprised you have heard so much. Are you spying for Albus of the Esquiline, is that it?"

Not answering, the girl shifted, started scraping his back with a strigil.

"I thought this was to be a massage," he observed, "not a clean."

"A clean will do you good."

"You are not wrong there."

The blade was not so much gliding as dragging across his skin – he again wondered about her experience.

"It's curious," she said eventually, "that you trust the Greens anyway. Do you know what they call you – your chariot masters?"

"What do they call me?"

"'Perfume Boy.' 'The widow's stablemate.' That sort of thing."

"Those are old taunts," Delphinius said, though in truth he was vexed – mention of his pampered past always got under his skin.

"And they say you are all but meaningless to them now – one donkey is as good as another, they reckon, and you are no better than Cyrnus of Corsica."

Cyrnus of Corsica was a notoriously inept charioteer who had once tumbled out of his chariot in the starting stalls and watched from the sidelines as his horses won the race without him.

"They speak in jest, if they really say that."

"They did not sound like they were jesting."

"Then you do not know them well enough," insisted Delphinius, sniffing. "Why do you tell me such things anyway? Are you here to make mischief?"

She was silent, still scraping away, and he wondered if she was in fact spying for the Greens. Making sure he was still loyal, intent on winning – he knew my father could be incorrigibly suspicious. So he added, somewhat declaratively, "Yes, jesting, I am sure of it. Picus knows he cannot win without me. He needs me now more than ever."

"Are you really certain he would not trade you to another faction, if the price is right?"

"Why do you say that? Picus would never trade me."

"Circumstances might force him to."

"Never."

"Then perhaps you would depart of your own accord? You are a freedman, are you not?"

"And why would I leave the Greens?" Now Delphinius was convinced he was being tested. "I love the faction as much as I love Picus. I have no desire to leave them – ever."

"You are that loyal to them, are you?"

"We are inseparable."

"And nothing would you make you consider otherwise?"

"Nothing."

She was silent again, so that he thought for a moment he had satisfied her – that she would shortly be reporting his loyalty to my father.

But then he experienced a brief, inexplicable image of Alector back in the Amuq Valley. He heard his mentor telling him to "hear" with his skin, with his hair, with the very air around him. And, at the same time, he detected movement in the atrium, an exclamation from one of his guards, and the scuffle of pounding feet.

Delphinius spun his body just in time. The girl, teeth bared, was slashing down with her strigil. Delphinius launched himself off the slab. The tip of the blade shrieked across the marble. The girl, crying *"Felix populus Veneti!"* – the rally cry of the Blues, raised the blade to stab at him again.

But just in the nick of time the guard stormed into the room and collected her with his sword. Her body jolted and stiffened. The strigil clattered across the floor. The guard drove the sword deeper and deeper. The girl, eyes bulging at Delphinius, seemed to be communicating some sort of unspeakable horror. Then she slid off the blade, bounced off the marble slab, and flopped across the floor.

Delphinius, his heart pounding violently, watched her twist and turn front of him. He watched the lustre fade from her eyes. And finally he exhaled.

"Who – who was she?" he asked, stunned.

The guard, still gasping for breath, said, "An assassin. She killed Thorax." Meaning one of the other guards.

"Then I am lucky to be alive."

"You are lucky I arrived just in time."

A frigid breeze at that moment swept through the villa, prickling Delphinius's skin. He said later that he "should have been exhilarated at having survived. Or furious with the girl for attempting such an atrocity". But instead, he later admitted with admirable candour, he felt "terribly intimidated by the forces that were arrayed against me, and not at all sure what I was going to do".

There were sixteen days to the races in the Circus Maximus.

# IX

CORAX KNEW THAT THE BRIGAND'S CAUSAL REFERENCE to fellow bandits could not easily be dismissed, just as he knew from experience that the highwaymen of Gaul – embittered remnants of tribes subdued by Julius Caesar – seldom gave up without a fight. He therefore considered heading south, for the safety of Arelate, before deciding that such a densely populated area presented daunting dangers of its own. So he resolved to stay in the hills.

But soon they found themselves on the edge of a steep gorge, at the bottom of which was a swift-flowing river. Heading north, seeking a point shallow enough to ford, they spotted tents and flaming braziers below – a Roman camp.

"A patrol?" ventured Magnus.

"No," said Corax, parting the bushes. "Look there."

Upriver, silvered by moonlight, was an immense three-tiered aqueduct,* its eastern end cloaked in scaffolding.

"Builders," decided Magnus, squinting. "Finishing their work, by the looks of it."

---

* Now known as the Pont du Gard.

"Not soon enough for us."

"And accompanied by soldiers, probably."

"If they are not soldiers themselves," said Corax – building projects in remote areas were often guarded against pillaging. "Let's have a closer look."

When they reached the aqueduct Corax scrambled up the blocks to inspect the span at closer range, and came down shaking his head. "We'll need to leave the wagon behind."

"You're thinking of crossing the aqueduct?"

"It's the quickest route."

"And the most perilous."

"All options are perilous now."

"But what if we're seen by the soldiers?"

"A risk we'll have to take."

"And the cargo? Cluvius Rufus's furniture?"

"The bandits are welcome to it. We can get replacement furniture – and another wagon – when we reach Massilia."

Magnus was doubtful. "There must be another route, Corax."

"No," said Corax, "we can ill afford to tarry now, with bandits on our heels."

("My protests," Magnus confessed to me later, "were borne chiefly of my morbid dread of heights. I had performed on tightropes, true, but never very far off the ground, and I remained terrified even of balconies. Though this was a weakness I was never keen to admit – least of all now.")

They found a builder's ramp and guided the horses to the aqueduct's top level.

"When the clouds part, that moon blazes like a lighthouse," Magnus grumbled. "I still don't like it."

Corax glanced up at the fast-moving clouds – cover would indeed be short and inconsistent – and nodded. "Then we shall go across one at a time, when the moon is fully covered. Cupido first, to encourage the others, then Andraemon, then Tuscus, and finally the cavalry horse. *Speed with vigilance,*" he added – one of the mantras of the charioteers' creed.

They went to the very edge of the gorge and waited until a thick caravan of clouds advanced on the moon. Then Corax bundled up Cupido and started across the shadowed span. He was thirty horse-lengths across when the clouds separated for a moment, the moon brightening the landscape like a giant lamp. Pausing just long enough for the curtains to close again, he hastened on, making it to the eastern side just as the light returned.

He dumped the goat in the undergrowth, waited for another suitable cloud, and raced back to Magnus.

Andraemon by this stage was so agitated that Corax's main problem was restraining him from a reckless charge. But as soon as the moon was concealed once more, they were ready. Corax whisked the stallion across the casing stones – Andraemon was reliably silent and uncomplaining – and reached the other side without incident. Then it was Magnus's turn.

"I had watched Corax in a species of awe," Magnus told me later. "One might have thought he was negotiating a stretch of the Via Appia, not an elevated strip of casing stones a few cubits wide. And I tried desperately to convince myself that I too could do the same, with even a fraction of the confidence."

He licked his lips, and trembled, and waited for the moment when he could no longer delay. But by now the cloud cover had thinned in both size and quantity. He had to hold off an excruciatingly long time, poised on the lip of the gorge, ruffled by the wind, chilled by the cold, and was finally about to sally forth – a warship-shaped cloud was ploughing towards the moon's brilliantly shining disc – when he heard noises below.

A soldier was emerging from one of the tents. He was waddling down to the river. Fumbling around within his leggings. And peeing into the water – a twinkling stream that seemed to go on interminably.

Then there was another noise, this time from behind. Magnus glanced over his shoulder. The scrub seemed to be shifting. He looked across the aqueduct. Corax, Andraemon and the goat were barely visible. He squinted up at the sky. The huge cloud was scraping across the moon. He checked the gorge. The urinating soldier was still standing by the river.

Then there was another noise from the rear – it sounded like someone had discovered the wagon – and Magnus decided he had no choice.

He seized Tuscus by the reins and launched onto the aqueduct. There were just a few handbreadths between themselves and empty air. They moved at a brisk but steady pace. The breeze was powerful. The moon was struggling to penetrate the clouds. The air smelled of woodsmoke. Magnus risked another glance down at the gorge.

The soldier was stretching.

Magnus checked the cloud – it was peeling away from the moon. And the aqueduct was brightening. The whole gorge was lighting up. He drew to a halt, frozen in place.

The soldier yawned. Tuscus nickered. The river burbled. A new, hunchbacked cloud approached the moon.

Agitated voices drifted from the brush behind.

The soldier in the gorge raised his eyes, looked up at the bushes, then across to the aqueduct. He seemed to be staring directly at Magnus and Tuscus. But he wasn't reacting. It seemed impossible that he hadn't noticed them.

Then the cloud reached the moon. The aqueduct was plunged into shade. And everything erupted.

An arrow, fired from behind, shrieked past Magnus's head. The soldier cried out. More arrows squealed through the air. A horn blared. The soldier dashed back to the tent.

Magnus, gulping, lurched forward, picked up pace. Sprinted across the last stretch of aqueduct, tried not to run off the edge. But he could scarcely see a thing. He almost slipped, almost plunged to his death. Gravel scattered from the casing stones. But before he knew it, he had reached solid ground. Arms were reaching out for him – Corax! – and assisting both him and Tuscus to safety.

"The bandits are after us!" he exclaimed, then looked back, catching a glimpse of dark figures swarming around the cavalry horse and flooding across the aqueduct.

"This way!" hissed Corax.

They scraped their heads, scratched their shoulders, waddled and stumbled, but never ceased pushing themselves forward. "Here!" Corax blurted, directing them down a rough-hewn path. The moonlight faded and brightened as from behind came neighs, curses, blares, hissing arrows and furious shouts.

They ploughed through glades and brush land until the ground fell away again – another gorge, another loop of the swift-flowing river. They were trapped.

"We can't cross the water here," panted Magnus.

"In here!" exclaimed Corax, indicating a grotto half obscured by scrub. "We can rest until we're safe!"

They tried to haul Andraemon and Tuscus inside, but the animals were surprisingly resistant. And the goat was shrinking away. Corax had to chase him down, scoop him up and carry him forcibly inside.

But Cupido continued to wriggle and squirm. And the horses, Andraemon in particular, were protesting violently.

"Great gods," cursed Magnus, "what's the matter with them?"

"They sense something."

"But what?" asked Magnus. "There's no one—"

There was a growl from behind. The men tensed, not sure if they had heard properly.

Another deep and bestial roar, and suddenly there was no doubt. The horses erupted from the cave. Cupido broke loose and followed. And the two men bolted after them, bowling through the scrub, fleeing for their lives.

"Of all the caves in Gaul," Magnus laughed later, shaking his head, "we had to choose one that was inhabited by a bear."

The enormous creature, flashing its teeth and slashing its claws, bounded after them down the slope as the shouts and curses continued behind.

# X

FOR ALECTOR AND SELENE, on board the former grain freighter transporting the vivarium to Rome, everything seemed to be going exceptionally well. The sea had been unseasonably smooth. The trade winds had been uncharacteristically cooperative. The ship's victuals, which included everything from seafood to salted pork, were surprisingly flavoursome. The three chariot horses, once they had become familiar with their growling companions, were reasonably settled. And Alector himself had found among the other passengers an agreeable number of fetching ladies upon whom to exercise his charm, even to the point of bragging about his feats in the Circus Maximus.

"Do you really think it's wise to boast, Father?" Selene asked at one stage.

"What does a man like me have, if he cannot boast?"

"I mean you might draw attention to the horses."

"On the contrary, I'm drawing attention *away* from the horses. But I see your point. We have more important objectives, it's true. Have you seen that raven again, by the way?"

"I don't believe so."

"Because he's flown away, that's why. Because he knows the race is lost."

But then, early on the ninth morning of the voyage, just as they were tacking south of Amorgos, a freakish black storm roared and flashed across the sky. The sea rose violently from its slumber. The sails swelled and the ratlines hummed. The rowers raised their oars. The beasts in the hold howled and hooted. Seasick passengers gathered on the deck, some of them, valuing the verdict of Alector above all others – charioteers were often glorified as helmsmen – even asked him what they should do. The captain himself seemed to be seeking his counsel.

"The Cyclades now," Sippas noted hoarsely. "In a storm such as this, the islands can be treacherous – more than treacherous."

"Can you not put in at one of the harbours?" asked Alector.

"Not during an easterly like this. The coasts here are littered with vessels that tried."

"Then can you not ride out the storm here, and try to negotiate the straits later?"

"That is potentially the most dangerous course of all."

In the arena Alector had very nearly been killed on six occasions, twice in the Circus Maximus and four times in the provinces. He had faced peril at sea before, too, on the voyage between Sipontum and Apollonia. And he had numerous times escaped the murderous clutches of cuckolded husbands like Theodorus. In short, he had faced death before. He had stared down Charon. And Selene, for one, was confident he could do so again.

"What should we do, Father?"

"Go through," he hissed.

"What did you say?" asked the captain, awed.

Alector looked over at him. "I said we should go through. We are men of Hellas, are we not? Sons of Theseus? Well, raise the sails and dip the oars, I say – we need to go through."

And such was his self-assurance that the captain could not resist. So orders were relayed, exhortations were made, prayers were muttered, passengers hung their valuables around their necks, and

Alector, glorying in his own powers, waddled to the stern, planted his feet on the boards and waved away the drunken helmsman.

"Tie me in place," he ordered Selene. "Bind me to the tiller so that I can steer this chariot to victory."

His daughter at that moment saw a man who – teeth clenched, eyes gleaming – "was summoning his enormous pride". A hero who was "reminding himself who he had been and who he still was". Alector the Great. Alector the Invincible. The charioteer in his purest form. The supreme master of destiny and the elements. A man who made a circus out of life, and life out of a circus.

So, speechless, she raced around collecting ropes and belts, and watched in fascination as her father, fastened to the ship's *clavus*, his hands clamped around the bars, prepared to pilot the *Concordia* between the landmasses – as if the islands were competing chariot teams in the Circus Maximus!

The sea was a rolling landscape of hills and valleys; lightning snaked through the clouds; spray whipped across the deck; and the *Concordia*, her sails billowing, ploughed through the waves like a team of stallions through a sea of grass. She veered towards one of the reefs, but Alector pulled hard on the steering oars. The vessel lurched to starboard, the rocks dangerously close. The Rooster, shouting his defiance, pulled even harder. Thunder blared at him, the waves blasted across him, the deck tilted one way and another, but he would not surrender. He was a ball of muscle and sinew, his teeth bared, his brow furrowed, his eyes squeezed to slits.

"But he must have heard the squeals, the groans, the screams, the growling animals," Selene enthused later. "He must have felt the ship straining, splitting, almost breaking apart beneath him."

He leaned back and cried out as the *Concordia* skirted the reefs and surged deeper into the strait. The ship climbed mountainous waves. She plunged into spuming troughs. Alector kept working the oars from side to side. Wide-eyed passengers crawled across the deck and stared at him. There were explosions of light as the heavens poured forth a deluge. A spotted panther erupted from the hold and gawped incredulously before retreating, terrified, back down the hatch.

But through it all Alector himself would not budge. He was twisting – and being twisted by – his imaginary reins. His every muscle was straining. His every pore was leaking. One moment he was pushing the bars forward, his shoulders hunched, the next moment he was leaning back, his neck tendons bulging like cords. And all the time the *Concordia* was responding to his will like a team of well-trained horses. As though she *wanted* to please him. As though she *feared* his wrath.

But now the passengers, crying out in alarm, could make out the flames of a lighthouse. The *Concordia* was heading for cliffs. Her oars were going to snap; she was going to impale herself on jagged rocks. The people turned again to Alector, who summoned his last reserves of energy. He had to dig deep, he had to shout out to his imaginary stallions, but somehow, like the champion he was, he found extra. He raised the steering oars just as an immense swell lifted the ship over the final obstacle. The keel scraped noisily across the rocks. Timbers separated, seawater leaked into the hold. But the *Concordia* was through. She was beyond the Cyclades and heading for the mainland. The storm grumbled but it had run out of energy. The clouds dispersed and the sun emerged from its prison. The passage had taken less than a day but had seemed endless – the people on board, surprised there was still sunlight, questioned their own senses.

There was no doubt, though, as to who had piloted them to victory. And it was not the captain, the drunken helmsman, or any of the crew. It was Alector of Arcadia. Alector the Great. The passengers edged forward and touched his cloak, his sandals, his skin. He was drenched, dishevelled and shaking uncontrollably. It was frankly astonishing that he had stayed conscious for so long. But he had done it. He had saved them from oblivion. And they cheered him like the crowds of the Circus Maximus.

"I had seen him winning races in the eastern hippodromes," Selene told me later. "I'd heard all his stories about his great victories in Rome. But I had never been prouder of my father than I was at that moment."

The sails were in shreds, the masts tilted and the rudder broken, but all the passengers and crew were alive, and only a small number of beasts had died in the mayhem. And in the crisp air of dawn, to further spirited cheers, the survivors spotted first the Temple of Poseidon at Sunium, then the glinting spear of the Athena Promachos statue high on the Acropolis in distant Athens.

There were fifteen days to the races at the Circus Maximus.

# XI

BEYOND AN AMUSINGLY CLINICAL DESCRIPTION from my father – that she was "still a formidable specimen" – I had no way of knowing, at that point, exactly what Xenia looked like. But in my mind she lived on as I remembered her: an uncommonly beautiful woman who, for all her lowly birth, could make highborn ladies quiver with inferiority (I witnessed this personally), while all the time bearing herself without a scintilla of affectation, wearing the simplest of clothes, adorning herself in scarcely any jewellery, and caring not the least for the latest powders and pastes.

But it is not for me to speculate how she felt in her heart about Alector. If anything, I suspect the Rooster was probably right when he declared that, being faultlessly practical, she would have favoured Corax for his reliability alone. She was not the type to be stimulated by worries about her man's welfare or constant doubts as to his fidelity. Nevertheless – as we shall see – she still thought fondly of Alector. Selene, who grew to love her as a mother, was certain of it: "Her eyes always lit up at the mention of my father's name. She admitted she often thought about him and seized upon any morsel of news about him with great fascination."

Indeed, Xenia would have been less than human were she not exasperated at times by Corax's nature. When his Stoical convictions seemed more like aloofness; when his devotion to horses seemed a form of misanthropy; when his refusal to argue with her seemed more like endurance than respect. And she must have wondered, too, if he had ever really given up on his Circus dreams; and if the Raven, when it came down to it, was really more reliable than the Rooster.

And now he was gone. Not to Narbo or any other regional racetrack, but to Rome. Melussa, despite being sworn to secrecy, had divulged the details prematurely. Corax and Magnus were smuggling Andraemon back to the Circus Maximus "to race in the Plebeian Games and save the Greens from destruction". They had stolen off in the darkness like thieves, in short, without the decency to furnish her with a personal explanation.

In fact, as Xenia later admitted to Selene, she had suspected that the two men were lying from the start. She was not even sure why she had not challenged them more vigorously. It was almost as if she had *wanted* them to deceive her, just so she might find some truth in the wash-up. So she might have an opportunity to test her husband – and test herself.

At any rate, after an initial burst of resentment, she attempted to lose herself in distraction. And it was not as though there was any shortage of things to do. Apart from the heavily pregnant mare, who had to be visited by the local veterinarian, there were horses to be fed and groomed. There were supplies to be purchased. Hay to be stacked. Repairs to be made. Farmhands to be disciplined. Not to mention all the usual wifely chores. She had managed all this before, when Corax was on the road, but she usually had Magnus to assist her, and her husband's absences were never particularly long. To be deprived of both men at once, and possibly for months, was infuriating.

"He said to tell you that he understands how disappointed you will be," Melussa assured her. "He said he wishes a lot of things did not have to be the way they are. He admitted that Magnus was initially to make the journey alone – that they had planned it that way, and not mentioned it to you because there was no need to – but with so little time available he saw that he would need to go as well. And he pointed out that Alector of Arcadia is bringing the rest of the horses from Syria."

*And what*, Xenia wondered, *is that meant to prove?*

She brooded on the matter until frustration overwhelmed her. "All men are dwarves in Rome," Magnus was fond of saying – an expression of his own yearning to return to the great metropolis. But Xenia too had yearnings. She too had lingering dreams. And she too enjoyed the prospect of putting everything – all her silly doubts and regrets – into perspective.

An eerie mist had settled over Tarraco when she informed the farmhands of her decision. She appointed toothless Atticus, so old that he had served drinks to Marcus Agrippa, to manage the estate in her absence. Then she filled her purse, packed a satchel with her necessities, and marched down to the port, seeking a captain willing to brave the November elements. She reckoned she had just enough time to get to the Circus Maximus in time for the races.

I have no way of knowing how much the possibility of meeting Alector influenced these deliberations, but again Selene was in no doubt:

"It was my father's spirit, I am sure of it, that hailed her across the sea."

232

# XII

QUINTUS CRETICUS TENAX, the vulpine horse breeder who had disguised Incitatus for my father, lived on a sprawling estate west of Massilia in southern Gaul. During the Julian Civil War, Massilia had allied itself with Pompey the Great and as a consequence had been punished by Julius Caesar, who moved the region's seat of power to the newly founded city of Forum Julii. The great general had also stripped bare the forests around the town, in order to supply timber for forts and bridges, so that parts of the surrounding countryside, once fragrant with pine-scent, became rain-sodden wastelands pitted with gnarly roots and tree stumps. Most of Tenax's estate had been that way when he acquired it, and only years of dedicated toil had turned the ruined fields into viable pastureland. From here he continued to supply horses to the Green Faction in eastern Gaul and Italy, and he still visited the Circus Maximus at least twice a year.

Tenax was "in bed with one of my slave girls" (he revelled in such ribald details) when he heard much muttering from the vestibulum. Assuming that it was his chamberlain Philocles speaking in the sort of shrill whisper he "always suspected was meant to wake me up", he pretended not to notice for a while, but when the exchange went on and on, sounding increasingly urgent, his curiosity got the better of him. Wrapping himself in a cloak and collecting a lantern, he bustled through the house to find Philocles at the door arguing with a man who looked like a soldier.

"What's this racket about?" he demanded, making sure he sounded annoyed.

Philocles was clearly pleased to relinquish responsibility. "This gentleman is requesting assistance, master, but I've already told him our villa is not some kind of rest station."

To which the man at the door said, "And I have already explained that I am here on a special mission and plan to tarry here not a moment longer than necessary."

"Oh?" Hoisting the lantern, Tenax found the man to be barrel-chested and strangely familiar. "You are a legionary, are you not?"

"I could be."

"You *could* be?" Tenax repeated, frowning. "You must understand, sir, that we need to be very discriminating here – we cannot offer lodgings to just anyone who shows his face."

"May I speak to you in private?"

"Why? Philocles's ears are my ears."

"Then I must mention the name of Lucius Cornelius Picus. And a stallion by the name of Hirnius."

Tenax was chilled. Hirnius was the trace horse he had disguised as Incitatus to fool Caligula. But only a handful of men knew that, and all of them were highly placed in the Greens. ("I should have recognised him right then and there," Tenax told me later, "because Corax was among that group.")

"Give me a few moments," he muttered hoarsely, and hastened back into the house to change.

Properly dressed, he joined the barrel-chested man, who guided him down the pebbled path.

"Do you mind extinguishing that light?" the visitor asked – it was a windy night and the flame was guttering. "We can be seen here from the high road, can we not?"

"Of course." Tenax sent Philocles back inside with the lantern. "Where exactly are you taking me?"

"Our horses are hidden among those trees."

"Horses?"

"Two stallions we have brought from Spain."

"All the way from Spain?"

"We have dodged Roman patrols. We have fled bandits. We have raced across bridges and forded rivers. We have been attacked by a bear."

"A bear?"

"We are unharmed but one of the stallions requires attention. He was clawed on the croup. Here they are now."

Amid a clump of windblown trees stood two shifting horses and a half-sized man wearing a headband over his ears.

"Greetings," Tenax said to the dwarf. "You too are with the Greens?"

"I am," said the little fellow.

"And you are seeking refuge for these horses?"

"For a day or two, yes. Then we must be on our way."

"To where?"

"To Rome."

"To Rome?" Tenax looked back at the barrel-chested man. "You are taking these horses all the way to Rome?"

"To the Circus Maximus – to race there."

"Then these are chariot horses? Belonging to the Green Faction?"

"They are."

"And Picus knows they are here?"

"He knows they are on their way," replied the barrel-chested man. "And he would do anything to ensure they are safe and well-tended."

"This way, then." Tenax was eager to get out of the wind and cold. "We shall get your beasts groomed and refreshed."

He directed the men to the empty stables and called for Philocles to return with the lantern.

"You are lucky," he observed. "Most of my horses have been requisitioned by the local legions. I could protest, of course, but it would do little good. Have you heard what is going on in Gaul and Italy?"

"It's one of the reasons we are traveling in disguise," replied the barrel-chested man.

"You don't say?" Tenax surveyed him more closely in the lantern light. "You know, if you don't mind my saying, I'm sure I have seen you before. Were you once a charioteer?"

"A long time ago."

"You raced in the Circus Maximus?"

"I might have."

"For the Greens?"

"For a few years, yes."

"Ah." There was something about the man's physical bearing, not to mention his manner – the terse way he spoke, the steely set of his face – that ignited a memory. "You are Corax, are you not? Corax of Campania? Who was once betrayed by Aulus Vitellius and the Blues?"

The man did not look pleased to be reminded. "A long time ago."

"Ah, so you are Corax!" said Tenax, oddly thrilled. "Hero of the Circus Maximus! My word – how did you know I was here?"

"When I was exiled, many years ago, Picus told me exactly where to find you should I require assistance."

"But I don't recall your ever calling upon me."

"Because I did not wish to put you in any danger," Corax said. "I beg your forgiveness, in fact, if I have put you in danger now."

"Nonsense, you are a free citizen now, are you not? And a famous horse breeder?"

"A freedman and a horse breeder, certainly."

"Well, your stallions must be special indeed, if the breeder himself is delivering them to Rome."

"One of them is, to be sure."

Tenax was about to go on, but then the lantern flame flashed across the left side of that special horse. And he happened to notice the scars. And his throat locked. He looked closer. And he saw something only he – the man who had disguised horses all his life – would notice at first glance. This horse had been masked. Indeed, the very invocation of the name Hirnius seemed a way of confirming it. And then, when he made out the stallion's milky right eye, everything became clear. He looked back at Corax, gasping.

"This horse . . ." he said, awed. "This horse . . ."

Corax nodded. "You are right," he confirmed. "He is."

# XIII

THE CAMPAIGN OF GENERAL MARCUS ANTONIUS PRIMUS that autumn has been covered extensively by historians more inclined to military matters than I, but I feel duty bound to recount some of its details before Primus reappears later in this chronicle.

Primus was the commander of the Flavian legions marching on Rome in the name of the rival emperor Vespasian. Fearless and charismatic, renowned for his good looks, outstanding oratory and preternatural luck, he was also indirectly responsible for what was, for the citizens of Cremona especially, one of the most tragic misinterpretations in history.

Cremona, three hundred and fifty miles north of Rome, had for seven months been the base of military operations for Caecina Alienus, the preening general whose battlefield victories in April had paved the way for Vitellius's own advance on the capital. Six months later it remained so vital that when Primus crossed the Julian Alps, taking Aquileia, Patavium and Ateste in quick succession, he knew he could not proceed further without first taking this city. He could not pass around it. He had to conquer it. And this was where his luck proved so consequential.

On the twenty-seventh day of October, he was scouting a few miles from Cremona when an advance force of Vitellian soldiers marched out to confront him. Though significantly outnumbered and inclined to retreat, the Flavian cavalry found itself unable to flee owing to the collapse of a bridge at its rear. So the cornered legionaries had no option but to fight, and to fight for their lives – none more inspiringly than Primus himself.

Then, when the Vitellians fell back, Primus summoned reinforcements and pressed on, engaging the full might of the enemy outside the city itself. The battle waged on through the night, with both armies appearing at times to have the upper hand, until three fresh strokes of luck tipped the balance in Primus's favour. The first was when the clouds dispersed in the eastern sky, leaving the Vitellians starkly illuminated by moonlight while the Flavians were concealed amid flaring shadows. The second came at sunrise, when the Flavians turned to salute the rising sun – a custom they had acquired in Syria – causing the Vitellians to panic and flee, mistakenly believing that enemy reinforcements had arrived. And the third came during the siege of Cremona itself, when the Vitellians, having run out of ammunition for their giant ballista, tipped the whole weapon down onto the heads of their opponents, only to breach the city walls in the process.

The Flavians flooded in and Cremona was seized. Forty thousand men had died in one night but the spoils of victory were theirs. Primus was nonetheless determined to be merciful and magnanimous. He knew that many of his troops had earlier in the year been humiliated by Caecina Alienus and would be itching for revenge. He therefore delivered a carefully calibrated speech celebrating their valour while exhorting them to remember who they were – Roman soldiers, paragons of nobility and discipline. Then he went to a commandeered villa to prepare for a triumphal parade.

But the troops, many of them indeed ravenous for payback, wondered if he had spoken out of formality, or even sarcastically.

And when Caecina Alienus came out of hiding, strutting around the city ramparts as though Cremona were still under his command, their fury spilled over. They hastened to Primus to ascertain his true intentions.

Now it so happened that at that very moment Primus was lowering his aching limbs into a bath. But the fires of the boiler had sputtered out and the water was freezing cold. So he cried out at the top of his lungs, "By Jupiter, let's heat things up around here!"

The arriving soldiers, many of them bearing flaming torches, needed no further encouragement.

By nightfall Cremona was a raging furnace.

By morning it was a smouldering, corpse-littered ruin.

This was the fire-scorched funnel through which Corax, Magnus and Andraemon would need to pass if they were to make it to Rome.

# XIV

Tenax's home was lavishly decorated with murals and mosaics featuring the legendary Greens victories: chariot teams in full flight, charioteers brandishing golden crowns, horses parading with the plumes of triumph. And while most of these works depicted products of his own stud farm, Tenax told Corax that he was planning to make a rare exception for Andraemon: a life-size statue – he had already purchased a slab of Lunense marble – to be sculpted and installed, once the stallion was retired or deceased, on a pedestal in his newly extended peristylium. "For such is my admiration," he said, "for a horse I dearly wish I had bred and trained myself.

"But I must be honest with you," he went on soberly. The three men were reposing near the murmuring fountains of the atrium, bathed in ripples of reflected sunlight. "A few weeks ago, Flavian legions loyal to the rival emperor Vespasian crossed into Italy under the command of a general named Antonius Primus. Virtually the whole of Venetia and Transpedana are said to be in flames."

"We can cross that bridge when we come to it," said Corax.

"Aye," returned Tenax, "but you might not even come to it. Another general loyal to Vespasian, this one called Paulinus, has

241

already conquered most of the towns in your path and is marshalling forces to merge with those of Primus. This is the very reason you have encountered such suspicion throughout Narbonensis."

"If Paulinus has declared for Vespasian," Magnus interjected, "then he is clearly no friend of Vitellius, and he would welcome the idea of the emperor being defeated in the Circus Maximus."

Tenax shook his head. "Paulinus is a practical man, with little interest in chariot races, and he would welcome your horses all right – into his cavalry. He is currently based at Forum Julii, the next major city on your route, and you would be lucky to get past him with a fairground pony, let alone a champion chariot horse."

"What about a ship, then?" Corax asked. "There are plenty of vessels in the harbour at Massilia, are there not?"

"Most have been seized by Paulinus in preparation for a naval attack. His men would scarcely allow you to put out to sea, in any event, unless you were on a secret mission."

"We *are* on a secret mission."

"Then your vessel would no doubt be boarded by Vitellius's navy well before you reached Rome. The invasion of Italy has raised this conflict to a whole new level."

Corax, lips compressed, considered in silence for a minute. "Then here's what we shall do," he decided finally. "Magnus will continue along the coastal road with Tuscus, pretending to transport supplies for the rebels. That should get him some distance into Italy, I assume?"

"What sort of supplies do you have in mind?"

"High-quality feed for the cavalry horses. Emetics and salves for the use of the veterinarians. Being in short supply, such items would raise few suspicions if searched."

"Perhaps," Tenax said doubtfully, "but what about you? What about Andraemon?"

"I shall be taking a different route entirely."

242

"You mean to go by sea? But I have already told you of the risks of travelling on a boat."

"I do not mean the sea."

"Then what other route is there?"

But Magnus, responding to the steely expression on Corax's face, was already chuckling. "By Hercules," he said, "he means the Alps."

"*What?*" Tenax said, looking back. "You mean to go across the Alps?"

"I do."

"With a chariot horse?"

"Hannibal did it," Corax noted, "with elephants."

"With elephants, aye, but not horses."

"With numerous horses – Numidians at that."

"But not delicate ones . . ."

"Andraemon is not so delicate, as he has already proved."

"With a goat . . ."

"Who will be in his element among the peaks."

"There will be scant fodder for the horse . . ."

"Andraemon thrives on scant fodder."

"There will be scant fodder for *you* . . ."

"I can take provisions in saddlebags."

"There will be bandits, driven into the mountains by Roman patrols . . ."

"We have already had our mettle tested by bandits."

"There will be much snow . . . snow on the passes."

"Not much if I move quickly. Hannibal crossed in the same season, or even later, if I am not mistaken." Corax stiffened, indicating that the argument was over. "Do you know of a guide who can lead me into the foothills, and set me on the quickest path?"

"I believe I know a trustworthy man."

"Then I thank you for your hospitality and promise that your efforts will not go unmentioned in Rome."

Corax was already on his feet, and Tenax was startled. "You are leaving already?"

"I must feed the horses, dress their wounds and freshen Andraemon's disguise. Crossing the Alps will add days to my journey, if not more."

"But really," protested Tenax, looking at Magnus and back again, "can you not stay long enough to enjoy a feast? Some wine? A slave girl? I am eager for good gossip, you know – for any sort of gossip at all."

Corax shook his head firmly. "No, I shall depart at dusk, or even earlier, if you can fetch that guide."

Tenax thought about it and laughed. "Well," he said, clapping his hands on his knees, "I can't imagine why I'm surprised. The charioteer spirit never really dies, does it?" He thrust himself to his feet. "All right, I shall send for that guide at once. And then sacrifice a calf – no, a whole bull – to Mithras, to ensure you make it safely through to Rome."

Tenax – who "could not work out why Corax looked so displeased at the mention of the charioteer spirit" – told me later that he had no confidence that the two men would succeed, and had only refrained from further protest because he could see there was little point. Considering "the inevitability of their failure", his only real consolation was that he could "finally go about getting the statue of Andraemon fitted into the peristylium, which was in dire need of decoration".

There were fourteen days to the races in the Circus Maximus.

# XV

WHEN THE *CONCORDIA*, battered and tattered and taking on water, floundered into the main harbour at the Piraeus, Alector's first priorities were to get the horses disembarked before setting about finding new passage to Rome. Accordingly, he was waiting impatiently with Selene in the hold – more oppressive than ever owing to the huge volumes of dung and vomit that the beasts had purged during the storm – when a salty shipping agent forced his way down the ramp.

"Poseidon's soggy arse," the man exclaimed, spotting the three horses. "Are these what I think they are?"

"And who are you," demanded Alector, "to be asking such questions?"

"I am Oxylos, Cornelius Picus's representative in the Piraeus."

"Excellent – then you will secure us passage on a new ship?"

"It is not as easy as that, my chariot racing friend. You are Alector of Arcadia?"

"I am."

"And these horses belong to the Andraemon Team?"

"The one sniffing at you now is Olympius himself."

245

"Then I am honoured to be sniffed by you, Olympius, though I take no interest in horses. My only task is to make sure that you are out of here as quickly and quietly as possible."

"Out of here? To where?"

"Just stay on board. Under no circumstances disembark until you see me again."

"Wait a minute," said Alector, taking the man by the arm. "Are you saying we are *expected*?"

Oxylos, prying the fingers free, nodded sternly. "Aye, and by all the wrong people." Then he was off.

"Father," Selene asked, "are we in danger here?"

"Keep your voice down."

They watched apprehensively as the other beasts – the whole growling, purring lot of them – were driven up the ramp. At one stage Oxylos poked his head in again, prompting Alector to renew his demand for an explanation.

"Just stay there," hissed the shipping agent, closing the hatch.

Meanwhile, the rowers dexterously pulled the ship away from the wharf, so that Alector and Selene wondered if they were already slipping out of harbour. There followed much shifting, swinging, creaking, many shouts, a thumping sound against the hull, and the only illumination – faint sunlight seeping between the cracks and grilles – disappeared entirely. The horses whinnied.

"Do you still have your blade on you?" Alector asked.

"Why, Father – do you think the horses are about to be attacked?"

"Not while I am still here. Not while I am here, I tell you." But Alector was fumbling nervously at the hilt of his own dagger.

Finally, the hatch burst open and Oxylos, sweating and panting, returned to the hold. "Very well – let's move your horses up the ramp."

"Are we safe now?"

"Not until we get out of here and maybe not then."

"Where are we?"

"In one of Picus's ship sheds."

"In the Piraeus?"

"Where else? Just get the horses on deck and then down the gangplank. We need to hit the road at once."

It took several minutes to work the horses into the darkness of the shed, which was like a massive timber basilica in which two great freighters, one of them in dry dock, were roosting for winter. On both sides, freshly sawn logs and planks of timber were stacked to the rafters.

"Picus ordered his agents in the ports to be on the lookout for you and your horses," Oxylos explained. "The emperor has assassins waiting for you."

"Assassins? Here?"

"Why do you think I had to take charge?"

"How do I know *you're* not an assassin?" Alector asked.

"Don't be a pelican. Are the horses disguised? Picus assured us they would be disguised."

"We had no time to disguise them."

"Then did anyone aboard recognise them?"

"I doubt it."

Selene felt obliged to interject. "We don't know, in truth – they might have."

"Hephaestus's hairless balls," Oxylos cursed. "We had better move like lightning, my friend, for words fly like swallows around here."

They entered a yard piled high with crates, fragrant timbers and shipping equipment. Here they hitched the horses to a dray loaded with empty flagons.

Oxylos jerked a thumb. "Who is this sprite, by the way?"

"She's my daughter."

"Is she good with horses?"

"There is none better."

"Then tell her to make them act like real dray horses."

247

"Two of them are yoke horses," Alector said, "and I can ride Olympius."

"I'll ride him," Oxylos said. "You get on that cart and tug your hood over your face. Let's go."

After bidding farewell to Sippas, who had been paid handsomely for his cooperation, the three riders made their way past warehouses and shipping offices and launched into a warren of streets. The setting sun was casting peach and purple hues across the rain-slicked brothels and watering holes. From the distance came the music of harps and sea shanties. It seemed innocuous enough, but all were tensed constantly for an ambush. Nevertheless, they made it as far as the crumbling city walls before a soldier wobbled out from the back door of a taverna.

"Hey!"

They whirled around.

The soldier, unsteady on his feet, wilted under their glares. "I . . . I was going to ask if you had wine in those flagons."

"Pickled squid," said Oxylos, "like you, my friend. And not for sale."

Then they were through the Aphrodisian Gate, climbing the statue-flanked path and wending into the dusk.

"Where are we going?" asked Alector.

"To the home of Chloros," answered Oxylos, "a wealthy merchant's son in Athens."

"Athens?"

"You will be safe there. And keep your voice down."

There were thirteen days to the races in the Circus Maximus.

# XVI

I N ROME, MEANWHILE, WITH NO AVAILABLE INTELLIGENCE about
the location of the Andraemon Team – not even from Albus
of the Esquiline – my father was spending most of his time
pacing around the Via Latina estate waiting for Corax and
Alector to arrive. It would not be accurate to suggest that he was
enervated by worry, since he derived great succour from being
at the heart of the crisis, nor that he refrained from leaving the
estate when strictly necessary, such as when he decided to make
a direct appeal to his old nemesis Rutilius Oceanus – the sort of
approach that, in better years, would have been an unthinkable
humiliation.

The meeting took place during the feasts that accompanied the
opening of the Plebeian Games: one in the Forum Magnum for the
plebs themselves, who owing to food shortages were fighting over
scraps like starving dogs; and one high on the Capitoline, where the
consuls, senators, equites, and Games administrators were gorging
themselves on thrush tongues, bearded mullets, fattened snails,
spiced mussels, ostrich brains, sea urchins and Pontic nuts (to say
nothing of a "Trojan Hog" which, when cut open, released forty
flapping finches).

Here, sitting primly under a blue-striped awning in the shadow of the great bronze quadriga, was little sun-wizened Rutilius Oceanus, revelling in what must have been for him a singular moment indeed. His faction had never been as powerful. His opposition had never been so weak. He had under his command the finest charioteers, the fastest horses, the most bounteous treasury, and – whether they were genuine or not – the most strident and numerous supporters. It was every *dominus factionis*'s dream.

All of which must have made it double annoying, and yet strangely delightful, when we – my father, Gryphus and myself – sidled up to him, in search of a quiet word, just as he was enjoying a syrup-coated pastry.

"Well, well, well," he said, dabbing his fingers in a bowl, "if it isn't Lucius Cornelius Picus, his loyal hound Gryphus and – who's that? – yes, his scribbling son Noctua. I should have known you lot might appear sooner or later, begging for mercy."

"We are in fact invited guests at this banquet," wheezed my father, "lest you did not notice."

"As it happens, I did *not* notice," Oceanus returned, sniggering. "Where pray tell have they got you sitting? On the Tarpeian Rock?"

"Not far off, if truth be told. And that is exactly why we have come to speak to you."

The Blues *dominus* was already shaking his head. "Do not expect to hear any pity from me, Picus. The Greens have wallowed in the grace of emperors for as long as I can remember."

"Not all of them. Tiberius and Claudius, for instance—"

"Then did you ever see me, or anyone associated with me, come to you in those days, begging for favours?"

"Come now, Oceanus, you must admit that—"

"Did Caligula not poison my horses? Did Nero not poach my charioteers?"

"Perhaps, but—"

"Perhaps! Let me tell you, Picus, I was *there*. I saw those horses *dying*. I watched my best charioteers – lads I'd recruited personally – prodded to your stables at the tip of a spear."

"*Possibly*," said my father, frustrated, "but all that had nothing to do with us."

"Nothing to do with you? Really? Then did you protest even once? Did you ever try to talk your imperial patrons out of it? Of course not. Because you were reaping the benefits with a grin, I dare you to deny it!"

My father heaved a sigh. "Oceanus, Oceanus, I bow my head in shame, and grovel to you for forgiveness, but I ask you now, when you forage about in that capacious memory of yours, to recall that no emperor has sought to annihilate an entire faction."

"You exaggerate, Picus, as you are wont to do."

"You *do* know that our best charioteer, Delphinius of Doriscus, was very close to being murdered last week?"

"That, as you are fond of saying, had nothing to do with us."

"Then how is it that you are aware of the incident at all, since we have mentioned it to no one?"

"How do I know?" said Oceanus, laughing. "Because Albus of the Esquiline told me – how else?"

My father nodded resignedly; he should have guessed. "Then perhaps Albus also informed you what the assassin was shouting when she attacked?"

"The Blues are not responsible for all who use their exhortations."

"What about your imperial patron, then?"

"What about him? If he's truly trying to exterminate your faction, as you presumptuously suggest, then he's not doing much of a job, is he? You are still here, are you not?"

"Barely, as you admitted yourself."

"You are still racing in the Games?"

"We are struggling to put together our teams."

251

"But you *have* teams. You exist. And that means the Circus will decide your fate, not I."

"The Circus, yes." My father leaned on his cane. "The Circus is everything – it decides all our fates. But there must be limits. There must always be limits. This murderous campaign against the Greens, for instance – it is not good for chariot racing, it is not good for the emperor, and it is certainly not good for Rome."

"For Rome!"

"Look down there at the Forum – they are tearing each other apart for mutton bones. They are biting each other like rats. And soon the Flavian legions will be at the Apennine passes. The conditions could hardly be more volatile. And you and I, as leaders of the two greatest chariot racing factions, are duty bound to avert a catastrophe."

"A catastrophe we are averting now, is it? The triumph of the Blues is a catastrophe?" Oceanus chortled wickedly. "But of course – that's always how it is when the Greens suffer a setback, isn't it? It's a scandal. It's a calamity. It's the end of the world! How intolerable is a little adversity to those who always get their way!"

My father was pained. "Come now, Oceanus, you *know* I am not blinkered by partisan issues. You *know* I can lose graciously. And you *know* that we have worked together in the past. Remember when I rescued your lads from Tiberius? And that business with Fabricius and his hounds?"

The latter referred to an incident, not thirteen years earlier, when Aulus Fabricius, magistrate of the Apollinarian Games, had refused to meet the financial demands of the factions and threatened to race chariots drawn by dogs instead. The Reds and Whites had surrendered meekly, but the Greens and Blues had stood firm, mutually defiant, and Nero himself had been forced to negotiate a compromise.

Oceanus shrugged. "That was in *both* our interests."

"*As this is now*," insisted my father. "As it is now. For what good can come of adding to the current unrest? Do the Blues not need the Greens just as much as the Greens need the Blues? Does the existence of the hawk not make the eagle soar higher? And are you really telling me you have no pity at all, in that formidable heart of yours, for a colleague who sees his life's work draining away before his eyes?"

For a moment it looked as though Oceanus might be relenting. And it was not as though he was a spiteful man, arrogant with power, and unfeeling to the plight of others. But then – you could see it in his little marmot eyes – he must have remembered how good it felt, at seventy years of age, finally to have the patronage of the Dominus of Rome. And how satisfying it must have been, to see his greatest rival resorting to all sorts of hyperbole to save his skin.

"Be off with you," he said, surrendering to some delicious disdain. "And let us sort it out in the arena, as real men do. If Jupiter – or Mithras, or Venus, or whomever it is you Greens worship down there – sees fit, then you will pull through. Do not blaspheme the gods by implying we are bigger than they, and dare not speak of the emperor so seditiously again. I shall not repeat what you have said to me today, I promise you that much, but there are sharper ears in Rome than mine. And let me tell you something else," Oceanus added maliciously, "straight off the grapevine. Did you know that that our noble emperor has recently added a *pedibus ad quadrigam* to the end of the card? That's right – just like the old days. A final race between the two best performed teams of the two best performed factions. A race that will decide the overall winner in the event of a draw. Think about *that* for a change, my civic-minded friend. Because to this point a deciding race has involved no other faction than the Blues and the Greens. And I would hate to see a great tradition dishonoured by circumstances."

It was cruel taunt and my father seemed momentarily disconcerted, possibly remembering a certain *pedibus ad quadrigam* from the past. "Very well, Oceanus," he said, stepping back, "then I shall bother you no more on the matter. But I sincerely hope you come to your senses before it is too late. And I ask you to remember, as you go about testing the waters of imperial patronage, that maiden voyages can be fraught with choppy waters and unexpected consequences."

"I've been around too long now," Oceanus assured him with a sneer, "to be surprised by anything, dear Picus – even tactless analogies from the likes of you."

When we returned to our table it was difficult not to conclude that our faction was at its lowest-ever ebb. Our best horses had been poisoned. Some of our finest charioteers had been poached or killed. Our finances were at the point of bankruptcy. Our major rival was openly mocking us. And we still had no idea as to the progress, or lack thereof, of Corax and Alector. All we could rely on were the revolutionary hooped wheel and the unquestioning loyalty of Delphinius of Doriscus.

But even the latter assumption, alas, was to prove a grave miscalculation.

# XVII

I T WAS THE FIRST TIME SELENE HAD BEEN TO GREECE, birthplace of the gods, and she found herself vaguely disappointed by the crumbling statues, dilapidated temples and weed-infested public spaces.* Alector on the other hand seemed both invigorated – to be back in the land where he was a panhellic hero – and on edge, no doubt remembering the powerful enemies whose thirst for revenge had compelled him to flee.

"Who is this Chloros?" he asked, as they passed through a deserted grove. "I don't believe I've heard of him."

"Worry not," replied the shipping agent Oxylos, "for he has heard of you. His late father so adored the Greens, in fact, that he named his sons after their greatest charioteers."

"His father?"

"A man called Lagos, a famous timber merchant in these parts."

"A friend of Picus?"

"Everyone in Greece who owns a tree is a friend of Picus – but especially Lagos."

---

* Much of Greece and fallen into neglect under Roman occupation.

They reached Athens just as the crescent moon erupted from clouds and bathed the temples and agoras in silvery luminescence. Even the columns of the Parthenon were limned with bluish light. Swinging east around the Acropolis, Oxylos guided them up the pine-covered slopes of Mount Lycabettus and down a series of twisting paths to a fortress-like mansion perched on a limestone ridge overlooking the city.

"Rest here a moment," said Oxylos, "while I announce your arrival."

Alector and Selene waited dutifully on the cart, glared at by a burly doorman, for what seemed an aeon.

"Should we be worried, Father?" Selene whispered.

"Prepare yourself for anything."

But the portly, salmon-pink and shaven-headed Chloros, when he appeared, could scarcely have been merrier or more accommodating.

"So this is the famous Alector of Arcadia!" he boomed, swooping down from the portico with outstretched arms. "My father would envy this day! And these are the horses of the Andraemon Team? Including the mighty Olympus? Discovered by my father himself? What a privilege this is!" He spent some time admiring the horses, patting and stroking their hides, before summoning a slave. "Have them led to the stables and nourished with the finest oats. And you, Alector, and you, young lady, come with me into my humble abode."

Alector and Selene were hungry for replenishment but the heavily scented Chloros, after seeing off the worthy Oxylos, seemed more interested in showing off his mansion: first the upper floors, which like my father's house were furnished with precious and well-polished woods, and then the vaults, where a profusion of life-size statues were clustered together like prisoners in a stockade. Some of these pieces were by famous sculptors, including Callimachus and Praxiteles, and most seemed to depict heroic Greens charioteers of various eras. But Chloros was eager to point out one recent acquisition in particular.

"Recognise him?"

"I think," said Alector, "I'm not sure . . ."

"But it's *you,* my friend!"

"Me?"

"Sculpted by Apollonius himself!"

Alector squinted. "But it doesn't look like me!"

Chloros laughed. "Not as handsome, you think? Not as charming? And yet innumerable women, and not a few men, had offered to purchase it, and some have even tried to steal it, merely to have your likeness in their bed chamber!"

If Alector had any doubts as to Chloros's authenticity, they dissolved at that moment. "Is that why you keep it here in the cellar?"

"I have hidden all the statues here ever since the Sublime Nero began seizing our most exquisite pieces. He would undoubtedly have taken this one, too, had I not hidden it before he visited."

"The emperor Nero himself was here?"

"In this very house. And yet we forgive him all his faults, all his rapacity, for his generosity here was of a species we have never before encountered from Rome."

Such was the popularity of "the Liberator" in Greece, in fact, that scores of shrines had been erected in his honour, and thousands of men had shaved their heads as a sign of respect when he died. "We fear," Chloros went on, "that he was assassinated – yes, we call it an assassination here – exactly because he was so beneficent to us in Greece, and that the new emperor Vitellius, should he get his way, will tyrannise us again with tariffs and taxes. That is why it is so urgent to us that he is defeated everywhere, including the Circus Maximus."

But Chloros – one of those heirs whose formidable inheritances encourage an interest in Epicureanism – showed no signs of urgency. He insisted that Alector join him at a banquet where a succession of young men, most of them similarly bald, rode in almost continuously from across Athens, having dropped everything when they heard that Alector of Arcadia and the great Olympius had arrived in the metropolis. The feast, which consisted of roasted pheasant, cuttlefish and delicious cheeses, then transformed into a symposium during which the men – most of whom fancied themselves as philosophers of various schools – waxed rhetorical about the ethics of organised contest, the human appetite for tension and conquest, the logic of courting death for monetary or spiritual reward, and the corrupting "martial spirit" of Rome. Someone recited a panegyric in honour of Hercules, said to be the first chari-oteer; there was a poem about King Oenomaus's legendary chariot race against Pelops; and – though Alector would not understand its full significance until later – an intriguing debate about the integrity of the sibylline prophecies. Listening to all this from the gynae-ceum,* Selene, recognising that the Greeks, like her father, were fond of dwelling on ancient glories, became so frustrated that she ventured to the door and beckoned impatiently.

"What's the matter?" whispered Alector, coming over. "Is some-thing wrong with the horses?"

"They are as fine as they can be, Father, but don't you think we should be on our way?"

"I've not yet discussed the situation with the men."

"If you leave it to them, the races will be over before they finish philosophising about them."

Unable to disagree, Alector returned to the chamber and demanded to know how the men were planning to get the three horses to Rome. Chloros insisted that everything was under control.

"There is no need for the slightest concern," he said. "In the coming days we shall escort you to Patrae, and from there you will board a ship bound for Sipontum."

---

* The women's room.

"Patrae?"

"We have good contacts there."

"But Patrae is a Roman port – with agents perhaps of Vitellius?"

"Imperial agents will be at all ports by now, but we can elude them easily enough at Patrae. For that matter, you are very much in the favour of the deities – though I am reluctant to say too much – so it seems unlikely you are in genuine danger. And while in the Peloponnese, you really must visit Olympia, where Lycomedes of Miletus won all the major chariot races this year – you will meet him, and he will be delighted to meet you."

Alector did not say it, but he had no desire to meet Lycomedes of Miletus or anyone else. Nor did he understand the reference to the deities, though he liked to think he was always favoured by the gods. And he was especially alarmed by the prospect of stopping at Patrae, because it was from there that he had fled the wrath of the vengeful Theodoros.

So, while he not admitting anything – and having signalled to Selene that he would not be shifting just yet – he made his decision even as he reeled out his thoughts on *thumos* and *hedonism,* on good strife and bad strife, on the philosophies of Plato, and in turn endured increasingly drunken interpretations from the younger guests. Meanwhile, while only pretending to sip from his own goblet, he proposed toast after toast and called repeatedly for more wine. But it was not until well into the morning – the bow-shaped moon, which had begun the night framed in an eastern window, now ornamented one in the west – that he was confident the others were sufficiently inebriated. Wasting not another moment, he picked his way across the chamber – half the men were asleep – and convened with his daughter in the courtyard.

"Get the horses ready," he told her.

"Are we leaving, Father?"

"As soon as I am sure the coast is clear." A steward and a couple of slaves were staring at them.

"Where are we heading, then?" she asked. "Back to the Piraeus?"

"North," replied Alector. "We're going north. We can make our own way to Rome."

"By going across land?"

"Why not? The ports are dangerous, did you not hear?"

Selene was sceptical but held her tongue. ("It was one of one my father's many endearing failings," she told me later, "that, as it was with money, so it was with distances – he seemed to think the whole world was the size of Campania, and had little grasp of the time necessary to travel from one place to another.")

With twelve days left to the races in the Circus Maximus, they escaped into the dawn.

# XVIII

A FTER CORAX DEPARTED FROM MAGNUS, and later from his Alpine guide, he rode Andraemon through gloomy gorges, alongside surging rivers, across pine-clad foothills and under drizzles of autumn leaves. Cupido was all the time racing ahead, presumptuously choosing paths and by sheer exuberance encouraging the others to follow. Their pace at this stage was brisk but steady, Corax halting now and then to massage the stallion's joints, lance his abscesses, reapply his leg bindings and handfeed him with poplar leaves and pine nuts wherever there was inadequate pasture. Keenly aware that the most taxing part of the journey lay still ahead, he was determined to keep the horse prepared for future ordeals.

As they climbed higher the pinewoods started to thin, their breath started to mist, and they glimpsed majestic peaks mantled with snow. But for three days they encountered no other humans apart from some weary Roman roadbuilders finishing up for the season. When he joined these men for a meal of roasted venison, and one of them noted his goat's resemblance to Cupido, Corax played innocent.

"Cupido?"

"The goat companion of Andraemon? You follow chariot racing, do you not?"

"Of course I know of Cupido," said Corax. "He's the most famous goat in the empire."

"Well, then, do you not think that your goat looks like him? The same stunted left horn? The same cleft ear?"

"He's darker than Cupido," decided another roadbuilder, squinting.

"Darker, aye," said the first, "but otherwise identical."

One of the others took an even closer look. "He *does* look like Cupido!" he said. "Like Cupido smeared with ash!"

Corax, taking inspiration from Magnus's audacity at the tavern, forced out a lie. "I see you men are not easily fooled," he managed. "And yes indeed, my goat in his natural state looks exactly like Cupido – so much so that I could no longer abide the constant comparisons. So I've taken to dyeing him repeatedly, simply to ward off the comments in advance. Even so, he's compared to Cupido almost as often as my half-blind horse here is likened to Andraemon."

The roadbuilders laughed, evidently satisfied, and got back to their venison. Corax, begging leave by virtue of his pressing itinerary, thanked them for their hospitality and promptly departed with his "lookalike" horse and goat.

A day later, he came across one of the precarious makeshift bridges the work gang had warned him about. A collapsed ledge in a limestone cliff face had been replaced by thirty cubits of splintering planks and frayed ropes. But while Cupido raced ahead without incident, Andraemon refused to take another step. Corax tried everything but the horse would not budge. Exasperated for a moment – he dreaded the prospect of wasting time, perhaps days, seeking a new path – he finally accepted that the horse would never be so stubborn, to the point of ignoring the lead of his beloved friend the goat, without excellent reason. So he coaxed Cupido back across the rickety bridge and turned them both in the direction whence they had come.

It was not long afterwards that they encountered a merchant guiding three donkeys laden with jingling merchandise – the first person they had encountered since the roadbuilders.

"The bridge ahead is unsafe," Corax told the man.

The merchant, gnarled as tree root, squinted sceptically. "Fallen away?"

"Not yet. But it will."

The merchant grunted and started to lead his donkeys past.

"I tell you," Corax said firmly, "the bridge ahead is unsafe."

"From around here, are you?"

"I am not."

"Then wind your neck in. I have been through here many times and suffered no ill."

"I warn you—"

"Let me past, you fool."

The merchant and his donkeys forced their way through, nudging Corax and Andraemon so close to the edge that they almost spilled over.

Corax considered following the man, and rescuing him if necessary, but decided he could not spare the time. He was moreover impressed by the fellow's aggressive confidence, which made him question Andraemon's wisdom. But he did not dwell on it.

The shadows were all-consuming when they reached the floor of the gorge. They picked their way along the edge of the stream and sometimes through the water itself. At dusk they reached the chasm under the rope bridge, whereupon Corax took in a sobering sight.

The baggage train of donkeys lay dead on the ground. Silver trinkets and cooking implements were scattered everywhere. The merchant himself, a strap of his satchel having snagged on a branch, was hanging upside down in an ash tree. Corax climbed up to shake the boughs, prompting a rain of amber leaves, but the man was definitely dead.

Corax buried the body under stones near the riverside. Then he collected the merchant's victuals, fed both himself and the horse, and in the morning resumed his journey, wondering how Andraemon might next prove his worth.

Two days later, as it happened, an intense blizzard swooped upon them from all sides as they were negotiating a precipitous mountain path. Snow filled their eyes, thunder rattled their teeth, and ice pellets the size of pullet-eggs thrashed at their skin. Corax's clothes were very quickly caked in ice, his beard was stiff with icicles, his teeth were chattering like clackers, and his fingers, even under lambswool wrappings, were swelling to the size of parsnips.

In the middle of all – the thunder, the howling wind, the pelting sleet – he heard what sounded like a horn blaring in the distance. Recognising what must be some sort of signal from the locals, he assumed for a moment that they, too, must have been in distress, before it occurred to him that such men do not get lost in their own dominion, that by their standards this storm was nothing unfamiliar, and they were very probably setting him up for an ambush.

He mounted Andraemon, took a grip on the ice-encrusted reins, and stared into the snow ahead and behind.

There was a tremendous crashing sound and out of the whiteness a huge boulder came slamming onto the path ahead and went bouncing off into the ravine. Then another boulder. A cascade of rocks. And lumps of displaced ice.

Corax understood immediately. He was being attacked, just as Hannibal's army had been, with a manmade avalanche.

But he could not retreat because the horns were sounding loudest from that direction; nor could he remain in place because the stones would inevitably start falling his way. So, with Cupido already far out of sight, he snapped the horse's reins and dug in his heels.

Andraemon, with an urgent whinny, galloped fearlessly and unhesitatingly along the ledge. Weaving between ice and tumbling stones. Hurtling through snowdrifts. Bounding over mounds of rock debris. Outrunning, finally, the avalanche. And through it all Corax marvelled afresh – that a Numidian stallion raised in Spain could respond to such wintry conditions as though having spent his whole life in the snow.

But soon the blizzard became so devouring that Corax lost all sense of perspective. He could no longer hear the bandits but neither could he see anything ahead. Fearing he might plunge over a cliff at any moment he was about to draw on the reins when Andraemon, of his own volition, dug in his hooves and shuddered to a halt. And Corax, his body already tilted forward, lost his grip. He speared over the horse's head. He sailed into the void.

He had the most incongruous notion – even as he was bracing for impact – that everything would work out well. And then his head hit a rock and his consciousness was snuffed out like a candle.

There were ten days to the races in the Circus Maximus.

# XIX

ALECTOR AND SELENE RODE THE REFRESHED STALLIONS through the morning to Oropus, where they stocked up on provisions before continuing to Tanagra and beyond. But Chloros's slaves had been protesting vigorously when they departed – one of the stable boys had even tried to prevent them from reclaiming the horses – so they could not be sure they had made it away without complication. As to where exactly they were heading, "my father," Selene admitted later, "seemed not entirely sure."

"Apparently the legions in Illyricum have declared for Vespasian," he told her. "That means we should be able to link up with the soldiers and join them on the march to Rome."

"But can we really make it in time to the Circus, Father, if we go by the route you are suggesting?"

"How long to the first race?"

"A week and a half, I think."

"Then we can get there if we don't delay."

"Are you certain of that, Father?"

"I steered a ship safely through a storm, did I not?"

"You did that, certainly."

"And Picus himself called me the fastest rider he had ever seen, did he not?"

"I remember."

"Then I can get three horses to Rome."

He was nonetheless fixated on the idea that they were being followed – "I have a sense for such things" – and determined to avoid all the major towns. But again and again this led them into sun-bleached wilderness where they had no idea where they were going, and repeatedly they had to return, humbled, to the rutted highways, bowing their heads and quickening their pace whenever approached from the opposite direction. And while Alector claimed to know these roads well, having crisscrossed the peninsula many times during his years in Greece, there were days, even on the major thoroughfares, where he seemed uncertain what town was next or even which *polis* they were passing through. Neither did it help that there were precious few signposts, milestones or roadside shrines, nor that the villages they passed were often so desolate that farm animals were grazing in the ruins.

"You should ask for directions, Father."

"I've never required directions in my life," he said. "Besides, there's no point advertising our route to assassins."

"Did you not say the assassins would be at the ports?"

"And they might be following us, too. That stable boy at Chloros's place was giving us a queer look when we left."

Selene suspected that he was too proud to admit that he was lost, and her frustration became so great that, when traversing the narrow mountain path where Oedipus had killed his father, she "came close to doing the same". After many hours of trudging across balding hills under a glaring sun, stopping only when earth tremors threatened to hurl them into the ravine, she prevailed upon him to seek assistance.

"Very well," he said. "If you really have such little faith in your father you can ask for directions at the next inn."

It was late in the afternoon when they came to a dingy roadside taverna called the Platanos. A nutbrown man with hair as spiky as porcupine quills was seated under a vine-festooned trellis, nursing a wooden goblet. He watched as Selene dismounted and headed inside looking for someone to consult. But the tables were coated with dust. The kitchen was empty. There was not a soul to be seen. It was only when she came out that he piped up.

"May I be of assistance, young lady?" His voice was as weathered as his skin.

"I'm looking for the owner of this taverna."

"I am the owner."

"Then might you be able to provide a traveller with directions?"

"No one knows these parts better than I do."

Selene glanced at her father, who was standing beside some cypress trees throwing stones at a raven. "We are hoping to reach Illyricum," she said.

"You are many days from Illyricum."

"But are we on the right path?"

"You are not on the wrong path. From where have you come?"

"From Athens via Thebes."

"From Athens, you say?" The man spared a moment to regard Alector and the horses – sizing them up like a butcher surveying livestock – before returning his gaze to Selene. "Then you should turn right at the next fork in the road. Otherwise, you will only end up in Delphi. By nightfall you should reach the district of Chaeronea, where one of the innkeepers will be happy to provide you with further assistance."

Selene relayed this to her father, who proved suspicious. "He looks like a bandit to me."

"He's too old to be a bandit."

"He no doubt has sons," Alector said. "Grandsons, by the look of him."

They nonetheless followed the old man's advice, diverting at the next crossroads, Alector all the time glancing over his shoulder and cursing under his breath. "I still sense danger."

"Do you wish to hide until it is safe?"

"I hope we don't regret this."

"I tell you, I am perfectly willing to hide."

"Keep your voice down."

It was an eerie twilight when they entered the outskirts of a lonely village flanked by reddish cliffs. But there was nothing to be seen but ruins and olive trees. The temples had collapsed. The public buildings were filled with grass and stagnant puddles. An owl's hoot echoed off shattered walls.

"I see no inns or taverns," Alector whispered. "I see no residents at all."

"This might not be Chaeronea yet, Father."

"It might be a trap, too. I told you I had my suspicions."

"What do you want to do?"

"We have to go on through, I suppose – it's too late to change direction now."

But when they rounded the corner, passing under a crumbling arch, they found the path hindered by a wall of fallen blocks. Alector dismounted for closer inspection. The road was completely impassable. A serpent coiled across ruptured flagstones. Alector was returning to the horses when they heard distant hoofbeats. Selene swung around.

Dark-robed riders were visible, approaching from the south. She gasped.

"Get off your horse!" ordered Alector, gesturing.

They hauled the three horses into a half-collapsed public building.

"Take them into the dark!" Alector hissed. The moonlight was just powerful enough to cast shadows. Selene dragged Olympius, Pertinax and Postumus deeper into the ruins. Her father was flattened against the wall, drawing his dagger. ("I have never been so scared in all my life," she admitted later.)

As the riders drew up, the hoofbeats grew louder – thunderous, ridiculously loud. The walls were shaking. The ground itself was trembling. And Selene belatedly understood. ("It wasn't just the sound of the riders. It was an earthquake – in the very middle of the attack!")

The wall beside her was bulging, about to collapse. Her father, no stranger to earth tremors from his days in Campania, sprang to his feet and dragged her away just as the blocks crashed around them. ("He saved my life.")

But now they had no option but to flee. The ground was shifting, pillars were toppling, dust was blooming, the horses were shifting and snorting.

"This way!" cried Alector, drawing the stallions though a narrow opening. The path was dark and riddled with debris. They crunched across stones, bounced off walls and burst through veils of dust, glimpsing hooded riders to the left and right.

Alector pointed south. They squirmed down another debris-cluttered lane, heading for the highroad. The flagstones were still separating but the tremor was petering out. They heard voices, scuffling sounds, shifting horses. Selene's heart was crashing around her chest. Alector gripped his blade, coiled for action.

"In here!" he whispered. They headed towards what looked like an empty agora but were not halfway there when two riders skidded to a halt in front of them. Alector and Selene wheeled around and raced back. But suddenly a hooded figure appeared in the open ruins too. They were trapped. They had to fight their way out. And Alector, summoning all his redoubtable courage, launched himself forward, shrieking in fury, raising his dagger and preparing to descend on the stranger – to stab him through the heart. But the stranger threw back his hood.

"No, my friend!" he cried. "It is us! Your escort!"

Alector stuttered to a halt. He surveyed the young man, speechless, then heard an irritatingly familiar voice from behind.

"Praise be to Hermes!" the fellow boomed. "We have found you at last!"

His blade frozen, Alector turned to find a bald-headed figure beaming down at him from horseback.

"Truly you must be adored by the gods! Many times we thought we had lost you, but now the very earth shifts to contain you!"

Alector lowered his dagger – "more dismayed than relieved" – as the grinning Chloros turned his attention to Selene.

"And you, dear girl, come forth with those precious stallions! Allow us to lead you all in safety to Delphi, where we can rest our weary limbs, drink from the Castalian Spring, and philosophise over fine wine and ewe's cheese!"

There were nine days to the races in the Circus Maximus.

# XX

NEARLY EVERY CHARIOTEER I HAVE KNOWN has been prone to some character weakness, be it insecurity, envy, resentment, suspicion, obsession or morbidity. It is difficult to imagine how a man could survive in the sport without one major flaw. But Delphinius of Doriscus might be unique in that he happily admitted, in his retirement at least, to have been a victim of all six – insecurity most of all. At the time of which I write, he was not yet a *milliarius*, a great deal of his wins had been at the reins of the Andraemon Team and, though his victory tally far outstripped that achieved by the likes of Corax and Alector, he still felt curiously inferior to the great charioteers of previous generations and continually embarrassed about his pampered past.

On the evening of the tenth day of November – I hereon rely on Delphinius's own self-effacing account – he was escorted to his villa from the Via Latina estate in a covered coach flanked by four hired guards. Since the attempt on his life, nine days earlier, he had been leaving home only to train with the Zephyrus Team, the horses he was scheduled to drive should the Andraemon Team fail to arrive. For security reasons there were no windows in the coach, no apertures at all, and Delphinius travelled in a heightened state of tension. The new guards were all charmless ex-gladiators – Crixus, the one who had saved him from the homicidal masseuse, had been laid low with a mysterious stomach ailment – and when the coach continued trundling down the street long after it should have drawn to a halt, he experienced a mounting sense of alarm. He took hold of the latch, and was about to sneak a look outside, when the vehicle jolted to a halt and the door cracked open. He recoiled, half-expecting an assassin to burst in with a drawn sword, but it was only one of the gladiators.

"Charioteer," the man said gruffly. "You're expected."

Stepping warily down from the coach, Delphinius found himself facing an opulent villa surrounded by building materials. And he did not need to be told where he was. He had witnessed the progress of the renovations from his own windows. He had even spotted the villa's owner standing on its balconies stuffing himself with sweetmeats. But as to what he might be doing here now he could not imagine. To be disposed of in the emperor's ancestral home would make all other racing scandals, including the one involving Corax and Alector, pale into insignificance. Nevertheless, it could scarcely be ruled out.

With a sense of fatalism, therefore, he followed a chamberlain up the stairs to an ivy-festooned chamber where Vitellius was conferring with a number of well-known chariot racing figures. Apart from little Rutilius Oceanus, *dominus factionis* of the Blues, these included the new charioteer recruits Leonides of Byzantium from the Whites, Cancer of Apulia from the Reds, and Delphinius's former stablemates Calliopus of Cappadocia and Crescens of Crete. All of them looked up self-consciously as Delphinius stepped tentatively into the room and the chamberlain dissolved into the darkness. A florid and sweat-soaked emperor welcomed him expansively.

"Delphinius of Doriscus! Step forward, young man, step forward – we've just been chatting about you. Would you care for some snails? Raisin pies? Falernian wine?"

"That won't be necessary," Delphinius told the emperor, dry-mouthed. "Though of course I am grateful for the offer, Caesar."

"I am not a Caesar."

"Then I thank you . . . Your Majesty."

"You do not have to thank anyone. But you must be ravenous, surely? You are still recovering from a scandalous attempt on your life, I hear?"

"The . . . assailant met a proper end."

"I am delighted to hear it," said Vitellius. "Damn gambling interests – they're ruining our sport, don't you agree?"

"If you say so, Your Majesty."

The emperor arched a bushy eyebrow. "You *do* accept that gambling interests were responsible, I hope? I know there are some wild rumours in circulation . . ."

Delphinius wondered why the emperor seemed to be inviting suspicion. "One hears many rumours in Rome," he said. "Only fowl-pluckers and singing girls believe them all."

Vitellius, who was eating honey-coated tarts from a silver plate, turned to the others with an admiring chuckle. "The boy is as diplomatic in the dining room as he is brilliant in the arena." Then, turning back: "You must remember me, Delphinius – from the days before I wore the purple?"

"I remember. You were very prominent in the Blues."

"And I still am. More prominent than ever, in fact. Though I have never been so blinded by my devotion that I cannot admire talent in other colours. And that is exactly why, as soon as I became emperor, I sought out the best charioteers no matter what livery they wore. You recognise these men? Some of them former faction-mates of yours?"

"Naturally." The charioteers were avoiding Delphinius's eyes.

"And Rutilius Oceanus?"

"I have spoken to Oceanus before."

"He tried to lure you to the Blues as soon as you became a freedman, did he not?"

"He did not have the money. Or the horses."

"Of course not. But I am heartened by your response, because you imply that you *would* have been interested, had the Blues the resources."

"I am always willing to consider an offer."

"Then allow me to *make* you an offer, Delphinius – allow me to make you an offer right now. May I do that?"

Delphinius felt queasy. "You may."

The emperor puffed out his chest. "Fifty per cent of your team's winnings – ten per cent more than I have arranged for anyone else here – and an annual stipend of half a million sesterces. A new mansion on the Palatine. The finest facilities in Rome. The best grooms, the most experienced veterinarians, the swiftest chariots. And look at our uniforms, custom-made by our tailors. Stand up, Cancer."

The charioteer known as Cancer, famous for having survived numerous crashes in the Circus, got awkwardly to his feet. He was wearing the traditional piped and padded tunic of the Blues but embroidered now with curious symbols – Delphinius had to squint to make them out.

"Crabs," said Vitellius. "Is not Cancer's emblem the crab? Well, we've had the crab threaded into his uniform. Just as we have had the spearhead woven into the tunic of Crescens and the lion into those of Leonides. And your emblem is the dolphin, yes? Well, we can have the dolphin stitched not just into your robes, but into banners all across Rome. We can have this done within days. You'll be more famous than ever, and more loved than any charioteer in the history of the Circus."

Delphinius knew he should have felt relieved, but in truth he struggled to look flattered. "Your Majesty," he said, "you honour me with such attention. But – I hope you understand – for me there is always more at stake than personal satisfaction."

Vitellius ruminated for a moment. "It's about the horses, is it not?"

"Well . . ."

"You yearn for Andraemon, Olympius, Pertinax and Postumus? You think you cannot win without them?"

"I did not say that . . ."

"No, but many others are saying that. *Many* others. Well, my boy, you have the perfect opportunity to prove them wrong. The Blues are now the only faction with horses capable of winning repeatedly in the Circus Maximus. Fulminatus himself has been reserved for you and you alone, you know."

"Fulminatus?" The emperor spoke of a four-year-old Sicilian trace horse, fresh to Rome, that had been weaned on the succulent fields surrounding Ætna and was said to possess "all the pent-up energy of a rumbling volcano".

"Fulminatus, no less. Named by veteran track watchers as the best chariot horse since Andraemon – better, in fact, by virtue of his youth and inexhaustible energy."

Delphinius was silent and Vitellius read his thoughts.

"Ah, you think that Andraemon himself has inexhaustible energy? Regardless of his age? Well, even if that is so, what does it matter in the end? You can't seriously believe you will ever see that horse – or the rest of the team – racing again in green?"

Delphinius, not blind to the implications, thought it best to remain silent. Vitellius smiled with apparent sympathy.

"Step this way, my boy, step this way."

Limping like a charioteer, the emperor guided Delphinius towards the garden. "I know how difficult it must be for you," he said, still nibbling on his tart. "You need time to think things over before you can cut your ties with those people, exacting masters though they are, and indifferent to your talents as they seem to be. But there is no reason for a moment's vacillation. I promise that you will nowhere find a more welcoming environment than under my patronage. Ask my troops from Germania – they loved me like an uncle. But there is more to it than that. When I took up the burden of power in Rome there had been nothing but chaos for over a year. So it was imperative that I give the people something to rally around, a force that resonated with imperial power. I chose to make the Blues my symbol – just as yours is the dolphin – and to assert my authority through chariot wheels. I imagined there would be few objections to that, considering the alternative, so you must understand how disappointed I was when some people – your faction in particular – seemed intent on thwarting my ambitions? For no good reason at all? And why I had to authorise certain actions I had hoped would not be necessary – for the good of Rome?" They had reached the arbour. "But I promise that I will apply no such pressure on you. I do not want you feeling the slightest unease with your decision, whatever it might be. And yet, I am convinced that you, Delphinius of Doriscus, the greatest charioteer in Rome, will not allow sentiment to cloud your better judgement. You will not let your emperor – your new *uncle* – down. Yes, of that I am completely certain."

Delphinius nodded, strangely intoxicated by the dilemma. He remembered for some reason the Greens' rally cry, *Fortius quo fidelius* – "Strength through loyalty". But also Alector's insistence that a ruthless commitment to winning superseded all else. And all his fellow charioteers who had recently come to sticky ends. Then he took one last glance into the villa – the others were chatting together stiffly – before turning back and asking in a whisper, "How long do I have?"

"To make up your mind?" Vitellius seemed disappointed, or just plain incredulous, as he released the charioteer from his sweaty embrace. "As long as it takes to be crucified," he said, plucking another pastry from the silver plate.

# XXI

Magnus did not believe in romantic love, or the after-life, or contemplating the stars, or sniffing a rose, or anything beyond filling his gut when he was hungry and calling upon a whore when he was lustful. What he did believe in was seeing things through, committing himself wholly to the task, working single-mindedly towards an end, and celebrating afterwards with as much wine as possible. And he was committed, above all else, to his best friend Corax. The Raven could be curt at times, he was as humourless as a stone, and would not countenance even the thought of getting drunk. But he had still done more for Magnus – rescuing his pride, smoothing his edges, drawing out his strengths – than any man alive.

All of which accounted for Magnus's palpable anxiety when the two of them parted a few miles east of Tenax's estate. They had agreed to rendezvous eight days hence, at the Mausoleum of Cyrax of Dertona – a monument in northern Italy well-known to charioteers – but the possibility that Corax, now in a sheepskin cloak and woollen trousers, could in the meantime negotiate the icy slopes, perilous paths, dilapidated bridges and bandit-infested passes of the Alps without injury, delay or death seemed to Magnus distressingly slim. Nor was it just for Corax that he despaired, for he had helped train Andraemon and felt a near-equal amount of affection for the horse. To see the two of them head off towards the peaks seemed tantamount to a final farewell, and it increased his sense of urgency to make it to the mausoleum well in advance, even if that proved a pointless achievement.

So he raced his horse and cart at a pitiless pace down the Via Julia Augusta. The road, which in many places was just ten years old, was paved sometimes with flagstones, sometimes wood, sometimes silex, sometimes gravel, and sometimes nothing at all. It swept through coastal villages, across sturdy bridges, past busy harbours and spume-flecked lighthouses, under a multitude of arches and along ridges suspended precariously between mountain and sea. Occasionally Magnus encountered legionaries or officials, but he always deployed his convivial mien to great effect, sometimes breezing past without raising a single eyebrow.

But outside Forum Julii there was a huge smoky barracks filled with ill-tempered soldiers preparing for battle. Wearing the aspect of a man on a mission, Magnus made it past the first checkpoint without incident, then through a knot of grim-faced troops, and he had the open road in sight – prematurely believing he had made it – when he was called to a halt by an officious quartermaster. Briefly entertaining the prospect of a mad dash for freedom, he at the last moment saw a column marching down the slope towards him. He reined his horses.

"Greetings, sir!" he exclaimed. "A splendid day, is it not?"

The quartermaster, who had a stylus lodged behind his ear, seemed in no mood for pleasantries. "And who might you be, that you are racing through here at such an ungodly speed?"

"My name is Flavius," replied Magnus, employing the family name of Vespasian. "And I am on my way to support the fighting legions in northern Italy."

"Support?" said the quartermaster. "How?"

"I've already explained this to the guard at the—"

"Explain it to me."

Magnus maintained his smile. "I have with me important supplies for the rebel cavalry regiments – articles which might prove crucial to the success of the whole campaign."

"And what could you possibly be carrying that would be useful to the cavalry at Cremona?"

Others were gathering now, attracted by the tenor of the exchange, and Magnus decided to confront the suspicions head on. "I trust you don't take me for a spy, sir? Because nothing could be further from the truth, as I've already explained to—"

"I have no idea who you are," spat the quartermaster, "but you still have not answered my question."

Magnus nodded. "I carry food and medicine for the horses – drenches, emetics and so on, all part of an urgent relief package thrown together by the veterinarians of Fifteenth Primigenia."

"Fifteenth Primigenia? Last I heard they were high in Germania."

"They have marched south, in anticipation of battle."

"And their veterinarians took it upon themselves to prepare this miraculous consignment?"

"They were determined to help the cause – as am I, in delivering it."

"You are a courier of the *cursus publicus*?"

"Merely a humble stablehand."

"Then why did they not send someone more capable, if the supplies are so important?"

"But I am very capable, sir. Not only am I to deliver the medicines but administer them as well. I know exactly how to mix and measure the potions, being the next best thing to a *veterinarius* myself."

"Is that a fact?" said the quartermaster. "Well, what if I retain you and your potions here? We've many sick horses of our own, some with colic and mud fever. Others will soon be injured, too, for we shall soon be in battle ourselves."

"And I'd be delighted to return here and assist, sir, as soon as my mission at the frontline is complete."

"This stallion, for that matter," noted the quartermaster, raising Tuscus's head, "looks too well-bred to be drawing hay carts."

"An old chariot horse, it's true, which is exactly why he was appointed to this mission."

"Old, you say?" The quartermaster was examining Tuscus's teeth. "He looks no older than eight."

"Old as in 'veteran of the circus,' I mean. Worn down by years of racing in Spain."

"Oh?" The quartermaster looked unimpressed. "What is the matter with you, stablehand? You carry no permits, you seek no rest, and you refuse even to change horses. Why should I believe that you are *not* some sort of spy?"

Magnus, still smiling, saw that he was beaten. Nor could he flee without having soldiers descend on him from all sides. So the best thing, he decided, was to cooperate gracefully, even eagerly, and then wait for the first opportunity to escape. It might take days, assuming there was any opportunity at all, but it was his only hope.

"You are right, sir," he said, "I can hardly deny that this might look unusual – I've thought as much myself. So I shall do gladly as you say. After all, my first priority has always been to assist the rebellion." He saluted for good measure. "Hail Antonius Primus! Hail Vespasian!"

In the end it took Magnus three exasperating days of toiling in the stables before a sympathetic centurion, recognising him from the Circus Maximus, engineered a distraction that enabled him to flee. Spurring Tuscus's flanks, he raced into the night and galloped without pause through Antipolis, Nicaea, Portus Herculis Monoeci and deep into northern Italy. By the time he reached Aquae Statiella, it was two days since he had left Forum Julii and eight days since he had parted from Corax. Exhausted, starving and foaming with sweat, horse and rider limped up the highway and collapsed beside the Mausoleum of Cyrax of Dertona.

It was there, on the grassy verge, stretching his stumpy legs and congratulating himself for making it on time, that he heard a stern voice from behind.

"Rest among the trees, if you really need to rest."

Magnus swung around, scarcely believing his eyes. For there in the gloom, sporting a massive lump on his forehead, was a windblown and haggard Corax, along with a patched-together Andraemon and a bedraggled Cupido.

There were six days to the races in the Circus Maximus.

# XXII

I N ROME, I JOINED MY FATHER AND GRYPHUS for the track inspection
of the Circus Maximus, a ritual that dated back to the days
when the arena was unshielded by grandstands and newly
laid sand was prone to blow away in the first significant breeze.
So, while surveying the track was not without a purpose, to do
so now, almost a week before the races – when the interim would
see the surface churned by numerous violent spectacles – made the
process seem even more ceremonial than usual.

As it happened, my father, shuffling and muttering under his
breath, was far too distracted to do any examining at all. Though
fully prepared to endure some favourable treatment for the Blues,
the obsequious deference now meted out to that faction by the
Circus curators – who were chatting to Rutilius Oceanus and his
retinue as if no one else existed – was proving hard to tolerate.
Moreover, while it was traditional for the Greens and Blues to lead
the inspection side by side, the Blues had now seized the vanguard
and were giving no indication they were willing to share it. And
then there were the Whites, who were making taunting comments
without having the good manners to explain themselves.

"Pity about Delphinius . . ."

"Shame about Delphinius . . ."

"Hope you can find a new Delphinius . . ."

My father turned to Gryphus. "What on earth are they talking about? Has some grief come to Delphinius?"

"Not that I know of," said Gryphus, blanching.

"Not that you know of? When did you last see him?"

"Two days ago, at training."

"Two days – ye gods! He could have been attacked again!"

"I'm sure someone would have told me."

"Do you still have his villa guarded?"

"Day and night."

"By reliable guards?"

"They were protecting me, before I transferred them to Delphinius."

My father scoffed. "The guards were unworthy of you but good enough for our most valuable charioteer, is that it?"

"No, I only mean to say that—"

"And you cannot be certain that Delphinius has not been murdered? Or had his arms broken?"

"I am as certain as certain can be," managed Gryphus, his face beaded with sweat.

"In the name of all that is sacred," breathed my father, "you had better hope that you are right, Gryphus. We have no idea where the Andraemon Team is, the decoy horse fooled no one, and now we are not even sure if Delphinius is still alive. If ever there was time for welcome news it is now, and yet all you offer me is ignorance and confusion."

Gryphus, who had spent so many years fielding my father's tirades that "his ears were calloused", was formulating a suitable response when members of the Red Faction sidled up – eager, it seemed, to talk.

"Such a beautiful day," said Decimus Maccius Pullus, the faction's *dominus*, "and yet so many clouds stain in the sky." Pullus came from a distinguished family of poets and was prone to speaking in tortured metaphors. "May we babble together for a while, dear Picus?"

"You may babble," said my father, who generally found Pullus insufferable.

"It's just that I would very much like to wave before you a dish that I have been preparing, in the hope that you find some of its aromas enticing."

"Wave away," said my father, sceptical as usual.

"Please do not misunderstand me," added Pullus, chuckling. "You know my main priority is the Circus. I love this place as other men love their wives. Indeed, I believe there is no man alive whose devotion to chariot racing is as consummate as my own."

"Your devotion has long been noted."

"You can surely appreciate therefore how unsettled I might be, as *dominus* of the Reds, to see the very foundations of the Circus undermined in such an ignoble way? Now it is true that none of our faction's horses have been poisoned and only two of our charioteers have been poached, but that is not to say that we do not share your alarm at the carnage that is being inflicted on the sport. For it seems to us that the Greens are not mere leaves on the tree – they are the very earth from which it sprouts."

My father was growing impatient. "You said you had a dish for me?"

"Indeed, I do, and I shall taunt you no longer. For it is merely this." Pullus shot me a suspicious glance and lowered his voice. "I wish to offer you the full resources of the Reds, dear Picus – in secret, naturally. And this means that we are prepared to collaborate with you not only on race day, as we do by custom, but *before* the races as well, in preparation and training. In fact, I shall go even further. We are prepared to offer you our finest horses and charioteers, simply to improve your chances of scoring some outright victories against the Blues."

My father was incredulous. "You are seriously serving such an offer on that dish of yours, Pullus? While seeking nothing in return?"

"I seek only that you *win*, dear Picus – win as many races as possible. Stave off the total dominance of the Blues. That cannot be allowed to happen. If the emperor gets his way, then his campaign of destruction will rumble on, and sooner or later he will set his sights on the Reds and even the Whites. And before long the whole edifice of the Circus will come crashing down around us."

"Indeed, indeed," said my father, impressed, "I share your sentiments, Pullus, and I am sincerely grateful of the offer. But I must be sure of something."

"By all means."

My father leaned in. "This is not some sort of tactic, I trust? A devious plot, hammered out with imperial agents?"

Pullus pressed his hand on his chest. "I swear to Consus that I speak with an undivided tongue." He looked genuinely hurt. "And allow me to add something else, to sweeten the dish further. For, as you know, I occasionally break bread with Vibius Cassus" – this being the *dominus* of the Whites – "and I can tell you now, off the record and notwithstanding the taunts you have heard from his men today, that he too is deeply concerned, and might secretly be willing to offer his resources to you as well, to the point of passing on intimate intelligence about the Blues."

My father glanced over his shoulder. "Vibius Cassus coming to the aid of the Greens? Now that I find hard to believe."

"And yet I assure you it is true," insisted Pullus. "For he also sees cracks opening in the pillars of the Circus, and he too is ready to do whatever he can to prevent a catastrophe."

My father decided that Vibius Cassus was indeed looking unusually subdued. He grunted with satisfaction. "Then I thank you, dear Pullus, with all my heart, and I am happy to take you at your word. I would be delighted to send around my people – my son Noctua here, for instance – to field your intelligence first-hand. And, as for your charioteers, would you have any objections if I met with them tomorrow in the Mithraeum under the Circus Maximus?"

"That is exactly what I was about to suggest."

"Excellent." My father felt relieved, most unexpectedly, of a great burden. "Well then, while the circumstances dictate that I cannot make a show of my gratitude, you may rest assured that the Greens are enormously grateful for your cooperation. There may still be clouds in that sky of yours, but there are surely a few rays of sunshine as well."

And truly, my father felt immensely warmed by the gesture, furnishing as it did a glimmer of hope in the midst of crisis, and reminding him that there were men, even in the cutthroat industry of chariot racing, who were not motivated entirely by self-interest.

"Oh, one other thing," he added, before Pullus could turn away. "You mentioned Vibius Cassus's men, and the taunts they have been directing at us today."

"I did."

"Well, do you happen to know what they mean? The taunts?"

Pullus seemed startled. "Do you mean to say," he whispered, looking left and right, "that you really have not heard?"

"Heard what?"

"About Delphinius of Doriscus?"

My father frowned. "What about him?"

Pullus, pale as a corpse, moistened his lips. "Then it gives me no pleasure to inform you," he said gravely, "that Delphinius of Doriscus has defected to the Blues. He is in the Circus Vaticanus right now, trialling the Fulminatus Team in the arena."

# XXIII

CONSIDERING CORAX'S TACITURN NATURE, in particular in relation to his own achievements, it seems remarkable that Magnus managed to draw from him as much about his Alpine journey as he did. In fact, Corax was initially more interested in Magnus's story, especially where it related to the condition and performance of Tuscus, and when he got around to divulging particulars of his own ordeal it seemed more in admiration of Andraemon than anything he personally had accomplished. "The horse performed magnificently," he enthused again and again, with a trainer's fatherly pride. Not only had the stallion saved his life, by refusing to cross the ill-fated bridge, but his later halt – the one that had sent him spearing into a rock – was nothing short of a life-saving manoeuvre. "He sensed that we were heading for a cliff and swerved just in time to toss me to safety. He even kissed me awake with his feathery lips, bringing me back to consciousness none the worse for wear but for this small lump on my head."

The lump, Magnus told me later, was "as big as quail's egg".

They rested a single night and were away before dawn, plying the Via Aemilia with the intention of crossing the Apennines via one of the less-frequented passes. But their attempts to rejoin the main highways were repeatedly thwarted by marching soldiers and military encampments.

"Are these legions fighting for Vitellius or Vespasian?" Magnus wondered.

"They are legions, at any rate," observed Corax. "Perhaps they will keep assassins at bay."

"And perhaps they will assassinate us themselves."

"You might be right. It would be best, I suppose, to avoid the main roads for now."

Shortly afterwards they were negotiating a narrow donkey track, with thick forest on one side and undulating cliff-face on the other, when Cupido, trotting ahead, started kicking his hind legs in the air.

"What's the matter with that damnable critter?" Magnus asked.

"I think he is working the cold out of his limbs."

"Or perhaps living up to his name. I noticed some nanny goats back there."

"It's late in the breeding season for goats."

"Not late enough."

Magnus, alone among those from the stud farm, had no love of Cupido. Prior to becoming a charioteer, part of his novelty act had been to engage ornery goats in "gladiatorial bouts", during which he had been gored too many times to count.

"The beast might still be recognised," he grumbled. "He might give the whole game away."

"I think we are safe enough on this lonely trail."

"It is precisely because it's a lonely trail that we are in added danger."

"You complain too much."

"I'm a jubilator, remember? It's my duty to issue warnings."

"It's your duty to issue encouragement."

"Very well," laughed Magnus, "then I encourage you to be aware of the dangers."

In the end, Corax seemed to concede the point, for he cantered ahead and scooped up the goat.

It was when he was remounting, the beast squirming in his arms, that Magnus – still behind, on Tuscus – heard, for the second time in two weeks, a whistling sound from over his shoulder. Then another whistle. A loud *thunk*. A shaft vibrating in the tree trunk next to him. A third shriek and his hair was ruffled.

"Corax!" he exclaimed. "An ambush!"

He dug his heels into Tuscus's flanks as more arrows streaked past him. He overtook his friend, who had just settled onto Andraemon, and the two of them galloped wildly up the path. Two swarthy riders had fallen in behind.

"They're gaining on us!" Magnus cried.

They continued at a furious pace, bursting out of the forest and racing across a rock-studded landscape. Corax took the lead. And Magnus, though he was urging Tuscus on with all his energy, found himself dropping hopelessly behind. The swarthy men were closing the gap. He feared he would be overtaken at any moment. Then they passed through a half-collapsed palisade.

They had entered a hamlet of huts, crude stone cabins and vegetable patches. Woodsmoke was clouding the air. Glancing behind, Magnus noticed that their pursuers had drawn up. They were refusing to follow them into the hamlet. Corax and Magnus reined their horses.

"Where are we?" Magnus asked. There was a foetid smell in the air.

"Are you well?" Corax said.

"Of course I'm well, but where are we? Why did they stop?"

"Get off your horse."

"What? Why should I do that?"

"Get off, I say – and slowly."

Corax himself was already dismounting. The swarthy men had meanwhile mounted a hillock. And Magnus, easing off his horse, noticed that Tuscus had an arrow protruding from his hindquarters.

"No wonder he slowed!" he exclaimed, surveying the wound.

But Corax was not looking at Tuscus. He was looking at Magnus.

"What's the matter?"

"Stay very still."

It was then that Magnus realised "with more wonder than alarm" that he had an arrow protruding from his own side. It was just above the pelvis and buried deep.

Corax, bent over with his fingers poised over the shaft, looked reluctant to touch it. "Do you feel nothing?"

"I don't know." Staring down at the arrow, Magnus marvelled at his own composure. "I don't know."

"I'll need to draw it out before it does more damage."

"Without so much as a swig of wine?"

"You've suffered much pain in the past."

"Of course I have," said Magnus. "I am a charioteer—"

Corax abruptly seized the arrow and ripped it out. The little man, howling with pain, dropped onto his rump. His head filled with light. And when he opened his eyes again, and wiped away tears, he noticed wraith-like figures in filthy rags emerging from stone huts behind Corax. They were hobbling forward. They had disfigured faces, boil-covered hands and black-furrowed skin.

"Corax—" Magnus breathed, gesturing.

Corax turned as the lepers surrounded him. But he did not move. Only Cupido was running around, still kicking his legs in the air. The swarthy pursuers were shifting around on the hillock. But for a moment, absurdly, it seemed no one would say a word. Then one of the lepers, who had gaping nostrils and ulcerated lips, spat a glob of phlegm at Corax's feet.

"Who are you to trespass here?" he hissed. "What business do you have with us?"

"We wish you no harm."

"Then get out of here – begone!"

"This man is injured."

"That is no business of ours!"

"Yet we cannot leave until we are safe."

"And what makes you think you are safe here?"

"We had no intention of disturbing you," Corax insisted. "We are on our way to Rome. To the Circus Maximus. These are our horses. We are under attack."

Now a woman, wearing a robe of animal skins, broke ranks. "The Circus Maximus?" she asked in a gravelly voice.

Corax turned. "That is correct."

"What is your connection to the Circus?"

"We are breeders and trainers, and once charioteers in Rome."

"Charioteers?" She squinted. "What be your names?"

"My injured friend here is Magnus of Noricum. And I am Corax of Campania."

"Corax of Campania?" The woman lurched forward to examine him more closely. Her one yellow eye, buried in a whorl of skin, raked him up and down. "Corax of the Scars?"

Corax stiffened. "I am."

"Corax who once raced against the ghoul Gaius?"

"The same."

"And who once knew Felix of Dacia?"

"I was honoured to do so."

"Who once, in the middle of a race, stopped to assist Felix when his horses crashed?"

"I believe I did that."

The woman drew back, grunting. "I was his lover, you know – his leper wife."

"Then Felix could not have been so unlucky after all, to have had a wife such as you."

It was the sort of platitude that only a man like Corax, who had never developed any mocking inflections, could have delivered without arousing suspicion.

292

The woman nodded. "Felix always spoke highly of you, Corax of the Scars. He said you and Alector of Arcadia were the greatest charioteers he had ever seen. The greatest of all time, if not for the ghoul Gaius."

"Then I am certain Felix would want you to help us now, when our own luck seems to be in short supply."

Magnus released a groan – the pain was overwhelming – and the woman seemed to arrive at a decision.

"Aye," she said, "show them your scars."

"I beg your pardon?"

"Show my brethren your scars. You seek our help, do you not?"

"I do."

"Then remove your tunic and display your scars."

Corax was discomfited but saw no choice. Very stiffly and reluctantly, then, like a maiden disrobing in front of the emperor, he removed his tunic and wrappings and stood half-naked before his hosts.

The lepers circled him, assessing his suffering. Amid the fresco of scars some of his old wounds had started weeping again, owing to the exertions of the journey, and the lepers made noises of sympathy. Even the man with the missing nose seemed impressed. And Corax, unblinking, unbreathing, endured the inspection wordlessly, stoically, just as he had done many years earlier in front of my father.

("As dizzy as I was," Magnus told me later, "I mustered enough strength to remove my own headband, to expose my missing ears.")

Finally, the woman made a noise of approval. "We shall not hinder you, my brothers, but neither can we attend to your wounds here."

"I understand," replied Corax, quickly redressing. "And yet it would be too dangerous to depart at this moment."

"Those curs are trying to stop you?" asked the woman, indicating the swarthy men.

"They are no friends of ours – nor of the Circus."

"Nor of us," the woman observed, "for they have mocked and belittled us here." She inhaled noisily and turned to the others. "Come, Gryllus and Nasica – in the name of the much-lamented Felix, round up the ponies and bridle them." She turned to Corax. "You have no objections to riding with our kind?"

"We would consider it a privilege."

"A privilege it will be, for no one will attack you when surrounded by the likes of us. We shall get you to the nearest town, my brothers – or at least the vicinity of the nearest town – but from there you are on your own."

"Your assistance," Corax told her, "will never be forgotten."

The woman huffed as a veil of smoke obscured her. "We have no wish to be remembered here."

Magnus told me later, "I wish I could recall more about these remarkable lepers, or indeed the frantic journey from the hamlet to Cremona, but alas, as soon as I tried to rise, I passed out."

There were just five days to the races in the Circus Maximus.

# XXIV

S O BEGINS A CYCLE OF ENCOUNTERS with figures from the past, proving, as my father used to say, that significant deeds in this world do seven laps before the race is over. In the case of Alector, his first unexpected rendezvous came in the port city of Naupaktos, on the north shore of the Gulf of Corinth, where he had allowed Chloros to lead him in the hope of finding safe passage to Rome.

He did so partly because he felt chastened by his failure to find the road to Illyricum but also because Naupaktos was at least not Patrae, where reigned the cuckolded merchant Theodoros (in truth, he could not be certain that Theodoros was still alive, and he had no interest in finding out).

You can imagine his surprise when, waiting with Selene in a briny harbourside shipping office for Chloros's contact to appear, he found an electrifyingly familiar figure erupt from a doorway and bear down upon him like a wild beast. Over twenty years older now, the man had acquired a Zeus-like majesty – enormous shaggy eyebrows and flowing white beard – that was so stupefying that Alector could not find the energy to flee.

But instead of striking him or flinging him against the wall, Theodoros – for that was Chloros's contact – seized Alector by the shoulders and appraised him like a lost son.

"By all the owls in Athens! I see you did not expect me to greet you in such a way!"

"I admit," said Alector, "that I am a trifle surprised."

"That I am not throttling you for what you did to my wife?"

"It crossed my mind."

"Bah." Theodoros made a dismissive gesture. "This matter is far more important than domestic squabbles. Did you know that you are the hero destined to save Greece? That your coming has been foretold?"

"Foretold?"

"In the Sibylline Books, no less!"

"My name has been mentioned by the sibyls?"

"In verses the meaning of which has only recently become clear!"

"What verses?"

"Ha!" laughed Theodorus. "I see you are eager to hear of your role in history! Then come, my friend – destiny tastes so much better on a full stomach!"

After repairing to a banqueting room for yet another Greek feast – oysters, cuttlefish and lamprey, all smothered in garum – Theodoros explained that Nero's abolition of port duties and tariffs meant that merchants like himself had made a small fortune smuggling goods across the Ionian Sea into Italy. It was therefore imperative that Vitellius be usurped before he could overturn these reforms, "and if defeating him in some silly horse races goes some way to achieving this, do you really think I would allow a grievance over a faithless wife stand in my way?"

"You are still married to Lysippe?"

"She was many wives ago – the chamber pot she bought me has lasted longer than her memory. Why? Do you wish to ravish her again?"

296

"I've no time right now," admitted Alector. "Though please tell me more about the prophecies."

"It is true! You have been identified as the one who brings down Vitellius in the name of Greece."

"I have?"

Theodoros looked across the table. "Explain it to him, Chloros."

Chloros smiled in protest. "I have been reluctant to mention it to this point, for fear of misinterpretation."

"Pig droppings," growled Theodoros. "What sort of misinterpretation could there be?"

"Do you not remember Croesus?"*

"But there is no ambiguity in this instance! Tell him!"

Chloros shrugged, dabbed his lips with a napkin and, with a brief show of reluctance, recited the full prophecy. "'*Upon three kings in twelve moons the vengeance of Ares will wreak, / One by sword, one by dagger, and one by rooster's beak.*'"

"Rooster's beak?" repeated Alector.

"Are you not the Greek Rooster?" asked Theodoros.

"Of course."

"Then to whom else can it refer? The rooster will end the reign of the third emperor in one year – Vitellius! And how can we, as mere merchants, argue with the sibyls?"

That very night, Theodoros went on, he was sending a spice ship to Italy with ample space in the hold for three stallions. "As long," he cautioned, "you are willing to risk the November waves? And make land with your horses at a tiny cove?" ("It was something of a challenge," Selene told me later, "but my father, swollen with his newly validated destiny, was not about to shrivel now.")

---

* Croesus, the ill-fated King of Lydia, had famously misinterpreted a prophecy from the Oracle of Delphi: "If Croesus goes to war with the Persians, he will destroy a great empire."

"I've already steered one ship to safety," Alector declared. "And as for the horses, they were transferred to a freighter in the waters off Seleucia, and are more than familiar with such operations." He leaned forward, clearing his throat. "But let me first be certain of one thing . . ."

"Of course."

"These prophecies, these Sibylline Books – there was no mention of a raven's beak, by any chance?"

"A *raven's* beak?" Theodoros glanced at Chloros with a chuckle. "There were no mentions of any ravens at all – why should there be?"

"No reason," said Alector, satisfied.

So it was that, after giving thanks to the magnanimous Theodoros and the equally charitable Chloros, Alector, Selene and the three horses were loaded into the hold of a creaky old vessel, which reeked of cinnamon, and then spirited at full sail across the sea – an uneventful voyage except for the presence of a grizzled old astrologer who refused to confirm or deny any claims about "the rooster's beak", or indeed to read Alector's fortune at all. ("He claimed he was seasick and unable to get a fix on the stars," Selene told me later, "though I wonder now if he saw something that rendered him speechless.")

When they arrived at the wreckage-strewn smuggler's cove just south of Sipontum, they found the waters too choppy to attempt a transfer of the horses. But Alector rowed ashore with a couple of seamen, anyway, and was guided up a series of paths and through the moonlit landscape to the port city, where he had been instructed to make contact with Picus's representative "be it day, night or anywhere in between". Since he had already visited the docks during his forced departure thirty years earlier, he had little trouble locating the portside office – a palace of oak and cypress fronted with gaily painted Corinthian columns – and was duly greeted by Picus's new agent, a man called Labeo, who was massive of head, lips, limbs and girth, and "curiously familiar,"

Alector told Selene, "though at the time I was too distracted to be ask questions."

"Alector of Arcadia!" boomed the agent. "Back after all these years! By all the gods, what an honour it is to assist you in your great journey to Rome!"

Without wasting a moment, the gigantic shipping agent summoned his best stevedores and, after seeing them off by boat, rode with Alector back to the landing site, where the spice ship was nowhere to be seen. Stricken, Alector raced around in a panic, but the agent himself seemed untroubled. "When coastal waters are unsettled like this," he explained, "vessels often retreat to sea until the wind drops." And, sure enough, it was not long before the ship reappeared, to Alector's conspicuous relief.

Now, under the supervision of Selene and the stevedores, the three blindfolded chariot horses were winched onto the skiff, then transferred to the shore, where Selene led them up to the clifftop to be reunited with Alector. It was no insignificant moment – the famous charioteer, after so many years, back on Italian soil with three equally famous stallions.

"It was dawn," Selene said, "and with the sun burnishing his face my father looked illuminated by his own destiny – a conviction that he had been born for this moment."

"Let's be off," he declared, grinning like a dog on a summer's day. And, as the entourage wound through the swaying grass, "What did you say your name was again?"

"Lucius Cornelius Labeo," the agent replied.

"You named yourself after Picus? As I did?"

"I did indeed."

"You were his slave?"

"I was a slave, yes, but not for Picus."

"Then why did you name yourself after him?"

"Because Picus awarded me a great deal of money once, then set me up for life with a job in shipping."

"Oh? And why did he do that?"

Labeo's eyes twinkled. "You really do not recognise me, do you, my friend?"

Alector squinted, trying to get a fix on the man's heavyset features. "You were a gladiator, perhaps?"

"A gladiator and a charioteer."

"A charioteer? But there are only two *essedarii* I knew of: Atlas of Lusitania and—"

"And Taurus of Crete," finished Labeo.

Alector looked at him wide-eyed. And Selene – who had heard all her father's stories – struggled to contain a gasp.

"You mean to say that you are Taurus of Crete?" asked Alector, astonished.

"I am."

"Who challenged me, when I was a mere biga driver, to a quadriga race in the Circus?"

"That was me."

"And who afterwards retired defeated, never to be seen again?"

"Until now, it seems."

Alector thought about it. "So old man Picus – he *paid* you to challenge me?"

"I'm afraid so."

"And you lost that race on purpose?"

Labeo chuckled merrily. "I hope this does not come as a disappointment to you, dear friend."

Alector brooded on the matter for so long that Selene worried that he was devastated. But finally he erupted into laughter, and slapped Labeo on the back like an old chum, and in great spirits they continued with their fearsome new entourage on the long road to Rome.

# XXV

General Marcus Antonius Primus was ten miles from Cremona, preparing his legions to cross the River Po, when an adjutant advised him that a man claiming to be Corax of Campania, the fabled charioteer, had arrived on "an urgent mission". Primus dropped everything and returned to his command tent, just outside the ruined city walls, to confront the fellow personally. (It is to the general's meticulous memory that I owe this account.)

"You say you are Corax of Campania," he said to the barrel-chested man, "and that you have journeyed all the way from Spain?"

"I do," replied the new arrival.

"It is a bold claim."

"It is the truth nonetheless."

"Did you know that I was once a devoted partisan of the Greens? That, on my very first visit to Rome, I was taken to the Circus Maximus to witness Corax of Campania racing alongside Alector of Arcadia?"

"You must have been quite young."

"I believe I was in my seventh or eighth year. But I remember Corax of Campania well enough. And I say that you look nothing like him."

301

"Then I would encourage you to look closer."

"I was close enough the first time," Primus countered. "After the races I was picked out of the crowd to meet the charioteers. I was as close to Corax of Campania as the two of us are now. I was introduced to him personally."

"As Marcus? Or Primus?"

"As Becco, my Gaulish name. I told him I had travelled all the way from Tolosa to be there. And do you know what Corax said in response? He said that—"

"He said that such bravery indicated you would no doubt become a man of great consequence."

Primus was speechless. It was one of his oldest, most cherished memories, but he had mentioned it to no one in years. So how could this man have remembered it, even if he was Corax of Campania? He stepped closer and scrutinised the fellow at arm's length. "By Jove," he whispered, dry-mouthed. "I believe there is a faint resemblance."

"I cannot claim to have avoided the ravages of time."

"And you truly remember me? After thirty years or more?"

"I believe you said you aspired to be a soldier."

"That's right, I did," admitted Primus, shaking his head. "I did indeed. But whatever allows you to recall such details?"

"I raced later at Tolosa and the memory of our meeting was rekindled."

"Well," said Primus, huffing, "that's remarkable. Truly remarkable. You truly *are* Corax of Campania."

"And you truly have become a man of great consequence."

Enervated by the moment's unreality, Primus offered Corax a seat. Corax said he would prefer to stand. Primus slumped into a chair anyway, still marvelling.

"I remember the day as if it were yesterday," he said. "There was some sort of tension between you and Alector, though I was too young at the time to understand it. But I could see, even then, that you were a favourite of the slaves. For your dignity. For the way you went about your business without seeking any sort of attention. And later, when you refused to race around those slaves, and then chose not to relinquish that race against Caligula, that gave the slaves of Rome – all the lower orders – something they would never forget."

Corax nodded. "It is dignity, or something like it, that I hope to restore to Rome right now. But I'm afraid I've not much time."

"Yes, yes" – Primus leaned forward – "you claim to be on an important mission? Please tell me more."

Corax informed the general of Vitellius's plans to destroy the Greens, and the consequent necessity of getting the Andraemon Team to Rome. He mentioned that Alector of Arcadia was heading from Syria with the rest of the horses, adding, "I myself had no intention of stopping here or appealing for your assistance, but my companion on this journey is severely wounded, along with his mount, and I saw no choice."

"Where is he now, your friend?"

"He is being attended to by your physicians."

"I shall make sure he gets the finest treatment. And the horse – is it important?"

"It is a minor trace horse called Tuscus. Nevertheless, I would be very grateful if your men could take care of him as well."

"They will do so; you may count on it. And as for the mighty Andraemon – you have brought him here as well?"

"He is among your cavalry horses."

"And Cupido the goat?"

"Not far away, as always."

"By Jove," said Primus. "This gets more amazing by the minute."

Outside, in the amber sunlight of late afternoon, Primus ordered a stablehand to bring Andraemon out of the corral, whereupon he inspected the horse and marvelled afresh. "He seems in excellent condition, for all the distance he has travelled."

"He is an excellent horse by any measure," Corax said.

"You have stitched his hide together recently?"

"With pack thread, which was all I had available at the time."

"I'll have our veterinarians attend to it at once. And I see you have tried to disguise him at some stage?"

"Alas, most of the dye has washed off."

"We can reapply some powder, too," said Primus. "But you believe that the false emperor Vitellius already knows that he is on his way?"

"His assassins must, since they ambushed us yesterday."

"And if they know where you are now, they will make even more attempts to stop you once you cross the Po."

"It is exactly what I fear."

Primus nodded decisively. "Then we shall do our b-b-best to make sure you get your horse to Rome, Corax of Campania," he said. "Are you ready to leave this evening?"

"I am ready to leave immediately."

"And why does that not s-s-s-surprise me?"

The general told me many years later, "I have no idea if Corax recognised how awed I was at that moment, or how difficult it was for me to contain my boyhood stutter. But I could never have imagined, when still a boy fresh from Gaul, that I would be encountering him again thirty years on, let alone that he would be calling upon me for assistance, let alone that I might be deploying him as a weapon against Vitellius. But now he was my Bellerophon and Andraemon was my Pegasus. I was to dispatch them to Rome in advance of my legions, and I had little doubt that – assuming they got through successfully – they would do as much damage as a thousand battalions.

"Which only made what happened later all the more distressing."

# XXVI

I N ROME, IT WAS THE THIRTEENTH DAY OF NOVEMBER, the Festival of
Jupiter, and the last of the beast hunts was being conducted in
the Circus Maximus. Delphinius of Doriscus, resplendent in a
dark blue tunic embroidered with light blue dolphins, was idling
with other recruits in the starting yard behind the stalls. In truth,
none of them wanted to be there – charioteers usually waited until
the last days of the Games before appearing in the Circus – but
Vitellius had insisted upon a preliminary parade to show off his
prize new acquisitions.

"Did you see him in the pulvinar?" groused Pamphilos of
Pergamum. "Looked like a brothel doorman."

"Made up with all sorts of powders and pastes," added Tatianus
of Galatia.

"He's putting on a show, that's why," grumbled Crescens of
Crete. "Turning the whole thing into a theatrical performance."

"Why not?" laughed Cancer of Apulia. "It *is* a theatrical
performance."

"But is that really what we've come to?" Calliopus of Cappadocia
asked glumly. "Are we actors now, not charioteers?"

It was customary for charioteers to gripe and growl, especially when forced outside their comforting routines, but Delphinius found the current business unusually dispiriting. At the Greens he had been warmed constantly by the raging fires of righteousness. Now, driven to the Blues out of fear for his life, he had only the feeble flames of pragmatism.

"What do you think, Delphinius?"

Prodded out his reflections, Delphinius realised how important it was to show some spirit. He was not, in truth, a natural leader – he preferred to let other charioteers find their own motivations – but clearly he was the most experienced and decorated of those present, and so felt obliged to dredge up something at least halfway positive.

"I think the emperor of Rome has a right to be respected," he said, "whatever he might choose to do."

Though he forced it through gritted teeth, without a scintilla of enthusiasm, he was surprised by the muted response. The others looked dismayed – ashamed of him. They were not even meeting his eyes. But then, very abruptly, Delphinius realised they were in fact looking over his shoulder, focused on someone else entirely. He wheeled around and discovered to his shock that Vitellius, the emperor himself, was standing at the other side of the yard, surveying them archly.

"Your Majesty," Delphinius spluttered. "We were just talking about you . . ."

The emperor stared at him, lips curled, and then, whipping a fly whisk back and forth, strode in. "Never mind the tittle-tattle," he huffed. "Let's get this farce over with."

But the way he moved, the way he spoke, the way he was not flanked by guardsmen, indicated to Delphinius that something was seriously amiss.

"You're not Vitellius . . ." he said.

"And you're not Hercules."

"Where then is the emperor?"

"Does it matter? We all have our roles to play, do we not? Which is your cart?"

"My cart?"

"Your carriage, dear boy – you're to steer me around the track, you know."

"Steer you?"

"In the parade, of course. I'm supposed to stand beside you in your cart." There was a blast of trumpets from the arena. "Come now, young fellow – do you not recognise a cue?"

The charioteers scrambled for their chariots, which were flamboyantly garbed with blue pennants and streamers, and Delphinius, with no time to argue, found himself standing side by side with the grotesquely disguised impersonator.

"Keep your distance from the audience, dear boy, lest they see through this wretched makeup."

The gates sprang open as a crier bellowed from the top of the stands.

"THE CIRCUS IS THE COSMOS AND THE COSMOS IS THE CIRCUS! CHEER NOW THE EMPEROR VITELLIUS WITH THE NEW STARS OF THE PLANETARY ARENA!"

Disconcerted, Delphinius drove his horses through the gates and onto the middle of the blood-soaked track, the portly actor clamping a hand on his shoulder.

"Slow down, lad – I've not been paid for stunts, you know."

"WELCOME DELPHINIUS OF DORISCUS! FAVOURED BY JUPITER! BELOVED BY VENUS! THE ENVY OF APOLLO! THE THUMPING HEART OF MARS!"

The applause, though suitably unrestrained from the Blues fans, seemed to Delphinius curiously desultory otherwise, as if the crowd were mocking him. He looked up, reflexively seeking out support from the Greens' seats, only to find seventy rows of faces glaring down at him pitilessly. Even old Erasinus, the faction's most loyal acolyte – a man who once claimed he loved Delphinius "more than a son" – was staring venomously. Delphinius tore his eyes away.

"Remember thou art only a man," the actor muttered unhelpfully.

But as they rounded the turning posts Delphinius reminded himself that he had no reason to be ashamed. Charioteers switched colours all the time; it was almost *expected* of them. Pompeius of Syracuse and Caramallus of Bruttium, the greatest charioteers of their day, had driven for nearly all the factions at one time or another. Corax of Campania, for that matter, had worn both green and blue. So why should he, Delphinius the Great – needing just a hundred and ninety-two more victories to have his name chiselled into the Wall of the Milliarii – commit himself to a lost cause? Why should he carry upon his shoulders – broad as they were – the hopes of an entire faction? It was too much to ask, as any impartial observer would surely agree.

Fortified, he allowed his eyes to creep back to the stands, this time into the Blues' benches. But even the response here, though wildly enthusiastic, seemed to bear a curious edge of rebuke. So Delphinius urged his horses on, over the blood and entrails, eager to get off the track and out of sight.

Outside the Triumphal Gate, however, waiting for them eagerly, was a group of racing fans – the usual mix of dying slaves, disabled war veterans and starstruck children. Most seemed to be seeking a quiet moment with Delphinius, who had been given a clutch of Blues figurines to hand out as mementoes. But at the end of the line was a blind boy who had come all the way from Venetia to meet him. When his turn came, the boy lunged forward and hugged his hero around the waist, sightless eyes spilling over with tears.

"Win for me, Delphinius! Win for the Greens!"

Delphinius, holding the last of the figurines, looked guiltily at the boy's father, not knowing what to say.

The father shook his head. "Never did I imagine the day would come," he whispered bitterly, "when I would be pleased the boy is blind."

# XXVII

WITH THE RACES OF THE PLEBEIAN GAMES just days away, the real Emperor Vitellius had yet to receive any intelligence on the progress of the Andraemon Team. If his calculations were correct, both Corax and Alector should by now have reached the shores of Italy. But there was nothing from the ports. Nothing from the highways. None of his cut-throats had returned to claim a reward. He had the deepening suspicion that something unpleasant was being concealed from him. On top of all this, the crossroads city of Cremona, according to military reports, had succumbed to the Flavian legions of Antonius Primus. And this possibility was so dreadful that Vitellius refused at first to believe it. He marched out of Rome, to see for himself, but made it only eighty miles before turning home after an immense flock of ravens, the symbol of Corax, blocked out the sun. Back in Rome he dispatched Julius Agrestis, a centurion renowned for his integrity, to assess the situation first-hand. But when Agrestis returned and confirmed the worst – the city in rebel hands, thousands dead on the battlefield, the legionary eagles seized – Vitellius launched into a vitriolic tirade, accusing the centurion of being an enemy agent. Trembling with humiliation, Agrestis made his famous valediction – "Then since you need compelling proof, it seems I have only one way left to convince you" – and promptly fell on his sword.

Vitellius, at the end of his tether, decided to visit Albus of the Esquiline.

The omniscient tavern owner, who in the past had been visited regularly by Claudius, Nero and Galba, was entirely unsurprised to see the latest emperor squeezing his bulk through the doorway and throwing back his mantle. "In fact," he told me later, "I had been expecting him." He folded his waxboards and ordered his loyal assistant Garrulus to locate a man called Duccius Valens.

The emperor, who was accompanied by two Praetorian Guardsmen, growled, "And who is this Duccius Valens, and what is his business with me?"

"Valens took out a bet that now needs to be settled."

"What bet?"

"Fifty to one that the emperor would not appear here in the Cornigera during the Plebeian Games. Looks like he forfeits a thousand."

Vitellius snorted and lowered his blubber – only slightly less substantial than Albus's – onto a tiny wooden stool. "Then I am happy to enrich your coffers."

"You have already enriched them."

"Then perhaps you might deign to consider some new wagers?"

"A man in my position will always entertain the prospect of a bet."

"Very well." With a self-conscious glance around the smoky little room, Vitellius inhaled and asked, "What odds might you offer on a Flavian advance on Rome?"

"That wager is obsolete," Albus responded flatly. "The Flavians are already advancing on Rome."

"Then what odds might you offer on the Plebeian Games being disrupted?"

"That's not a wager I would ever contemplate."

"Why?"

"You yourself have the power to disrupt the Games."

"I have no plans to do so."

"So you say."

"All right, then, what odds on the Flavians reaching Rome before the end of the Games?"

"A thousand to one."

"A thousand to one?"

"That is what I said."

"They are not going to make it, are they?"

"Not before the end of the Games."

Vitellius shifted; the stool protested. "And the odds of Andraemon Team making it to Rome in the meantime?"

"The odds on that are pending."

"Why?"

"I await intelligence from my informers."

"Have contacts within the imperial legions, do you?"

"I never divulge my sources."

"In the *cursus publicus*, perhaps?"

"I said I never divulge my sources."

"Well, you can tell me this much. We have reason to believe that Andraemon himself is being brought across land – is that not so?"

"Who are your sources?"

"What makes you think *I* am willing to divulge them?"

"Expediency," replied Albus. "Who are your sources?"

"It's none of your business. Someone intimately connected with the Greens, that's all I shall say."

"Then you should be more discriminating with your intelligence."

"You are telling me that our source has lied to us?"

"I am telling you your source might have been lied *to*."

"And Andraemon is *not* being brought by land?"

"That I do not know."

311

"I thought you knew everything."

"There are limits to everything."

Vitellius sharpened his gaze. "You're not protecting the horse, by any chance?"

"I take no emotional interest in the outcome of the races."

"I wonder if that is true."

"I'm a businessman, not a sentimentalist."

"And still I wonder."

"Wonder all you like – it makes no difference to me."

Vitellius considered a moment – the pigeons were flapping about in the loft – and leaned forward again, the stool squealing. "Very well, one last question. What are the odds on the Greens winning the Plebeian Games, should the Andraemon Team make it to Rome?"

"Three to one," Albus told him.

"Three to one! Those odds are rather short, don't you think?"

"Glauco of the Viminal is offering fifty to one. You are welcome to take your wagers to him, if my odds displease you."

"I might just do that," said Vitellius, grunting. "I might indeed. But you were offering two thousand to one a few weeks ago – what since has changed?"

"You are here, are you not, asking me questions?"

"What has that to do with it?"

"It means you failed to stop the horses."

"Do I need to stop them?" Vitellius scowled. "Even if they make it through, they will have travelled a thousand miles or more."

"A thousand miles is a trial run for horses like those."

"They are horses, not gods."

"You flatter the gods."

Vitellius stared at him. "Have no emotional interest, do you? You're a businessman, are you?"

Albus lowered his eyes to watch a weevil crossing his table.

Vitellius's anger boiled over. "You *are* protecting them, aren't you? You're protecting the Andraemon Team. Because you *want* the

Greens to win. Because you want me to *lose*. Well, let me remind you of something, my salt-encrusted friend. I am the emperor now, not some common gambler, and you are the slimiest slug in Rome. I can have you squashed, if I so wish, with a turning of my thumb."

Albus crushed the weevil under his own thumb and looked up.

"Kill me, if you wish," he replied. "I died a thousand times in the salt mines. But you should remember how much of your riches I hold here. How much of *Rome*'s riches I hold here. And then you should ask yourself who really is more powerful – you in your golden palace or me in this stinking room."

The weevil flattened, Albus rolled it into a ball, flicked the tiny carcass into the shadows, and returned his ghostly eyes to the emperor.

Tongue-tied, Vitellius fought his impulses. Remembered the extravagant amounts he had tied up in wagers.

"You might regret talking to me like that," he said at last.

Albus reopened his waxboards. "Would you like to bet on it?"

Vitellius harrumphed, on the verge of a scathing riposte before fizzling into impotence. He hauled himself to his feet and said, "I might have cause to return."

"Provided you can squeeze your gut through the door, you are as welcome as any other citizen."

Vitellius chortled – it really was something for Albus to mock another man's weight – but in the end, immensely frustrated, he and his guardsmen bustled out the tavern in a whirl of foul air and stifled rejoinders.

"He might have slept in the Domus Aurea," Albus told me later, "but I think, at that moment, I made clear who really reigned as Emperor of Rome."

# XXVIII

LATER, MAGNUS WOULD FONDLY REMEMBER his farewell to Corax. The little man was resting on a pallet, stitched by "the butcher surgeons of Third Gallica" and half-drunk with wine – "a concession granted to me by Primus" – when the Raven entered the tent to inform him that he was departing for Rome.

"There's a bridge of boats ten miles east of here. It's the safest route across the river, I've been told, though even it is not without danger, for a Vitellian detachment has been spotted on the southern bank."

"You are intending to ride into the midst of a Vitellian detachment?" asked Magnus, brow creased.

"It has not been seen for two days, and General Primus has promised me an escort of his finest soldiers."

"You will need them, I should think, if there is an army to get through."

"I shall need them even more on the way to Rome. We were identified once and it's likely we will be identified again."

"It's that accursed goat that does it, you know. If not for Cupido announcing us like a herald, I might not even be here now."

"You certainly would not be here now, for neither would Andraemon."

"Well," chuckled Magnus, "I can hardly argue with that. Champions choose strange friends. Speaking of which, I shall do everything possible to get out of this charnel house and see you in Rome."

"Just make sure you have recovered sufficiently before you try anything foolish."

"I can look after myself, Corax – it's not like the old days."

"Then please keep an eye on Tuscus as well."

"From what I've heard," laughed Magnus, "the horse is recovering better than I am."

"That's because he was struck in the hindquarters, not the flanks."

"If only that arrow had struck me in my bony arse, eh? Ah, well, let me hug you, brother – not too tightly, though! – and wish you the best."

For Magnus, Corax's subsequent embrace was "as close to affection as he had ever deigned to offer me", so he "made every effort to remember it, lest I never see him again".

Corax then went to meet with the hard-bitten riders of his escort and to collect Cupido before joining Primus on the ride to the crossing point. On the way, they passed through blood-soaked battlefields thickly decorated with the bodies of soldiers and steeds.

"Two great battles were fought here six months apart," Primus explained. "The vultures had barely completed one feast before we served up another. One grows accustomed to the stench."

At the tenth milestone on the Via Postumia, as darkness descended, they steered through a series of dense thickets to the banks of the swollen and fast-flowing Po. Here they found the pontoon bridge – boats and barges fastened together with ropes and planks – as well as a cohort of Flavian troops guarding the approaches while watching attentively for activity on the far side of the river.

"It's a risk," Primus admitted to Corax. "The Vitellians need the bridge as much as we do, but equally they can destroy it as quickly as we can."

"The mist should help conceal us," Corax suggested.

"But it's lifting as we speak – I feel a breeze on my legs right now. So go now, Corax of Campania, wait for nothing, and with luck no one will even notice that you have crossed."

Corax instructed one of the guards to gather up Cupido and hold him tight. "And make sure you ride in advance of me," he added, "so that Andraemon is always in sight of the goat." Then he turned back to Primus. "I am grateful for your assistance, General."

"And I am g-g-grateful for your presence, Corax. But please – you've known me longer than anyone in the legions here, so you have a right to call me Becco."

"Becco," Corax repeated. "What does it mean?"

"The r-r-rooster's beak."

"The rooster's beak?" A frown flickered across Corax's face – "as if he sensed some curious significance," Primus told me later, "though he could not rightly account for it" – before he nodded. "Then I hope to see you at least one more time, Becco."

With that, and after a further short conference with his bodyguards, Corax rode down to the bridge as the gap boat was rowed into position to complete the crossing. A posse of troops, meanwhile, had crept down the riverbank to create a din – a crude distraction. Primus himself cantered up a crest to survey the action.

And so it was that, on a rise overlooking the moonlit Po, General Marcus Antonius Primus, once known as Becco, watched Corax, Andraemon and their escort of soldiers thunder down the riverbank and head at full gallop for the ramp. He saw them pour onto the wooden causeway and charge across the first boat. Second boat. Third boat. Flashing across the boards, leaping over gaps. Fourth boat, fifth. Everything seemed to be going extremely well. But then, just when he thought they would make it across without incident, Primus was alarmed to notice Vitellian troops flooding out of the mist on the far side of the river. They were all over the bridge like locusts. They were pouring sulphur across the decks. They were setting the vessels aflame and hacking at the ropes. Caught between the urge to assist and the need for dispassionate caution, Primus watched helplessly. The Flavian escorts, including the soldier carrying the goat, had drawn up in their tracks. But Corax himself – caught up in his own irresistible momentum – had forged ahead, heading still for the opposite side of the river.

But the boats around him were loosening. The causeway was coming apart. The vessel holding Corax and Andraemon swung free. Primus saw Corax spin around as if abruptly deciding to retreat. But it was too late. The boat had already been swept up in the current. It was separating, twisting, colliding with other vessels. Flaming arrows and incendiaries were streaking past. From a distance Corax looked strangely resigned to his fate.

And this was the last the general saw of them: Corax and Andraemon – without Cupido, without escorts, without, it seemed, a chance in hell – coursing downstream on the overpowering current, melting into the fiery mist as other boats, lit up like braziers, caromed wildly around them.

"I cursed myself for letting them go through," Primus admitted later, "just as I challenged the gods for not intervening on the side of the just. And I immediately dispatched riders down the riverbank in a frantic attempt to locate and rescue them. But though they found the wreckage of their boat – it was strewn across a sandbar near Castra Majora – they found no trace of either man or horse.

"And thus we had no way of knowing if Corax and Andraemon were alive or dead."

There were four days to the races in the Circus Maximus.

# XXIX

ITH THE CONCLUSION OF THE BEAST HUNTS, the focus of the Plebeian Games shifted briefly to the Circus Flaminius for military parades, gladiatorial bouts and, once the arena was purposely flooded, a reenactment of famous naval battles. The Circus Maximus itself had been dressed for the culminating race day, the walls washed of dust and blood, the stalls and stewards' boxes set in place, and team banners and standards, predominantly blue, hung in places of prominence.

My father – now based permanently at the Via Latina estate, and still refusing to accept defeat – was meanwhile running me off my feet with a range of tasks including liaising with the Reds and Whites, consulting with Albus of the Esquiline, and attending the stall draw as an unofficial observer. It was prior to this last task that I managed to squeeze in a brief visit to the family home.

My mother, by that stage in the late autumn of her life, had lapsed into a state of near-complete incapacitation and insensibility. Propped up in her bed by her handmaidens, she failed to recognise me at first and babbled something unintelligible as usual.

"Xenia was here, she was, she was here."

"Yes, Mamma."

"Gone now, gone now, coming back, she says, coming back."

"That's good to hear, Mamma."

I was hastening out, typically dejected, when old Priscilla, matron of the slaves, intercepted me at the door.

"It's true, you know – what your mother said about Xenia."

"I beg your pardon?"

"She was here at the house."

I stared at her. "What are you talking about?"

"Not long ago. She asked to be remembered to you."

"Our former maid?" I asked, blinking. "The wife of Corax?"

"None other."

"She was truly here? With her husband?"

"She was alone."

I suddenly remembered the need for caution – the slaves had been told nothing about the return of the horses – and I lowered my voice. "Then did she mention him? Or anything related to him?"

"She wished only to greet us and pay her respects to your mother."

"And where is she now? Where did she go from here?"

"She is lodging with old Chartos and his family."

"Chartos still lives in the Subura?"

"He does."

Being a scholar all my life, my athletic feats have been confined chiefly to sauntering between libraries and lifting scrolls off shelves. Nevertheless, the speed I achieved in my race down the hill would have shamed a Greek sprinter. The timber block of insulae where resided Chartos, our former head cook, had been reduced to a pile of ash during the Great Fire but tenements of Alban stone had sprung up in their place. When I found the little apartment of Chartos on the fourth floor I was told by the old fellow that Xenia had gone to "make her devotions" at the Temple of Venus Erycina.

"The one on the Capitoline or the one on the Quirinal?" I asked breathlessly.

"There's one on the Quirinal?" said Chartos, blinking.

I hastened over to the Capitoline, weaving between the crowds, and it was in racing up the temple steps, panting like a dog, that I passed a distinguished-looking woman heading in the other direction.

"Manius – is that you, Manius?"

I stopped and turned, disconcerted – I had not been called Manius since childhood.

"Manius?"

The woman – leathered of skin, silvered of hair, gilded by the late afternoon sun – had halted in her tracks and was staring up at me with her fearsome mahogany eyes.

I was frankly astonished that she, like her husband, could recognise me before I could identify her. "Let me catch my breath," I said, struck dumb by her presence. This was, after all, the woman who had nursed and educated me. Who had instilled in me a love of reading. Who, I am embarrassed to say, was the object of my very first infatuation. "When . . . when did you arrive, dear Xenia?"

"Yesterday, by boat. Why, Manius – have you been looking for me?"

"I only recently learned of your arrival. But how did you know it was me, when I have gained such weight?"

"You were always overweight, Manius."

I fought a blush. "Is Corax not with you?"

"He does not yet know I am here."

"But he is on his way?"

"To the best of my knowledge, he is. You have received no word from him?"

"We have not."

"And Alector?"

"Neither has he arrived," I admitted, wondering why she'd asked. "But please," I said, ushering her into the safety of the temple's shadows. "Have you visited my father?"

"I've arranged to visit him tomorrow morning." She looked conspicuously unimpressed by my earnestness.

"But you must be careful, Xenia. Many would like to stop you."

"Nonsense."

"I speak the truth. They will do anything to prevent your husband from getting to the Circus Maximus."

"That is entirely a matter for my husband."

"They could kidnap you, Xenia."

"They have no reason to know who I am."

"But you have already made your presence known to our household slaves."

"You are not suggesting my fellow slaves would betray me?"

"They only have to gossip."

"Don't be foolish, Manius." She turned for the steps.

"Please, Xenia," I insisted. "Think of Corax. Think of his safety. He – and my father, for that matter – would never forgive you if you put his life in danger."

In retrospect I am surprised I managed such manipulations. But perhaps even scholars, in the heat of the race, can find extra. And Xenia, looking back at me, considered awhile – I suddenly remembered that this was the vey place where she had ambushed Corax prior to the race against Caligula – before relenting.

"Very well, Manius, if that is the way of it. Unlike others, I am not completely impervious to reason. What do you expect me to do?"

"It would be best for everyone if you stayed indoors – in Chartos's place if necessary – and tell no one else that you are here. I shall inform you immediately when your husband arrives."

"And if he does *not* arrive?"

I gulped. "Then I shall inform you immediately of that too. Why exactly did you come here, may I ask?"

"Does it make a difference?"

"I'm a historian now – I am interested in people's motives."

She made a noise of amusement. "Dear me, I hope you are not planning to include me in one of your little chronicles, young Manius?"

"Historians are duty-bound never to make promises, dear Xenia."

She reflected for a moment and then sighed. "All right, I suppose there's no avoiding the truth. And the truth is that I came to confront my husband. What I do after that I cannot say. But it is important, I feel, to be honest with myself."

"I see." I sensed I should not enquire further. "Then as soon as possible I shall inform my father that you are here." I bowed. "It has been an honour to speak to you again, dear Xenia."

"And it has been a pleasure to have been lectured by you again, young Manius."

She had barely taken a step, however, before she turned back.

"Oh, Manius?" she called. "Might you do me a favour?"

"Of course, dear Xenia."

"Can you inform me when Alector arrives as well?"

"I can," I said stiffly. "I can do that."

I was deeply troubled, of course, for I had always been partial to Corax, and was loath to imagine him suffering any more than he had already. But I had no time to dwell on it, for a nearby burst of trumpets reminded me that I was already late for the stall draw.

# XXX

IN THE FORUM MAGNUM, where the draw was being held in public for the first time, four gaily decorated platforms had been erected to contain each faction's legal counsel, administrators and star charioteers. Crowded around them, assembled on temple steps and hanging from scaffolding, was a vociferous audience of Circus acolytes, chiefly Blues, while in centre, on a dais made up like a sacrificial altar, the gold-uniformed magistrate of the games was spinning coloured balls in a double-handled urn.

Delphinius of Doriscus, looking decidedly ill at ease, was seated among an ensemble that now included Venustus of Venusia and Tamarix of Tridentum, the latest recruits from the Greens. The platform designated to the Greens themselves was virtually empty: all I could see were Gryphus and the faction's florid lawyer Camelius Petrus. This notable absence of champion charioteers was a source of great amusement for the Blues partisans, who openly speculated that they might have been poisoned:

"Where hides Primulus of Prusa? Is his tummy troubling him?"

"Has his tongue turned green?"

"Has his face turned yellow?"

"Has his shit turned black?"

And as much as I sought to ignore them, and to remind myself that under similar circumstances Greens supporters would be equally odious, I could not quite overcome a draining feeling of despair. I might have slipped away early, in fact – I was eager to inform my father of Xenia's unexpected presence – had not the draw been arranged in a heavily contrived order, so that the minor races were called first and the most important ones last. To add to my frustration, Camelius Petrus seemed under specific instruction to prolong the proceedings as long as possible.

"May I ask the honourable magistrate," he boomed, "if there are currently any limits to the number of races a horse, or team of horses, may contest in one day?"

And: "May I ask the honourable magistrate how many horses of an established team need to line up in the stalls to qualify as an established team?"

And: "May I ask the honourable magistrate if a charioteer needs to be officially registered in the faction's books to qualify for a race?"

All this rules-parsing seemed a further admission that the Greens were stretching their resources painfully thin. But, if so, they elicited little sympathy from the Blues fanatics.

"Tell them to yoke their chariots to donkeys!"

"Tell them to yoke their chariots to dreams!"

"Tell them to recruit monkeys as charioteers – they couldn't be any dumber than Rufus of Britannia!"

Laughter echoed around the Forum and up into the Palatine, where Vitellius could be spotted surveying proceedings from a sunlit balcony. Finally, amid much anticipation, came the draw for the first major race. But now, surprisingly, the blue ball did not drop first, meaning that Delphinius was assigned the unlucky number seven stall – no manipulations being required, it seemed, since he was such a certain winner.

But when the green ball fell – stall number eight, even worse – and the Greens were obliged to identify their own team and charioteer, Gryphus rose and muttered something so meekly that the magistrate had to ask him to repeat himself.

"I said we are able to name neither at present," Gryphus managed.

Wild derision and trumped-up outrage from the crowd, fading only when the magistrate appealed for calm. "What is the meaning of this? The new rules state explicitly that both team and charioteer must be declared two days before the race!"

But the pompous lawyer Camelius Petrus now launched dramatically to his feet. "Far be it for me to correct the honourable magistrate," he bellowed, "but if the definition of 'two days' derives strictly from the calendar – and indeed it must, by any reckoning – then we have until sunset on this day, the fifteenth of the month, to announce our teams and charioteers."

The magistrate, calming the crowd, said, "But this is a spurious point of order, and you know it!"

"It may be so," returned Petrus, "but we are entitled to make use of it, and indeed we shall."

The crowd chose to sneer and laugh, clearly inferring that the Greens were having trouble putting together any quadriga teams at all.

The magistrate settled on a growl. "Very well then, you have until sundown."

"With gratitude, your honour."

As it happened the sun had already sunk low over the Capitoline, and its steady progress towards the horizon became a source of great interest, not least because virtually every major quadriga race was accompanied by the same confession from Gryphus: "The Greens can name neither team nor charioteer at this stage."

The mockery and imprecations became louder as the sun fell even lower, the shadows deepened, and only the highest entablatures remained aglow. The penultimate draw was announced and still the Greens could proffer no names. As the urn was spun for the final time – the twelfth race, in honour of the emperor himself – everyone leaned forward expectantly.

The blue ball dropped first. And Caius Manlius Scaevola, the flamboyant secretary of the Blues, shot out of his seat to declare, "Our horses for the last race will be the mighty Fulminatus Team driven by the immortal Delphinius of Doriscus!"

Thunderous acclamations from the crowd.

"All hail Delphinius!"

"May his horses wear the plumes!"

"May he be crowned in gold!"

"May he ride across the sky!"

To which Delphinius rose and offered a perfunctory wave before settling back into his seat. ("I had a powerful feeling," he told me later, "that something unexpected was about to happen. The incessant queries of Camelius Petrus, all the hedging and bluffing, made me suspect that Picus had a surprise on the way.")

When the green ball dropped, everyone turned to the faction's dais, where Gryphus pushed himself reluctantly to his feet. The crowd was murmuring. The sky was darkening. And for a moment Gryphus looked as though he did not know what to say.

"Your honour . . ." he began, then glanced around as if for inspiration.

The sneers and scowls quickly faded when it became clear something was happening behind the dais. Someone, amid much commotion, was forcing his way urgently through the crowd. I stood on tiptoes to see.

Then someone was ascending the stairs to the Greens platform. Two people, in fact. The first, surprisingly enough, was my father himself – still using his walking stick but suddenly looking half his age. But the figure beside him was truly confounding: a weathered-looking man wearing Greens regalia and a wicked grin. No one seemed to know who he was at first – he seemed too old to be driving chariots – but this did not stop him standing tall and proud and gazing out upon us haughtily, cockily, exuberantly, as though the whole world knew his name.

Then, in a flash, I *did* recognise him. And almost instantaneously I heard an accelerating ripple of whispers as many others identified him as well. Though none of us could rightly believe it, even as he made his dramatic pronouncement.

"I, Alector of Arcadia, shall be the charioteer in all six of the undeclared races!" he cried. "*Fortius quo fidelius!*"

Multiplying gasps from around the Forum, not just because the Rooster had returned to Rome – and was acting, for all intents and purposes, as if he had never left – but because this meant that he would be driving against Delphinius of Doriscus, his erstwhile apprentice and rumoured son!

But that, astonishingly, was not all. For, as soon as the commotion had subsided, Alector made one more stunning declaration.

"And in three of those races I shall be driving the Andraemon Team!" he exclaimed, as the last rays of light vanished from the Palatine, the emperor, and the whole city of Rome.

# XXXI

THE JOURNEY OF ALECTOR, Selene and the three horses from Sipontum had not been without incident, not least when a fierce ambush was launched on them outside Corfinium on the Via Valeria. But Labeo and his men not only repelled the assault but were even more ferocious in their counterattack, scattering the assassins like cockroaches while shielding their charges from harm. In the three subsequent days of relentless riding across the spine of Italy through rugged hills and valleys and a multitude of villages – on flatter roads the chariot horses were transported in wheeled vehicles of my father's design – no other assailant managed to get close. And Alector, by the time they were close enough to Rome to spot its ornaments glinting through the haze, was exhibiting an almost spiritual reverence for his destiny.

"I sense her," he whispered to Selene.

"Rome?" she asked.

"Xenia, of course. The goddess is there now. I feel her presence – she is expecting me." And he urged the horses on, as though Xenia was waiting to greet him on the outskirts of the city.

In fact, it was my father who was at the Via Latina estate to welcome them. "Where have you been?" he chided cheekily. "I have been expecting you." (A messenger pigeon from Sipontum had alerted him to the Rooster's arrival in Italy.) He embraced Alector, whom he had not seen for three years, and kissed Selene – "What a fine young lady you've become!" – before inspecting the three horses and making sure Labeo and his men were well rewarded. He was always at his best in such moments: charming, sincere, meticulous, generous, inspirational – I wish I had been there.

But he was not forgetting the proper order of things. "Have the horses watered, fed and groomed," he told the stable boys. "Have the veterinarians examine them thoroughly. Administer nothing without first consulting me. And have them guarded like the treasures that they are."

Then he turned again to Alector and Selene, summoning great platters of food and wine while casually informing them that Corax and Andraemon had failed to arrive. Alector, despite being the victor of the unofficial long-distance race, went so pale at this news ("most probably because of what it meant regarding the presence of Xenia," Selene decided later) that my father misinterpreted his concern: "Ah, I see you are worried about Corax, your brother charioteer! Truly time heals all wounds! Alas, you might never get the chance to be reunited now, for I suspect Corax has been tangled up in this accursed civil war. So let me confess something before it is too late – yes, now is definitely the time."

He went on to admit that he personally had manufactured the rivalry between the two great charioteers, nourishing it with flagrant distortions and outright lies, and had borne the subsequent shame for his mendacity through the succeeding decades.

("My father looked further troubled," Selene noted later, "this time genuinely, it seemed to me, for what it meant about his relationship with Corax.")

"Have you ever told Corax of this?" asked Alector.

"I have, though that is a moot point now. For the present, we must forget all about him, for there are important races to win."

My father went on to explain the strategies and blocking tactics that had been devised in collaboration with the Reds and Whites, as well as the intelligence he had managed to acquire about the Blues. He mentioned the iron-rimmed wheel that would be publicly unveiled for the first time on race day. But when he listed the chari-oteers who would be racing for the Greens – those who had not been poisoned or poached – he was forced to admit that Delphinius of Doriscus had defected to the enemy.

"Now it was I who was stricken," Selene admitted later, "for I adored Delphinius and could not imagine what could have accounted for such a betrayal."

But Alector, in contrast, was jittery with excitement, for he had been waiting years for just such an opportunity. "No one knows the horses better than I," he argued. "And no one knows Delphinius's weaknesses as I do. It is indisputable, I tell you – I am the charioteer best-equipped to drive the Andraemon Team to victory. Not just the Andraemon Team, but all your teams. Fortuna herself has divined this to be so – did you not hear about the Sibylline Books?"

Here he revealed the prophecy regarding "the rooster's beak", an argument which my father, always receptive to any augury that aligned with his own inclinations, found persuasive. On top of which, "I have always put the greatest stock in self-assurance," my father admitted to me later, "and what I saw that day was an irresist-ible confidence I had not witnessed in anyone since the halcyon days of Alector himself."

So it was that the Rooster made his surprise appearance at the draw and then spent the following day training with the hooped-wheel chariot – he did not approve of it at first, claiming it slowed him down – and so it was that, when race day came, he participated, for the first time in decades, in a *pompa circensis* through the streets of Rome.

"I followed him all the way from the Capitol," Selene remem-bered, "struggling and squirming through the crowd, which in places was ten deep. It was exhilarating, not least because my father was obviously in his element."

Indeed, Alector was bowing and waving and blowing kisses just as he had done in his prime. Even his horses – the noble trace horse Zephyrus had replaced Andraemon – were arching their necks and prancing extravagantly. And while there was no shortage of catcalls mocking his advanced age, it was immediately apparent that he and his team carried with them a remarkable amount of goodwill, not just from the Greens but the Reds and Whites and even some of the Blues.

"All the same," Selene admitted, "I feared some form of attack, even out in the open, and had my eyes peeled constantly for danger."

They nonetheless made it through unharmed to the Forum Boarium, where the competing teams had assembled in preparation for their entry into the Circus. Here Alector ducked away to empty his bladder into a stinking vat installed exclusively for the use of charioteers (the urine was sold later as a hair restorer) and he was on his way back to his horses, which were being in held in place by Selene and the faction's moratores, when he found himself passing his erstwhile apprentice.

"Glory be!" he exclaimed. "If it isn't Perfume Boy of Doriscus! Who told himself the Andraemon Team would never get to Rome and so defected to the Blues for fear of being shown up as the pretender that he is!"

Delphinius, though he appeared distracted for some reason, had been charioteering long enough to develop some facility with pre-race taunts. "And if it isn't Alector of Arcadia," he returned. "There's no point trying to fool me, old man – I know you better than you think."

"And what do you know? Or think you know?"

"I know that you are always at your most obnoxious when you are most nervous."

"Oh really?" Alector chuckled. "Then tell me this, Boy-Beard, do you still fill your gut with wine before each race, to quell your doubts and fears?"

"The only reason you yourself do not drink before a race, old man, is because you fear your bladder will burst – the very reason you have drained it just now."

Alector sniggered again. "Ha, ha, your sparring has improved since the old days – has the widow paid for training? Anyway, don't kid me that you are not worried, being at the reins of some trumped-up colts which you know are no match for the Andraemon Team."

"The Andraemon Team it may be, but I see no Andraemon. And my own team might be trumped up but at least it's not clapped out. Good luck, Alector – I mean it. Good luck. You'll need it."

"I never need luck, as you well know. And I need no fresh horses, as I'll shortly prove. But you, Delphinius – you *know* you are at sea without the Andraemon Team. And I can tell that you are nervous, because I've never seen you looking so ashen. *Castor and Pollux!*"

In fact, Delphinius's anaemic appearance may have had more to do with his first sight of Selene. ("He had gone as pale as milk," she told me later, "though I offered him nothing but a glare – registering in the harshest way possible my disappointment.")

"Hey, Downy Cheeks." It was Alector again, his brow knitted severely. "Get your eyes off my daughter. She is not for the likes of you."

Resuming his place in his chariot, Alector was ushered through the narrow streets around the Circus Maximus, through the Porta Pompae, and onto the sunlit track where he paraded with seven other teams, including a separate Green team driven by Primulus of Prusa. The roar of the crowd shook the earth so violently that dust loosened from cracks in buildings across Rome. The three horses of the original team – Olympius, Postumus and Pertinax – were so delighted to be back that they were stamping proudly. Passing the pulvinar, where Vitellius sat clenched in his curule chair, the charioteers were required to salute respectfully. But Alector performed his own gesture so theatrically, thrusting his chest out like a pigeon and puckering his lips like a trout, that a good portion of the crowd dared to laugh with approval.

As the chariot teams entered the stalls, Delphinius came close enough to Selene to address her for the first time. "I regret that it has to be like this," he told her.

But Selene, not even deigning to acknowledge his presence, headed instead to her father, who was fitting the reins around his torso.

"I'm sorry to hear about Xenia, Father."

"What are you talking about?"

"I am sorry that she has not made it to Rome."

"Oh, she is here, all right."

"But Picus said—"

"I heard what he said. And I am telling you she is here. She is in the Circus Maximus right now. I sense her. So stand back as I win this race, and then watch as I present the palm of victory to her, and later the golden laurel to you."

Marvelling at his composure, Selene retreated to the shadows, assuring herself that there were sound reasons for her father's confidence. They had, after all, just pulled off a minor miracle by bringing three chariot horses all the way from Syria. In intense trialling, Alector had proved himself to be still the most capable charioteer in the Greens. And, notwithstanding the absence of Andraemon, he was now at the reins of the most famous chariot team in history.

"*Fortius quo fidelius!*" he shouted presently, at the top of his lungs – specifically it seemed to needle Delphinius.

Then there was a thumping of drums and fanfare of trumpets and much muttering in the crowd – Selene could hear it through the starting-gates – which mounted to a crescendo before tapering off, then a reverential silence of a type not heard anywhere outside a temple, and the moratores withdrew, and truly a sparrow could be heard cheeping in the eaves, and either the emperor dropped his *mappa* or the magistrate waved a flag – from the stalls it was impossible to say – and suddenly a mechanism was released, there was a huge groaning sound like a keel scraping over a reef, and the bolts flew back, and with a *bang!* the brightly painted gates burst open, and into the arena, like arrows released from their bows, shot the eight quadrigas drawn by thirty-two gnashing steeds, which amid a whirl of hooves and flashing whips raced frantically for the breakline.

"I was convinced at that moment we were going to win," Selene recalled later, "because of my father's infectious confidence, because of all the ordeals we had been through to get there, and because I could see no conceivable way the gods would now permit us to lose."

The first race of the Plebeian Games was underway.

# XXXII

**B**UT THE ROOSTER DID NOT WIN THE FIRST RACE. I was watching from the lower tiers. And I saw a charioteer who, for all his enthusiasm, looked like he had not driven in the Circus Maximus for thirty years. A former champion who, for all his confidence, had failed to keep pace with modern skills and tactics. A driver who was comfortable enough with the fundamentals but conspicuously out of his depth with the finer points. A charioteer, in short, who had lost his edge. He crossed the finishing line a miserable fifth, a half-lap behind the winners, Delphinius of Doriscus and the Fulminatus Team.

We were dismayed, naturally, but like all faction acolytes we fell back on expedient excuses. It was only the first race. Alector had been terribly unlucky. If not for this, if not for that, he might have won. And he was still finding his feet. He was refamiliarising himself with the Circus – the sheer size of the arena, the roar from a hundred and fifty thousand throats, the smoke, the sparking sand, the dazzling shafts of light. He would come good eventually, we were sure of it. And besides, there were other Greens charioteers eager to take the reins.

But in the second race, which did not feature Alector or Delphinius, Greens stalwart Primulus of Prusa came third behind new Blues recruit Cancer of Apulia and Whites veteran Proculius of Latium. And again, we resorted to rationalisations. Primulus's performances had always been erratic, his horses had been unfairly hindered in the fourth lap, it was still early in the day, and the Blues were showing signs of overconfidence (all such bluster seemed reasonable enough at the time).

In the third race Alector was back, this time driving the Nitidus Team. We were hoping that, having gotten the first race out of the way, he would be demonstrably better and more composed. But he crossed the finishing line second last. The hollowness in our bellies was matched only by the despair on our faces. And our conviction – that all was not lost – was looking very tenuous indeed.

But then, in the fourth race, a biga special, there was a flicker of promise when Betulinus of Belgica – a promising apprentice making his Circus debut – came from well behind to claim our first thrilling win of the Games. We told ourselves that the tide had turned, that the spirit of victory had been ignited, that a new surge of self-belief would propel our other charioteers to victory as well.

But in the fifth race Primulus of Prusa, though he put in a heroic performance, was pipped at the post by new Blues recruit Tamarix of Tridentum – and an honourable second was not, whatever you might call it, a recorded victory.

The sixth race was another feature event matching Alector against Delphinius. Despite our waning spirits we experienced a surge of hope when Alector's horses, the Corinitus Team, completed the first lap three lengths ahead. We were genuinely excited when he finished the third lap five lengths ahead. We were increasingly tense when we began the sixth lap neck and neck with Delphinius. And we were in the doldrums again when he finished in second place, four lengths behind his apprentice.

The Greens had lost five of the first six races and overall victory looked all but impossible.

By this stage it was time for the midday entertainment. I believe it was a re-enactment of Vitellius's victory at the first Battle of Cremona, though in truth I was too distracted to care. I was meant to head down to the Forum Boarium and check on the charioteers, but I remained rooted to the spot, fearful of what I might find on Alector's face, and trying desperately not to imagine my father's reaction when he learned of the results.

In fact, Alector "was confused, maybe even distraught, but he had not given up hope," Selene told me later. "He still believed in his destiny. He was convinced he was going to bring down the emperor. It was true he could not immediately explain what had gone wrong on the track, but this did not stop him hunting around for all sorts of excuses."

He could hardly blame the condition of his horses, for he had lost without the Andraemon Team as well as with them. Nor could he credibly blame the Reds and Whites, who were clearly doing as much as possible, without exciting too much attention, to assist him across the line. But he was able to point out – quite rightly, as it turned out – that track attendants on the spina were employing all sorts of underhand tactics to disrupt his horses. He was able to argue that Zephyrus, as good as he was, was no Andraemon. He was able to note that the other horses made available to him would not in normal circumstances be considered the best in the Greens stables.

Most of all, he was able to blame the iron rim on his chariot's right wheel. He went directly to the faction's wheelwrights, in fact, and insisted that they remove it at once. When they told him that would make the chariot more volatile, he said, "I don't care. It's slowing me down. It's like an anchor in the straights." When they protested that they could not perform such an operation without damaging the wheel itself, he replied, "Then get me another chariot entirely – something with untouched wheels." And when they said the only such chariots in the vicinity were banged-up models that had been pillaged for spare parts, he said, "So be it. I am Alector of Arcadia. I can drive anything with an axle."

While waiting for this replacement he headed off to the nearby Temple of Fortuna – my father had introduced him to the faith – where he supplicated before the god's graceful statue and emerged muttering *Audaces Fortuna Iuvat*\* repeatedly.

"*Audaces Fortuna Iuvat*," he whispered. "*Audaces Fortuna Iuvat*." And, as though to remind himself, "Rooster's beak, rooster's beak."

When he lined up with the Andraemon Team for the all-important seventh race – a three-lap special – he was feeling so excited, so eager to hurl himself into the fray, that he seemed not even to register the taunts of Delphinius of Doriscus:

"You have done well, Alector, considering you have travelled so far – let no one tell you different." ("In fact," Selene admitted later, "I was not even sure if they *were* taunts.")

Whatever the case, Alector was so clearly kindled by purpose, so transfixed by his own determination – teeth clenched, eyes unflinching – that he no longer cared. He did not even bother to respond.

He romped out of the stalls, crossed the breakline in first place, led at every single turn, and won the race by seven lengths. We were beside ourselves. It was a stunning turnaround. And of course we told ourselves that the second half of the card would be completely different from the first. Though I am not sure if we really believed it.

But Primulus of Prusa and the Caelistis Team won the eighth race by a similar margin.

Alector himself and the Nitidus Team won the nail-biting ninth race by a single length. Incredibly, and against all the odds, the Greens were now just a single win behind the Blues. And abruptly

---

\* "Fortuna favours the bold," an inscription above the statue.

we found ourselves looking for reasons to temper our hopes. We did not want to get too presumptuous, after all – we did not want to invite the displeasure of the gods.

But then Betulinus of Belgica, who would later become such a champion, won his second biga race, the tenth race overall, by a half-lap.

And Rufus of Britannia, the faction's most eccentric first-rank charioteer, performed well above himself to win the eleventh race by two lengths, albeit with some brilliant blocking by the Reds and Whites.

The Greens were now leading the Games by one race. It was astonishing, too good to be true. We entered a giddy world where, should we be successful in the twelfth race, there would not even be a need for a deciding *pedibus ad quadrigam*. The unthinkable had become a genuine possibility. And the plebeians of Rome, recognising this, had finally found their voice. They were stamping their feet. They were howling their approval. It was as though a great spirit, swollen to bursting point, had exploded out of a locked trunk. And Vitellius, high in the pulvinar, looked aghast – face shiny with perspiration, his hands fastened knuckle-white to his chair.

"When my father lined up in the starting stalls for his third race with the Andraemon Team," Selene recalled later, "he had rediscovered his dignity. He had remembered who he was."

"The goddess has taken me to her bosom," he told her (Selene was not sure if he meant Rome, Fortuna or Xenia), before noticing his apprentice nearby. "You have done well, Delphinius, considering the standard of your horses – let no one tell you any different."

But now it was Delphinius, staring ahead, lips pressed together, who did not respond.

In the profound hush that followed, as everyone awaited the starter's signal, Selene heard her father mutter *"Audaces Xenia Iuvat!"* under his breath (she was convinced he said "Xenia" this time). And then he gave himself over to destiny.

He exploded into the darkening arena and was first across the break line.

He completed the first lap well ahead of Delphinius and Appius of Calabria.

He completed the second lap four lengths clear of Delphinius and Pamphilos of Pergamum, who had worked his way into third.

He completed the third lap five lengths ahead of Delphinius and Pamphilos.

He completed the fourth lap six lengths ahead of Delphinius and Teres of Heliopolis.

He completed the fifth lap eight lengths ahead of Delphinius with no clear third.

He completed the sixth lap literally half the straight ahead of Delphinius.

As he headed into the seventh lap he was flying. A hundred and fifty thousand people were on their feet, bent forward in sheer excitement. Half of them were chanting his name. He glanced into the crowd, as if spotting someone he knew – I saw this with my own eyes – and he smiled in recognition.

*Xenia favours the bold.*

As he shaved the golden turning posts for the final time, leaning hard to the left, there was every indication that Alector of Arcadia, the Greek Rooster, would be the hero of the greatest Circus Maximus comeback of all time.

And then his right wheel disintegrated.

# XXXIII

MEANWHILE MY FATHER PICUS, at the Via Latina estate, had come as close as he ever had to terminating his life. He had spent the first part of the day watching the pigeons flap into the atrium, and with the appearance of each new blue-painted bird his spirits sank a little lower. Shortly after midday there were five blues and only one green, and when a courier rode up with a full report on the early races my father accepted the news with equanimity. But inside, he told me later, he was devastated. He had failed. The hooped wheel had failed. His impetuous decision to invest his faith in Alector had failed. Vitellius would have his precious victory.

Over the next three hours, too sickly even to check the colour of the newly arrived pigeons, he wondered if suicide might now be the noblest option. He did not want to live on only to have Vitellius grind him into the dust. Perhaps, if he sacrificed himself now, the faction itself would be spared. And he was an old, old man – he had lived well. He had built some magnificent ships. Enjoyed the company of famous men. Introduced Rome to some extraordinary horses and charioteers. Even sired some children who perhaps weren't so disagreeable after all.

He was hobbling to the tepidarium, in any case, perhaps to draw a bath and slit his veins ("I genuinely wasn't sure"), when he heard a flurry of activity outside. And the whinnying of a steed. A slave bustled his way into the atrium, looking aghast.

"What is it, Strouthos?" asked my father, anticipating more bad news.

But before the slave could stammer out an answer a visitor appeared: bloodshot, blistered, lean, lined, whiskered, sun-reddened, with a wound on his forehead and a haunted look in his eyes. For a moment my father mistook him for a courier.

"Well?" he asked. "What do you have to tell me?"

Looking disconcerted, the man answered hoarsely, "I am Corax of Campania, master."

"Corax?" My father leaned in, squinting. "*Corax*?"

"It is I, master."

"Ye gods, what has happened to you?"

"It was a difficult journey, master."

"But are you well?"

"As fit as ever, master – as is Andraemon."

"Andraemon is here?"

"He is outside."

"Then bring him in" – my father motioned to Strouthos – "bring him in, for heaven's sake! And Corax, Corax, come closer – let me have a better look at you." He dragged the charioteer into the sunlight. "Yes, yes, it is you, after all – please forgive me. It's my terrible eyesight."

"I am sure I look worse than I feel, master—"

"Stop calling me master."

"But I have not much time. I ask you to have your carpenters assemble a ramp at once."

"A ramp? What are you talking about?"

Corax was about to explain when Strouthos reappeared with a dye-streaked stallion.

"Andraemon?" my father asked. "This is Andraemon?"

"He too is in far better shape than his appearance suggests," Corax assured him.

"He is not run down?"

"My greatest difficulty was in holding him back."

"And the goat? Where is the goat?"

"We lost Cupido on the Po."

"Cupido has drowned?"

"We do know not where he is."

"And Andraemon does not miss him?"

"Andraemon is grieving but he has adapted like the champion he is. And now I must ask for your carpenters to prepare a ramp."

"Yes, yes, this ramp – what are you talking about? Why do you need a ramp?"

"Because the city is ringed with soldiers."

"But of course. Vitellius has thrown up a cordon specifically to stop Andraemon getting through. Are you saying you have already tried to breach it?"

"I was unable to do so. And that is why I need another means of reaching the Circus Maximus."

"You still aim to reach the Circus?"

"Is today not the day of the races?"

My father been so overjoyed by Corax's return that he had almost forgotten the parlous state of the Greens. But now he sighed. He gestured to the edge of the fountain. "Let us sit down, Corax, and commiserate together. Let us resign ourselves to reality."

"I'm not sure I understand," said Corax, as my father slumped onto the fountain's rim.

"I mean that there is no longer any point worrying about the Greens."

"But why? Is there no chance of winning the Games?"

"None. And I say that because our principal charioteer – none other than Alector of Arcadia, your old comrade – has failed miserably."

"Alector is here? He made it too?"

"He did indeed – with Olympius, Pertinax and Postumus."

"And he has been racing them in the Circus?"

"Regrettably so."

"Regrettably?"

"He has proved a miserable failure."

Corax still looked perplexed. "Then it is more urgent than ever that Andraemon is reinstated to his team!"

My father shook his head. "It makes no difference now."

"But it makes every difference. The Andraemon Team is never complete without Andraemon!"

"Corax, Corax" – my father shifted on the fountain's edge – "I am tremendously moved by your determination as always, but how would you get Andraemon to the Circus, even if it would help? The horse would need wings to fly over the cordon."

"And there is a way of giving him wings. Did not Alector himself, as a youth, ride horses on the aqueducts of Campania?"

"What of it?"

"Well, does an aqueduct emerge from the hills no great distance from here?"

My father might have been amused under any other circumstances. "I see," he said. "You need the ramp to gain access to the Aqua Claudia, so you can ride Andraemon all the way into Rome."

"If Alector can do it, then so can I. I have crossed an aqueduct, in fact, on this very journey to Rome."

My father chuckled softly. "Your audacity, too, does you credit, Corax. But I say again, all such efforts would be futile – just look at the pigeons."

And Corax, at this point, did look at the pigeons. And his brow creased. And he turned back at my father. "The pigeons that signal victories in the Circus?"

"Of course."

"The pigeons by which you tell which faction is winning the Games?"

"Yes, yes – why do you look at me like that?"

With that, my father turned and took a fix on the birds that had assembled on the eaves. And though it took him a while to blink and focus and make sure his eyes were not deceiving him, he eventually ascertained that of the ten pigeons present, five of them were now green.

He gasped, scarcely believing it. Then he turned to Corax, who nodded resolutely.

"Please assemble that ramp," repeated the Raven, already heading for Andraemon. "The race is never over until the finishing line is crossed."

# XXXIV

To MY SHAME AS A HISTORIAN, I can offer no account of Corax's four-day journey from Cremona to the Via Latina estate. The drama that succeeded this accomplishment extinguished anyone's desire to ask too many questions, and certainly Corax himself was not forthcoming with any details. Nor am I able to offer more than a superficial account of his dramatic late-afternoon ride across the Aqua Claudia into Rome. Only my father's assurance that Corax did indeed ascend to the aqueduct via a hastily assembled ramp, along with the fact that that he indisputably arrived at the Circus with Andraemon, prevents me even now from dismissing the whole idea as incredible.

Consider for a moment that the aqueduct, though only thirty years old, was at that stage temporarily unused, crumbling, and riddled with gaps in its topmost tier. Then imagine what Corax would have to have done: led or ridden the empire's most famous horse over a ribbon of casing stones, no more than seven cubits wide, for eight miles, over outlying meadowland, over the other aqueducts, across lines of soldiers and sentinels, above the menagerie near the Praenestine Gate, and then over the Gate itself, before negotiating a zig-zagging course through the heart of the city and arriving at the aqueduct's terminus on the Aventine Hill.

And yet numerous witnesses – soldiers, shepherds, guards, thieves and philosophers – emerged in time to confirm this extraordinary feat. And what they saw, collectively, was a wild and unkempt man with a ferociously determined look on his face – this was evident, it seemed, even from ground-level – riding a filthy stallion high over their heads, kicking up dust, scattering stones, driving roosting birds into the air, and dodging spears and arrows as he closed in on the city walls. It was, one poet in the Valley of Camenae told me, "one of the most bracing sights I have ever beheld – a horse and rider flashing past my fourth-floor window, framed with the nimbus of the setting sun, just as I was beating the dust from my Sidonian rug."

At the Circus Maximus one of the Greens track officials – all of whom were standing outside the starting stalls in a state of shock – remembers being approached by a haggard man leading a dye-streaked stallion.

"Where is Gryphus?" the man demanded.

"Gryphus?"

"Or whoever is in charge."

"Gryphus has gone to the spoilarium," the official reported blankly.

The haggard man started heading in that direction before stopping in his tracks. Through the Porta Pompae, which was wide open, he had caught sight of the chariot wreckage that littered the track. And this, combined with the palpable atmosphere of dismay, told him that something was terribly wrong.

"What happened?" he asked, turning back.

"What?" the official asked.

"What happened in the arena?"

"It's the Andraemon Team."

"What of them?"

"They've crashed. The right wheel of the chariot collapsed on the final turn."

The haggard man, paling visibly, said, "And the team itself?"

"Zephyrus looks to have broken a leg."

"Zephyrus?"

"The proxy for Andraemon."

"The other horses?"

"Uninjured."

"And Alector?" the man whispered.

"Trampled by other horses and taken to the spoilarium to die." The official narrowed his eyes. "But who are you exactly, to be asking such questions?"

The haggard man, still coming to terms with what he had heard, had no time to explain. "Look after this horse," he said hoarsely. "Look after him with your life. I must go now to the spoilarium."

"But who are you? Answer me that!"

The haggard man turned back to the man – to all the Greens officials – and said tonelessly, "I am Corax of Campania, come from Tarraco to deliver Andraemon to the Circus Maximus."

And then he was gone.

The officials – among them a few old enough to have known Corax in his prime – now erupted into argument:

"Corax – that man was Corax of Campania!"

"Impossible!"

"Not only was that man Corax, but this horse is Andraemon – he said as much himself!"

"Andraemon! You jest?"

"Look at him – it's Andraemon, I tell you!"

"But Andraemon is white as a dove!"

"He has been inked up, can you not tell?"

"But how can we be sure?"

348

"Fetch Cupido himself – fetch the goat."

What I have refrained from mentioning until now is that two of Antonius Primus's men had that very morning smuggled Cupido into Rome, having transported him all the way from Cremona just for the possibility that he might be reunited with Andraemon. And when the anxious goat was brought out of hiding and introduced to the crudely masked stallion, the two beasts indicated through their manifest pleasure that they were indeed the famously inseparable companions.

"By Hercules!" one of the officials exclaimed. "It is Andraemon, after all! Let us get him prepared at once!"

In the blood-spattered spoliarium Zephyrus had been put out of his misery and Alector, as wrecked as his chariot, was lying on a slab with Selene weeping over him. When he heard mutterings that Corax of Campania had arrived, he spasmed awake and shot glances around the chamber.

"Corax?" he rasped. "Corax is here?"

Corax, looking very sombre, pushed his way to his old comrade's side.

"Corax," said Alector, gasping, "so you made it too!"

"Not before you." The two men seized each other's hands.

"You met old man Picus?"

"I did."

"And you've brought Andraemon to Rome?"

"I have."

"I almost did it, Corax. I brought Olympius, Pertinax and Postumus all the way from Syria and very nearly won the Plebeian Games by myself!"

"I have heard that."

"If only Andraemon had been in the team, I am sure I would have succeeded!"

"I've no doubt about it," said Corax. "Alas, I was too late to assist you."

"There is still time!" Squeezing Corax's forearm, Alector tried to raise himself. "There is a *pedibus ad quadrigam*, you see, to decide . . ."

As her father struggled to speak, Selene insisted he should not exert himself. But Alector, reclining, only chuckled.

"My daughter refuses to believe that I am dying, Corax. Will you look after her for me? She is as good with horses as you are."

"I shall."

"I can leave this world happy knowing that she will be with you and the goddess. Did you know the goddess is here too, Corax?"

Now Corax frowned.

"The goddess Xenia," Alector whispered. "I said I would race before her again, and so I have. And now she has given me her blessing, and now . . . now I can go in peace."

Then, as the last breath fled his body and Selene erupted again into tears, the Rooster made one final gesture, compelling the Raven to turn.

And Corax saw, standing in the gloom at the other side of the spoilarium, his wife, Xenia.

He stared at her, perplexed, and she stared back defiantly – apart from Selene's sobbing there was not a sound in the chamber – until finally they both seemed to understand something unspoken, a truth they had known for years, and then both simultaneously crossed the room and embraced, and kissed, and Xenia shook her head and said softly, "What foolish boys you sportsmen be."

And Corax knew at that moment, simply because her rebuke had been no more stinging, that he had her blessing too.

"We must continue," he declared, turning to the Greens officials. "We must never give in." He looked at Gryphus. "There is to be a *pedibus ad quadrigam*?"

"It's true," said Gryphus. "Under torchlight, with the novelty races first."

"The *pedibus ad quadrigam* will decide the victor of the Games?"

"It is so."

"And it will be between the Blues and the Greens?"

"It will."

"Then are our horses fit enough for one final race?"

"If you mean Postumus, Pertinax and Olympius, certainly. But Zephyrus is no longer – and who will replace him?"

Corax did not need to respond. Because news of Andraemon's arrival had by now swarmed through the stadium and the crowd was chanting his name:

"ANDRAEMON . . . ANDRAEMON . . . ANDRAEMON!"

They were *demanding* to see the horse in action.

"Andraemon has travelled a thousand miles to be ready," Corax said. "Strap bindings on his legs. Groom him if there is time. Then harness him. That horse will let no one down."

Gryphus was awed by Corax's astonishing mettle. "But who will drive him, now that Alector has left us?"

Again, Corax did not to reply. Because another development had now swept through the Circus Maximus, and the crowd was chanting a whole new name.

"CORAX . . . CORAX . . . CORAX . . . CORAX!"

# XXXV

I HAVE BEEN ASSURED BY A MAN of unassailable authority that Vitellius had already begun conspiring with stewards to apply some sort of disqualification should the Greens happen to win the deciding race. But when news arrived that Corax of Campania was intending to drive their horses – having travelled a thousand miles or more and looking "as though he had stepped out of a furnace" – the emperor, who might by rights have forbidden him from racing on a technicality, opted to allow the race to proceed, "because he had seen Alector of Arcadia literally crushed and thought it delightfully appropriate that Corax would be defeated too, along with the Greens as a whole, in a *pedibus ad quadrigam.*"

Selene, meanwhile, with tears still leaking from her eyes, spared enough time to race to the Forum Boarium – ignoring Delphinius, who again tried to speak to her – and confront Corax as he strapped padding to his legs. The clouds overhead were blood red.

"Is it true what you said?" she asked. "That you are to take my father's place in the final race?"

"Your father himself asked me to do so."

"But you must be cautious – they'll try to sabotage you, just as they tried to sabotage him."

"Of course they will."

"The emperor's agents on the spina, I mean – they will be flinging hot ashes, studded balls . . . everything!"

"I am familiar with all the tricks of the Circus," Corax assured her grimly, "and I know how to deal with each of them. So let us meet again after the race, dear girl, and honour your father together."

At which point Selene, overcome with emotion, reached out and hugged him tightly, feeling in her heart a presentiment of fresh horrors to come.

The light towers had now been set ablaze and a new chant was ringing around the arena:

"CUPIDO . . . CUPIDO . . . CUPIDO . . . CUPIDO!"

Among those of us in the stands this caused considerable confusion until we noticed the famous goat being bustled into the lower level so that Andraemon might see him from the track. And then, to thunderous cheers, the mighty stallion himself emerged from the stalls with his fellow horses and Corax of Campania. Following closely came Delphinius of Doriscus and the Fulminatus Team. The two teams paraded side by side to the breakline, whereupon the charioteers stepped down for the first-lap footrace. A new chorus began:

"CORAX . . . ANDRAEMON . . . CORAX . . . ANDRAEMON!"

Many of the crowd would not even have been born when the Raven raced against Caligula. But they would have been aware of his story. More than that, they must have heard the whispers that the Flavian forces were at the foothills of the Apennines and that Vitellius was teetering on the edge of defeat. So, in the cauldron of the Circus, it was easy to see how the fabled charioteer, forced into exile by imperial corruption, had become the symbol of justice denied, even to supporters of the Blues (in whose colours, after all, he had been so notoriously framed).

Delphinius himself later claimed he was unperturbed by the acclaim. "Though I had heard much about Corax I had never met him or even seen him, and was able to dismiss the crowd's fervour as the usual caprice. It was the death of Alector – the news of which reached me as I was preparing for the *pedibus ad quadrigam* – that really unsettled me. The circumstances of his crash, not to mention Selene's refusal to accept my condolences, had me battling a profound feeling of despair and confusion."

The two men limbered up wordlessly as the horses were held in place at the line. Corax – though it was difficult to see him properly in the fluttering light – looked leaner and darker than I remembered but otherwise seemed remarkably at ease – as if, instead of participating in his first Circus Maximus race in twenty-nine years, he was preparing for a friendly joust with a favourite nephew.

A great sense of anticipation swelled in the arena, the crowd hushed, the emperor Vitellius rose to his feet, he gazed around pompously, he raised the *mappa*, he released it – the crowd roared – and the footrace began.

It was, at first, a dispiriting sight. Delphinius bolted away like a cheetah while Corax staggered after him – debilitated, worn out, ancient. By the time he reached the western turning posts Delphinius was already ten lengths ahead, a sight so draining that even Corax's staunchest supporters could not resist a mirthless chuckle. Because it looked for all the world that the race was already over – lost ignominiously before the horses had even started. Small wonder that Vitellius, foreseeing such an outcome, had allowed it to proceed.

When Delphinius completed the first lap and sprang into his chariot, Corax was still halfway down the Palatine side, reviving painful memories of his race against Caligula. It seemed inevitable that Delphinius would lap him before he had completed the foot-race. But – just as he had decades years earlier – Corax, with an impressive burst of energy, was able to bound through the final few lengths, lunge into his chariot and launch his horses into the race before his opponent could pass him. An ironic cheer erupted from the crowd.

Nevertheless, there was no denying that the Andraemon Team, with their lead trace horse back in the harness, was a force like no other. Like a bolt of lightning, they shot down the Aventine side. They took the turn at top speed – to this day I do not know if Corax was aware of his hooped wheel – and tore up the dust of the Palatine side. They gained eight lengths on Delphinius and the Fulminatus Team in a single lap. And the crowd – perhaps, like me, they had forgotten just how awe-inspiring the horses were together – were no longer laughing.

"CORAX . . . CORAX . . . CORAX . . . CORAX!"

He made up a further seven lengths in the third lap.

And another seven in the fourth.

And so it continued, under the flames of the giant braziers, under clouds of fading crimson – Delphinius lashing his team and shouting exhortations, Corax all the time bearing down on him, plumes of dust sparkling, axles grinding, hooves pounding, hubs smoking, *spartores* dousing the wheels with water, and spectators in the stands shouting so thunderously that flames swirled and sputtered around the arena.

As the trumpets announced the sixth lap, Corax, incredibly, was almost level with Delphinius. He was urging the Andraemon Team to overtake. And Delphinius, his head twisted, was looking at him with astonishment. And resignation. Because there was nothing more he could do – not whipping, not shouting, not calling upon the gods. The Andraemon Team was just too good. They were drawing level. They were surging ahead. They were seizing the lead. And Corax – who had spent the entire race maintaining his distance from the spina, to avoid interference – was now steering left, directly in front of Delphinius. He was depriving Delphinius of the inside track. And still extending his lead. Two lengths. Three lengths. Four. He was going to win. The Andraemon Team was going to win. The Greens were going to win. The crowd was heaving and roaring with excitement.

This was the moment when Selene, watching from the starting stalls, noticed one of the attendants on the spina tilting one of the standing braziers. She had already seen, just a couple of laps earlier, the *spartores* hurl over Corax's wheels what she assumed was cooling water. But now, as embers rained down in front of the approaching horses, she was seized by the appalling suspicion that what had actually been hurled over his chariot was pitch.

Then the team was passing through the falling embers and the chariot wheels were bursting into flame. The wickerwork frame was catching alight. Corax himself was on fire.

A cry of massed horror erupted from the crowd.

From behind, Delphinius, appalled, saw a flaming Corax steer his chariot into the open area at the turn. He saw the old charioteer rein the horses, leap onto the track and roll his smoking body in the sand. He saw ground attendants, together with Selene, charge out bearing buckets of water.

But, at the same time, he knew the path was now open. The race was his for the taking. All he had to do was take the turn, reclaim the lead, and drive unchallenged through the final lap.

"But I could not do it," Delphinius told me later. "Not after winning the race against the ill-fated Alector. Not after seeing what they had just done to eliminate Corax. I could not claim victory in those circumstances, whatever the consequences."

And so, to gasps of surprise from around the arena, Delphinius hauled hard on his reins. He drew the Fulminatus Team to a halt. He got off his chariot. He went over to Corax and, together with Selene, assisted the veteran charioteer to his feet. Corax was singed and smoking but did not appear seriously burned (his habit of clothing every inch of his flesh had very likely saved him).

"Typically," Delphinius remembered, "he was more interested in the welfare of the horses than he was in himself. But apart from a couple of minor burns the stallions were untouched. All the flames had been extinguished. The reins were still usable. The wheels were blackened but intact. He asked me, in fact, why I had bothered to stop.

"I told him simply, 'Castor and Pollux' – and he looked at me, tremendously moved. It clearly meant something special to him. Then he seized me by the hand. He was proud of me. And when I asked if he wanted to resume the race, he said, 'Of course I want to resume it. The race is never over until the finishing line is crossed.'"

Selene was aghast, thinking that Corax was in no condition to continue. But her new guardian advised her to make as swift an exit as possible, for only authorised attendants were permitted on the track during a race. Then he turned back to his chariot.

The crowd, which had spent the whole time shifting and murmuring uneasily, now watched the two charioteers stepping back into their vehicles. Sorting themselves out. Checking that they were ready. Conferring with the stewards on procedure. And lining up again, side by side, with one lap to go.

Then, at a signal from the stewards, they were off again. At full speed. Driving abreast for a few moments. Cleaving down the Aventine Side for the last time, side by side. Yet as they gained more distance the Andraemon Team again began to assume the lead. One length, two lengths, three. They were simply unbeatable.

"Let no one say," Delphinius told me later, "that I did not give it my all. But I knew the Andraemon Team as well as anyone, remember. I knew that they always responded best to special occasions, and in particular to the touch of a sympathetic charioteer. And I knew that, when they were racing in harmony, no team in the empire could get close to them. So the outcome was more or less inevitable."

Indeed, the Andraemon Team seemed if anything more determined and energetic following the sabotage. They scythed through the sand. They tore around the final turn. They speared down the

Palatine side and crossed the line to a cheer so loud it was heard as far away as Ferentium.

Against all the odds, the Greens had won the Plebeian Games.

His tunic smouldering, Corax turned his chariot, reined the horses, stepped down to the track, and glared up at the emperor, whose face in the torchlight looked as purple as his robes.

# XXXVI

**M**Y PALATINE INSIDER ASSURES ME that Vitellius was beside himself at this moment. Just three days earlier, he could never have imagined that such an outcome might be possible. He had done everything to prevent it. He had secured for the Blues the finest horses and charioteers. He had poisoned, maimed, blackmailed and sabotaged the drivers of the Greens. He had the vociferous support of the Blues partisans, the patrician class, and all of his sycophantic court. Moreover, he had no good reason to believe that the Andraemon Team would ever make it all the way to Rome.

Even when it became clear that three of the stallions had somehow broken through, he was not overly perturbed. His spies had assured him they were in dreadful condition, much as you might expect of horses that had braved a multitude of hazards all the way from Syria. And when it was announced that they would be under the command of Alector of Arcadia, his drinking companion from the days of Caligula, it seemed to Vitellius that the Greens were mocking the very idea that they had a chance.

And so the races had played out for the first half of the programme. The dominance of the Blues was so pronounced that

Vitellius was concerned not so much about overall victory – which seemed assured – but by the spirit of the crowd, which fell far short of expectations. There was no rowdy acclamation when he entered the arena. No roars of approval when he dedicated the races to Jupiter. No great show of pleasure when he celebrated the victories of the Blues. Indeed, the faces he could see were pallid, gaunt and full of spite. And there was audible discontent, too, about the underhand tactics employed by the attendants on the spina – so much disapproval, in fact, that he had to order the stewards to scale back on the interference for a while.

And yet, when he retired to the Palatine during the midday break, he was feeling more than satisfied. The Blues had won five of the first six races. The Greens, though they had done their best, were on track for humiliation. Everything was going to plan. He was so content, in fact, that when his military advisers insisted on seeing him, bearing more bad tidings from the north, he sent them away without hearing a word.

But returning to the pulvinar he found the reception again disturbingly understated. Worse, the obnoxious Alector seemed inexplicably to have found form – driving the Andraemon Team with such brio, while Delphinius in contrast seemed to have developed a sudden reserve – that it seemed almost as if they had exchanged bodies midrace. And the other factions, too, for all his warnings and threats, seemed to be colluding in the Greens' favour. Vitellius nonetheless assumed that the Blues' lead was too great to be seriously challenged. And it was only by mid-afternoon, when the Greens had registered four victories, that he summoned the magistrate of the games.

"What in Hades is going on?" he asked. "How has this been allowed to happen?"

"A combination of unforeseen circumstances," replied the quivering magistrate.

"A combination of unforeseen circumstances that might see you exiled to Planasia?"

"Excuse me, Imperator – am I to understand we have permission to engage in sabotage again?"

Vitellius blew out his lips. "Do what you can . . . but discreetly. And be ready to administer penalties for some indiscretion or another – you know what I mean?"

"I do, Imperator."

"It is no more than Nero and Caligula did, in favour of the Greens."

"I well remember, Imperator."

Shortly afterwards Alector was involved in the fatal crash and Delphinius crossed the finishing line in first place, meaning the Blues and Greens were level on wins. Everything now came down to the *pedibus ad quadrigam* – a risk the emperor felt disinclined to take.

A devious new plan, suggested by the magistrates, which involved declaring the Andraemon Team no longer eligible now that Zephyrus was dead – an established chariot team is allowed no more than one replacement to its normal line-up – came to naught when Andraemon himself arrived just in time for the deciding race.

But then came the astounding news that old Corax of Campania was seeking to take over from Alector. And Vitellius finally relaxed – revelled, in fact, in this delicious twist of fate. Because victory again seemed assured, in the most fitting manner imaginable.

But now, unbelievably – and thanks in no small part to the complicity of the wretched Delphinius of Doriscus – it was worn-out Corax of Campania who had won. Corax whose name was being acclaimed by the crowd. Corax whose horses were being affixed with the plumes of victory. Corax who was limping to the pulvinar stairs, seeking to be crowned with the golden laurel.

Vitellius, affecting the most insincere of smiles, went into hasty consultation with the stewards and, by the time the Raven had hobbled up to the platform, he had made sure all were primed to play their roles.

"Corax of Campania," he exclaimed in his most senatorial voice. "Rome salutes you for your astounding victory!"

361

In point of fact, he was having trouble looking the Raven in the eyes. He was not sure how many knew of his role in framing the charioteer twenty-nine years earlier, but he was not so self-serving that he could not recognise a moment of supreme irony.

"And now, in the name of Jupiter and Mars – in the name of Romulus himself, whose residence overlooks us all – I reward you and your team with—"

But exactly on cue there was some commotion beside him and he pretended to be caught off-guard. He leaned forward to hear the magistrate. The crowd was shifting menacingly. Corax wore a withering stare. Finally Vitellius nodded, raised his hand for silence, and with a show of dismay stepped aside.

Accepting a freshly inked scroll from a sweating steward, a crier moved to the edge of the platform, flanked by giant braziers, and started reading:

"All hail Vitellius! All hail the Circus Maximus, symbol of the cosmos! It is by celestial law that the planets wheel through the cosmos and by terrestrial law that chariots wheel through the Circus! Let no one deny then the primacy of law and the need . . . the need of all to submit to the rules of Rome!"

The crier, for all his experience, had faltered because there was a groundswell of anger from the crowd, as if the plebs had already guessed where this was heading. Vitellius meanwhile maintained a sombre countenance.

"During the last race of the day" – loud jeers – "during the last race of the day, the *pedibus ad quadrigam*" – howls of displeasure – "during this race a girl was observed to cross the track in violation of—"

But the crier did not get a chance to finish. The crowd, snarling and hissing, spilled onto the track, heaved against the barrier, and forced their way onto the pulvinar stairs. Half-eaten food and fragments of brick sailed through the air. A chunk of tufa glanced off Vitellius's head, causing him to drop the golden laurel. In response, the Praetorian Guard mobilised around their emperor and, with breathtaking efficiency, bustled him through a hidden passageway into the Palatine. But not before he had glanced into Corax's eyes – which were burning with reflected flames – and heard the charioteer declare something utterly bewildering.

"That girl is now my daughter."

Then he was back in his palace, spurning the generals who had arrived with yet more unsavoury news, and listening all night to the riots that convulsed the city.

Vitellius's fall, over the course of the next four and a half weeks, was the most humiliating of all in the Year of the Four Emperors. He ate so much he could barely get out of bed. He grew increasingly ill. He tried to distract the populace with more games, more shows, more feasts. He refused to believe that Antonius Primus was descending on Rome. He rejected an offer of hundred million sesterces and safe retirement in Campania. And when he did concede some notional power to Flavius Sabinus, the older brother of Vespasian, his last lingering supporters swarmed over the Capitoline Hill, burned down the Temple of Jupiter and brutally murdered Sabinus.

Rejoicing in righteous indignation – a cheaply purchased licence at the best of times – Antonius Primus's legions stormed into Rome and soaked the streets in blood. After taking refuge in a palace room meant for dogs, Vitellius was dragged out and smashed to death on the Stairs of Lamentation. His disembodied head – still snarling and spitting, if some reports are to be believed – was paraded through the streets on a pike as his gas-bloated body floated down the Tiber and exploded at Ostia.

It was the twenty-second day of December in the year the Raven and the Rooster returned to Rome and raced the Andraemon Team in the Circus Maximus.

# EPILOGUS

I HAVE MENTIONED THAT MY FATHER WITNESSED just one race in the Circus Maximus during his entire reign as *dominus factionis*, and that race was the *pedibus ad quadrigam* which saved the Greens from extinction. As soon as Corax left him at the Via Latina estate, he set about making his way into the city – a not uncomplicated task, for he first needed to penetrate lines of (admittedly distracted) soldiers – but in the end made it just in time to witness, inasmuch as his failing eyes allowed him to witness anything, the monumental victory of Corax and the Greens.

I wish I could report that what followed was relief and celebration, but of course the possibility of reprisals compelled us all – Corax and Delphinius included – to seek refuge far away from Rome. Even when Vitellius was overthrown we did not regard the city as entirely safe – Flavian soldiers were carousing through the streets, looting and settling scores – and it was not until Vespasian himself appeared in the autumn that we judged ourselves ready to come out of hiding.

The new emperor proved no great patron of chariot racing, however, lavishing funds on the construction of the Flavian

Amphitheatre* while letting the Circus Maximus take care of itself. Nor did he prove much of a friend to Greece, where he reinstated the taxes and tariffs that Theodoros and the merchants had been so keen to avoid. But his factional impartiality at least allowed us to return to the arena and complete the crowning ceremony that Vitellius in his panic had abandoned.

The curator opened up the Circus for principal figures from the Greens – sixteen people in all, including Selene and Xenia – and a suitably embarrassed Corax drove the victorious team around the empty track, waving to the minuscule crowd, before ascending to the pulvinar where my father was waiting with the golden laurel.

"Enter now the halls of immortality," he announced, placing the crown on Corax's head.

To which Corax, enduring the charade out of respect alone, replied, "As you wish, Imperator."

This was intended as my father's valedictory act as *dominus factionis*, his farewell gesture to chariot racing, but I regret to say that he could not quite relinquish the job of restoring the faction to financial stability, a thankless task that occupied him day and night for the next four years and ultimately became more enervating that invigorating. He expired halfway through the reign of Vespasian, consoled to some extent, I hope, by the knowledge that his achievements had been respectfully recorded by his scholarly son.

Delphinius of Doriscus rejoined the Greens and went on to drive the Andraemon Team in another sixty-five victories. Before my father's death he was proud to see his name chiselled into the Wall of the Milliarii. His final tally of wins was one thousand and twelve victories in both quadriga and biga, his career prize money

---

* Later called the Colosseum, after Nero's colossal statue nearby.

amounting to nearly twenty-five million sesterces.* More significantly, in personal terms, he became a close confidant of Corax, as well as the lover, for a season or two, of Corax's adopted daughter Selene.

Selene herself had been taken to the Spanish stud farm – she never again saw the Amuq Valley – where, as Magnus's successor, she became the estate's most reliable assistant and horse trainer before emerging as a charioteer in her own right. Her stormy relationship with Delphinius, which promised to produce such highly pedigreed offspring, famously crumbled after she contentiously defeated him in her first race in the Circus Maximus.

Magnus recovered from the deep wounds sustained in Liguria but was never again to ride a horse. He became, however, one of the most recognisable figures in the taverns and brothels of Spain, and never tired of recounting his heavily embroidered stories of the great adventure.

For a while Gryphus took over as *dominus factionis* of the Green Faction – the first freedman to do so – but reigned without distinction, his most memorable achievement being to retain the Greens' immaculate record in the Plebeian Games.

The profits of Albus of the Esquiline – who also, remarkably, made it into the Circus to witness the fabled *pedibus ad quadrigam* – were at the end of Vitellius's reign said to be "too great to contemplate". He passed away on the roof of his tavern, still gazing possessively over his empire, his corpse in his tomb said to be so well-preserved that even today he appears "eerily alive".

General Antonius Primus co-ruled Rome between the reigns of Vitellius and Vespasian but afterwards receded into the shadows,

---

* Delphinius's victory tally fell well short of the records later achieved by Scorpus of Hispania (2,048) and Pompeius Musclosus (a whopping 3,559). His career prize money was, however, close to that earned by Diocles of Lusitania, reckoned to be the most financially successful sportsperson in history.

content that he had played "no small part in the security of Rome". He lives today in Tolosa, Gaul, for "birds and old soldiers, at the end of the day, like to return to the nest".

The exceptional forbearance of the goddess Xenia was tested to its limits when her husband's ailing body prevented him from fulfilling his training duties and she was compelled, in combination with Selene, to take full control of the stud farm outside Tarraco. She still presides there, bemused, no doubt, to find herself playing such a crucial role in the ridiculous sport, but proud, one hopes, that the horses she now dispatches to Rome are renowned for characteristics so ample in herself – beauty, nobility, feistiness, and a supreme tolerance of human foolishness.

Corax crossed the finishing line some years ago, succumbing to exhaustion and injury, including perhaps whatever wounds he sustained during his final journey to Rome. Inasmuch as he kept my father's golden laurel on display in his vestibulum, rather than burying it in the pit with his other trophies, it seems to me he had finally accepted that an honourable man can step into arena occasionally without entirely abandoning his virtue. He is buried beside his son Falco under the chestnut tree outside Tarraco and is remembered today with universal affection – not the most victorious charioteer in history, but certainly the most admired and consequential.

The great journey of the Andraemon Team soon became the subject of frescos and friezes all the way from Gaul to Galatia. Quintus Creticus Tenax decorated his peristylium with an exquisite marble statue of the team; my father commissioned a smaller version for the family residence; "Old Man" Sterninius (who still lives in Picenum) installed a likeness of Corax on prominent display in his stud farm; Chloros had a new statue of Alector added to the Avenue of Immortals in Olympia; and I continue to notice celebratory bas-reliefs, frescos and mementos all around the empire.

The four stallions themselves, together with Cupido, were laid to rest in an elaborate mausoleum on the Via Appia where acolytes of the Greens, and fans of chariot racing in general, lay tributes to this day. Alector is buried nearby, in the Cemetery of the Charioteers, under a statue of weeping Fortuna.

The wooden stands of the Circus Maximus went up in flames again under Domitian, but the emperor Trajan, under whose reign I write these words, has now begun extensive renovations, including new starting stalls, colonnaded arcades and even stands of stone. When passing the construction site on a recent visit to Rome I was pierced by the notion that my father was now surveying his most cherished dream through the life he had transmitted to me.

I am no colt myself these days, and must content myself with the possibility that this chronicle might wind up being my only contribution to history. My father used to say that there are only three immutable laws in life: fire consumes wood, rocks don't float, and everyone dies unsatisfied. It is perhaps for that reason that I am haunted by an unusually poignant exchange between himself and Alector, which I present it to you now before sealing these manuscripts for posterity.

It came about late on the night before the fabled race that saved the Greens. Alector, having just completed a successful day's training, had joined my father in the tablinum for a cup of wine.

"Is it true what you said," he ventured, "about your having manufactured those disagreements between me and Corax?"

"Alas, it's true," my father admitted with a sigh. "I had an idea it would propel both of you to greater glory. How inglorious are men when we attempt, like gods, to manipulate the lives of others!"

Alector thought about it and shrugged. "Well, the gods got their way in the end, did they not, because we *did* propel ourselves to greater glory? And I have ended up here, have I not, just when you most need me – on the cusp of my greatest-ever victory?"

My father smiled. "It's an agreeable way of looking at it."

They were silent for a while, sipping their wine, until Alector – who had, it will be remembered, immersed himself deeply in Greek philosophy – became surprisingly sombre.

"Still in all," he said, "I sometimes wonder if it all matters in the end. If anything really matters at the close of day. Did I ever mention that cave I visited near Tarsus?"

He went on to inform my father of a rock cavern in Cilicia, discovered by some limestone quarriers, which was found to be decorated with fabulous wall-paintings of woolly horses surrounded by handprints. The images, which were thought to date back to the days of Hercules, had struck a deep chord with Alector, who owing to his celebrity was one of the few notables permitted to visit the site.

"Because it moved me," he said, "to think that someone, a few hundred years ago, might have loved horses so much – loved anything – to record them on the wall of a cave. I was supremely haunted by the paintings, in fact – so much so that I made a point of returning there the next time I was racing in Cilicia."

But this time he was in for a rude surprise, for the sublimely decorated wall had already been demolished – sacrificed ruthlessly to the quarriers' picks.

"And I was curiously wounded," he admitted, swilling the last of his wine. "Riven, really, that all the painter's love and effort had been extinguished by a few indifferent blows. And it got me wondering if all my achievements, too, would one day be torn down and forgotten. I mean to say, when we perish – and we are all tied to our bodies like oysters to their shells, are we not? – will anyone care to remember the things we achieved? Are all men not dreams of shadows?"

My father, finding it remarkable to find himself discussing mortality with the Rooster, assured Alector that he had already commissioned a written history, written by someone they both knew rather well, which would cover in great detail his career in the Circus Maximus.

"Everything?" asked Alector.

"Everything."

"All my great victories?"

"Most of them."

"The race against Caligula?"

"Of course."

"My rivalry with Corax of Campania?"

"And your friendship, too."

"And the goddess Xenia? Her role in our rift?"

"How can such a thing be avoided?" my father said, then chuckled gently. "So you see, Alector, while the oyster itself might perish, its pearl will live on, more lustrous than ever."

Alector nodded reflectively. "It still might not be enough," he decided. "Because what's to say that the written history itself will not perish? Be tossed by some peasant onto a fire? To warm his hands on a winter's night?"

My father assured him that some ingenious method would be found to preserve the manuscripts, but Alector remained unsatisfied.

"In any case," he went on, "how can words hope to capture what it was really like? To win a crucial race in the Circus Maximus? To be spirited around the track by the fastest horses in the empire? To weave between your opponents? To cross the finishing line in first place? To receive the crown of triumph? And then to leave the arena into the light of the setting sun, knowing that everyone is admiring you? Will anyone really appreciate the pure exultation? In a hundred years? In two hundred? Will anyone care about Alector of Arcadia? Or Corax of Campania? Will they understand why we turned against each other? Or will be brothers only in dust?"

"You were always brothers," my father insisted.

Alector looked at him, seemed on the verge of admitting something personal – it is tempting to conceive of something self-deprecating, perhaps even than Corax was a better charioteer than he – but in the end he took refuge in whimsy.

"Just think of what the two of us, Corax and I, could have achieved if we had ever shared the reins of one chariot. *Thumos* and *hedonism* together. The irresistible combination. The soul split across two bodies, hauling and driving the chariot at the same time. But it is not to be now. It can no longer come to pass. Only in death can we reunite. Ah, well," he said, "the ordeals of the journey enhance the lustre of the destination – have truer words ever been spoken?"

He nodded, as if answering his own question, and my father found himself lost for words. ("I wanted to believe he was referring to the great effort it had taken to get to Rome, but could not shake the suspicion that he was foreshadowing his own death in the Circus.")

Then Alector looked into his empty goblet, shrugged and smiled, and plonked it onto the table.

"Anyway," he finished, with a hearty sigh, "my cup is empty and I deserve a good sleep."

# ACKNOWLEDGEMENTS

Anyone who writes on the subject of the Circus Maximus, or chariot racing in general, owes an incalculable debt to John H. Humphrey for *Roman Circuses: Arenas for Chariot Racing* and Alan Cameron for *Circus Factions: Blues and Greens at Rome and Byzantium*.

I also consulted *Chariot Racing in the Roman Empire* by Fik Meijer; *Equus: The Horse in the Roman World* by Ann Hyland; the various academic papers on chariot design by Bela Sandor; *Cruelty and Civilization: The Roman Games* by Roland Auguet; *Spectacle Entertainments of Early Imperial Rome* by Richard C. Beacham; *The Roman Games: Historical Sources in Translation* by Alison Futrell; *Animals for Show and Pleasure in Ancient Rome* by George Jennison; *Leisure and Ancient Rome* by Jerry Toner; *Roman Passions: A History of Pleasure in Imperial Rome* by Ray Laurence; *Festivals and Ceremonies of the Roman Republic* by Howard Hayes; *Handbook to Life in Ancient Rome* by Lesley Adkins and Roy A. Adkins; *A Cabinet of Roman Curiosities* by J.C. McKeown; *Life in Ancient Rome* by F.R. Cowell; *A Walk in Ancient Rome* by John T. Cullen; *Rome the Cosmopolis* edited by Catharine Edwards; *24 Hours in Ancient Rome, Ancient Rome on 5 Denarii a Day* and *Ancient Athens on Five Drachmas a Day* by Philip Matyszak; *Daily Life in the Roman City: Rome, Pompeii, and Ostia* by Gregory S. Aldrete; *Rome: Its People, Life and Customs* by U.E. Paoli; *Guide to the Aqueducts of Ancient Rome* by Peter J. Aicher; *A Topographical Dictionary of Ancient Rome* by Samuel Ball Platner; *Travel in the Ancient World*, *The Ancient Mariners* and *Ships and Seafaring in Ancient Times* by Lionel Casson; *Cities of the Classical World* by Colin McEvedy; *Roman Alpine Routes* by Walter Woodburn Hyde; *Roman Roads of Europe* by N.H.H. Sitwell; *Roman Roads* by Raymond Chevalier; *Hannibal Crosses the Alps* by John Prevas; *The Romans in Spain* by J.S. Richardson; *Roman Spain* by S.J. Keay; *Graecia Capta* by Susan E. Alcock; *Greece Under the Romans* by George Finlay; *Age of Conquests: The Greek World from Alexander to Hadrian* by Angelos Chaniotis; *Power Games: The Olympics of Ancient Greece* by David Stuttard; *The Ancient Olympics* by Nigel Spivey; *The Mysteries of Mithras: The Pagan Belief that Shaped the Christian World* by Payam Nabarz; ORBIS: The Stanford Geospatial Network Model of the Roman World; and, on the subject of the Year of the Four Emperors, the books by P.A.L. Greenhalgh, Gwyn Morgan, Kenneth Wellesley, and Nic Fields. Thanks to Robert J. Harris, Debby Harris, Zara Fram, Dave Bowden, Megan Duff, Professor Hélène de Montgolfier and the ever-reliable Ariel Moy. And of course David Forrer at InkWell and the hardworking team at B&W, especially Emma Hargrave, Campbell Brown, Ali McBride, Thomas Ross, Tonje Hefte and Hannah Walker.